CW00738658

Call of the Goddess

Call of the Goddess

Book One of the Stormflies

Elizabeth N. Love

COPYRIGHT (C) 2014 ELIZABETH N. LOVE
LAYOUT COPYRIGHT (C) 2014 CREATIVIA

Published 2014 by Creativia

Book design by Creativia

Cover art by http://www.paperandsage.com/

This book is a work of fiction. Names, characters, places, and incidents are the product of the author's imagination or are used fictitiously. Any resemblance to actual events, locales, or persons, living or dead, is purely coincidental.

All rights reserved. No part of this book may be reproduced or transmitted in any form or by any means, electronic or mechanical, including photocopying, recording, or by any information storage and retrieval system, without the author's permission.

Acknowledgement and Dedication

Thank you to my late mother, Genevieve, for insisting that her daughters be more than the sum of their parts. On occasion, I find myself channeling her spirit.

Thank you very much to my husband and my children, who have waited patiently (but usually impatiently) while I put these thoughts into words.

And to all of my friends asking me now and again if I was ever going to get this finished - perfection takes a long time (and it still isn't perfect).

Contents

Chapter 1

Changes

On the planet Bona Dea, the fourth planet of ten orbiting binary stars in a gravity-driven waltz, the last vestiges of the human race make their home. Thirteen ships traveled to a new world to begin a new way of life free of persecution, free of poverty. They located a temperate planet occupied by a variety of animal species, but devoid of civilization.

Our story begins on the 21st day of the month of Trimont, in the year 307 after the Landing of the generation ships.

+++

Axandra's brain tickled. She remembered the sensation from two decades ago, when she was a small child. She knew what the feeling meant. The Goddess was coming. The Sliver called to it, *I am here!* and it followed that call.

Leaving her cottage after giving her lover an excuse that she wanted a short walk, Axandra went to the beach to wait. The sand beneath her bare feet radiated leftover warmth from the day's sunshine, even though the suns had set more than an hour ago. In the night sky, distant stars blazed. She could see hundreds of thousands of them, each a tiny point of light, an unbelievably small fraction of its true size. Though some nights she tried, she could never hope to count them all in her entire lifetime.

Low upon the horizon in the west, one point of light moved. It seemed to be flying just over the ocean. The closer it came, the less like a star it appeared. The tiny point grew larger, to the size of a firefly, then larger still, the size of a fist. A glow reflected off the water, then the sand.

Axandra breathed deeply and dug her feet into the beach. She had waited years for this moment to come, ever since she fled the Prophets' guardianship as a child, when her name was Ileanne. She tried to prepare herself for what would happen when the Goddess found her. The orb of light grew large enough to envelop her as it flew over the white beach. Before she could to react to shield herself, it was upon her.

The sensation plowed through her body with a thousand times more power than the Sliver. She flopped to the ground. Her body quaked against the sand as the glow shrouded her with sparks. She struggled against its hold, but force bound her limbs and paralyzed her. Blinding her, the brightness entered her left eye. Panting for breath, an orgasmic ripple coursed through her nerves, melding pain and pleasure into euphoria. Ringing filled her ears. Generations of experience swelled her brain. Images she'd never seen before filled her eyes. Memories of a lost childhood snapped into vivid clarity. Curiosity tempted her to try to see everything. The sights flashed by too quickly to understand. Overwhelmed, her mind shut off.

+++

1st day of Unimont, in the year 286, after the Landing

"**I don't want** to stay here!"

With white knuckles, Ileanne bawled and gripped her mother's hand. A pale Prophet woman touched her shoulders as though to comfort the child. Having never seen a Prophet before, Ileanne recoiled. The mystics kept themselves segregated from the rest of the population. She knew the Prophets served the Protectress in a magical way that frightened her.

Elora, crouched down to the eye level of her six-year-old daughter. "You have to stay, my darling. The Prophets are going to teach you everything you need to know to be the Protectress when your turn comes. Please don't cry," her mother begged, cradling the girl against her breast. "You're breaking my heart."

After several minutes of consoling, Elora framed Ileanne's face with both hands and looked into the child's green eyes. "You'll be fine."

Behind the frail woman, Ileanne's father said nothing. He barely even looked at his daughter, his typical expression toward her. He stood there with his hands held together in front of him and twitched his fingers, waiting impatiently for the scene to end.

The little girl kept her lips tightly shut, refusing to say goodbye. Ileanne did not want them to leave her. She wiped her cheeks dry with her hand, but the hot tears kept streaming down into the creases of her lips. Her cheeks felt raw.

Her mother cried, too, but urged her only child to stay with the strangers. Ileanne witnessed the pained look upon her mother's face, a frightful look of sadness. The girl hated her parents for turning their backs and climbing into the car to leave.

Beneath the Great Storm, the wind whipped at gale force, blasting sand in gigantic swirls. As the car engine began to hum, the same gateway that opened to allow the car into the Haven reappeared as though by magic. The car disappeared through the Storm, seemingly untouched by the sand. Lightning flashed all around, bolts striking the ground and fingerlings groping out in every direction.

Yet, in the Haven the destructive winds stayed away, as though the Good Goddess cupped her hands over the mountain to stop the air. The thunder was muffled, and the lightning stayed in the sky. A shell of peace existed here in the center of the Storm.

"Welcome, Ileanne. I am Jala." The Prophet woman said to her, smiling kindly in hopes of easing the transition. The Prophet woman wore her light brown hair in a loose braid that looped around the back of her head. Her face was almost white, typical of all Prophets whose skin was never touched by sunslight. "Come with me. We must get you ready for tonight."

"What's going to happen?" Ileanne questioned, her feet reluctant to move. Jala gripped her wrist and pulled just hard enough to start her feet walking.

Tonight is very special, Jala thought. *Tonight you will learn the true honor of being the Protectress.*

Protectress. Instead of that word giving her a sense of accomplishment, it only made the girl angry and sorrowful. All her life, Ileanne had watched her mother, the Protectress, work every hour of every day, strained by the people to the point of breaking. Many nights, she had listened to her mother and father snarling at each other bitterly. Sometimes, her mother wasn't even around, for the woman was out traveling across the countryside. Thinking of these things, Ileanne slouched on the stool where she was planted and pinched one palm with her fingers. "Oh."

Jala proceeded to braid the child's hair in a long, simple plait down her back. She helped Ileanne changed her clothes into an unadorned gray shift reeking a metallic odor that stung the eyes.

I am so proud of you, Ileanne. You are about to embark on a most wonderful Journey like you can't even imagine.

Ileanne scowled as Jala led her down to a large room where many of the Prophets were gathered. Her tiny body began to tremble nervously. At the front of the room, the elders stood before a large stone platform. Everyone was quiet.

One of the elders directed her to the platform. Jala helped her up to sit on the edge and introduced the gray-haired man as Tyrane, their principle elder.

Ileanne looked around at the large collection of eyes focused on her and could not keep her limbs from shaking. Amidst them, she saw the man whose face felt familiar to her. She remembered dreaming about him once, and in the dream he came to her room and kissed her gently on the brow, the kindest gesture anyone had ever shown.

"Relax, child," said another of the male elders. The voice caused her to jump.

Tyrane approached the platform with purposeful steps, a smile curving his lips upwards with a sickly sweetness that made Ileanne's heart race. "Ileanne, as your mother before you, and all of her mothers before her, you will be host to the Goddess. She will keep your path straight and guide you in times of trouble."

Confused and terrified, Ileanne pinched her brows together. She didn't want anything in her. "What are you talking about?"

Someone entered the room carrying a small box fashioned of silver metal. The smooth surface of the box gleamed as though powered from within.

Tyrane offered the box to Ileanne and instructed her, "Open this vessel, and from it learn the purpose of your life. The Goddess lives within her chosen ones. Now, she will live within you as well." Tyrane flashed that smile again, his eyes gleaming in the light of the glow stones.

Cringing, Ileanne shook her head. Unwillingly, she felt her hand lift from her lap. She wasn't moving, yet she could see her fingers stretching toward the flawless metal. As she reached out to touch it, she felt a buzzing in the back of her head. The closer her hand moved, the stronger the buzzing became until she thought she would be sick. Something invisible grabbed her hand when she tried to resist the tug, keeping her steady until her fingers touched the box. The surface felt hot to the touch, burning her fingers. The lid seemed to melt away and the box lay open in her hands. Inside was a small, shining mirror, and Ileanne saw her own face and green eyes.

Then something incredible happened. As she watched, her face began to glow with a purplish light. A glowing bead, like a firefly, floated up and toward her eyes, then flashed and disappeared. In the mirror, her eyes changed color, shifting from pale green to violet, like the open sky.

Her brain tickled. She giggled at the sensation. Her lips tingled, and her nose itched.

Hello, young one, came a voice inside her. It was not one of the Prophets, for it did not come from outside her mind. She wasn't sure how she knew that. The voice just felt different.

Hello, she replied in thought, her inner voice sounding soft and weak. *What are you? Where are you?*

I have been with your family since the Journey was finished. I come from a distant place but I now live with your mother. This is a sliver of me, so that my whole can find you when needed.

The words and phrases overlapped each other in her mind, and several moments passed before she could make sense of what the thing tried to tell her. Her brain filled with pictures of objects and places she had never seen before. She flew through space without a ship, passing stars and planets. She lived on a dirty world, colored with strange orange dust and black mold. She traveled on a ship alone, in space again. Each life was shown to her in a storm of small pieces, all crammed into her small mind.

Hands held her, keeping her from falling. Her eyes refocused on the face in the mirror.

Her eyes looked like her mother's now. She stopped smiling. She did not want to be like her mother. Her chest felt tight with fear.

I don't want to be her.

+++

6th day Unimont, 286

"She's gone?" Elora screamed, her delicate face distorted in horror. Her violet eyes spilled tears down her crimson cheeks. "You lost my only child! I trusted you with her safety, and you betrayed me!"

"We have looked everywhere, Your Honor," Tyrane informed, his eyes appropriately downcast with apology. "We have searched for several days."

Elora marched the length of the room, arms stiff at her sides with rage. Her breaths seethed between her teeth. She stopped and jabbed her finger at the old man. "Days? Why didn't you tell me she was gone?"

"We did not want to cause alarm if she could be found," he explained, immediately realizing his mistake. The mother's ire flew at him from across the room, slamming into him like a physical blow.

"*You—!*" Elora shrieked. She stared at him with disbelief. "You liar! I don't EVER want to see you again! Any of you!"

She lifted a heavy book from a table and flung it at him. The book sailed past to his right, landing harmlessly with a thud on the rug. Then she grabbed a vase, which sailed directly at his head. He ducked while the porcelain shattered against the door with a deafening crash.

"Get out of here! Out! Don't ever come near me again!"

"Protectress, there is still time for you to have another child. Patrum can—" Tyrane began to suggest, holding his arms out as a shield against the next flying object, another book. It struck his forearms, sending a bruising sting through his elbows. "We will help you."

"I can't!" Elora screamed, filled with rage. "I won't let any of you touch me again! Get out! Guards! Guards!"

The door rattled behind him, but he had locked it upon entry. In another moment, the guards would bust the door to get in.

"Protectress, I implore you. Let us help you have another—"

"No! I won't let you near me!"

Wood splintered against his back and he went down in a tumble of human bodies. The guards wrested Tyrane's arms behind his back, lifting him like a doll back onto his feet.

"Get him out of here!" Elora ordered, her left arm stiff in the direction of the exit. "And don't ever let him back in."

"Yes, Madam," a guard acknowledged.

Spinning Tyrane around, the guards roughly guided him toward the stairway, down into the main hall and out the main door where his car and his traveling companion waited. The younger man narrowed his eyes in confusion at the elder's undignified treatment.

"Home," Tyrane stated simply, signaling he wanted no further conversation on the matter. The two Prophets drove out of the city and back into the Storm.

Nothing of Ileanne was ever found. Her parents feared she crashed the car in the Great Storm and perished, her body disintegrated by the blasting sands. After almost a year of searching the entire continent, the people resigned themselves that they would never know her fate.

+++

Axandra woke when the first sun rose, still lying on the sand, the tide licking her feet. Every nerve ached. Rolling onto her side, she covered her face, blocking the bright rays that climbed skyward east of her home. She was not alone, for the Goddess rested in her mind, a quiet presence for now. Her head felt like a boulder upon her neck. She lay still and breathed against the sand. Grit coated her tongue and mouth. She could not bear to lift her body through the force of gravity.

"Axandra?" came a shout from the direction of the cottage.

Jon must have just realized she never came to bed the night before. He called again, his voice fading in volume as he turned away from her. She opened her mouth to call back to him, but only a croak came out. Her mouth and lungs felt arid. With a moan, she positioned her knees against the ground beneath her and pushed up. Each muscle trembled like jelly.

Jon dashed down the beach toward her, shouting her name over and over as he came. His knees hit the ground beside her and sand flew up, hitting her skin in a cool layer of stinging.

"Axandra, are you all right? What happened? What are you doing out here?" Jon's hands grabbed her and tried to help her as she lifted her head from the ground. A wave of darkness swept over her, and she felt her body spinning. She thrust her arms straight as braces against the beach. Her dark hair shrouded her face from the light of day. Jon's fingers gently tucked the curls behind her ears so he could see her. "You look sick. Did you get stung?"

Coughing from dryness and sand, Axandra managed a meager nod. Being stung seemed a good explanation. The throbbing felt reminiscent of a jelly sting. She could have stepped on one of those nasty critters in the dark. The blue jellies packed a heavy dose of toxin that, while not fatal, sickened a healthy man Jon's size for several days. Heaving her lungs, she tried to calm her hacking with an intake of fresh air.

Shifting his arms, Jon cradled his lover and lifted her above the sands. "Let's get you inside. I'm so sorry. I went to bed. I didn't think—"

He blamed himself for not checking on her last night. She'd been lying unconscious in the sand for hours. Resting against him, she stopped fighting the pain in her body and tried to let it flow out of her.

Jon lay her down on the bed inside. The air felt cooler and smelled of the flowers cut from a roadside yesterday. Axandra closed her eyes and lay still, listening to the sounds of the water, of the birds, and of Jon rattling around in the kitchen as he looked through the herbs to find the best one to help counteract a jelly sting. She wondered if the remedy would help with this pain.

As she lay in bed, with Jon fussing over her, Axandra had no idea how much time passed. Much time elapsed with her unaware of her present surroundings. Drifting in and out of waking, she found herself in strange places, dream-like worlds. She watched flying reptiles soaring over jungles. She stood in a city of buildings so tall, they blocked out the sky. Trees did not exist. Night skies looked hazy.

Jon washed her face with a damp towel and dribbled a tea made of the herb onto her tongue. The mixture tasted bitter and coated her teeth and gums with an oily layer. By evening, the aches in her muscles eased away and her joints loosened. Her foggy brain cleared.

Jon stayed by her side, seated on the edge of the mattress while he watched her. Opening her eyes, Axandra felt as though she woke from a bizarre dream. Jon looked worried, his bearded face scrunched and frowning. She shifted her body so that she could look up into his face.

"I should've stayed awake 'til you came back," he scolded himself, shaking his head. "What'f something—"

"I'm fine," she tried to assure him, though her weak voice lacked conviction in those words. Brushing her hands across her skin, she felt decidedly grimy. The idea of a warm bath popped into her head. Immediately she could smell the aromas of soaps and oils and feel the tickle of popping bubbles on her skin. Blinking rapidly, she pulled herself back to the moment.

"You looked really horrible out there on the beach. I thought you were dying," Jon said with great distress. "I didn't want to leave you, not even to get the Healer. I couldn't find where you were stung—to put the herb on—so I made tea."

Pursing her lips in a sour expression, she told him, "It tasted awful, but it seems to be working." She laughed softly, amused by his concern. Reaching up, she touched her fingers to his tan cheek, stroking the soft whiskers of his full beard. "Thank you for taking care of me."

Jon jerked back from her touch, his eyes abruptly wide. Her hand hung alone in the space between them.

"What's wrong?" Axandra asked, leaving her hand there for him to nuzzle. Jon did not move toward her again, so she slowly withdrew.

"Y-you gave me a shock or—er, something. Maybe it's all the sand." He forced a smirk, but his lips turned down again quickly. He reached out to take her hand, but stopped himself uncertainly. "I'll fill up the tub. You'll prob'ly feel a lot better after a bath."

Her companion sensed something wasn't right. As he left the room, Axandra held her hand in front of her, staring at the bluish lines across her palm, trying to see something unusual in her veins. Only sand and dust and bitter tea.

Water splashed into the shallow metal tub in the next room. They didn't have a large tub in this cottage by the sea, but she fit inside the round basin if she bent her knees. Jon usually stood, using the hose to rinse himself with warm water. He looked awkward if he tried to sit.

Sitting up in bed, she listened and waited for Jon to return, thinking he would help her out of her clothes and use the sponge to wash her skin. He usually enjoyed shampooing her hair.

"Tub's full," he called. He escaped past the bedroom and into the main room, not even casting a glance in her direction.

A sinking sensation weighed in her chest as she sighed. She prayed his jitters would pass soon and that they could return to normal. She made no plans to reclaim her old life. The people would simply have to make do without a Protectress.

Using her arms to push herself up from the bed, she went to take her bath.

+++

23rd Trimont

A majority of the residents in Port Gammerton assembled to hear the official news. In the meeting hall on the village square, the people sat on long wood and lacquer benches arranged in loose rows. The unofficial news already spread rampantly of the Protectress' demise in the form of chatter trickling among the townsfolk.

Still feeling ill from the prior day, Axandra leaned against Jon. She sensed tension in his embrace and a strong desire to move away from her. Though weak and desiring his comfort, she straightened her spine and tucked her cold hands between her thighs, being careful not to touch him again. She knew that Elora, the Protectress, was gone. The Goddess could only be released upon the death of the host. The arrival of the spirit delivered this news without words.

The Principal of their village addressed the people, his sun-darkened arm waving to ask for quiet. "Everyone, I have very sad news. Very sad news. The Protectress—Our Esteemed Matriarch—has passed away." He made the announcement in somber tones, his eyes cast down toward the floor. He fidgeted uncomfortably as he listened to the gasps and bursts of sobbing that circled the room. Others sat silently, stunned by the news.

Again, the Principal raised his hands to request stillness. "This is official from the People's Council. They ask everyone to give a few moments to honor her in her passing."

And so everyone present sat quietly for a few minutes, giving their thoughts over to thank the Protectress for all of her good deeds. Axandra could hear those thoughts, making the air too heavy to breath.

Then, people began to ask questions. "When did it happen?" asked Nellie from the far side of the room.

Axandra slouched mournfully on the bench feeling drained. All morning, she struggled with the noises in her head. The fight exhausted her. Voices spoke to her from nowhere and from everywhere. Some she recognized as neighbors. Others came from unknown distances. They weren't really speaking to her, yet she felt as though everything she heard was meant for her. The voices distracted her again.

Who will show us the way now? Someone worried. What will happen to our peace? If only her daughter was still alive. That poor girl.

Rubbing her temple, Axandra attempted to block those voices. Since the Goddess had come to her, she found herself unable to form even a simple barrier to close her sensitive mind from others.

She so wanted to lean against Jon for support, to draw strength from his presence. He had shifted several centims away from her on the bench since they sat down. He kept himself withdrawn, his hands tucked beneath his arms and his eyes forward. He wouldn't even look at her.

"She was very ill," the Principal responded to a second question Axandra had not heard. "The Council informs us that she has been so for some months. Her passing was, unfortunately, expected."

"Do they know who will take her place?" asked Janette, raising her age-withered hand above the heads of the crowd to be noticed.

The Principal shook his head of salt and pepper hair. "They did not say, Ms. Nariss. I suggest that we all go home and take a few minutes to honor her. The Council will let us know as soon as they have any further news." With these words, he stepped down from the raised platform and walked away, sagging sadly as he exited the building.

The crowd split off into small groups. Some left the hall and headed for home. Others stayed, conversing about the tragedy. Axandra waited to see what Jon was going to do. He did not move immediately.

Janette, who sat to her right, bumped her shoulder. "Oh, dear. You look terrible. You're taking this quite hard."

Did she look so grief-stricken? Janette touched her bare arm, and the woman's mind flew at hers with little effort. Axandra backed away slightly.

"Jelly sting," Jon announced flatly. "Farenseve. Been sick ever since."

"Oh, is that what we call it now," Dora, Janette's life-partner, commented from the far side. "Were you that jelly, Mr. Jon. I'd say there is something else causing these shakes."

"It isn't like that," Axandra vehemently denied the accusation that she might be pregnant. She met Janette's eyes momentarily. "I just haven't been well the past couple of days."

"Well, something sure feels different about you," said Janette. Having no children of her own, she often fussed over Axandra like an overbearing mother, giving no thought to touching her so casually or blurting out every comment that came to her mind. "Did you see the Healer? Maybe she has a remedy."

Shaking her head, Axandra assured, "It will pass." She shivered, feeling a sudden chill across her skin.

"Well, my dear, I do hope you get better. Our garden needs tending again. You know," Janette swiftly changed subjects, "I don't believe I have ever noticed your eyes to be so brightly colored before. I know they've always been that unusual shade of purple, but today they seem remarkably deeper."

Axandra raised her fingers to the soft flesh around her eyes, as though she could touch the color of them. "I suppose I should take that as a compliment." Would anyone else notice?

Jeanette switched gears again. "I feel so sorry for the Protectress—having lost her daughter all those years ago— Twenty is it?"

"Twenty-one," Axandra stated too matter-of-factly. This caused Jeanette to peer at her suspiciously. "I, uh, I believe it's been twenty-one years," she stammered, pretending to be less knowledgeable.

"Twenty-one," Janette echoed. She held a crooked finger to her lips thoughtfully.

Panicking that she gave away too much, Axandra tugged at Jon's sleeve. "I need to go home."

"All right," Jon allowed and grudgingly helped Axandra to her feet. As soon as she was up, he released her and started away.

"So, when are the two of you going to get married?" Dora asked loudly, without qualms. Other heads turned in their direction. "You've been together so long now, you might as well."

Ignoring the old woman, Axandra followed Jon through the remnants of the crowd.

In the square, many of the villagers milled about, not quite sure if they should return to their work or go home to mourn. The only service being provided for the time being was spirits at the tavern.

"I'm going to head over to the pub to get the rest of the scuttlebutt," said Jon, his eyes wandering in that direction. "Will you be all right to walk home by yourself?"

Axandra hadn't expected to be abandoned so quickly. She opened her mouth to say no, that she needed him. Jon's instincts urged him to run away from her. He didn't understand why, but the need to flee overpowered any other emotion. Closing it again, she nodded to him. "I should be all right. I just need to rest."

"Thanks," he said and quickly ditched her where she stood. She heard him call out a hello to the operator of the tavern. Jon often worked there, cooking and serving food to travelers and locals.

"Let me walk you home," said a voice behind her. She recognized Lilsa's inflection. The friend came to a stop beside her, looking off in Jon's direction. "He's acting very strangely today," Lilsa observed, offended that anyone treat a friend of hers in such a manner.

Axandra looked to Lilsa's freckled face. "You don't have to do that. It's out of your way."

"Nonsense," Lilsa dismissed lightly. "I don't mind. We haven't talked in a week. You've been hiding out at your place."

"I wasn't feeling well," Axandra offered as an excuse, then scowled. Saying that would only give fuel to the rumor that she might be pregnant. She didn't want everyone to think it was true. Hurriedly, she tried to clear up such suspicions. "With a bug. Fish flu or something." She started walking toward the road that would pass her cottage about a kilom outside the village. She chose consciously not to look back at Jon. Lilsa kept pace beside her.

"Don't pay any attention to those old ladies. You're definitely not pregnant," Lilsa told her confidently. "You know I have a knack for those things."

"Why didn't you become a Healer?" Axandra asked her, knowing that Lilsa had been approached to join the respected profession, just as she had, a couple of years ago. They were both a little older than the typical recruits.

"Why didn't you?" Lilsa asked in return, signaling she would share if Axandra did. Each knew the other would keep her own secret.

"Well. I'm relieved to hear that," Axandra said, skipping back to the diagnosis. "I'm not ready to have a baby."

"I didn't think so—but you don't have the flu—and I heard your story about a jelly sting. I don't believe that either," rejected her dearest friend. Lilsa tucked her short brown hair behind her ears, only to have the sea breeze tickle the strands loose again. "Jon isn't listening. Do you want to tell me about it?"

Not answering immediately, Axandra walked quietly with Lilsa along the narrow road. Leaving the village proper, they entered a realm thick with leatherleaf and umbrella trees. A large colorful parrot perched in a small tree nearby, watching the two ladies pass him as he clung to a narrow branch. The strong wind from the open ocean clapped the heavy leaves together overhead. The ocean waves sounded gentle, muted by the thick vegetation. They walked alone. This road was rarely traveled except by the residents of the few homes along its path.

"I'm not really certain what to tell you," Axandra admitted, cautious of revealing anything. Her pace slowed. She felt exhausted from her exertions. If her head would quiet down, she thought she might be able to get some sleep. Even now, hints of voices echoed in the space between her ears. "I'm very tired. I don't feel like myself."

"When did Jon start acting so strange?" Lilsa prompted. "Usually he's fawning over you, ready to respond to your every whim? Today he just abandoned you in the street."

"A couple of nights ago," Axandra replied honestly. She remembered it too clearly, the spooked look on his face when she laid her hand upon his cheek. "It's my fault."

"Your fault?" Lilsa asked, abashed.

Axandra nodded. Her eyes followed the ground in front of her, concentrating on counting the dark pebbles along the way, hoping the exercise would clear her mind. "I've changed."

"People don't change overnight," her friend rebuked. Lilsa bent to grab a stone from the side of the road, the black surface scratched from decades of treading.

"I can't explain it, but I know Jon doesn't want to be with me anymore."

"Sounds like he's the one who's changed," Lilsa insisted. She was not willing to let her dear friend take the blame for the fouled relationship.

"Lilsa, you've been a very good friend to me," Axandra said gratefully. "I hope I've been the same to you."

Her companion stopped her, reaching for her hand and holding it tightly, a gesture reserved for the most intimate of friends. "Of course you have. And I will always be your friend, no matter what happens."

Yet, even as Lilsa said this, the expression on her face changed. Her charming smile fell away and was replaced with a perplexed wrinkle of her high forehead. She reached out with one hand to touch Axandra's face. "You do feel different."

Lilsa's mind seeped into hers like water through the seams. Her pink lips quivered. "You're in pain. Someone is hurting you." *Why is someone hurting you?*

Lights flashed in Axandra's eyes, and she sensed the Goddess reaching out to Lilsa with hurtful intentions.

Shaking her head, Axandra shrank away from her friend's touch and stifled the Goddess, at the same time wresting her hand free. "Stop! Don't! You sh-should go."

Axandra turned and dashed over the impacted ground, leaving Lilsa where she stood. Her friend did not follow.

First Jon. Now Lilsa. Axandra didn't want to scare anyone, but she did not have control over the power the creature possessed, nor control over the flashes in her mind of memories both hers and not. The noise in her head pained her. Stopping her ears with her fingers, she continued up the road, not looking back.

Before she realized what she was doing, she packed a travel bag with a few of her belongings—clothes, shoes, a couple of books and a necklace Jon had given her as a token of affection when they first began their romantic relationship.

The half-packed bag rested upon the mattress. She paused in her work and stared at it, confused that she felt an undeniable urge to flee her home. The compulsion was so strong, she continued packing even as she tried to restrain herself. Her body continued to act in ways her mind did not wish.

Her hands, moving independently, closed the packed bag and lifted the strap. Forcing herself to stop the progression, Axandra suddenly understood why she yearned to leave.

The Goddess wanted to return to Undun City. The creature belonged to that city, with its host standing in a position of power before the people as it had for centuries. Images of the stone city impressed upon her eyes, red granite buildings with terracotta shingles, a hill topped with a large white structure like a fortress. The spirit pulled her back there.

I don't want to go. This is my home!

Her body jerked, her resistance limiting the forced movements. The being forced her to pull the strap of the bag to her shoulder. The weight dragged her down so that her feet scooted across the floor, the soles of her sandals scraping the wooden planks. With a surge of force, her feet propelled her to the outer door. Throwing her arms out stiffly, she blocked her own exit.

No! You cannot control me! Even as she thought to it, her brain became saturated with more images. Ocean waters lapping at the hull of a ship. The wind whipping her hair and dress. Roads. Bumping over gravel and brick. The Palace, brightly lit by the afternoon suns.

Voices swelled in her ears. *We must come to a resolution soon. The people are already growing restless to know who will act as Protectress. (But there is no one else.) There must be someone—*

"Stop!" Axandra screamed aloud, raising her hands to her ears. Unsteady on her feet, she felt her spine meet the door frame as she stumbled. The heavy pack caught up in gravity and dropped like a stone in the sea. *Please stop! You're hurting me!*

The Palace stayed in her mind, as though the creature said, *Go there. We belong there.* The pressure of the image felt as though the building itself sat upon her chest.

With tears, Axandra conceded to go. "All right. I'll take us to Undun City. But why would they believe me?" she asked it. Worn down from the fight, she slid to the ground, her head to knees. "They think I'm dead."

A face fixed before her eyes, an old man, very pale with a full head of silver hair cut short. He possessed a round, bulbous nose pock-marked with scars. Red patches of capillaries dotted his pasty complexion. The likeness evoked a sense of familiarity in her. He was a Prophet. She did not remember his name. She long ago banished those people and their identities from her memory.

Without conscious movement, she stepped over to the writing desk and retrieved a few sheets of paper and a pen bloated with indigo ink. Her hand scripted a letter to the Head of Council. Her eyes watched her cursive script on the paper, but she did not compose the letter herself. She didn't even know what it was going to say until she read each word that appeared. Her fingers folded the letter and sealed it with a dab of sticky from the bowl on the desk. After addressing the outside, she slipped the letter into the pocket of her dress. They would send it from the town office before they set sail on a ship to cross the Ocean.

They. Two creatures locked together. She wanted to be herself again.

Axandra insisted that they write a second letter to Jon. The words that flowed on paper this time were her words. She apologized for frightening him. She explained that it was time for her to go home, a journey that required her to go immediately and one that required she go alone. As tenderly as her crude vocabulary allowed, she reminded him how much she loved him. Usually, she did not need words to express these things. She only needed to touch him, kiss him and let her gifts open up to him. Lastly, she invited him to come to Undun City and find her. "*I will be waiting for you. But I understand if you do not want to see me again,*" she added. "*All my love, Axandra.*"

This letter she folded once and used the sticky to post it to the door where he would most certainly see it.

With the pack on her shoulder again, she left the cottage and began a long journey.

Chapter 2

The Newcomer

30th Trimont, 307

The letter arrived in Undun City seven days after leaving Port Gammerton.

Addressed to the Head of Council, the folded parchment arrived in Nancy Morton's hands unopened. The outside bore no return address and only a single word in the upper left corner. "Ileanne."

Pursing her eyes and mouth, Nancy cracked the sticky seal and unfolded the sheet of paper with a gentle, curious touch. She reviewed the words written in elegant swirling characters that were almost difficult to read.

"Esteemed Councilor Morton,

I have carefully considered my obligations to the citizens of our small planet and believe it necessary to reclaim an identity I long ago relinquished when I fled the Prophets and disappeared.

While I do not expect to be believed at first, I am certain you will find that my true identity is that of Ileanne, daughter of Elora and Mitchum Saugray, though I have not gone by that name since the age of six.

I expect to arrive in Undun shortly after this letter is received, and I am prepared to submit to whatever tests you may require in order to prove or disprove my claim.

Sincerely,

Axandra Korte."

The Councilor frowned at the letter. Nancy feared that someone would attempt to lay claim to the identity of the long missing child. In fact, she anticipated many such claims as the weeks tarried forward. Her plan to deal with them consisted of politely acknowledging each claim. Then she would send a representative to explain that the enthusiasm to fill the shoes of the Esteemed was appreciated, but at the same time unwelcome. So far, this was the first such claim to be made. Unable to send a representative to the claimant, she would wait for the impending arrival.

The Council would indeed require tests to provide proof. Only a few individuals possessed the ability to confirm the identity of this mysterious visitor. And she would share this letter with no one but the few whom she needed. No use giving the people any false hope.

The audacity of anyone to pretend to be a long dead child! A distasteful grab at honor! Nancy could barely palate the thought that anyone would make such a bold and clearly false move.

Sitting at the wide desk in her office, Nancy read the letter a second time, focusing on different words of the composition, seeking out anything in the language that would indicate who this woman was or where she was from. The letter contained no regional references and no date. The family name meant nothing to her. Nor did the letter contain any details that were not publicly known. The letter represented a feeble attempt to excite her. Nancy felt no excitement. She suspected that no one would come. She dreaded her duties if the writer of this letter actually arrived. The visitor would not be welcomed kindly.

5th Quadrember

Councilor Morton kept watch over the front entrance of the Palace for several days, distracted her from her other duties. The staff observed her preoccupation, and they attempted to discover what secret she kept while staying well out of her way. Nancy caught one of the kitchen staff snooping in her office one afternoon and chased the young man out with a disgusted shout.

However, on a planet inhabited by people with telepathic abilities, secrets proved difficult to keep, especially when on the forefront of one's mind. Nancy couldn't help thinking about the letter. After six days, she grew restless waiting. She was about to give up that anyone would step forward to claim the note. Her inquiries into the location of a person named Axandra Korte turned up nothing. No one could find record that such a person existed. A fictitious name on a fictitious piece of drivel.

Miri caught the first stray thoughts about a visitor coming to Undun City, an important visitor, though the reason for the importance remained indiscernible to her from a mere peek. Morton shielded the thoughts whenever Miri lingered nearby.

But Miri let slip to other staff that the Councilor anxiously anticipated a visitor. Everyone in the Palace began to keep an eye on the front entrance to catch a first glimpse of the awaited stranger.

A council aide overheard that an Heir was coming to claim the Protectresship. He babbled this to everyone in the Palace, unable to contain his excitement that soon the Protectress would be with them again.

Morton frowned realizing the news spread around the staff like a prairie fire, deepening the creases in her already dour face. She reminded herself to keep her mind more shielded.

The seventh day after the letter arrived, a visitor appeared on the front walkway. From her office window, Nancy found a woman dressed in pale pink being escorted through the front doors of the Palace. She was a petite woman with dark brown curling hair loose about her shoulders.

For days Nancy had practiced how this first meeting would proceed. She decided she must march into the room with a cool head and skeptical temperament. She would dictate the tests to be performed. She half-expected that the show would quickly fizzle, that the imposter would give up immediately. If not, the Healer stood by to gauge the woman's state of mind and truthfulness. A Prophet would arrive tomorrow to determine the identity of the stranger, one of the Prophets who had last seen Ileanne the child.

Morton waited impatiently, tapping her foot on the stone floor beneath the window ledge. Frustrated with waiting for notification, she started out the door of her office just as Miri arrived with the news.

"Councilor Morton, Miss Axandra Korte awaits you in the Library," the young woman announced, careful not to display her own excitement that the visitor had finally arrived. The server kept her pink-painted lips in a straight line, but her pale blue eyes betrayed her hunger to hear the verdict.

"Thank you, Miri. Have tea served. I will be with her momentarily."

"Yes, Councilor." Miri bowed and turned from the office, leaving the door open as she left.

Alone for a moment, Nancy breathed deeply and steeled herself for the task ahead. She very much doubted that the woman could be the lost daughter. The child had undoubtedly perished under the Great Storm. To attempt to pass oneself off as the lost child displayed gross impudence.

These thoughts set Morton in a sufficiently sour mood, so she headed to the Library on the second floor of the Palace to find out just who this woman thought she was.

Stepping into the expansive room lined with bookshelves, Nancy first saw the woman's back. She observed a short woman, slender yet curved. A pink dress with one slightly tattered hem flowed over the slight frame down to her knees. Miss Korte wore only light sandals on her feet. An islander. The woman handled a book from one of the shelves and read the first page.

Looking up as she sensed someone watching her, Axandra Korte turned to the Councilor as the elder woman entered. She drew a somewhat sheepish smile on her sun-kissed face, perhaps already aware of the distrust brewing in her host.

"Greetings, Miss Korte. Welcome to Undun City," Morton greeted flatly, making the gesture less of a welcome and more of a formality. "From where did you travel?" Nancy asked curiously.

"I came from Gammer Island," replied the young woman without hesitation, trying to retain her smile despite the less than cheerful welcome. "From the village of Port Gammerton."

"That is quite a distance" Nancy stated. She knew well for she too was from the Western Islands, though not from Port Gammerton. "I judge by your arrival that you are determined to see this through."

"I am," Axandra replied seriously, more closely matching Morton's demeanor. She replaced the book carefully on the shelf before more formally addressing the Councilor. "As I suspected, you have doubts about my claim."

A server arrived with tea. Miss Korte waited silently with Morton while they were served. Neither moved to sit down among the lavishly upholstered furniture. Nancy watched the visitor as the woman surveyed the room from ceiling to floor.

When they were alone again, Axandra reminisced, "I loved the Library. My mother would let me hide in here from time-to-time to read picture books."

Nancy scowled listening to such a contrived story. The books on these shelves were rarely touched and the Protectress-Past had never mentioned her daughter's love of books. Elora rarely mentioned her daughter at all in recent years, and when she did, the thoughts sent the sick woman into a fit of grief.

"Let's get down to business, shall we?" urged Nancy. "With your permission, I have arranged two identification studies to be performed to validate your claim."

"Of course," the young woman agreed.

At that moment, Nancy took a good look at the woman standing a meter in front of her. Though disheveled from her travels, her resemblance to the Protectress-Past was unmistakable. From her oval face to her large almond-shaped eyes, round nose and soft lips painted in a natural shade of pink. Dark tea-colored curls contrasted her ivory skin tone, tanned from time under the suns. Miss Korte must have spent much of her time outdoors. Her mother's skin had never darkened to such a shade.

And those eyes—those lavender-colored irises that seemed to swirl like clouds in a whirlwind. Only the women of the Protectress' family were ever documented to have such color of eyes. The longer Nancy looked at them the more she decided that their color was true and not a trick of the light.

"First, our staff Healer will examine you physically and mentally to determine if you are being truthful. She will compare your physical examination to notes made by the Healer who would have cared for you as a child. Any birthmarks or scars will help determine the authenticity of your claim. She may also request a blood sample for further comparisons. Secondly, a Prophet who is familiar with the child Ileanne will examine your thoughts. I believe his examination may be the most definitive."

With that, the Councilor summoned the Healer, a middle-aged woman named Eryn Gray, who politely asked for the Councilor to wait outside while she conducted her examination. Nancy imagined the procedure to include a thorough examination from head to foot, making notes on a sheet of paper of paper, and then continuing with the entrance into the mind. For privacy, Nancy felt no concern being asked to vacate the area. When the door to the library opened, Nancy noticed Miss Korte fastening the last button of her dress and rising to her feet from where she had perched on a wall-mounted bench. Eryn slipped a vial containing a blood sample into her pack.

"I find no reason to believe that this woman is lying to us," the Healer announced openly. "She bears a pink stain birthmark between the spine and left scapula, similar to the one described in Healer Cardra's notes. I will compare the blood sample to those records as well."

"Very good," Nancy bowed gratefully to the Healer. "Thank you for your assistance." She ushered the Healer out of the Library and stood alone with Miss Korte once again. She thought she spied relief in the young woman's eyes. One obstacle overcome successfully.

"Tomorrow, the Prophet will arrive. I will summon you at that time to meet with him. I trust you're prepared to allow him to enter your mind."

"I have nothing to hide, Councilor. I wish you to understand the truth, as improbable as you believe it to be." Morton observed that Axandra remained calm about the situation, as though she had no doubt what they would find.

"Very well. We'll proceed. Do you have accommodations? I take it you just arrived in the city." Nancy eyed the wrinkled dress the woman wore and the stuffed travel bag that rested to one side of the doorway.

"I came straight here," Axandra confirmed. "This is a very urgent matter for many people. I'll find a suitable inn in the city."

"Nonsense. You may stay here in the Palace. I will have Miri show you to a guest room."

Nancy thought the woman about to protest, but saw her think the better of it. Miss Korte appeared tired and in need of rest.

"Thank you. That is much appreciated."

"You're welcome," Morton said with a snort, still putting on an air of distrust. She turned on her heels and marched from the room. She sent Miri in to see to her guest's needs and returned to her office for a final task of the day. As part of her daily ritual, she cleared her desk of all papers and arranged her personal items suitably on the dark surface. While doing so, Nancy discovered that her staunch disbelief of the young woman's claim was quickly replaced with overall acceptance. This both relieved her, as the office needed filled desperately, and disturbed her. Miss Korte's emanations emitted a pervasive pulse of persuasion.

Once the task was complete, Nancy left the Palace for her residence.

+++

Releasing a breath of great relief, Axandra allowed her shoulders slump as soon as Councilor Morton exited the room. The Head of Council, to her credit, did not allow the prospect of filling the position blindly lead her into accepting the claim. As frustrating as it was to go through the rigor of people stepping into her mind and eying her body, the ritual was also comforting. Not just anyone would be able to pose as the lost Heir.

And at least the Goddess rested quietly for now, having kept its promise to calm her mind if she came to Undun City. The creature still weighed heavily in her head, a physical weight that strained her neck. She hoped she would get used to the burden.

Soft pattering footsteps alerted her that someone else approached. Straightening her posture, she made herself ready for another round of questions.

Miri, the young blonde woman who had greeted her in the main hall, appeared in the Library again and asked that Axandra follow her. The aide moved lithely and quick, every move purposeful. They walked quietly up a flight of stairs in the center of the Palace and turned right into the south wing of the elaborate edifice, where the guest residences lay opposite the Protectress' residential suite.

Many memories from her childhood returned, things she had long ago buried in her strife to be someone else. She was never allowed in the guest wing, though she had wandered down this corridor a couple of times. She'd been just four or five then. The details were unclear, except for the feelings she remembered, a curiosity about everything and the desire to explore. She used to escape from her nanny and tutor and sneak around all over the Palace, much to their chagrin.

Antiquities and art lined the corridor, depicting a faraway world from the past. A large painting illustrated a pastoral scene, a picnic of ladies and gentlemen dressed in fine fabrics and buckled shoes. Heads nodded toward each other as though conversing. The grass lay green and the sky soared blue—not the lavender color of this planet's atmosphere.

Miri guided Axandra to a suite halfway down the corridor and on the east side of the building, where she stopped to open an ornately carved door.

"We refer to this as the Fairytale Room," Miri explained cheerfully, her pink lips beaming a welcoming, toothy smile, "since the door is carved with fairies and nymphs. That isn't official though." She lowered her voice to a whisper at the last remark. She went immediately to the double doors of the balcony and pushed back long silken drapes to let the sunlight filter in.

"I understand you've traveled quite a long distance, Ms. Korte. I can have your clothing laundered and bring up a meal when you're ready. The chef is preparing stuffed lettuce for supper."

"Thank you very much," Axandra accepted both offers, handing Miri a majority of her luggage.

"The Head of Council says you may have your run of the Palace. She only asks that the north wing of this level be regarded as off limits. That's the Residence."

Axandra nodded in understanding. "I will respect that."

Miri moved quickly to continue her business, heading for the door. "I am at your disposal during your stay. Just let me know if you need any assistance."

"Oh, for the moment, I'm just going to rest. It's been a long trip."

"Very well." Miri disappeared, closing the wide door behind her.

Breathing in the air of the room, Axandra found it fragrant with flowers from a planter covering a small table. She went out onto the balcony and looked down at a lush garden filled with native blossoms and hedges, some so tall as to block the paths from view of each other. The grounds stood divided from a forest of broad-leaf trees by a two-and-a-half meter wall. The trees lined the banks of a shallow river that ran wide and clear. Sunlight glinted off the water.

As Axandra sat down on a lounge chair draped with a small canopy for shade, exhaustion settled in her bones. The cushions of the chair felt luxurious compared to the lodgings aboard the sailing ship and riding in a bumpy solar bus for hours.

The trip had taken sixteen days of dreaming up scenarios of how this meeting might go. She imagined any number of results, from being welcomed back with open arms to being forced back out the door without consideration. The event landed acceptably in the middle. Things could have gone much worse.

Thoughts about the day began to melt away, replaced by contentment to be lying against the soft shams, her toes kissed by the suns. The garden gave the air a sweet and moist aroma. It was Spring, and every plant glowed brightly with new growth. The suns basked the world in a warming light. A cool breeze brushed her skin and ruffled her dress. Her eyelids grew heavy.

Floating in the front of her brain, she saw her mother's face, the adoring face she remembered from childhood. The face wore a warm and inviting smile.

+++

Miri woke her when the suns were nearly set and an orange-pink glow belted the lavender sky. As the shade darkened to indigo, the stars began to shine. A subtle patch of the Milky Way melted across the middle of the skydome like a leftover cloud.

"I apologize, Ms. Korte," Miri said at waking her. "I thought you might be ready for dinner now. It's nearly eight o'clock."

Axandra opened her eyes to the pleasant and friendly face, then sat up slowly on the lounger.

"Yes," she said after considering the growling of her stomach. "I am. Thank you. I was much more tired than I realized." She quickly combed her fingers through her curls to revive them and pushed herself up to her feet.

The balcony table lay set for one with a covered plate and silverware on a cream-colored table cloth. "It's a very pleasant evening," Miri began to chat. "Is there anything else you need at the moment?"

Axandra sensed Miri's curious questions running rampant through her mind. "I would enjoy a conversation that doesn't involve sailing or fishing," Axandra said with a depressed laugh. "If I can make use of you for that purpose."

Invitation accepted, Miri slid herself onto a seat across the table. "Certainly. Go ahead with your dinner. I've already eaten. Where are you from exactly?"

While Axandra nibbled at the wraps, which were stuffed with a mixture of vegetables, fruit and mushrooms glued together with a nutty sauce, Axandra explained that she had traveled from about the farthest point away from Eastland as was possible and that she had sailed across the open Ocean instead of coming by land. "I've been seasick for almost two straight weeks." The rich food made her stomach rejoice, for she had eaten very bland meals supplied by the sailors with limited supplies. She hadn't even eaten lunch today. As soon as she made landfall, she got on the bus to come to Undun, another six hours, wasting no time on trivials such as meals.

For dessert, there were chilled berries in cream. After devouring the wraps, Axandra took to those greedily with her spoon. The cream tasted sweet with a pinch of sugar.

"You enjoyed that I see," Miri gestured to the empty plate. "The chef will be pleased. Why is it that you've come to us, Ms. Korte, if I may ask? You've traveled a very long way when surely a letter would have sufficed." The young woman thought she was being clever, fishing for hints.

Axandra answered carefully, however. Until the final verdict was reached, she would not be announcing to anyone in general that she was the Heir. "In this case, it was not sufficient. I'm sorry that I'm not at liberty to give you any details. It's currently a matter of personal concern."

The aide looked at her more seriously. She leaned close to the table and glanced around as though to check for any other listeners.

"You are Her aren't you?" Miri asked insistently. "You are the daughter."

Axandra emulated Miri's secretive posture and prepared an ambiguous response.

There came a knock at the door. Miri jumped up and grabbed the dishes, making herself look busy.

"Come in," Axandra called.

The door swung open to allow Councilor Morton and a second figure to enter the suite. The Prophet had apparently arrived earlier than expected. Morton saw no point in wasting time today.

Miri escaped with the dishes before Morton had a chance to shoo her out.

Axandra recognized the Prophet immediately. He looked slightly older, but essentially the same as he had twenty-one years ago, his pale face scarred with craters. His presence elicited a cringe. "Elder Tyrane."

"It is I, Ileanne," he nodded in confirmation. "I am surprised and pleased to see that you survived."

Morton's eyes widened at the passing tones, apparently taking this as the confirmation that Axandra was indeed whom she claimed to be. Immediately, her distrustful expression softened. Prophets were truth-seers. No one had ever been able to pass lies anywhere near them. Their abilities were too powerful. "You recognize her?"

"I do indeed. I recognized her aura as soon as I came near the Palace," Tyrane stated in a tone that mixed relief with somberness. "The presence is very strong. Though it has been a long stretch of years, an individual's base emanations change little over time. They are something about ourselves that we cannot change."

His voice was laced with disappointment as well, perhaps at her choice to disappear and remain hidden, rather than return to her rightful place. Axandra felt the manipulative fingers of his telepathy envelop her. Though wary, she opened up to him as she promised the Councilor she would.

Why did you flee? He asked her mind, addressing her without sharing his conversation with Councilor Morton.

Before Axandra could answer, Morton cleared her throat, addressing them both. "You have passed this test," Nancy said. "Now we await the more physical evidence that will validate your claim, your blood sample comparison. Then we will decide how to proceed further."

Taking Tyrane with her, Morton left. Axandra stayed alone in her suite. Darkness reigned outside and the city below turned on the lights. The broad vista of sky filled with stars of every magnitude, the same stars seen from her cottage on the island when she had stared into the sky, looking into the past.

The past caught up with her quickly now. She could not turn back and return to the islands and to Jon. Breathing in a deep sigh, Axandra contemplated her decision to leave the Haven and run away and wondered exactly why she had left. A six-year-old's reasons seemed far too simple now that she was an adult. Fear and hate had been her motivation then, wanting nothing more to do with the Prophets or her parents and their violation of her body with the Sliver. Had Tyrane frightened her off, when she had accidentally seen into his thoughts? He had been thinking of the future then, of something hideous. She did not remember the images in any detail, only that they horrified her.

Whatever the reason, her life played out this way and could not be redone. She had not learned anything about being Protectress while growing up, but perhaps that would give her a better understanding of the people whom she intended to watch over. Her life paralleled her constituents, instead of one catered to and pampered. Her past could only make her a stronger person in the future.

+++

Councilor Morton took Tyrane to the Council Chamber on the first floor of the Palace. In the large room of risers and desks gathered three of the seventeen elected members of the People's Council.

In this room they created rules and guidelines to protect the people and continually interpreted the laws as laid forth in their Covenants, preventing the citizens from destroying this world as Old Earth had been destroyed centuries ago. The Council met just three times per year for one week. For the most part, governance was kept at a minimum, impacting little in the routine lives of the people. After three centuries, the general public was adept at keeping themselves out of trouble. The Council dealt mostly with natural disasters and the equitable distribution of resources.

These three members composed a special group, the few who knew the secret that the Protectress would always carry.

Nancy heard them speaking in quiet tones to one another. They sat in the front row of desks.

"Why do you think she's called us here at this hour?" asked Franny in a gravelly voice of complaint. "I was just about to go to bed when March came knocking at my front door."

"It must concern the woman who came to the Palace today," answered Casper. "There is a rumor—"

The three turned immediately toward the clomping footsteps, and Casper left his statement unfinished. They sat in the front row of desks.

Once again, the loose lips of the Palace staff had taken care of much of the work. The Councilors' eyes looked up at her curiously, though no one dared ask the question that teetered on the tip of each of their tongues.

Nancy Morton suggested that they move to her office and they quickly departed from the large room to a hallway that hid several smaller offices used by the Councilors during their vigils in the capital city. The Head of Council's office lay immediately opposite the Council Chamber door.

Seating themselves in the chairs around a small tea table, they waited quietly for Morton's report.

Nancy sat in the largest chair and looked carefully at each of her cohorts before speaking. She sensed their eagerness for any tidbit and their awareness that, to be called together at this hour, the news offered a solution to a very difficult problem.

"As I'm certain you all know, thanks to our talkative staff, a woman arrived at the Palace this afternoon. She is the writer of the letter I shared with you all last week." Each of them leaned forward in his or her seat, just enough to decrease the space in the center of the circle. "The Healer is doing her job to compare this woman's attributes, inside and out, to the Healer's notes of record. She will complete her task tomorrow, but is already satisfied that our visitor can be believed. This man, Elder Tyrane of the Prophets, will voice his opinion to us now."

Tyrane had not taken a seat with the Councilors but remained standing, positioning himself near Morton's chair. "This woman is indeed Ileanne Saugray, Elora's daughter. I can feel that the Goddess is with her. The Goddess will seek out only the one whom it has touched."

In general, the sense of relief saturated the room. Surprise surfaced as well, tempered with curiosity and satisfaction. How could the young girl have stayed hidden so long? Who raised her? Thank the Goddess she had returned!

"Then the blood test should prove that she is physically the daughter?" Foster Tremby asked of Morton, still harboring a doubt or two. This had come about too easily. "It will be needed as proof to the general public." He was often the voice of public relations, understanding what the people wanted and needed to hear and making it understandable when situations did not come clearly cut. This was definitely one of those times. The citizens remained unaware of the Goddess and her existence inside their leader, a secret kept all these centuries for good reason. They were not about to make it public now.

"Yes, I expect the sampling will offer the definitive proof. Eryn will tell us tomorrow."

"What has she been doing all this time?" questioned grouchy Franny Gilbert. Her old face seemed squashed with age, her eyes narrow and her flesh sagging. "How did she survive?"

Tyrane offered his thoughts on the matter. Ileanne had taken one of the cars, which were easy to operate, and headed west out of the Storm. When she emerged, she was taken in as an orphan and raised by another family. "I sense she suffered no strife. Though my contact with her was brief, I find her mind is that of a woman who was brought up in a happy, productive home."

"But she didn't try to come home?" Franny disbelieved. "A child wants to be with her mother and father."

"I cannot explain her intentions at that time, since I did not have access to her mind after she left the Haven," Tyrane said flatly. "It would appear that she did not want to be found."

Nancy staved off further questions with the statement, "When the blood sample results return tomorrow, we must be prepared to reintroduce the Heir to the people. She is to become our Protectress. The people will know something by morning with all the chatter around here. Questions are coming our way, and we must be prepared to answer them. She will require a great deal of training to make up for lost time."

"But you told us she was likely an imposter," Foster argued, crossing his arms glumly over his chest.

"My beliefs were misplaced. I will arrange for everyone to meet her tomorrow, and you will see that she must be Ileanne." Morton made no further apology.

They all agreed to draft an introduction speech and training regimen while gathered in session that night.

"You will find," said Tyrane "that training a Protectress requires little effort. The Goddess contains the life experiences of every previous Protectress our world has known. Her service will come to her naturally."

Morton scoffed his sentiment. "Her service isn't so simple. She shows no poise and no restraint. The last thing the people need is a free spirit jumping into the lead." She grabbed paper and pens for each of them and rejoined them at the table. "We are finished with you for now. Go make yourself comfortable in one of the guest rooms." Nancy brushed her fingers through the air to dismiss him.

To that, Tyrane excused himself. Nancy glanced up briefly as he walked out to make certain he closed the door behind him.

+++

At a quarter past nine, sleepiness crept through her body again. The Palace, this room, was the safest place she had slept in a fortnight, yet Axandra remained uneasy about being here. Outside her door, she sensed that people kept passing by, their thoughts curious about the occupant of this room. Their expectations loomed about her in the air. *Is it really her? (Has she come to stay?) Perhaps she will be the greatest Protectress of all time. (She lived among the real people, people like us.) I wonder what service she offered before she came here?*

She tried to block them out, but the strain of the day depleted her defenses. Tiny noises bothered her ears, like the hooting nighthawk in the garden outside. She wanted it to fly away and make noise somewhere else. Letting her mind drift, she imagined the static sound of the Ocean and let it wash over her senses.

The knock on the door startled her, bringing her back to where she sat in an ornately carved chair. Who was bothering her now? She sensed the Prophet outside the door. She did not want to be alone with him, yet she rose and loosened the lock.

Don't control me, Axandra chided the entity harshly. *I will make my own decisions.*

"Good evening, sir," she said politely, though without smiling. "I wasn't expecting you to return tonight."

"Morton rushed me away before my visit was complete. May I come in?" Tyrane opened his hand toward the chairs set in the front of the room.

Glancing at the furniture, she still dreaded being alone with him. But what harm could he do to her here? They were surrounded by people in the building. "I guess that would be all right. For a few minutes. I'm very tired."

"I only came to see how you were doing," he gave as reason for his visit. In this private meeting, his expression softened to one of fatherly concern. He followed her and sat only after she lowered herself into one of the fine chairs. "Receiving the full Goddess is not a pleasurable experience. Usually the receiver returns to the Haven for assistance in accepting the gift."

"Not a pleasurable experience," she echoed with wry smirk. "That, sir, is the grandest understatement I've ever heard. I have never felt such pain in my entire life." The lamps from the sleeping area shown through the silk partition, silhouetting the colorful fairies that carried the theme of the suite. She studied the figures for a moment before focusing her eyes upon Tyrane again. This time, she resisted the floating touches his mind sent out to her. "I am fine now. I have … adjusted over the last two weeks."

He sat with a straight spine in a spindle-legged chair and waited patiently for her to continue. His posture urged her to keep talking.

"I'm tired," she admitted, rubbing her eyes and flaring her nostrils as she drew in another deep breath. "It keeps my mind open when I want to block things out. I don't feel any rest."

"That is typical," Tyrane responded. He sat very still and kept a respectable distance, though Axandra witnessed tension in his muscles. He probably wanted to reach out and give her help. She created a barrier over her torso with her crossed arms.

"I am pleased that you chose to return to your true life," Tyrane said to her, expressing genuine gratitude. "We worried a great deal that you had perished in the Storm, that the Sliver of the Goddess was lost. We could not ask for another. Your mother believed you were still alive. She only wished to see you one more time."

If his words intended to make her feel guilty, they succeeded in giving her such a twinge. Axandra avoided his brown eyes and struggled with her feelings toward her mother, the woman who never seemed to have time for her daughter. When Ileanne was six, she felt nothing but anger at being sent away. Her mother had just been frightened knowing what was to come.

"Tell me why you ran away."

Axandra felt herself pulled into the past for a brief moment, remembering in flickers the day she escaped. Fear, hate, lightning, and sand were all she could see.

"I will not explain myself to you," she denied, staring him down. "It is too late to change what happened. And I don't appreciate being saddled with guilt for my mother's grief. I saw her three times in my village when I was growing up. Not one time did she look at me and know it was me. You would think a mother would know her own child." Axandra said the last part under her breath, more to herself than to him.

"Yet here you are, completing the cycle," Tyrane reminded her.

"When the Goddess found me, I realized returning here was inevitable," she explained, her shoulders slumping sadly. "I left behind my home and my loved ones—I don't think I will ever see them again, not in this life."

The conversation agitated her. Now that she vocalized what she had truly given up, her calmness ended. "It seems inescapable."

Tyrane placed a hand under his chin and rested a finger along his pale cheek. His skin glowed chalky white and his hair gray and thick. He looked the part of elder, old enough to be her grandfather.

"This is where you have always belonged, Ileanne. It will be your home again—your true home. You will do great things. It is your time."

Axandra brooded, pursing her lips. "Great things. That is an indistinct foretelling. It could be a great blunder. Don't you see things more clearly?"

"I wish you goodnight, Ileanne," Tyrane said as he rose to leave, giving no acknowledgment to her scathing remark. "And welcome home."

Axandra scowled at him and locked the door in his wake. Worked up from his visit, she fretted it would take another hour to settle down to sleep. She set to work relaxing immediately.

Chapter 3

Acceptance

In the year 285

"**Mother,** may I go play in the garden?" asked the small child. Ileanne leaned her elbows on her mother's lap and looked up at the oval face and dark wavy hair.

Those strange violet eyes peered down at her with a smile. "Not right now. I need you to go with Corey and learn your lessons."

"I'd rather go outside," the girl replied matter-of-factly, testing her mother to see if she might change her mind.

"After your lesson. Go now," her mother insisted, returning her attention to the pages being handed to her by a dark-suited woman who often worked at her mother's side.

Lips curled in disappointment, Ileanne dragged her feet to leave her mother's office.

"Please put your shoes on, darling," said her mother, looking to the girl briefly.

"Yes, mother."

"And I love you. Have a good day."

"I love you, too, Mother." Ileanne said it out of habit. She didn't feel it at the moment, but she said it anyway. She wanted to go outside, not into the stuffy library. And she hated her shoes.

They were too sweaty in the summer and made her feel hot all over. She couldn't feel the grass in her shoes or the soft carpet or the cold stone floors.

She started toward the Library, walking slowly and dragging her fingers along the wall of the long corridor. As she walked, she avoided various pedestals holding urns and statues, pieces of art from places on this world and one faraway that she would never see. Why did they keep this old stuff? She wasn't allowed to touch it or play with it. The pieces meant nothing to her and most of it smelled dusty and old.

The suns beamed in through the western windows. High suns, just after lunch time. She felt sleepy from lunch. Going outside would keep her awake, not her lessons.

Corey waited for her outside the Library door.

"I'm glad to see you back, Ileanne," he said with a gentle smile. "As a reward, I will forego the ritual of strapping on your shoes."

She brightened a little.

"And we will make it a short lesson," he said, gesturing her inside. "Just a little reading."

After she read through just a few pages of her primer, Corey dismissed the lesson and took her down to the sunny garden. Gleefully she ran down from the veranda and into the paths, dashing left and right, chasing insects and birds.

"Don't go too far," Corey called out to her, following her in between the hedges. He laughed as she played. She would take her specimens to him and ask for identification, showing him insects, leaves, flowers and a quick-moving reptile that crossed her path.

But always, something else walked in the garden with her, a strange feeling that someone stared at her. Ileanne felt it whenever she was out here. She kept that to herself.

+++

Axandra opened her eyes to a glaring gray that appeared smooth and unending across the stratosphere. The doors to the small balcony spread wide open, letting in the thick, wet smell of rain and the soft pulse of water droplets pounding on stone and leaves.

Stretching, she sat up in the soft bed and leaned on her bent knees, keeping her eyes on the view outside. She breathed in deeply to bring herself fully awake, drawing the cool moisture into her lungs.

Though she had been away for over twenty years, everything about this place wafted a familiar scent, from the native plants to the aged must of the tapestries and paintings and the tang of the peculiar rain that fell just this side of the mountains.

All of the land within one hundred kiloms of the Great Storm was affected by the churning, ionic atmosphere and the concentration of certain atoms that existed within the contained region. Why the Storm remained stationary was not understood—by all scientific rights it should flow eastwardly with the currents of the atmosphere. Yet it hovered, held by some undetectable force, swirling in a myriad of purple, orange and pink, brightened by flashes of cloud lightning that could be seen over the peaks of the jagged young mountains. The rain from passing storm clouds secreted a more acrid aroma absorbed from those peculiar atoms in the Storm.

Axandra looked out opposite the Storm, east toward the horizon. Except for the columns of trees that lined streams and rivers, the land stretched out in broad, flat plains of tall grass, dotted here and there with herds of grazing animals. Two roads wound out from the City within this panorama. One headed almost due east, toward the shore towns—Otsmouth, Port Galient and Ocean Pointe. The other steered northeast toward Steward Falls and Towton. The roads were paved with chip rock and tar seal. The east road appeared to be in need of repair. A small solar-powered car headed in from the east road, tires bumping over potholes and sloshing in the muddy water.

Stepping out onto the veranda, which was half-covered by a ledge above, Axandra held her hands out into the rain. The sprinkles cooled and refreshed her skin.

Barefoot and in her robe, she decided she would go for a walk.

Moments later she reached the garden and walked among the carefully cultivated vegetation. She let the rain soak through to her skin. The air moved in cool drafts, and goose bumps popped up on her arms and neck. Though she had tied it up in a loose knot, her should-blade long hair dripped and clung to her neck.

The spitting droplets washed the color out of everything from the sky to the ground. Only the vibrant reds, purples and pinks of the blossoms remained, stark against the gray. Some flowers bloomed in tiny bunches. Others splayed large petals, and water pooled in the bells and cups.

As she walked among the hedges and along the paths, she thought back to her dream, the churned up memories of a four-year-old wanting nothing more than to go outside and experience everything she could lay her hands on. She laughed as a bird, startled by her approach, flew out of a nearby bush, splattering her with water from its wings. She opened her mouth as though to ask her tutor what kind of bird it was, then remembered she walked out here alone.

Further along the path, Axandra let her mind empty and thought of nothing more than the flowers and the rain, leaving her anxiety and sadness behind her. Her senses floated in the air just outside herself, listening to everything. A nest of hatchlings lay hidden in the hedge. The mother bird nestled them warmly beneath her breast. Plump raindrops burst into smaller droplets each time one struck a leaf.

Miri approach. Axandra sensed the vibrant young woman long before she arrived.

"Miss Axandra!" Miri exclaimed from under a large umbrella. "You're soaked to the skin. You'll catch fever!" Prepared as she always seemed to be, Miri wrapped Axandra's shoulders in a dry blanket and sheltered her with the umbrella. Axandra took notice that the portable shelter was stitched out of some sort of waterproofed fabric, rather than the gigantic leaves of the umbrella tree prevalent on the islands.

The gentle shower continued to fall steadily as they headed toward the covered portion of the large veranda that stretched across the back side of the Palace.

"The walk was very refreshing," Axandra explained with a cheerful laugh. The blanket felt warm on her skin. She hugged the fleece closer.

"And a bit chilly," Miri complained. "If you get sick, Morton'll scuttle me down to basement work."

On one of the ironwork tables steamed a pot of tea. Breakfast lay served as well, in this case hot fruit and cream.

"It's not that bad. I'm fine," Axandra assured with a dismissive wave of her hand. "Thank you for the blanket. This smells wonderful."

As she ate, the warm food and tea heated her from the inside and made the goose bumps recede. Miri waited patiently nearby.

"What time is it?" Axandra asked.

"Ten o'clock" Miri answered.

"Oh," she responded, somewhat taken aback. She thought it much earlier and hadn't bothered to look at any clocks. "It's difficult to tell time in the rain."

"I thought it best to let you be. You've been on a long trek to get where you are," Miri explained as she refilled the mug with tea. Steam drifted into the air and was swept away by a puff of wind coming out of the rain. The precipitation began to thin just a bit, but the wind picked up beneath the clouds.

"The weather watchers says it'll rain for the next few days. It'll be perfect for the spring crops," Miri said, offering idle chatter for her charge.

But at that moment, Axandra stared into the garden, listening to another voice. She couldn't make out the whisper of thought that brushed her mind, but the Goddess reacted to it like a prairie cat to an intruder, arching its back and hissing, claws extended and ready to strike. The presence concealed itself nearby, watching them.

"Miss Axandra, are you all right?" Miri's voice filtered in when the young woman gently touched her upper arm, a soft but quick gesture only to gain her attention. The woman's mind felt strong and comforting, not painful.

The nudge was enough to bring her back to where she sat, away from the static-like noise made by the strange presence.

"Are there predators in this area?" Axandra asked abruptly, squinting over toward Miri.

Eyes glancing to the side briefly, Miri answered knowledgeably. "A few, yes. Mostly the packhounds that hunt the prairie. They are usually nocturnal, though they do hunt in the rain frequently. The mud slows the bustles or something like that. Why do you ask? They can't get in this garden. The walls are too high."

Miri must have caught a hint of her worry that one trespassed in the garden, the image of a large dog-like creature snarling and baring its teeth as it watched, secluded behind a hedge.

"Oh, I was just curious," Axandra dissuaded, looking away toward the garden again. "I thought I heard something," she said honestly. "I should have known about the wall."

"Well, the garden was only walled in about nineteen years ago," Miri told her. "You couldn't have remembered."

"That makes sense then," Axandra agreed, taking some relief in that fact. Yet, it also stirred up the fear that she had sensed something worse than a packhound stalking nearby. The presence felt extremely old and patient.

"Well, I should clean up and get dressed," Axandra rose up from the table, still wet, but warmer. She wanted to the leave the strangeness here. "I think I'll take a warm bath to take off the chill."

"I'll get one ready for you," Miri agreed. She hurried ahead, her blue skirt swaying about her slim hips.

Axandra followed more slowly, tarrying across the rug to the main staircase.

"Oh, good morning, Ms. Korte," greeted Councilor Morton, who just stepped into the main hall from a side room. Once again, the Councilor dressed in formal silk suit, this one maroon flecked with gold in the jacket and slacks. On the right breast of the jacket, she wore a large gold and jeweled broach, an emblem of her office. Ruby stones accented four graceful curves in progressively smaller sizes—the two suns and two moons, the symbol known as the Four Circles.

The Councilor's eyes surveyed her up and down, frowning at her dripping state. In an indignant gesture, she fluffed the curls on the back of her cropped gray hair. "I trust Miri is taking care of your wardrobe. I expect to have the results of the blood sample comparison reported to me this afternoon. Healer Eryn is working on them now."

"So soon? Uh, yes. Miri is taking great care in her work," Axandra assured the Councilor who seemed in doubt of Miri's abilities.

"Very good. I will summon you later. Good day." Morton already turned and started away.

The Councilor already knew the truth, yet she continued to try to downplay the situation, hoping to avoid any premature leaks of information. It was also clear the Morton disliked Axandra and thought her naïve and unprepared. Axandra admitted to herself that she was both of these things.

"Good day, Councilor," she wished more kindly. Then she headed up the staircase.

The bath warmed her thoroughly and washed away a great deal of grime from her trip. Then she dressed in her freshly laundered blue dress and sweater. Outside the rain still fell and the air felt damp and chilly.

Axandra waited now, not quite certain what to do with herself while the hours stretched before the inevitable news was shared. No doubt the Council needed to make decisions about how best to proceed with reintroducing her to the world-community. They would take great care to limit the shock.

She had no work to do, no chores and no hobbies with which she could entertain herself at the moment. The rain made it less than desirable to explore the town that lay below the Palace, even with an umbrella.

That left exploring the Palace, which she did not feel welcome doing even though Councilor Morton gave such permission, probably with a grudge.

Axandra looked back down at the garden. She stood on a high enough level to see into most of the space between the hedge rows, even into some areas secluded by dwarf trees.

Several uniformed individuals stalked along the paths, clearly in search of something. Axandra thought they must be members of the Elite, the Palace security force. Dark gray rain cloaks covered the uniforms, but as one tossed back his cloak to reach for a pocket, she saw the golden emblem of the Four Circles emblazoned on his chest. The uniforms themselves were dark gray flecked with metallic gold. Each member wore a cap that supported an oil skin against the rain. She counted five visible, possibly more further into the garden that extended over a half-kilom of land. In their hands, they carried small devices the like of which Axandra had never seen before. Non-lethal weapons, she surmised. The humans, upon coming to this world, had discarded all lethal weapons and all knowledge of their construction. Guns, swords, and other devices of war existed only in ancient books that had survived the Journey.

Miri must have mentioned her guest's concern about the packhounds in the garden and asked the guards to check for a stray animal inside the high stone walls. The server seemed very attentive to others whims.

Settling on her occupation for the next few hours, Axandra headed for the Library one story below. She slipped on her sandals and went out into the corridor, closing the door softly behind her. Despite the carpeted runner down the center of the hall and the variety of tapestries hanging along the walls, loud noises still echoed off the stone. She did not want to attract much attention, and she knew that some of those guards lurked in the hallways of the Palace.

In the Library, she searched the shelves for something to pique her interests. She found an illustrated field guide to the local plants and animals in Eastland. She immediately looked in the index for the packhound and turned to the pages describing the creature. The visage rendered in pen and ink struck her as quite gruesome. The drawing depicted a tall animal with a sleek body and nimble legs built for quick bursts of speed. The head sprang like an oversized knob from the body, sporting a mouth filled with sharp teeth. Two long fangs jutted down from the upper jaw. Oversized ears pointed straight up, each turned in a different direction to listen independently for the slightest sound. Thick fur bristled high on the back, and the tail tucked low.

She certainly did not want to encounter the likes of such a beast. The captioning stated that attacks on humans were rare, mostly because humans stayed out of the way of these beasts and the hounds kept to the open prairie, away from homes. However, packhounds would eat whatever they could catch and had little fear of people. They traveled in packs of at least eight adults. Only sick or dying animals ventured off alone, if they escaped being eaten by their own pack.

Amazing, she thought, that the wall had not been erected around the garden earlier. The Palace stood on this hill for the last two hundred fifty years and the packhounds roamed here long before humans left Earth.

Holding onto the book for further reading about the indigenous flora and fauna, Axandra moved on through the shelves. She pulled out a recently penned volume by a Southlander entitled *Tales of the Journey: A Collection of Short Historical Fiction.* The introduction made a quick read, explaining that the author based his fiction upon stories passed down through his family. It was printed in the year 304.

With a slight creak, the left side of the double entry door opened inward. Miri found her once again.

"Miss Korte, Councilor Morton would like you to meet with her and the Council members in the Council Chamber."

"Already? That was much sooner than I expected," Axandra said, instantly feeling her heart race in anticipation. Breathing in deeply, she lifted her shoulders, letting them fall again with the exhalation. Books under her arm, she followed Miri out into the corridor. The aide closed the Library door behind them and began the march to the Council Chamber on the main level of the building.

They stepped into a small anteroom just outside the main doors of the chamber. These heavy wooden doors were carved with a large tree beginning with a curled but thick trunk that wound from the roots toward the left, slightly to the right, and then left again with a small twist. Brass leaves covered the numerous branches. Tiny serif lettering etched many of the leaves, bearing the names of those who had served as Councilors. The mentions included all members since the Council's formation, just a few years after the Landing. The years of service followed each name. The names began in the bottom section of leaves and worked up to the most recent Councilors. Layers of unetched leaves waited to honor the future classes.

Axandra focused on the base of the tree for a moment, taking a deep breath as they paused before these doors.

Outside the open archway of the anteroom, the staff slowly gathered. They tried not to seem obtrusive. Miri smiled at them and rested her hand on the door handle. "Are you ready?" she asked with an encouraging smile.

Axandra handed the young woman the books and nodded. "I am." She raised her head and straightened her spine.

Miri opened the doors.

Axandra walked straight into a round room set with desks upon rounded risers. At each desk sat a member of the Council, save a single councilor's seat. A second empty seat in the front of the room remained reserved for the Protectress.

Nancy Morton rose to her feet and wasted no time on pretense.

"Ms. Axandra Korte, the blood sample comparison confirms your claim of relation to the Protecting family. Tyrane of the Prophets confirms that you are Ileanne, the lost daughter of the Protecting family. I offer the Councilors the opportunity to challenge the claim."

One rose, a younger man with a cynical expression. He donned a drab suit with a high keyhole collar. His raven hair was cropped below his ears, but slicked back at the sides. His skin gleamed deep bronze.

"Mr. Osander has the floor."

"Ms. Korte, I find your timing impeccable. You waited to come forward when no one in the family is left alive to confirm your identity, and you wasted little time after the Protectress' death to come forward to claim your title. Do you do this simply for the fortune of the Protectresship?"

Believing that the overall presence in the room accepted her has the Heir, Axandra felt encouraged, not intimidated, by this man's harsh tone.

"The Protectress has no fortune," Axandra reminded those present. "She exists to serve and protect her people as a voice in their stead. I have come to you now to fulfill the obligation I have owed since my birth."

"You could have come to us long before now to begin fulfilling your duties," Osander demanded. "What possesses you now? Glory? Fame?"

What an odd way to phrase the question, Axandra thought, for he did not know the true secret. Only three did, she remembered this from what little training she had received from the Prophets. Three Councilors knew about the Goddess—the only people in the world outside of the Prophets.

"If I could fulfill the duties of the office in obscurity, away from public eyes—I would prefer it. I have no desire for everyone to know my face or adore me," Axandra stated honestly. "I understand these things come as part of my service. I want only to preserve that which our people hold most dear—our way of life."

Morton interrupted the young man. "Thank you, Councilor Osander. She has sufficiently answered the questions. Are there any other challengers?"

No one else came forward.

"The Council has already voted to validate your claim and to begin your installation as Protectress. Do you accept this office?"

A quiver coursed along her muscles from her feet to the neck. She hoped no one could see her shaking.

"I do," Axandra replied, willing the words to form on her breath.

"Then the Council orders it so. Your formal training will begin tomorrow morning. Your installation will take place in two weeks. Welcome home, Ileanne," Morton said, smiling at last.

The Councilors applauded and rose to their feet.

Cheers and applause also came from the main hall as the staff heard the news. No doubt, as the news spread, everyone everywhere would be very excited.

The Councilors filed from the risers to introduce themselves. As they did so, Axandra tried to remember each one, but her mind reeled with the surreal sensation that she was truly about to become Protectress, a fate she long avoided. Here she stood in the Council Chamber, where she would take part in setting an example for the citizens. Her quivering intensified. She tried to take in a deep but discreet breath.

Each Councilor bowed to her in greeting and welcomed her back to the City. She appreciated the common courtesy of avoiding touch. They wouldn't be able to feel her trembling.

Eventually, the Councilors divided into smaller committees, each with a task to write the official announcement or plan the training schedule. They moved off to smaller meeting rooms.

At last, Axandra stood alone with Morton.

"I am pleased," Nancy began, "that my doubts about your identity have proven misplaced." Beneath the face value of her words, Morton retained other doubts about Axandra's abilities in the tasks to come.

"Thank you, Councilor. I know it hasn't been easy to convince people that I am ... me."

"Oh, on the contrary, it's been quite simple to convince most people," Morton assured, clasping her hands behind her back. "That is one reason why I was so skeptical—to protect everyone. Most were convinced the moment they saw you. I erred on the side of caution."

"Please make yourself more at home, Ms. Saugray," Morton went on, emphasizing the use of the familial name of the Protecting Family, rather than the name Axandra had adopted. Morton gestured her toward the main entry. "Miri has already moved your belongings into the Residence. It's your home now—again."

"Thank you."

Axandra walked out into the main hall. The staff members scattered back to their duties, disappearing quickly into hallways and doorways, eyes flickering with excitement.

Two Elite, the standing guard of the Protectress, waited outside the doors. As Axandra walked by, they fell into step behind her.

Miri waited on the bottom step of the main stair, unable to quash a grin from her freckled ivory face. "I knew it was you," she said excitedly. "This is so wonderful! All of your things are in the Residence now. I'll show you the suite—"

"I know it," Axandra stated, her own enthusiasm fading out now that the decision was final.

"Oh, right. I'm sorry. I—"

"Don't worry about it. It's very strange for me too." Axandra gestured for Miri to lead the way.

Miri fussed for several moments after they entered the official suite, showing Axandra where necessities were kept and offering to bring up a meal.

"No, thank you," Axandra refused, too nervous to think about food. Every few minutes, her mood changed in an almost manic swing, from anxiousness to depression, from sadness to pride. She didn't want to touch anything. She stood in what seemed relative safety in the center of the bedroom. "I would just like to be alone for a while."

"Of course, Your Honor," Miri addressed, bowing in respect. "Please summon me if you need anything."

"I'm not the Esteemed Protectress yet," Axandra reminded upon hearing the title of respect. Bashfully, she requested. "Please don't call me that. I'm not ready."

"Yes, Miss Saugray. My apologies." Miri bowed again, backing from the room.

After Miri left the Residence, Axandra moved back into the great room, blind to the objects that filled the space.

The goal of being established as the Heir had been realized. The Council recognized her for who she was supposed to be. Everything happened so quickly, without time to absorb the moments or strategize what to do or say next.

The suns bowed just past high noon. Until tomorrow, she had little to do. Free time gave liberty to her brain to think. She would rather occupy her time with some laborious task than think.

This was Home, the place of her birth. Her world began here. She feared exploring, afraid that her parents had never cleared her room of those things left behind by her departing. Had her mother left the room a shrine to her lost child?

She would only know if she went to the room, the one in the northwest corner.

Her feet took her there, to that room, and her hand opened the door.

She wasn't sure if she should be disappointed or relieved that the room was empty of anything personal. A wide bed draped in a thin canopy, a dresser, and a vanity and mirror furnished the child's room. No toys, no drawings or children's books. They had taken it all away.

Chapter 4

Murder

11th Quadrember, 307

For the next week, Axandra woke at the break of day and spent hours engulfed in information on rules and laws and protocols and procedures. She returned to her rooms in a trance when evening came and fell asleep quickly after dinner, which she always took alone in the suite.

Lunch she took with whomever her instructor happened to be on that day, as several of the Council members took turns giving her lessons in certain aspects associated with her service. Moonsday she took part in visiting with citizens about the city, strolling the avenues with young Carmen Offut and introducing herself to the individuals who performed their services for the Palace community, including tailors, farmers and the mechanics who maintained the cars.

On Tinsday, she took part in the Council session, observing how each member contributed proposals to distribute surplus foods from their respective regions and discussed the most logistical and equitable options. The fishers in the southeastern areas of Westland were graced with a bountiful harvest of greenfin this season due to a bloom of the algae the species fed upon.

Much of the fish could be shipped cold and served fresh. The rest would be dried for storage.

The third day she toured the hidden areas of the Palace that she would not normally see–the Archives, the Laundry, the Recycling and the Holds in the basement where emergency food and general supplies were stored. She toured the tunnels and the bunkers where she might be housed in a weather emergency, a place stocked with rations and water, cots and even games to keep the occupants entertained until the threat passed.

As her main function, the Protectress provided a visible, physical link between the rule makers to the rule followers. She represented the community as a whole, a single soul with the responsibility of hearing and seeing the needs of everyone in order to maintain their world as a safe and peaceful home. She was a balancing force between the Covenants and the people required to interpret the ever-changing world.

Publicly, this appeared to be a symbolic duty. Even with telepathy, a person did not have the capability to know all the needs of the people everywhere in the world. Even a powerful and adept telepath possessed a limited range. Admittedly, Axandra was the strongest remoter she knew, even if she kept her abilities reigned in. With the Goddess, hearing and seeing farther became possible, for it amplified her own mental talents. The Goddess filled her head with the voices of the people, even those hundreds of kiloms away. She could literally hear the concerns of the people in her mind. She could see what they saw. At night, when all was quiet and she lay still, her head flooded with the lives of strangers. However, the Goddess's involvement was kept secret.

Axandra understood why the Prophets trained so vigorously in blocking. Even that training, much forgotten over time, did not help her now. Sometimes, blocking anything seemed an insurmountable obstacle. The Goddess held her mind open, allowing everything to flow in. She begged at night for it to give her rest.

Tonight, the voices cried with distress, people in a small village somewhere south. They felt very afraid, but she could not pinpoint why. Their voices sounded like whispers where one could only hear the hisses of breath. In her dreams, blurs of darkened faces clashed with the sound of someone running, panting with strained lungs.

In the morning, Miri woke her early. The suns barely kissed the sky with dusty pink light. "Miss, a messenger came with terrible news. Councilor Morton needs you downstairs."

Groggy from the restless night, Axandra pushed against the mattress to rise slowly, pulling her legs from beneath the light covers. She knew immediately that this news concurred with her dreams. She dressed quickly in whatever clothes the assistant pulled out for her, ignoring her hair and face to get downstairs in a hurry.

Residents of the village of Cutoff found a man dead in his home, violently killed. At first the Safety Volunteers suspected an animal attack, but the home was shut tightly with no way for an animal to enter or escape. The neighbors heard no cries for help, and no predatory animals were sighted near the village that evening. The Night Watcher discovered the body after noticing late in the evening that the lights in the house were still on, long after the owner typically went to bed.

They did not know who or what caused his death. The villagers were frightened to be vulnerable inside the assumed safety of their homes.

Along with this report, delivered in person to Axandra, Councilor Morton and three other councilors, came word that one of the villagers of the community remained unaccounted for.

"He was last seen by the Day Watcher 'round six o'clock yester evening. He lives alone, so nobody sent word out he was missing 'til late this morning when he didn't show up at the canning kitchen," the Night Watcher stated. He appeared visibly exhausted and shaken by the incident. A tall man with thick upper arms, he stood before them in Morton's office, clutching his round cap in his hands. He could easily overpower another man or perhaps even a charging antelope, yet he stood before them white-faced and terrified. He had not rested since seeing the body.

"We grieve with you for your loss," Morton said when the report ended. The Watcher sighed, struggling with sleeplessness and sorrow. "Please take rest here in the Palace. We will send assistance to your village immediately to find the missing man."

"Thank you, Councilor, and thank you, Protectress. We are very happy to have you with us again." But he said this without happiness, for he could feel none.

Axandra bowed in his direction. "I wish you a comfortable rest. The Assistors will work as quickly as they can." She sent out her sympathy to him. Just the sound of her voice seemed to ease his distress. One of the Elite escorted him from the office.

"I will go with the Assistors," said Antonette Lelle as she stepped forward before the small gathering. "These are my people."

"As you wish, Ms. Lelle. We await your return."

The councilor left immediately to gather the Assistor team.

The tension in the room escalated since the beginning of the report. The others let their imaginations get the better of them.

"Very strange circumstances," voiced Casper Ross, opening the air for discussion.

"Surely this was some sort of accident," Nancy purported, unwilling to accept the worst possible scenario, the one not yet voiced.

Axandra felt lightheaded. She tried to listen as the councilors spoke, deciding for the moment that she would only listen. Her midnight dreaming had not revealed any more information than the Watcher's report gave them. She eased into a seat, signaling the councilors to follow suit, and reached for a nearby glass of water.

"I've never heard of anything like this," said Sara Sunsun in disbelief. "No one on this planet has been... *murdered*," she whispered the atrocious word, "by another human since—since ought-six, at the end of the New World Conflict." Sara's eyes glistened with moisture as she glanced upward toward the ceiling. One hand moved to cover her lips and hide a quiver.

The transplanted humans long ago discarded acts of brutality such as murder. The appointment of the first Protectress and her endorsement of the Prophets established peace centuries ago. Without peace, this planet would become like the world they left behind—disordered and destroyed.

Blood pounded in Axandra's temples. Her stomach cramped. Blinking rapidly, she attempted to remain alert.

"Now, now," Morton soothed. "There is no proof that it is murder. We still cannot rule out other causes. The man may have done this to himself."

The Goddess pulled at Axandra's mind, pulling her down and away from the present, pulling her into yesterday, when she had followed Sara Sunsun through the basement and observed the staff taking inventory of food, paper, toiletries and various sundries stored in the Holds. A sick feeling welled up in her stomach as she was pulled back. She leaned more deeply into the chair.

Stop it, she begged, trying to focus. It kept drawing her back in time. The last few days flashed by in reverse.

Then the world went gray.

+++

When she woke again, Axandra found the only people present were Miri and the Healer, whose name she couldn't recall. It was the same woman who performed the examination upon her initial arrival. With sticky eyes, she oriented herself to her location—Morton's office. She lay on the settee.

"Slowly, Miss," the Healer instructed. "Eat this." She gestured Axandra to open her month and inserted a sweet nugget of cone fruit, which melted on her tongue like pure sugar. "Miri tells me you ate very little lunch yesterday, no dinner and no breakfast."

"We didn't have time for breakfast this morning," Axandra defended. The sugar woke up her brain with a buzz.

"Well, your blood sugar dropped and your brain dropped with it," the woman explained. "Feeling better?"

The sugar dissolved to a small sliver. "Yes. Thank you, Healer." She began to sit up. Her head still ached with each heartbeat. Her sinuses felt dry.

"Slowly, please. Miri, breakfast immediately. She needs to eat regularly."

"Yes, Healer Gray," Miri disappeared to procure the meal.

"How long was I out?" Axandra asked as her body began to stabilize and the churning in her stomach settled. She didn't dare move from her seat. Her eyes swam as she tried to focus on the Healer's richly freckled face.

"Oh, just about fifteen minutes," the Healer replied, sharing an understanding smile. Healer Gray helped her over to a small table where breakfast was being set and waited while Axandra ate several bites of whole grain bread with creamy butter.

"And seriously, Miss. Eat when you need to. This will happen again if you don't."

"It's never happened before," Axandra countered, sipping her tea.

"You've never been under this kind of stress before either, I'll bet," the Healer inferred.

"No, I haven't. That's true. This is a lot different than my old life." Axandra continued to eat, though her stomach did not want her to continue. The organ cramped as more food filled the space.

"I will check on you later this afternoon," said the Healer. She packed her small bag and readied to leave. "Miri will keep an eye on you and report to me. Lunch and snacks."

"Yes, Healer," Axandra agreed like a chastised child. She bowed her head in thanks.

"Take care," Gray wished, then excused herself, her pouch slung over her shoulder and across her torso.

Councilor Morton returned to the office, her face expressing annoyance at being evacuated from her space for someone's fainting spell. "It is good to see you feeling better, Miss. You gave us all a start," she said insincerely, as though fainting were a common occurrence. "The Assistors are gathering in the City Square. They intend to leave shortly. Do you have a message for them?"

A short speech of encouragement was customary when Assistors left home to aid in calamities. Words from the soon-to-be Protectress needed to be hopeful yet truthful. She paused a moment as she decided just what to say.

"I wish them speed and success in finding the missing. And I thank them for their service."

She felt inadequate, like there should be more to say, more of an explanation of why they were going. She hoped for the best, but feared the worst would come. The missing man most likely committed the ultimate sin against his fellow human.

Then what? The law supported no punishment for such crime other than detainment. Murder had been erased from their culture. The last murderer, by account, committed suicide out of guilt, punishing himself.

"I will tell them. We will continue with our training tomorrow. Hopefully we will have news by then."

"I hope so, too. Thank you."

"Take your time," Morton offered, though Axandra sensed she really wanted to say Hurry up and get out of here. "I have an appointment with Principal Noel about restoration of the city gates." With that, the Head of Council left the room again.

Miri, the young blonde, was appointed her personal aide by the Head of Council's decision alone, and not yet officially. Miri simply took over caring for Axandra's needs during the short time she'd been here. The woman's eyes looked at her brightly just now, and Axandra could see in them loyalty, faith and honesty. As any good server should do, she held her tongue in company, but often vocalized her opinions in private.

"She's been rather rude to you," Miri said quietly after the Councilor passed from earshot.

Axandra left the comment alone, though inside she agreed. Perhaps Morton had the right to treat her in such a manner. After all, she had shown up out of nowhere with no idea how to do her job.

"Miri, I never got a chance to ask about the Elite in the garden earlier this week." The memory came to her mind as she thought of the dead man and the description of his wounds. "They were looking for something—in the rain."

Miri answered quickly. "After you asked about the pack-hounds, I thought it best to have the garden searched just in case one got in. They didn't find any unusual animals, but a gate was left open at the back of the garden, on the River side."

"Can the gates be opened from the outside?"

"No. Only from inside the garden, Miss Saugray."

"That's good to know." Axandra returned her thoughts to her hopes that the missing man would be found alive and innocent and attempted to finish her meal.

Chapter 5

The Palace

17th Quadrember, 307

On the ninth day of her new life, Axandra, sleepless from the voices and phantasms in her head, wandered about the Palace. She meandered with only the minimum of direction, downstairs first to look around at the Council Chamber while it sat vacant.

She rested there for a short while at one of the Councilor's desks, and she found herself trying to decide how she would best address the latest inquiry about more busses on route from village to village. She felt much too nervous to get up in front of the Council members and start spouting off her reasons in favor of such a project. If she prepared herself properly, she hoped the anxiety would lessen. Just sitting in the vast chamber made her feel more comfortable with the place.

Her wandering took her up a side set of stairs, which she discovered half-hidden at the dark end of the north corridor. Of course, there would be additional stairways throughout the Palace, allowing for quick exit in emergencies, but she also thought about how Miri seemed to move about the large building so swiftly. This staircase rose narrowly and only went up the second floor, into the hallway occupied almost solely by the Library, save for a pair of closets hiding brooms and dusters.

Axandra crossed the second floor from north to south and thought about her shadows—an Elite guard following her almost everywhere she went. Not the same one the entire way, to be sure. As she moved from level to level, a new one appeared, taking over the watch of the last. The objective was to keep a set of eyes on her wherever she roamed. These were standing orders of their Commander, Ty Narone, whom she had not yet met, but had been told would meet her the next day to discuss further security measures. She found this security less comforting and more of a burden, and she felt self-conscious about her every action and inaction. What if she needed to scratch an awkward itch when she thought no one was looking? She avoided making any possibly inappropriate motions unless she was in the lavatory—where thankfully no one followed—or in her suite. The Residence was the one place where the Palace eyes did not see her. She stayed there when she didn't need to be anywhere else.

On the south end of the Palace, the second floor looked down upon the Grand Hall, which was being decorated for her installation in just seven days. Below her, the room took a significant portion of the south wing. Each side wall was lined with stained glass and beveled windows, each about a meter wide and three meters high. The windows spread the colors throughout the room as the last of the evening sunslight seeped through.

A skeleton of stone ribs supported the vaulted ceiling, bearing the weight of the arched roof. The Grand Hall stood three stories high and extended from the front of the Palace like an extra limb. From this vantage point, she could see almost every corner of the open room. There were no chairs, but a runner of blue carpet and metal stands separated her procession aisle from the soon-to-be crowd. Though not yet finished, the backdrop behind the dais depicted the symbolic objects she would receive, carefully hand-painted in vibrant colors in larger than life images.

The installation of a new Protectress happened once in a generation. The people expressed great pride in celebrating the occasion with exceeding flourish and artistry.

Continuing on to the south end of the long corridor, Axandra found, as she suspected, another stairwell. This one led in both vertical directions, opening into the basement tunnels below and above to the third, fourth and fifth levels. Noises echoed here in spite of the carpeted runner on the stone steps. From above, she heard instruments playing and voices singing.

Curious of the origin, she climbed upward past the third floor to the fourth and poked her head out the doorway into the corridor. This door already hung ajar, allowing the sounds to bleed into the stairwell. The music sounded louder here, but the source remained unseen.

These rooms housed many of the resident staff, affording them shelter and the basic necessities in exchange for their service to the Palace community. Each member was afforded a small apartment with private baths and small kitchens. During her tour of the Palace, Axandra was given a brief look inside one currently unoccupied. She wasn't expected to ever come up to this level, let alone need to know the layout of any of the servers' quarters.

Stepping out of the stairwell into the corridor, she noted that these walls displayed decoration to the same degree of the public floors. One side of the corridor broke with windows every few feet, hung with dark violet drapes tied back for the view. At a certain point, the windows stopped and a room, one on top of similar octagonal rooms below, jutted out from the east side of the building. This room harbored the source of the commotion, and Axandra crept toward it softly.

She recognized the song being sung and sang along in a whisper, "... *went out on the ice and CRACK he fell right through.*" One of many songs often taught to children and loved by adults.

Axandra came to the doors of this room, a double-wide door that was closed on one side and open on the other, and peeked in with hope of not being seen. Inside, there were staff members from many of the Palace functions—the laundry, the kitchen, housekeeping, etc. She didn't recognize them by name, but she had seen many of these faces on her tours.

On the window-side of the room gathered a trio with lutes, guitars and drums on their laps. They rested between songs at the moment and one man strummed lazily on his guitar strings while the three talked over what to play next. At a table to the right, another group played a raucous card game. A chorus of light-hearted boos rose up as the participants of the game lost to a single player, who cheered for herself.

Seeing them relaxed like this gave Axandra a twinge of jealously. She once could go to the pub and join in the evening's play, sip at an ale and sing a loud song. She missed those evenings. She hadn't had a free moment to just sit and play since she had left home. Either her brain occupied her with the images of the long-lived Goddess or she was simply too exhausted. Even during the ship voyage on the open ocean, she had occupied her time doing chores for the crew, cleaning up or helping prepare meals as trade for her passage onboard. And she doubted she could walk right in and enjoy this fun without everyone in the room going out of their way to bow and give her the most comfortable seat.

She listened as the players began their next piece of music. It sounded like a lullaby, a tune she did not recognize. The woman with the small hand drum began to sing, her lilting voice mesmerizing. "When the winds blow 'cross the prairie, my heart goes to find you—"

"Miss!" exclaimed a voice in the corridor.

Abruptly, everything stopped. The occupants of the room looked up and saw her near the door. Chairs scraped on the stone floor as people stood. Everyone rose at once, shock reddening their faces. Staggering their motions, some suddenly re-membered to bow. Others followed suit.

Miri came up the corridor accompanied by another young woman, Lynn. Startled by Miri's loud voice, Axandra jumped back and one foot turned as though ready to run. But her sense of reason held her in place. Having already been spotted, turning to run the other way exhibited childishness, even if she hadn't wanted to be seen. Miri and Lynn picked up the pace of their walk, hurrying to her.

"Miss, what are you doing up here? Did you need me?" Miri asked almost frantically. She excelled at sensing when Axandra needed her assistance and worried she failed in her relatively new duties.

"No, I was just wandering. Please, everyone. Go back to what you were doing. I didn't want to bother anyone." Axandra waved them back, but no one seemed willing to move. They all waited for some other sign, uncertain what to do while she stood in their presence. "Please, you don't have to stand. Just go about as you were. Good evening."

Axandra moved away from the door so that they might think her gone. Her face blazed hot with embarrassment. As she moved farther down the hall, Miri followed her.

"I didn't need anything. I heard the singing and wanted to see what was going on," she explained to her aide. "I couldn't fall asleep."

"Let me get you something that will help. Eryn keeps several herbs—"

Axandra waved her off. "No. Nothing like that." She rubbed her brow for a moment, starting down the hallway again. The static in her brain became suddenly loud and obnoxious. "I just needed to get out of my room. Let her—the singer—know that she has a lovely, lovely voice. I would like to hear the end of that song sometime. Goodnight." She increased her pace, finally leaving Miri behind. She hit the stairway down and escaped back to the Residence, her brain throbbing.

"Stop, please," she begged the Goddess, trying to block out the noise. Her eyes witnessed dark trees around her, and she smelled the moist decay of a forest. Struggling, she stacked gray bricks starting at the ground and building up, blocking out the scene.

Whose eyes are these? To her left, she heard voices calling out, *Over here! Look over here!*

The gray bricks trembled. She didn't have any strength to cement them together.

Stubbing her big toe on a piece of furniture brought her back to her own realm immediately. Hissing curses, she hopped holding her toe with her hand. As she breathed in, the scene around her returned to the sitting room, a comfortable room scented with the garden through the open windows. A cool wind rustled the curtains.

Axandra breathed in deeply, her hands to her waist feeling her lungs fill up, relieved that the episode seemed to be over. The mistiness of her vision persisted. Moving into the bedroom just beyond, she sat on a chair to check her aching toe, but saw no visible damage, though pain flared through the bone. She sat with her head in her hands trying to think about what she saw, but it all seemed erased so quickly. Only the voices echoed on. She didn't know who they were or where or what was going on.

At the mirror, she began the ritual of brushing her long spiraling hair, the motion soothing her until her eyes drooped a little. She washed her face and hands and climbed into the oversized bed, pulling up the warm algodon covers that kept off the nighttime chill. She slept with the windows open every night, like she used to in her cottage. But she did not hear the ocean surf here, nor the clicks and chirps of the ocean-dwelling curana. Below, she heard the wind in the trees and in the distance, the rumble of thunder from the Great Storm. She lay awake listening, afraid of what her eyes would see if she closed them.

Chapter 6

The Covenants

20th Quadrember, 307

The peaceful society of the small world of Bona Dea succeeded based upon each individual's service to the greater community. Time spent in service guaranteed the basics of living and allowed the pursuit of personal interest without strife. No one went hungry when food was available. Everyone had shelter in a comfortable home, books to read, instruments to play, tools and other items. In service, some cared for children or taught lessons. Others helped construct new homes or repair roads or maintain the general infrastructure. There were always jobs available, from recycling, sowing and reaping the crops, preserving food, treating wastewater and so many other vital tasks. Masters such as clothiers, potters, masons, carpenters, weavers and other craftspeople, trained apprentices in the perfection of their arts. Goods were distributed equitably. Rare items or local treasures were often bartered among neighbors.

In her old life, Axandra took her turn as teacher and nurse. She volunteered as an Assistor for two years when she turned sixteen, after her father, Reiko, passed away. After meeting Jon and joining him in his home by the sea, she used her hobby of fashioning jewelry to trade for special wants, and she assisted the elder neighbors with their chores. For her contribution to the community, she received food, shelter, and other amenities for a contented and quiet life.

As Protectress, Axandra's service to the world-community would be complete—she would be provided anything she needed or desired for the remainder of her life. She no longer needed to volunteer to teach or harvest or nurse, yet she would do all of these things in the course of her life-service. She would serve the people in whatever manner they needed her and was expected to do so without grudge or complaint and only to question if the needs conflicted with the Covenants.

In that respect, she was responsible for knowing the Covenants by heart.

Everyone shall have the Free Will to believe as they wish to believe.
Humans shall not kill humans.
Everyone shall live in Harmony with the World.
Everyone shall be fed, clothed and housed.
Everyone shall receive medical care as necessary.
Everyone is expected to perform service for the good of the community.

These guidelines on living life in peace as a whole seemed simple when read to oneself. For over three hundred years, the humans of Bona Dea had lived life so simply, wanting for nothing, contented with their existence.

Axandra understood the simplicity masked a more complicated system or there would be no need for the People's Council and Protectress as they were described in the extended body of the Covenants document. It was the nature of human beings to disagree and argue. She participated in many arguments with those who did not share her views. Argument created an exchange of knowledge. Humans also shared the desire to grow and to better themselves and their world for the children who would follow them. Conflict nurtured innovation and tempered overachievement.

Axandra studied the Covenants a little every day and discussed them with whichever Councilor acted as her tutor, particularly the Covenant of Free Will.

"Does Free Will overrule the other Covenants?" Axandra asked Casper as they sat in the Archive vault looking through the records of her mother's service, reading pages upon pages of natural disasters that took place across the continent. "Free Will gives us the right to choose our individual paths. What if someone chooses not to provide service? The other covenants will still give him food and shelter, even if he provides nothing."

"Dear," Casper said with a fatherly smile of his almost lipless mouth. Cataracts clouded his dark brown eyes. He leaned upon his cane with his hands and chin. He didn't see very well, but who needed sight when the emanations of others indicated who was nearby. "Yes, Free Will gives everyone the right to refuse to provide services—but such action will have consequences. It then becomes the Free Will of others in the community to deny him food unless he collects it himself."

"Then the effects of one person's actions begin to break down the system," she concluded.

"Yet the system is still in place," Casper reminded, a gnarled finger tapping the air in her direction. "And I have known several young people in my time who have tried what you suggest, to live without working, to be served without serving." Casper swayed on his seat as he spoke, his eyes straying toward the high ceiling and the books stacked on the shelves. "They always find that, unless they sit like a lump on the ground, they are always providing something to someone else. Even if it is only to provide conversation to an old man."

"So no one feels the need to withhold," Axandra followed, wondering where his story originated, "and the Covenants are protected from failure. I see." She nodded, understanding his reasoning.

"And you must set an example by serving when and where needed. The people look up to you. If you stray, they will also."

"I understand," Axandra told him. "I must be the perfect moral compass for the citizens."

"Oh, not perfect, my dear. Just Human."

Nancy Morton's answer differed somewhat.

"Miss, Free Will is imaginary. No one is absolutely free to do as he or she wishes," Nancy scoffed. Axandra dreaded her days with the Head of Council, who never smiled at her and always seemed inconvenienced to be giving lessons. "Those around you always affect your decisions, even in the smallest way. You can't escape influence unless you live under a rock."

"So while we have given ourselves the freedom to make choices, you say that our choices are made for us," Axandra paraphrased.

"Yes," Nancy confirmed. "From the day you are born, you are told how to think and how to act. You believe that you had the Free Will to run away and escape the life you were born into," Nancy told her bluntly. "Yet you are here. Was that your Free Will?"

Axandra began to defend herself, but no words flowed from her tongue. At last, she said, "The people need me."

"You are welcome to believe that." And Nancy left the discussion at that.

+++

23rd Quadrember

Two days prior to the installation, Axandra and the Councilors practiced the ceremony and unlocked the artifacts from the safe in the basement Hold, bringing each out of its customized case.

The collection consisted of five objects, one for each of the regions that made up the continent and islands, simply named Eastland, Westland, Southland, Northland, and the Great Storm. The Gifts had originally been presented to the First Protectress as symbols of the people's acceptance of her leadership. Viewing them against black velvet on a long table, Axandra and the Councilors admired the artistry of each piece. Axandra listened with amusement at everyone's tendency to whisper around the objects, as though their very voices might crack the centuries old antiques.

Eastland presented a square tablet of white and gray granite carved with the figure of a woman and children, perhaps a teacher or a mother nurturing the young ones. This symbol represented their permission to be nurtured and instructed to become better individuals and therefore a better community. The granite came from the same quarry that had given the stones for the Palace, near the base of Mount Zetnic near Undun City. Below the carved image was etched the phrase *With Love Comes Peace.*

From the Northland came a wooden staff about two meters tall, which made it stand above Axandra's head by almost a full third. Sturdy, it also possessed flexibility, with enough give that it could be bent in a smooth arc. Upon the staff was carved A tree bends to the will of the wind, but breaks if it does not yield.

An amethyst medallion touted to be the smallest and lightest Gift in the collection. Southland was noted for the gems mined in a network of natural caves that wound in labyrinths beneath the highlands. Simply mounted in a sterling silver claw, the crystal hung on a long chain that would be placed around her neck during the ceremony. The Southlanders felt that their stones exhibited special properties capable of enhancing the telepathic abilities of the wearer. While this claim bore no scientific basis, the legend of the stones continued with each passing of this medallion. She would wear it for the first week of her service, then it would return to the hold for safekeeping, coming out only on special occasions.

Westland gave the First Protectress a gavel carved from a curana bone, a heavy ivory substance that was rarely seen. The aquatic creatures headed for deep water at the end of life, their corpses sinking into the deepest abysses of the Ocean. Occasionally the bones washed ashore or a curana would perish upon beaching and scavengers would clean the flesh from the bones. These rare objects were prized by those who studied the Ocean as well as those who believed such gifts were delivered to them to remind all humans of the fragility of life. The surface of the gavel depicted the animals of the oceans—the fish, the curana, the corals and others, crowded along the head and handle. The First Protectress had been asked to ensure that this new world never became like Old Earth, a vacant ball of toxic gas, devoid of all life except human.

Lastly, the Prophets of the Great Storm gave her a mirrored box. The silvered glass lay in a smooth silver metal frame, hinged so that is folded like a clam shell. Axandra recognized it, for the sliver had come from a smaller such box. Had this been the method of instilling the First Protectress with the Goddess herself? Was this case to protect the entity if there was no new host to inhabit? Councilor Morton recited that the mirror showed the Protectress a reflection of herself to remind her that she was one of the people she served, not a goddess to be adored and waited upon. A humbling thought.

I am the Goddess, Axandra thought as she set the ornate item back on the cloth. *I can't forget that now.*

In the same order in which they were originally given, the Gifts would be presented to the next Protectress, as they had for generations. The group practiced several times over two days, making certain Axandra could handle each piece with care and move about the dais without stumbling. Axandra never thought of herself as graceful. She carefully measured every stride to prevent tripping over her own feet.

To adorn the new Protectress, a dressmaker designed an elaborate gown that complimented Axandra's features. From the strapless, fitted bodice of periwinkle silk, the skirt cascaded in layers of gathered gossamer in metallic gold and grayish shades of blue, clear to the floor. At her neck, fastened to the bodice with a gold and jeweled broach, a long scarf of the same gossamer fabric went over her shoulders and draped down her back about half way down the skirt. Numerous fittings took place to size the gown just right and test the fabrics. Several things changed in two weeks—the designer did not like this color or that gather or that stitch. Two days before the ceremony, the gown still lacked the hem and all of the fasteners. With all the things she had to worry about, Axandra dismissed this from her mind. She trusted the tailors to finish on time.

Now all that remained was convincing herself that she was up to the task. Axandra didn't feel ready, not for service of this magnitude. The last two weeks, she'd seen the slimmest example of what lay in store for her for decades to come. Perhaps she never would be ready. But her parents—her adopted parents—taught her to follow through with her commitments, and that is what she would do.

Chapter 7

The Ceremony

25th Quadrember, 307

The ceremony would begin at five o'clock. At four o'clock, Axandra dressed and sat at the vanity while Lynn and Miri styled her hair in cascading tresses held in place with gold, sparkling hairpins. The girls chatted excitedly while they worked, commenting how beautiful the Heir would be processing down the aisle and how they wished they could be on the floor.

"But we'll have an even better view from the mezzanine," Lynn said. "I hope to get up there early, if Marta doesn't think I need to be somewhere else."

Axandra applied color to her lips while listening to them pine their lowly status.

"But it would be so much nicer to down among the principals and governors, right near the Gifts," Miri bemoaned, pinning up a hunk of curls. "I've always wanted to see them up close instead of in photographs."

A knock came at the main entrance of the Residence. Lynn hurried to see who came calling. When she returned, she had only a message. "Councilor Morton wishes to see you in her office in a few minutes. There is word about the missing man from Cutoff."

The two women finished the preparations so that Axandra could get downstairs. Axandra hoped to hear good news. Following her to keep the train of her dress from dragging, Miri and Lynn scurried to keep up the pace down the wide staircase and into the Council wing.

In Morton's office gathered four other Councilors. The Night Watcher from the village of Cutoff had returned to Undun City with the Assistors. With everyone present, he gave his report.

"He's been found, Your Honor. However, he's not well. The Healer says he isn't likely to survive. He shows signs of malnourishment and dehydration to the point that his body is shutting down. A smaller group of Assistors stayed in Cutoff to help the Healer care for him." He was clearly distressed. Like everyone in the room, he hoped to bring better news. He continued with the details of the search. "We found him a two days ago in the woods," the Watcher described, "curled up at the trunk of a broken tree. He clutched a small kitchen knife. He wouldn't move or speak. I've known this man all of his life—and the man we found wasn't the one I remember. He looked like a ghost and only mumbled nonsense." He looked to the councilors with pleading eyes, seeking explanation. Finding nothing, his eyes fell away again to his memories. "He's very sick. I pray the Healer can find what's wrong with him."

Axandra must have witnessed the Assistors in the forest those few nights ago, as she remembered the trees and the smell of decay. Perhaps those voices calling out were the ones to find the man. Had she continued to share the moment, perhaps she would have witnessed him too and seen what the Night Watcher described.

Axandra approached the man. The Councilors took notice and tensed, uncertain what to expect from her.

"May I take your hand," Axandra asked the man, holding her own hand palm up toward him.

Timidly, he lifted his hand, one roughened from work and weather. He hesitated before placing it in hers, gulping so that his prominent larynx bobbed up just below his chin. Despite his height and bulk, he behaved like a timid child.

At the touch, the images of the lost man filled her vision. Pale and ghastly, he appeared like one already dead. Lips thin, he trembled, the only sound he made a hissing noise and slight moans as he shook.

While sharing these thoughts, Axandra projected comfort to the Watcher and offered him strength. He clung to it, for he felt weak and helpless against this unknown thing.

"I promise we will do everything we can to discover what happened to your friend," Axandra told him aloud.

"I trust you, Protectress," the messenger said, his voice calmer. "You won't fail us."

He held such conviction, as though she stood as a divine creature with mystical powers. If only he knew how right he was.

Releasing him, Axandra backed away.

"I'd like to go now," the man requested. "I'm going to visit his family here in Undun. His sister lives in the city."

"Of course. Please offer our sympathies," Axandra allowed, bowing to him as he in turn bowed to her.

Still clutching his cap in his hands, the Watcher was escorted out by one of the Palace guards.

"Is it a virus?" asked Councilor Sunsun. "Or a mental illness?" She asked the questions aloud, well aware no one in this room had the answer. "We should have several Healers investigate the illness, examine the man. We don't want to spread anything this terrible."

"Agreed," said Axandra. The other councilors present nodded as well. "And check others in the village for symptoms. If it is contagious, we will need to control it quickly."

Antonette once again stepped forward for service. "I will arrange it, Protectress."

"Thank you. Report to us as soon as something is discovered."

"I will go as well." Osander rose and addressed Axandra. Once a staunch opponent of her claim, his distrust suddenly lessened. "We should inform neighboring towns to watch for these signs. By your leave, Protectress."

Morton raised a hand. "Councilors, she is not the Protectress yet. Not for another thirty minutes."

Antonette bowed with respect to Morton and Axandra. "Your pardon, but she has proven herself to be the Protectress today. We will address her as such."

Even Osander agreed to this. The Councilors all bowed to Axandra. It was an overwhelming display of respect and adoration. The emotions warmed her heart.

What caused this sudden change in their attitude? Though they accepted her as the physical Heir, they each retained their doubts that she would fit the part, having been raised outside of the Palace. They reserved uncertainties about how she would handle situations such as this one, faced with a possible catastrophe. Her collapse the other day had not given them much cause to give up those doubts.

Now Axandra sensed confidence and trust washing away those qualms. They wanted her here with them as they served the people. They did not see her as an outsider any longer. She was the Protectress.

Only one last person viewed her as any less, and that was Nancy Morton.

What must I do to prove myself to you? she wondered at the woman.

"And the ceremony starts in just a few minutes," Morton prompted. Clapping her hands, she called the Councilors to attention. "Places, everyone. We have a Protectress to install."

Four voluminous bars into the brass fanfare, the main doors of the Grand Hall swung open and allowed the seventeen members of the People's Council to enter two by two, with Nancy Morton following up at the rear. Each wore silk robes of their station in colors that signified their region. They all smiled cheerfully, for it was a momentous day to welcome a new Protectress. Most of the Councilors exited the procession as they came to their contingent of Principals and Governors. Only five proceeded forward, those elected to bestow their respective tokens.

Behind Morton, Axandra strode gracefully down the blue runner, aware that all eyes were on her as she approached the raised stage. She graced her face with her best smile, pulling the expression from the admiration the councilors had shown her just moments ago, the happiest idea she could muster.

She could see the finished mural now, each of the Gifts rendered larger than life in spectacular color. Behind her, a contingent of twenty Elite marched, led in by Commander Ty Narone, wearing shining gold breastplates over sleek grey shirts and crisp charcoal pants. Their caps sported arm-length white feathers that bounced up and down with each high-kneed step. Between the ranks, the Elite transported the Gifts in their cases, handling them with reverent care.

At the raised stage, Morton oversaw the delivery of the Gifts to the tables set and draped with gold cloth. The fanfare continued throughout this ritual, played by a quintet of brass players seated openly to the right of the stage. Their tones reverberated off of the arched ceiling and melded into each other. The last notes died away before Morton addressed the congregation.

"Citizens, welcome," Morton bowed to them. She smiled proudly, possibly the first real smile Axandra witnessed on the woman's face since their first meeting. Nancy typically scowled, her lips straight or down-turned, disdainful of anything that might be considered a breach of protocol, to which Axandra was prone.

"We come together this day to receive into service Ileanne Saugray as the Protectress. Our Covenants state: The Protectress, a service heretofore distinguished by these covenants, shall serve the people and the planet. She shall be the voice of the people. She shall be the eyes of the people. She shall be the heart of the people. And in this service, she shall protect the people. She shall be born of the same family as her predecessor, so there may be no feud of power, and she shall remain the Protectress as long as she lives, removable only by death itself." Morton recited the paragraph of the Covenants that described the position. Agreeing noises came from the audience. "Ileanne is the daughter of Elora, one of many women descended from Amelia, proven by birth to be the only true Protectress. Ileanne, do you accept the terms of this service, knowing that you are obligated to continue it throughout your life?"

"I do," Axandra accepted, her own voice echoing in the hall. She stood as straight and as tall as her body was able.

"Do you accept the responsibility of protecting our way of life and our lives, even as it may interfere with your own life?"

"I do." Though she had practiced listening to and understanding these words, the reality of their meaning felt heavy. There would be no leaving now. Her decades of hiding meant nothing. She had not escaped what had frightened her all those years.

"And do you, Ileanne, vow to hear, see and feel the needs of the people and provide for them and comfort them, so long as you live?" Morton asked the questions without expecting any answer but those practiced. She would not be surprised today.

"I do, Your Honor." Axandra bowed at the waist after this final answer, first to Morton. Then she turned to the audience and bowed to them, signifying a bow to the entire population. She climbed the three steps of the dais and stood beside Morton, facing the crowd. She reminded herself not to try to count their number, to think of them only as one, a less intimidating digit.

"At this time, I invite the regions to bestow their gifts. Foster Tremby from Eastland."

Foster came forward from the left, where four of the five presenters awaited their participation. Climbing to the table, he retrieved the granite tablet, then approached while holding it out between his hands. "From Eastland, Honorable Matriarch, our finest stone. A master engraver created for you a portrait of a teacher and children willing and eager to learn from her example. We accept you as our protector and are ready to learn from your example." Bowing, he extended the tablet.

Taking the heavy stone, Axandra raised it over her head, calling out that she accepted the gift and thanking the Eastlanders, who raised their voices in loud cheers. Morton set the tablet on the table for display.

"Sara Sunsun of Northland."

The slender young woman collected the wooden staff and offered it horizontally with the words, "From Northland, Your Honor, a gift from our strongest tree, the rockwood. It grows in rock and ice, and thrives in winter. This staff may bend, but it will never break. We accept you as our Protectress. May you bend as the needs of your people change, but never break or fail to uphold our values."

Again, Axandra took the gift and raised it toward the ceiling. "I accept this gift and I thank all of Northland for their support." Cheers and hoots rose from the Northland contingent.

"Franny Gilbert of Southland."

For her age, obvious by the creases in her skin and the thinning strands of gray hair wrapped in a loose bun, Franny lithely scaled the steps to the table and retrieved the medallion from its small case. Though her fingers looked gnarled with arthritis, she had no difficulty grasping the thin chain of silver.

"Esteemed Protectress," Franny spoke in a ragged voice. The hall grew even more still as she spoke very softly, and everyone wished to hear her words. "From Southland I bring you our most prized stone, this violet amethyst from the caves of Mt. Measure. We believe wearing this stone gives strength and power to the mind. As it is your duty to be our eyes, ears and hearts, we give this to you so that you will see, hear and feel all that we feel. With this gift, we accept you as our protector." Franny bowed, then proceed to adorn Axandra's neck with the faceted and polished stone.

Bowing to the Southlanders, Axandra graciously accept the gift and thanked them for their contribution.

"Casper Ross of Westland." Morton called out to the fourth presenter.

The white haired, cocoa-skinned man moved less nimbly as he walked up the stairs, back hunched. One hand held the front of his jacket as gravity pulled the lapels forward. Slowly he moved to collect the bone carving and carried it carefully over to her.

"From Westland, Esteemed One, I present this gift. The bone of the curana is a rare find and, when one is given to us by the Ocean, it is cherished and celebrated. To you, I give this rib, as it as been sculpted by a master artisan with the life of the sea, to remind us that we share this planet with life that was here long before we came. We must all protect that life. We give this cherished gift to you and ask that you keep the planet safe from any harm. We accept you as our protector."

At last, the ceremony neared its end. Only the final gift remained to be presented, the mirror.

Morton called out among the audience. "Will the Prophets please come forward to present their gift?"

They had instructed Axandra that the Prophets would remain hidden until they were called for, as they preferred to remain apart from the public. From behind the dais, three Prophets emerged, having come into the hall through a hidden door. Tyrane was among them, his hood lowered and face visible. The other two hid their faces with their hoods pulled far over their heads. These two stood to the side, waiting.

Tyrane came forward to retrieve the token, holding the metal casing between his pale hands. He did not bow as he approached, but opened the mirror toward her.

"Your Honor," he said. "We, the Prophets, provide you with this mirror so that you are constantly reminded that you are one of the people, lest you forget that you are a human being. Peer into the mirror and see yourself. Peer into the mirror and see your people."

Looking into the mirror, Axandra saw her face and her violet eyes, and remembered exactly the opposite, that she was more than one of the people. She would always be reminded by those eyes.

With that, Tyrane placed the mirror in her hands and turned away. Then the three Prophets disappeared once again, back into seclusion.

Morton turned to the audience now.

"Citizens, please give honor to our most Esteemed Protectress. May she guide us in our living so that we may continue to share knowledge and live in peace with this world."

"It is by the will of these people," the gathering recited in unison, "that we accept the leadership of the Protectress."

Cheers rose up from the Hall and spread to the gathering outside the Palace. The words of the event had been channeled outside on speakers, so that as many as possible could bear witness to the installation. Axandra waved and bowed again to the crowd.

The time came to speak a few words of her own. With some assistance from the Councilors, Axandra had composed a short statement, hopefully to explain her absence without admitting to any character flaw that would undermine her position. She wanted to be as open as possible, but the councilors coached her that doing so might not be the best idea.

"Citizens," the Protectress began. She had practiced for many days, memorizing the words, rehearsing the intonations. "Thank you. I understand that many of you have wondered about my absence from Undun City since my childhood and many of you are relieved and exhilarated that I have returned to take my place here. To truly understand the people I speak for, I have lived among you. I have experienced firsthand the way of life I must protect. I have a much better understanding of what I am charged with preserving, and I thank everyone I met along the way for teaching me the lessons other protectors have been without. I will serve the people for the good of all people. Thank you. Enjoy the celebration."

As the applause rose up, Axandra descended from the stage and, preceded by two Elite and more following behind, made her way toward the main doors and out into the crowded courtyard in front of the Palace. She told the Councilors of her plan to do this instead of escaping through a rear door to avoid the crowd, as some had suggested. They warned her that many would want to touch her, as though it would bring them luck to do so. To solidify her own statement about being one of the people, Axandra insisted she walk among them. She braced her mind for these contacts.

The Elite watched the crowd carefully as Axandra extended her hands to the people. Each touch was brief, but each mind touched hers all the same. They felt overwhelmingly happy. Some hands felt warm, others cool, some clammy, some dry, some smooth, some rough. Each mind left an imprint on her, from the grandmother who watched her young grandchildren during the day, to the young boy who pictured her in a fairy tale. Yet one touch sent a different emotion through her body. It wasn't anger, but it was powerful. Someone wanted to cause harm. Resentment clung to her

You do not belong here.

The touches changed so swiftly, she could not pick out which person thought these things. The line of people swept her along. Thousands wanted to be close, but she knew she would need to stop soon, before she suffered from shock.

The Elite began to lead her away from the crowd. She waved and bowed again to the gathering of people before she walked back into the Palace to prepare for the banquet with the Councilors, Principals and Governors.

The Commander of the Elite led her escape back into the Palace. He directed her off to a narrow hallway that led along the front edge of the North wing, taking her away from the crowd in the main entry. Soon, the Grand Hall would be reset with tables and chairs for the banquet. For the moment, Axandra was taken away to refresh herself.

In a quiet room, Axandra gestured for Ty to give her a moment of his time. The Commander, a stocky man with bronze skin, acknowledged her by removing his feathered cap. At attention, he stood a half-head taller than Axandra. "How may I serve you?" he asked, bowing his head in her direction.

Through the windows, they could hear the cheering crowd outside. The glass and stone muted the deafening sound.

She looked directly into his dark brown eyes. "Outside the Palace, does anyone ever know of an attempt on the Protectress's life?"

"Madam, no one has made an attempt to harm the Protectress in the last 200 years," he stated firmly.

"I believe someone is going to try."

"They would be unsuccessful," he said with even more conviction.

"I hope so. Someone in the crowd touched me, and I felt they wanted to do physical harm. I believe toward me."

He didn't take her seriously, she sensed, but he kept that hidden from his face. His service was to protect the Protectress, to keep her safe to the best of his ability, even if it meant accepting possibly ridiculous notions.

"As I said before, Madam," Ty leaned forward to emphasize his point, "they will fail."

She thanked him and asked for a few minutes alone, to which he exited the room, no doubt hovering just outside. After using the lavatory and looking herself over in the mirror, she sat down to wait for summons to the dinner. She sighed tiredly, though she didn't feel sleepy. In fact, she felt quite restless, in need of a long night of activity to release a lot of pent up physical energy. She'd spent so much time inside, studying, reading and talking, that she hadn't even taken a walk in the last week.

When the Councilors beckoned her to make her entrance and join the party, she did so eagerly. Everyone ate a lavish meal while she moved among the guests and spoke to them each personally, even if only for a few minutes. She didn't try to remember any of their names; she knew this was an impossible task. But she did make an effort to remember something about them. No doubt she would see many of them again.

Hours later, exhausted from the celebration and tipsy from the wine, Axandra got out of her evening gown and into her nightgown. After some tea, a bitter-flavored remedy for the post-alcohol headache, she crawled into her bed and went to sleep.

+++

Around the world, in every community, the people celebrated the day. The wine makers and distillers broke out their best barrels and passed them around. Food was cooked and served for almost thirty-six hours straight and everyone ate until they were stuffed.

In Port Gammerton, a great deal of talk circulated about the woman who had left their number more than a month ago.

"Had you ever thought that she might be the One," asked Jeanette of her other elder friends gathered around the table.

"She did have those unusual eyes," replied one. "Not many have violet eyes like those."

"But she never even hinted at it," Jeanette went on, feeling it was her duty to tell what she knew. "Not once did she give it away, and she knew the entire time. What a secret to carry around!"

"She kept it pretty well," hummed Dora, who sat next to Jeanette on a chair at their table. "I wonder what she'll do about the baby?"

"She wasn't ever pregnant, you poop," Jeannette scolded.

"Coulda fooled me."

"What about poor Jon?" asked another. "They seemed so happy together and she just up and left. If they were having a baby, why did she run off?" It was somewhat of a scandal. The gossipers of the village wondered why the young woman had left them behind without so much as a word goodbye. When they didn't see her for a few days, they'd asked Jon, who told them bluntly that she had left town and she wasn't coming back. And he gruffly explained to everyone that she was not pregnant. He was quite bitter about the break up at first.

"Who knows why love changes? And she wasn't ever pregnant," said Jeanette as she sipped her glass of red wine. Her wrinkled hand held the bowl-shaped glass very gently around the stem. "A least that puzzle is solved. We know she's all right and we have a new Protectress. Everything turned out well."

"He's not taking it all that badly." One pointed to Jon, nearby in the same tavern, smiling and doting on another young woman who was unmarried. She was slender, curvy and sported brilliant auburn locks. She almost met his height, where Axandra had always been dwarfed by his tall stature. If seeing pictures of his lost companion bothered him in anyway, Jon wasn't letting it show. He didn't look as though he even cared about the celebration, other than it being an excuse to fill himself with ale and fill his hands with a beautiful young woman.

"She'll do a wonderful job," Jeanette told her friends. "We won't be disappointed. I wonder why she wanted to live all the way over here instead of going back to her home."

"I heard she hated her parents," Dora offered, her words already slurred with intoxication. She lifted her mug of ale to her lips, trying to focus her bleary eyes on its contents. "She's a runaway. Remember when they first thought she'd been kidnapped? By one of the Prophets, no less. Those creeps. Never did trust 'em. Now she's told everyone she left on purpose."

"Oh, that tripe about living as one of the people—" Jeanette guffawed loudly. "Why would anyone want to do that when she could've lived at the Palace, up to her ears in luxury. I think somebody conned her into leaving. She was just a little girl at the time. She was probably lured by the Prophet with the promise of something sugary and was never allowed to even think about going home. Well, she's home now. I, for one, am happy for her."

The villagers around her all raised their voices in cheer.

+++

In Northland, a large group of celebrators gathered at the site of the Landing just a bit before the installation began.

The Believers, as they called themselves, believed that a Goddess, a divine and all-knowing being, had shown herself to their ancestors before they had ever left Old Earth, giving them the command to leave that toxic place and come here, to the New World. And it was at the landing site of this spacecraft, Sojourner, that the Goddess had come with the people, keeping the fleet of ships safe on the Journey—for so many times the ships narrowly escaped destruction. They believed the Goddess protected them still, through the Protectress.

They gathered here each time a Protectress was inducted, honoring the divine Goddess as she passed from the old to the new, in hopes that she might return here and they might catch a glimpse of the Goddess's true form.

The remains of the ships that lay grounded were maintained as they had been left, like museums to the distant past. Caretakers guarded the skeletons of the craft, the carcasses that had been cannibalized in the beginning to create shelter and storage, and later became tombs for the dead.

The Believers camped around the main entrance of the monument at the starboard side of the ship. They watched, prayed, drank ale and ate bread, celebrating and calling to the Goddess to come to them.

Around eleven that night, a glow rose up over the Sojourner. At first, the people thought it must be the Northern Lights, sparkling in the night sky. But the glow came too low in the sky to be the aurora. It seemed to hover just above the hull of the derelict ship, compact and bright.

"She is here!" someone cried out, pointing to the light. Others joined in the shouting until everyone came from their tents. They all stood and stared at the light as it hovered, dancing slightly to and fro in the air. Some muttered prayers to her, praising her immortal wisdom and asking her grace to lead them to perfection. Others lost their words, stunned to see her naked form.

The light hovered many minutes more, then began to pulse, dimming and brightening slightly, over and over in a slow, purposeful rhythm.

Everyone watching began to fall silent, hypnotized by the pulse. Only a few whisperings continued. Minutes later, not even the night noises could be heard.

In a brilliant flash, the light disappeared, leaving behind only euphoria among the Believers. They smiled at each other or cried happily, falling to their knees.

The Goddess was here. They knew the truth. They were chosen. They would spread the word.

Chapter 8

On the Road

In the weeks following her installment, Axandra continued her training and began to travel about the continent to villages within each of the four Regions, a tradition for generations.

For the long trips, the visiting group took a short convoy of electric cars. The vehicles were composed of aluminum frames and panels. A solar battery powered each conveyance, charged by the panel composing the cabin roof. For comfort, the interiors boasted luxurious padding for comfort over the unpaved and bumpy roads.

Knowing how susceptible she was to motion sickness, Axandra asked the Healer for something that would keep her stomach from churning. Throwing up the hospitality of her hosts at every stop seemed unproductive in the effort to put forth a good face.

Eryn gave her a supply of dried chickle leaves in a small glass vial with instructions to steep them in her tea or to chew them directly. One dose—the leaves were already cut into dose-sized strips—would stave off motion sickness for an entire day.

"Oh, I've heard of this, but it's difficult to get them in Gammerton. We can rarely obtain anything nearly as effective. Thankfully I rarely traveled."

"It's local to Northland," Eryn explained as she finished checking her Healer's pouch for supplies. She joined the entourage on their trek to Southland, their first tour of villages. "Sara brings the leaves for me when she comes to town. It's the most effective remedy I've found."

In one car, outfitted to seat seven passengers with ample comfort in the rear compartment, loaded Axandra, Eryn, and Councilors Morton, Sunsun and Lelle. The driver operated the vehicle from inside the front compartment and a secondary driver sat on the right. In the second car rode four Elite, their commander and Miri. Their luggage, mostly for the Protectress, embarrassingly enough, stowed neatly in a compartment at the extreme rear of each car. The other councilors from Southland had left Undun a few days before to prepare their villages for the Protectress' visit. Arranging themselves comfortably in the compartment seats, Eryn shared the bench with Axandra and the other three sat across from them. Axandra made sure to face forward, in hopes the position would stave off sickness.

"May I sit in the middle?" Sara asked the two older Councilors. "You know I have such long legs."

Batting her gray eyelashes in annoyance, Morton conceded. "Yes, Sara. You may." It took several minutes for everyone to shift and settle.

In six hours, if the traveling went well, they would arrive at Range End, aptly named by the people who settled where the mid-continental mountain range faded back in low rolling hills. On the way, they would stop in Redding for lunch.

As they started out from the Palace, they drove slowly through the main thoroughfare of the city, a broad avenue paved with hand-formed terracotta bricks. The streets ramped up to the doorways of shops and homes along the street.

Along the route, a man kneeled on the bricks, replacing a few that were cracked and worn. He moved aside to let the cars go by, waving to the drivers as they passed. Then he returned to his work, prying up the ruined bricks and packing down the new ones.

They left town to the west, toward the towering sharp peaks of the mountains, and on to a fork in the main road heading south. The driver did his best to smooth out the ride on the somewhat eroded pavement. A kilom later they passed a paving crew just beginning deconstruction of sections of collapsed roadway.

They departed around eight in the morning, planning to arrive before dinner. The eastern suns glowed upon the mountainside, accentuating the crevices, crags and boulders that designed the slope. Flecks of mica sparkled in the pink and gray granite.

For practicality, Axandra wore a pantsuit of earthy red in hue. She had taken off her jacket and stowed it, neatly folded, in the shallow bin above. At the moment, she held onto a book she brought with her, for she hadn't had the luxury to start on the collection of short stories she'd borrowed from the Library. She gazed out the window instead of reading, her chin perched on her folded hand. Stretched in the space in front of her, her legs crossed at the ankle.

"Join us in a game of rummy?" offered Sara with a welcoming smile. The councilors folded down a table top between the seats and pulled out a deck of playing cards.

"I haven't played that game," Axandra declined uncomfortably. She labored over what attitude to take with other people. Should she distance herself from those in her everyday life? She did not want to be lonely, but the possession of her mind by the Goddess made her feel distinctly alone. She also felt particularly friendless, knowing no one in Undun prior to her recent arrival and having no opportunity to make friends prior to becoming Protectress.

"Oh, we'll teach you. I promise the time will go by much faster if we have a little fun." Sara Sunsun gave a little wave for Axandra to join them. Sara exuded pleasantness and good-humor. Of the individuals Axandra had met in Undun City, Sara was the most amiable, always ready to start a conversation about anything cheerful and making even mundane tasks less tedious.

"You're right," Axandra admitted. The sixteen day voyage from Gammerton to Undun had felt like years.

Sliding over on the long bench seat, Axandra agreed to join them. The cards were dealt, and they took turns explaining the rules. After a few practice hands, Axandra began to understand the nuances of the games, and the play became somewhat raucous, each competitor playfully blaming another for their losing a hand.

While they played, they visited about both personal and business topics, openly sharing troubles and joys alike. At least this was true for Sara and Councilor Lelle. Nancy barely afforded anyone so much as a glance during the games, and especially not in Axandra's direction.

Sara spoke of her life-partner. "Suzanne is very upset about the incident in Cutoff. She worries about my traveling to Undun for the Council. She's suddenly nervous that we'll be attacked by some stranger along the road. But she's always been prone to an overactive imagination."

"Where do you live?" asked Axandra for she knew little about the council members and thought they all lived in Undun City. But it seemed logical that the Councilors would live with their constituents.

"In North Compass," Sara explained. "Almost five hours to the northwest of Undun. Suzanne keeps our home there and is a teacher of music and an artist. Fortunately, I'm not usually away from home this much. The extra travel is worrisome to her, now that strange things are happening."

"She must love you very much." Axandra felt envious. Jon had not yet written to her, and she doubted he much cared now. For the last week, she deeply regretted having left her lover without saying goodbye, without explaining herself in person. The

Goddess had receded into the back of her mind during the past few days, giving her relative peace and quiet. Now her mind renewed worries of her former life, of abandoning her village and her friends. And especially of abandoning Jon and of frightening his soul so that he was terrified to be anywhere near her.

"She does. I don't think I can love her as much as she loves me—and that's a great deal, I'll admit," Sara chuckled. She examined the cards in her hand and pulled the top card from the draw pile, slipping it in place and discarding the card from the left of the fan. Axandra noticed the beautiful ring on Sara's left hand, silver metal and blue stones. Sara possessed slender hands of pale pink. She stood several centims taller than Axandra on her slender frame. Often, Sara wore open-necked blouses that bared a graceful clavicle and modest cleavage. Her pink, freckled face smiled more often than not, as though she enjoyed everything in life. Her blue eyes sparkled, especially when she spoke of Suzanne.

"Does she want you to retire?" Nancy inquired, her tone stern. "It's your turn, Madam," she whispered aside to Axandra, who had lost track in the conversation.

Axandra took the card from the discard pile, laid down her completed sets, and discarded her final card. "I'm out," she said timidly. This was the tenth hand she reigned.

The councilors turned to her with dismayed looks.

"Again?" Nancy tossed down her cards disgustedly, then took up a pencil and score pad. "Points, please."

They added up their totals and saw that Axandra won the game. "Beginner's luck," Antonette grumbled under her breath.

"I hope you all aren't letting me win," the Protectress probed. Though she possessed the capability to reach into their minds, she left their thoughts to themselves out of moral principle.

"I wouldn't dream of it," Antonette crowed. Her hair was short, white and straight. Jowls framed her thin lips and wrinkles framed her eyes. "We should be stopping for a break soon. We're almost to Redding."

Outside the window, she could see a small town in the short distance. The car moved at a good clip on a smoother section of road. Getting out to stretch their legs would feel good but they still had three hours to Range End, their first official stay-over in Southland. "We've just crossed the border," Antonette continued. "Welcome to Southland, Protectress."

Within a few minutes they stopped outside a small house in the loose collection of homes known as the village of Redding. After a moment a tall man, round about the gut, strode out. He wore blue slacks and a white button shirt with the collar open. Suspenders held up his pants. Mud caked the sides of his leather-leaf boots, each of which had frayed laces.

As the travelers piled out of the cars, Antonette moved forward to introduce them to the local Principal. He bowed in welcome.

"Please come in for a rest. We have lunch spread for you. I hope it suits your needs." He gestured to a shelter house that stood to one side of the center of the small village, where several tables stood laden with food and drink, and where the majority of the townsfolk gathered.

For about twenty minutes, they rested and took their lunch standing and milling about with the local people. They stood to stretch their legs, knowing they would be back in the car for another lengthy period in less than an hour.

Despite the herbal remedy, Axandra's stomach still bubbled. Finished with her small bite of lunch, she listened to the Principal's proposal to expand the communications network in order for each village to possess up to ten communits for public use. Currently, each village had one or two communits reserved for government or emergency use only. Resources existed to commit to the increased number, and the new units would allow residents to quicken communications between family members and colleagues across the continent. The Principal had done his homework, and knew that convincing the Protectress favored his desired outcome.

Much too soon, Nancy reminded everyone that the time had come to continue the trek. Plates and cups returned to the tables, and the travelers exited the shelter to return to the cars.

"Thank you very much for your hospitality," Axandra bowed graciously to their hosts and directly to the Principal. "And for your ideas. I will take them to the Council for discussion."

"It was an immense pleasure to meet you, Esteemed Protectress." The Principal bowed deeply.

The traveling party climbed back into the cars. This time Axandra rode with Nancy, Miri and two of the Elite. The secondary drivers took the wheels, relieving their counterparts. The next few hours passed in subdued silence. Axandra once again attempted to read her book, yet could not concentrate on the black words printed on the thick flaxen pages. The movement of the car frame over the cracked pavement made it hard to focus. That and the silence laced with solemn seriousness.

The Elite focused on their duty of protecting their charge, thinking of little else. Each one kept his or her face locked toward the windows, eyes scanning the road and landscape in all directions. Ty and Morton shared brooding glances with one another, each of them concerned with some matter they were not ready to discuss in present company, but one that marred their enjoyment of any companionship. Ty was all work, anyway. Axandra wondered if he ever relaxed. And Morton just plain disliked her. Axandra made many attempts since her arrival to make herself more appealing to the Head of Council, futile as they were. Soon, she promised herself to stop expending the energy to try.

Miri was the only one not consumed by her duties at the moment. The young woman worked on a needle point of a name bordered by vibrant flowers.

Axandra chose to break the unbearable silence, speaking to her aide. "What are you working on, Miri?"

"It's for my niece," she explained. "She was just born last Tinsday. I've been working on it for months." Miri passed the work to Axandra to examine.

"It's lovely," Axandra praised as she studied the threads. The stitches looked perfect. Nothing seemed uneven or out of place.

"I've made several for friends and family."

"Is it your own pattern?"

"Yes. I took this idea from the Palace garden," Miri blushed slightly, then gestured for the hoop. "I still have trouble with a few stitches, and I know I have much to learn about patterns and colors. I wish I could stitch one like the tapestries that hang in the Palace."

"Tapestries are woven, dear," Nancy informed her condescendingly.

"I know, but I would like to stitch one. The work would be something different." Miri looked dreamily out the window for a brief moment, then returned to her stitches.

Nancy cleared her throat and began to go over the itinerary for the next few hours days.

"When we reach Range End, the Principal will greet us and take us to our accommodations. There is an inn there, so we will all be housed in the same location. We'll change and head to dinner in the square. The entire community will be there and probably some out-of-towners. Before the meal, you'll give your small speech—the one we prepared last week."

Axandra nodded. She'd memorized and practiced the words of the blessing but she didn't feel right saying them, especially the end "... and all will be well." Simple words, but she felt them untruthful. She sensed that matters were not going well at all. First the murder, then the strange news that the Believers at the Northland Landing claimed to have witnessed a light—what to them was the Goddess—to which a new flush of recruits gathered to worship.

The Goddess had not gone there that night. At no time did Axandra believe it left her body. With its constant mental interruptions and the physical presence of it weighing on her head, she felt certain she would notice its absence. Nor did she believe it could exit her for quick jaunts about the world. The presence was so entwined with her physical being now, she feared that only death could separate them.

So what *thing* had appeared?

The event worried her just as deeply as the murder. Three hundred people attested to the appearance of the light. Was it a new life form? Did it come from a far away planet to this one that teemed with life? Humans no longer doubted alien life, though they had not crossed anything with the human level of intelligence or capability. Many animals on this world possessed considerable, though wild, intelligence, such as the sea mammals, the curana.

Axandra could not shake the sensation that something watched her from nearby. Like that first visit to the Palace garden, she sensed a presence just on the margins of her mind. The Goddess reacted defensively, sending out defensive vibrations to warn the intruder away. The presence never came close enough for clarity. Over the last three weeks, Axandra sensed the nearness four distinct times in different locations. The mind behind the presence remained watchful for now.

"They will want us to stay up for drinks, but I suggest we turn in by nine. We have another long trip to Midsouthton tomorrow for another dinner and a concert. Then another five hours over to Lazzonir the next day. We'll stay two nights there before the eight hour trip home."

"Lazzonir is the Southland Landing site, correct?" Axandra quizzed. Hence the two-day stay. They planned to tour the site for several hours. She looked forward to that portion of the trip.

She had only ever been to the Eastland Landing when she was four—she barely remembered what the place looked like. All of the Landings had been converted into museums and libraries, open places for the citizens to view the history of the Journey and reach back to their ancestors. Axandra hoped to see what Old Earth looked like in the past, and perhaps learn to understand why the Journeyers left behind their home with hopes of starting something new.

Though ten generations removed from those travelers, Axandra nurtured a healthy interest in their history. Choosing to leave one's home and never return was possibly the bravest action any person could ever take. The fact that so many had left in search of a place to make a safe home and having no idea what they would even find when they got there was an incredible feat.

And now she had memories from the Goddess to fuel her fascination with the past. The Goddess gave her many glimpses of life aboard star-spanning ships—brief though they were. Centuries of information was now stored inside her. She would never know it all.

"Yes. But we may be sharing it with a large contingent of Believers," stated Ty. He sat stiffly in his gray uniform. The gold circles appliquéd on the breast sparkled in the rays of the midday suns even though the darkened glass of the windows muted the light. "We have been informed of large gatherings at all of the Landings, awaiting another appearance of the Goddess."

The Protectress glanced toward Nancy, who kept her eyes on Ty. They would get an appearance, but they would not know it.

"That is their right, as long as they do so peacefully," the Morton allowed. Any group of citizens could peaceably assemble without permission, even in light of a special visitor.

Ty pledged, "I will keep them under observation."

They all fell silent as the travel continued. Axandra set aside her neglected book and returned her gaze to the terrain passing on the mountain side of the car. The peaks grew shorter and more worn. Jagged rocks gave way to soft slopes covered with feathering grasses and bushy shrubs. She let her mind wander to less corporeal ideas, allowing herself to float away with the icy clouds in the stratosphere.

Chapter 9

Lazzonir

Lazzonir, the village, mirrored its name from the space faring ship that led the Landing in the South. That vessel was named for its designer and primary funder, Paul Lazzonir. Each of the dozen generation craft used in the Journey was unique in design and construction. Across Earth, groups of individuals with unique mental gifts, independent of each other, designed and stocked the vessels. Just months before many of the ships planned to launch, the groups discovered each other, each seeking the same freedom, and began to collaborate, picking these stars and this world on which to set foot.

Fleeing persecution by the Normals, as they called the non-telepaths of the day, the collection of pilgrims left Earth forever and hoped, by some twist of fate, that they might actually reach a new world to call home and to shape as they desired. Those who began the Journey never saw its end, over one hundred years in their future.

Rolling into the village, the Protectress and her companions were at once surprised and dismayed by the massive numbers gathered in the streets. The Believers recently recruited many new worshippers, all awaiting a glimpse of the Goddess. The wide streets teemed with people, almost to the point that the cars could not pass safely. The cars paused for a moment and the Elite climbed out. The five intimidating guards began politely but firmly clearing a path.

Seeing the Elite, the Believers immediately recognized who rode in the cars and began to move closer. If the Protectress was here, then the Goddess would come. They tried to see into the tinted windows, hoping to catch a glimpse of the Protectress.

Axandra sensed that most of the onlookers were harmless, their minds still wrapping around the idea of the Goddess incarnate. They hoped only for a chance to feel the euphoria the Northlanders described, a taste of utter happiness. Yet their proximity gave Axandra a nervous itch. Despite the fact that they could not see in, she pulled back from the glass.

In front of the inn, the entourage climbed out of the cars and headed inside with their luggage. The early afternoon suns shortened their shadows. They had plenty of time to relax before the next dinner.

Two Elite went straight to bed. Assigned to night duty, they watched the inn while the others slept. The other two claimed their stations outside the Protectress' suite. Ty disappeared somewhere, presumably to his own accommodations, but also likely, off somewhere with Morton.

After Miri set up the room, Axandra lay down on the soft bed, thinking she would also fall asleep. Despite the cushions in the cars, the potholes still jarred her bones and the strain of trying to keep herself steady exhausted her pampered muscles. She decided she needed to find a way to retain her muscle tone that had always been naturally firm simply from performing the labors of her typical day. Sitting and talking did not provide for much exercise.

Instead of being able to rest, the surge of minds outside kept her awake. So many focused on her. She found it difficult to shut them out. Through the glass, she could hear them chanting in a low rumble of voices.

We are your chosen ones. Oh Goddess of our hearts. Come to us (we need you)

We feel you near and ask you to give your grace. Forgive us our sins (we have few)

Comfort our Souls and we will give ourselves to you freely.

Let us see your face! (the Goddess's face!)

Stray thoughts filtered in, jumbled with their words. The horde pushed down every defense she could muster. She looked down upon an amassing crowd of people in the avenue, their faces raised toward her room. Their lips moved as they continued to make their prayers.

I see her! (she is beautiful)

There! (in the window)

Come to us! We want to touch you! Be our strength!

She gasped and moaned, overwhelmed by their sentiments. As more of them arrived, the din rose in volume.

As though on cue—for she had just thought to seek out the Healer—a knock came at the door of her modest suite. The Healer announced herself.

"Come in," Axandra allowed. She stepped away from the window. *When did I get up from bed?* she wondered. The suns cast dual shadows of her across the polished wood floor. The glare blinded her to the dark areas of the room. The light shot pain through her skull. She rubbed her temples and covered her eyes with her hand.

"They are affecting everyone," Eryn informed. The thin woman stepped inside and closed the wooden door behind her, sealing them in mock privacy. She slipped off her pouch and set it on a small table near the door. Before she retrieved anything from the kitbag, she asked Axandra to sit on the bed.

"May I touch you?" Eryn asked politely.

Axandra nodded. One of her ears rang with a high-pitched stinging noise. She rubbed her finger against the small knob of cartilage, pressing closed the hole, but the ringing did not stop.

To heal among a telepathic race, the Healers trained to heal more than the body. The honor of Healing required more than a decade of training and an inherently strong telepathic nature. Adolescents were usually chosen to begin the training as early as age fifteen. Not all completed the rigorous education. The service was honored almost as much as that of the Protectress and commanded a great deal of respect from the community. A Healer's needs were provided without question.

Very gently but with purpose, Eryn touched Axandra's hands, which rested on her lap as she sat. She watched as the Healer slowly rotated the hands palm up and massaged the pale, soft portions, holding each just a few centims above her legs.

"Look at my face," Eryn instructed, her voice taking on a lower pitch and softer tone. "I will come into your mind only to dam the flow. You may have your eyes open or closed. Trust that I will not intrude where you do not wish me to go."

"I trust you." The massage relaxed her arms and helped focus her mind. Eryn's hands felt cool and luxuriously soft.

Axandra let her eyes close, her last vision Eryn's green eyes looking directly into her.

The static in her mind filled her ears and her eyes with fuzzy and dizzying white. Flashes of color painted her eyelids. Figures blurred together. Laughing and crying flew into her from the minds surrounding her.

Come to us, they continued to call

Then a small green circle of color appeared in the center. The circle had undefined edges at first and was barely larger than a pinhead. Axandra latched onto it. The circle was Eryn.

Without words, the outer arc clarified and the circle expanded, pushing away the maelstrom little by little. There was no telling how much time passed as the circle grew in miniscule bits. Time remained irrelevant inside the mind.

As the green circle expanded, the noise in Axandra's ears faded in volume until all she could hear was breathing. Involuntarily, she sighed. The relief felt almost as overwhelming as the onslaught of minds had been. Her body and her room became very quiet.

Opening her eyes, she found Eryn still watching her and still clasping her hands.

Your mind is very strong, Eryn shared her thoughts, her mental voice an echo of her physical one. *You would have made a fine Healer.*

I was asked, Axandra responded silently. *I declined. I was not up to the challenge.*

Eryn's lips curved slightly in a smile. She understood.

Rest now, the dam should hold through the morning.

With her arm, Eryn supported Axandra's back as she settled onto the mattress and pillows.

+++

Dinner with the Governor of Southland that evening passed in a less than pleasant way. While Axandra and her companions received relief from their Healer, the village's own Healers failed to keep up with the demand for aid. Every resident of the village suffered the irritating effects of the swarm of Believers.

Mark Tornedon, the regional governor, sat at the head of the table, bleary-eyed.

"We allowed them to come, but we didn't know there would be so many. We aren't equipped to care for the needs of so many people," he told them. "They didn't bring anything into our community but their ideas, but we've given them all we can. They've been here only five days, and we've almost exhausted our resources."

He barely ate his dinner of grilled freshwater fish and boiled grains mixed with spicy red and yellow peppers. He rubbed a hand up across his hollow face into his thin blonde hair. His skin was very tan from spending time outdoors. He told them he often rafted on the rapids in the Range River that ran nearby, when he wasn't serving as governor. His short sleeves displayed hardened muscles and a line between his tan and the skin that spent most of the time covered.

"I haven't slept well for the last three nights because of them."

"Have they explained what they're expecting to see?" asked Antonette. Lazzonir was her home town and she was familiar with its ways. She expressed great agitation at the invasion of the religious fanatics.

"The Goddess!" Tornedon moaned, his eyes rolling up. "I hoped they would be disappointed enough to leave by now. If they are not on the way out by the time you leave, Protectress, I will have to ask them depart."

"You must do what is necessary for your community," Axandra approved, as she sensed he sought agreement from a higher power. Once a group began to cause harm, they could be dispersed. "What supplies do you need replenished? We should organize relief."

Tornedon beamed, pleased with the offer as he leaned his right arm on the table toward her. "We have plenty of drinkable water, but we have little left of food. While having this dinner for you, Protectress, many have nothing but bread and meager pickings from a garden or two. Some of the visitors do not appear to have eaten for days. The Healers are overrun just making rounds on them. A few extra healing hands would be beneficial as well."

Councilor Lelle tapped her stubby fingers on the dark wood tabletop. "If only we could give them what they want."

Axandra inhaled a sip of wine down her windpipe and hacked loudly. Her throat burned from the alcohol. She recovered quickly by clearing her throat and giving a little tap to her chest. A wave of anxiety swept hotly through her torso, mixed with the concerns of her entourage that she might be choking.

"What nonsense—this goddess!" Antonette continued, mumbling somewhat—perhaps an effect of the wine. "Never seen any proof she exists. They're just wasting time they should be devoting to their own communities."

"Is there anything else we can do, Mr. Tornedon?" Axandra returned her focus to the needs of the village.

"We just need to get back in harmony again," he said, satisfied. "You will still visit the Landing tomorrow?"

"Yes. I am looking forward to it," Axandra promised. She was still excited for the moment, at least for the historical perspective. The crowd would still be there, still focused on her and the Goddess they believed would show herself.

Dinner ended at that point, and everyone returned to their rooms at the inn. Ty instructed them to meet at ten in the morning to walk to the Landing, less than a mile away. The later start would give everyone a chance to sleep in and have breakfast on their own.

Miri helped Axandra get ready for a bath and bed, packing away today's clothes and setting out tomorrow's. The aide carefully put away the jewelry Axandra wore that day, including the amethyst amulet she donned in honor of visiting the land of its origin.

"Miri, may I ask you a somewhat personal question?"

The blonde puffed out a short laugh, her straight hair falling over her shoulder as she bent to pack a pair of shoes. "You may, Madam. May I have permission not to answer?"

"That's fair," Axandra agreed. She offered a warm smile. It was probably quite unfair for the Protectress to ask anyone personal questions when she was supposed to hear and know everything.

"Do you believe in the Goddess?" she asked the young woman, her tone inquisitive and carefully non-judgmental.

Miri slowed in her work and pondered if she would answer. "I do," she said at last, folding a jacket and pressing it into the trunk. "I used to belong to the Believers sect in Eastland, but it lost its magic after a couple of years. We never witnessed the Goddess or any type of miracles, so I gave up spending my time waiting for her. It seemed wasteful."

"But you did not lose your belief." Axandra noted.

"No. I still believe she existed and that she had a great influence in bringing our people here." Miri looked wistfully toward the stars outside in the darkening sky, absently caressing the silk of the tunic in her hands. "If she still exists, she is probably far away from here, helping another species in their darkest hour. It's selfish to think she exists only for us. May I ask you the same question?"

Axandra should have expected to be caught in a trap of her own making. Miri was quite bold to ask, and this made her blush. She didn't feel prepared to answer.

Miri came to her at the vanity mirror and began to brush her dark, spiraling hair. Axandra noticed how long the strands had grown, half-way down her back. She decided a haircut was in order when they returned to Undun, to bring her tresses under control again.

"I used to wonder why people needed to believe in something larger than themselves or more powerful than the community," Axandra explained as she watched in the mirror's reflection. Miri deftly braided her hair in neat, uniform plaits. "I don't believe in a self-conscious, omnipotent being in the sky."

Finished with the braid and the conversation, Miri excused herself for the evening.

Axandra soaked in her bath for several minutes, cleaning off the residue of the last couple of days travel, that grimy feeling that comes from sitting in a car for hours. The warm water soothed tension from her muscles. With her mind free of others' thoughts, thanks to Eryn's ministrations, and the discomfort of the body fading away, her thoughts drifted back to her old life. She stepped into a memory of walking along the beach in the evening, the suns, one yellow, one blue, descending into the open Ocean. Dry warm sands brushed between her toes while she walked barefoot, her sandals dangling from her fingers. In the memory, she walked the beach alone.

She realized this wasn't a single memory, but a collection of several, similar moments when Jon left her at home alone in the evening or for the night while he stayed in town. She never viewed her companion's absence as loneliness. Those evenings gave her freedom to eat simply, since Jon usually insisted on cooking meals with several courses. Nor did she feel tied to make conversation with him. He typically talked about the townsfolk—who was up to what and when and what others were saying about each other. His mind did not open to discussions about literature or history or even musings about the sky or the ocean. He hadn't read a single full book since she had met him. He only read the few pages of the local gossip sheet passed out at the tavern each week.

What did we ever have in common? she wondered.

After a while she climbed out of the deep tub, dried the moisture from her skin and shimmied into a algodon nightgown, comforted by the coolness of the fabric on her skin. Feeling exhausted and weak, she burrowed beneath the soft covers of the bed and listened to the chirping insects outside the open windows.

While Eryn's "dam" held, she dreamed in green hues. But she dreamed of Jon. He was smiling with her, making love to her, laughing with her. Then he was gone. She saw him walking away down the village street—only they weren't in the sea-side village. She recognized the structures of Lazzonir. He walked toward the derelict spaceships, dressed in a long drab robe.

She hurried toward him, calling his name. She touched his shoulder, but as the figure turned to her, it wasn't him anymore. A stranger looked at her, perhaps one of the faces that infringed on her mind earlier that day. Others came. Smiling with sickeningly sweet passion, bodies in drab robes surrounded her. Her body prickled, every hair standing on end.

Fear! Fear! FEAR!

Pale hands groped her, the fingers pinching her skin, tangling in her hair. Spinning, she slapped at them, knocking some away. She could not deflect them all. Her limbs became entrapped by their hands. They pulled her in every direction, stretching her joints—

Waking, she found the room cast in the purplish glow, the mix of the gray and red hued moons. A bright swatch of stars bisected the sky.

A silhouette blocked a portion of the stars, ambulating in jerking motions as it climbed in through the open window.

She froze, staring at the figure, squinting to see some detail.

It is you (she is here)

Who are you? she asked of the figure whose mind infringed upon hers. She extended tendrils of her mind to touch the stranger. *Stop where you are. Don't come any closer!*

Arms outstretched, he did not stop moving toward her. *I want to touch you (feel your power) Do not run (stay, stay, stay!)*

"Help!" Axandra shouted at once, her heart jumping in her chest. As the intruder reached for her she rolled from bed, hitting the floor on her stomach and knocking the wind from her lungs. The covers twisted around her body, trapping her arms and legs. Thrashing her limbs, she worked herself free even as she heard the bed frame clatter. The arm of the stranger loomed from above, touching her face.

Scrambling to her feet, she sprinted for the door, which exploded inward toward her. Struck squarely in the forehead, she now saw stars inside her room. Knocked backward by the force, she hit the wooden planks of the floor a second time, leading with her elbow. Pain shot through both halves of her arm.

The light from the hallway illuminated the floor. The Elite lunged in with aggressive grunts. While one grabbed her up from the floor and shoved her outside the room, the other blocked the attacker and quickly subdued him, wasting little effort on wrestling the thin figure to the floor. The first continued to shield the Protectress with his body, pinning her roughly against the wall opposite her room. She could not see past his barricade and the flashing lights in her eyes. Gasping, she shielded her face from the bright lights of the corridor.

The councilors and others spilled into the hallway from their rooms, checking on the commotion. Narone and the other two Elite pounded up the stairs, fully dressed. Ty reviewed the scene, seeing that the Protectress was out of harm's way. Then he went into the room where the intruder was held.

Rescuing her from the almost crushing protection of the guard, Eryn grabbed her by the arm and steered her down the hall, an Elite close behind. They went to the Healer's suite, where Eryn closed the door, leaving the guard outside.

Shaking, Axandra could hardly breathe. She paced the floor in her bare feet, shaking her hands at her sides, trying to catch her breath. Pain still shot through her skull. Touching her brow, she felt the lump forming.

Eryn touched her without asking permission, hoping to help her gain control, but instead the touch only worsened the anxiety.

"No!" Axandra heard herself shriek, though the rational part of her mind begged that Eryn help her.

Instead, Eryn used the connection formed earlier that day— touching her mind, pushing calm in place of fear like a levee between the river and the land.

Slowing her pace, Axandra sensed the instinct to fight or flee diminish. Her breathing steadied. Instead of pacing, she clenched and unclenched her hands slowly. She moved involuntarily in this manner, pieces of her still feeling the urge to run.

"You are fine, Protectress," Eryn spoke firmly. Without a single touch, the Healer coaxed her to settle on the tousled covers of the bed.

The green shade in Axandra's brain, the color of Eryn's eyes, pulsed in a lulling effect, blocking other outside influences. "Settle down, please. Breathe deeply. That's good. Let me see where you're hurt. Careless guards," Eryn muttered, examining the head injury visually. "They should have sensed you behind the door."

At some point, Miri arrived. She brought hot tea and a robe for her mistress, along with a cold pack for the bump on the Protectress' head. Eryn convinced Axandra to drink, placing the mug in her spasming hands. Then Eryn instructed Miri to hold the ice to the growing lump over Axandra's right eyebrow.

"What if I hadn't woken up," Axandra kept sputtering. "Why did he come in? Who is he?"

She felt relieved to be alive and relatively unharmed. But even realizing this did not calm her agitation any further. Her tea rippled above her quivering hands, threatening to spill over the lip of the cup. She stared at the dark surface of the liquid frightened and embarrassed by her lack of control. She'd never been given a reason to feel so frightened in all her life.

After a few sips, Axandra noticed that the tea helped calm her nerves. Eryn must have slipped an herb into her drink to help sedate her. She felt slightly unnatural, like her head was filled with hot air. Blinking forcefully, she attempted to clear the unwelcome state of mind. The strangeness enveloping her did not change, but wavered around her as though she were underwater.

"Ty will be here shortly to ask questions," Eryn explained while she got dressed in pants and a light shirt.

"I can't even think," Axandra complained. Even the steam of the tea tranquillized her nerves. She handed the mug to Miri to discard the rest, refusing anything else from the aide's tray, distrustful of the contents.

Ty arrived a few moments later and asked without pretense what transpired. Axandra explained how she awoke to see a figure coming through the window and escaped his reach. "The guards acted amazingly fast," she praised when she had finished her description. "Though too fast for me to stay clear of the door."

"They will be commended," Ty promised, then he revealed what he had learned from the intruder. "He carried no weapon. He claims he wished only to touch you, that it might bring the Goddess to them. He says he came with others to the inn, but they did not enter. They must have fled when you screamed, because we found no other intruders."

"Believers?"

"It would appear so. I suggest we cancel the visit to the Landing tomorrow—"

"No," Axandra protested, raising a halting hand between them. "It will send the wrong message."

"But it will keep you safe," Ty argued. Safety first, apologies later, his thought came to her as words he would not say. She was certain he did not intend for her to hear them.

"Postpone it until later then, but we're going. I will not run away from them. They are still my people," Axandra stated staunchly, allowing no room for further argument, even though her insides still quivered with fear. If she gave into those fears, she would have ordered them all home right that moment.

Ty resigned from the argument. "Noon, after lunch," he proposed. "I will secure the location personally before you arrive."

"Very well. After lunch." Nodding curtly, she accepted his compromise.

Ty turned to Eryn. "Healer, I respectfully request your assistance."

"Certainly." Eryn nodded. "Please, Protectress, make use of my room to sleep. Excuse us."

Sleep seemed the farthest thing from Axandra's mind as she sat there, her thoughts still a jumble of the dark images, the man coming at her and not knowing what he planned to do. She watched them leave with her brow furrowed anxiously.

Miri, gentle and persistent, convinced Axandra after several minutes to lie down. Doing so, she soon felt her eyelids grow heavy. She insisted the lamp stay on. She stared at the window, half expecting someone to climb in. Miri sat nearby keeping watch.

+++

Ty took Eryn back to the Protectress' room, where the Elite detained the intruder. The Healer was not certain what she expected to see, but she understood what the Commander expected her to do.

The robed man sat slumped on the bed under full lighting. He appeared to be about thirty-five years old, his hair sandy in color and his skin smooth and lightly colored like that of someone who spent most of his time indoors. His eyes appeared sunken, and the bones of his wrists protruded sharply due to deterioration of muscle and fat tissue. No wonder it had been so easy for one Elite to apprehend him. Hearing soft noises from the captive, she realized he wept, his chin touching his chest as he slobbered with tears.

"I wasn't going to hurt her," he mumbled over and over again through his sobs. "I would never hurt her. Please believe me."

He spoke at the two Elite who guarded him, one standing at the doorway and the other at the window to prevent any attempts to escape. Eryn doubted he was in any shape to make such an attempt due to his weakened condition and by the fact that the guards had tied his wrists together behind his back.

"Sir, this is Healer Gray. If you will allow, she will be able to verify your claim and you will be set free."

The man raised his eyes to the tall woman, squinting through his tears to see her more clearly. He sniffled and, frowning, shook his head. "No. No, I can't let her in my mind. Only the Goddess can enter my mind. This woman will stain me."

"Sir," Eryn spoke, "I will not go anywhere you do not wish. I have taken my vows and adhere to them." She spoke in assuring tones and emanated trust to him. She met resistance to even her light projections.

Still he shook his head. His entire body trembled and he looked away. "No. No Believer lets anyone but the Goddess and her chosen in his mind. Bring her here and she will know the truth."

Ty refused with a harsh tone. "That will not be possible, and you know it. Healer, you may stay if you wish."

"Clearly this man needs physical attention," Eryn stated, still concerned about the man's malnourished appearance. She addressed the stranger again, moving herself in front of him, more deeply into his field of vision.

"What is your name?"

"Carter," the man answered.

"If you will allow me, Carter, I will tend only to your physical needs."

Again, he looked at her, breathing heavily and rapidly so that his shoulders moved up and down in massive heaves. New tears swelled in his eyes. He nodded that he would allow this. "I don't feel well. I haven't had food in three days. The locals have begun to refuse us any meals. I will not steal, but others have taken from the gardens. They anger the Goddess. They are why she will not appear to us. She does not abide stealing for any reason."

Eryn knelt in front Carter, careful to view his symptoms without touching his flesh. She asked if she could touch his hands briefly with her mind closed. He grudgingly agreed. She checked his fingernails, pressing them down so that the pale pinks turned white. The veins beneath his skin glowed blue and raised the thinning epidermis. "The Governor tells us that there is no food left to give you," she explained. "The village stores are not stocked to supply so many people."

"He lies," spat the man. "They have food. We saw the dinner they prepared for you. They shouldn't let people starve."

Eryn ascertained that his only ailment was the lack of food and politely ordered one of the Elite to locate at least a loaf of bread. When the bread arrived, she oversaw that he ate a portion of it, then wrapped the rest in a clean towel for him to take.

"Commander, I believe the man is speaking the truth," Eryn announced to everyone in the room. "His demeanor is that of a true Believer, and they have an even stricter set of rules than the rest of us regarding harm to another. You should set him free. Carter, please tell your companions that we regret their situation. Unfortunately, we will not be able to provide them with that which they seek most."

"But the Goddess is here," he pleaded with her to understand, his brown eyes turned upward to her, searching her for sympathy. "If only we could speak with the Protectress, we could have what we desire."

"I am sorry. The Protectress cannot help you in this matter." Eryn expressed herself as clearly as possible, but understood that the man would continue to insist that he was correct. She instructed him to take the bread to his camp and give it first to the children. "I will see if I can locate more," she promised.

The Commander watched the exchange without expression or comment. He breathed deeply, his nostrils flaring as he considered the situation. "Release him," Ty ordered his underlings, "and escort him back to his camp. I suggest you inform your companions that this behavior will not be tolerated."

With that, Ty signaled the Healer to come with him again. She followed with a soft sigh, annoyed with his demands. She wanted to return to the Protectress and see that she was getting back to sleep. They exited out into the corridor and the commander led her to a room at the far end of the hall. After closing the door, he turned to her without inviting her to sit.

"The Protectress' condition," he ordered. After a silent pause, in which she gazed at him patiently, he added respectfully, "Please, Healer. How is she?"

"She was harmed only by the guards attempting to protect her, struck by the door when they forced it open. Your people need to work on their mental training. The injury could have been avoided," Eryn told him tersely, allowing her temper to flare for a moment. "Fortunately the bump to her head is not serious. Otherwise she shows symptoms of emotional and psychic shock. She is very much disturbed by the intrusion. Her anxiety level is quite high. And the 'noise' of the Believer's minds is continuing to press in on her, despite my treatment. I do not expect that she will take must rest between now and tomorrow morning unless I reinforce the blocks I made earlier today."

"I am not a student of the mind, Healer," Ty stated, stoically refusing to allow himself to be embarrassed by his ignorance. "Please explain to me how three hundred people can cause such a gross mental disturbance when the City of Undun's three thousand people do not."

Eryn pressed the palms of her hands together before her, forming her answer carefully. "The almost three thousand citizens of Undun each have their own individual thoughts concerning their daily lives, and most of them are not actively emanating their thoughts into the atmosphere. These three hundred Believers are focused on one congruous purpose and often share a collective thought. They emanate this thought to summon their Goddess. Since the Protectress, by association, is the focus of their thoughts, she is severely affected. Bystanders are affected as well."

"I see," Narone hummed at the end of her explanation. Eryn sensed he did not understand completely. He was not prone to sharing his mind with anyone outside himself, not without opening his mouth. "You will see to it that she is protected?"

"Yes," Eryn vowed, understanding that Ty cringed at being forced to give up control of the Protectress' safety. He could only protect her physically.

"Do you think she will allow me to cancel the tour when she is more reasonable?"

Shaking her head, Eryn felt she knew exactly how the Protectress would respond to the idea. "No. The tour of the Landing is the dominant reason we came here. It demonstrates that the Protectress is aware of our cultural history and will endeavor not to repeat past mistakes."

His eyes dropped to the floor momentarily, a rare event in his body language. Narone always stood at attention, his eyes fixed upon his subject. This signaled that he contemplated his next steps when dealing with his stubborn queen. Her mother almost never quarreled with his recommendations. A moment later his copper-brown eyes returned to the Healer. "Very well. We will attend the tour when she is ready tomorrow. Please assure her that she will not be bothered by any intruders again."

Eryn did not doubt he would keep his word. Commander Ty Narone took the Protectress' safety very seriously. This knowledge gave Eryn comfort.

Chapter 10

Pictures of Old Earth

10th Pentember, 307

By morning, the town was ghostlike. The hordes of Believers vanished, leaving behind only visible traces of their existence, such as trampled grass and litter. The residents wandered out of their homes and looked about the town curiously, wondering where the out-of-towners had gone.

Miri called Axandra to the window when she looked out to see the general weather. They both looked down upon vacant streets. A breeze blew, and the trees swayed gently. A few locals retrieved baskets from their homes and began to pick up the trash that the wind blew around.

Not a Believer in sight.

"Get Ty. I want to know what happened," Axandra demanded, her first reaction leading her to believe he was behind this, that he chased them off. She did not know him well enough yet to assume that he would always comply with her intentions. He definitely viewed his first priority as her safety, regardless of the image his actions may advertise to the public.

Waiting for Ty to arrive, Axandra dressed in the clothes Miri brought from her room, since she had yet to return to the scene of the trespassing. Realizing this, she briefly wondered where Eryn was.

At the knock, she called for Miri and Ty to enter, recognizing their emanations. Ty looked as though he came fresh from a good night's sleep, his uniform neat and tidy and face clean shaven. She doubted he had slept since the incident.

"You requested my presence," Ty acknowledged.

Axandra gestured out the window to the street below. "Can you explain this?"

"I can. They decided to leave," Ty stated with a plain, matter-of-fact tone. Good riddance, his mind reflected. Axandra blinked at receiving his stray thoughts again. Normally she did not pick up one's unspoken pieces of conversation. Long ago, she trained herself to block unintentional sharing. Blocking was a skill all remoters needed to learn.

"Just like that."

He nodded succinctly. "We released the intruder after we decided that he no longer posed a physical threat. At that point, the Believers began to pack up their belongings and leave."

"And you had no influence in their decision."

"Other than capturing their representative, no." Though his face remained impassive, Axandra detected a note of amusement in Ty's words. "It was not your desire, Madam, to force them to leave. I will not go against your wishes, as long as your wishes do not place you in foreseeable danger."

Axandra went back to the window, as though she might find a straggler. The village remained relatively empty.

"Madam, I have been with the Night Watchers since we released the intruder. Several Believers passing us muttered disappointment that the Goddess did not come. I do not know what our friend may have said to them that caused them to leave. But the situation has made my duty much less difficult," Ty elaborated, fulfilling her unspoken desire for more information.

"That's fine, thank you," Axandra said to conclude the discussion, though not entirely satisfied. It seemed strange that so many people could all leave in the dark to go to their own towns. Many had come dozens of kiloms to be here. They gave up, just as the Governor had hoped.

"What time is it?" she asked.

"Eleven, Madam. Time for lunch," Miri replied. After the intrusion, Miri kept watch over her mistress. The younger woman's pale face reflected the lack of sleep in bluish circles beneath her eyes.

"Then let's eat and go on our tour. I can't wait to go home tomorrow."

+++

The Landing made a fascinating sight. Within one square kilom, two gigantic generation ships, each carrying approximately fifteen hundred people, landed on this grassy plain, creating their final resting place. Once grounded, the ships never flew again. They rested here, like ancient temples to the stars.

From the outside, open panels and ragged edges marked where sections of the vessels had been removed and recycled to build temporary homes or salvaged to construct a ground vehicle or any number of things necessary to the survival of the pioneers. One of the derelict vessels, the *Lazzonir*, towered above them, a curved shape of dark gray alloy dotted with clear portals, all dark from the inside. The troupe walked toward the ramp that led to the main entry doors into the shadow of the mighty hull.

Imagine, people of all ages walking down the gangplanks of these vessels, and not one had set foot on a planet before. All born on the Journey, they knew only the interior bulkheads of their ships with everything supplied for them through machines. They breathed only mechanically recycled air and walked on hard deck plates, nothing like the sponginess of real soil beneath their feet.

The new adventure must have felt exhilarating and terrifying, Axandra thought. So many unknowns. What perils would they face? Would they survive the year?

Inside, the custodian greeted the group. He explained that he also worked as an archeologist, and while he enjoyed his digging through the people's history, he was more often found digging into the planet's secret past. Tired as she was, Axandra accepted his welcome only as a passing blip in her mind, looking at the man's face for only a moment as they bowed to each other. Then she allowed the others to surround her, letting them take the brunt of the information being spouted at them.

The custodian took the Protectress and her companions on a tour of the museum housed in the once space-bound structure. He explained that the second ship, the *Ulysses* had been sealed about fifty years after the landing, for it had been used to entomb the dead. The humans were not certain what effect their remains might have on the ecology and tried to prevent too much interference. The sealing of the tomb came when it was determined that cremation would be the best method of interring the deceased. Those original bodies still rested peacefully inside, undisturbed for centuries.

Inside the *Lazzonir*, the ship remained preserved as the crew left it. Solar generators supplied power to several of the machines and computers, and much of the equipment was carefully maintained in working order. Data from the Journey was easily accessible at several of the control stations in this large area at the bow of the vessel. The arena had long ago been used as a scientific station, where the explorers gathered information about the space around them and marveled at the mysteries of the universe.

"The *Lazzonir* is the only one of the generation ships that is kept in this phenomenal condition," the custodian explained.

"The other ships exist merely as memorials to their crews and families.

"Fortunately, the records from all of the ships were downloaded into the *Lazzonir's* computers. Not only is there data from the interstellar flight, but a great deal of information archived from Old Earth. I am able to show you the world that our ancestors left behind," said the custodian as they stopped in front of a large display screen. On a keypad, he typed a command and called up still images of a nasty place.

"Humans lived there?" Eryn asked, scrunching her nose in disgust. "Why is the sky orange? I thought Earth's sky was blue."

"It was blue when it was clean," the custodian replied. "The term we find in the records is smog. The pollution was so thick, that humans were not allowed to breathe the air outside of their homes and buildings, where it was filtered before being pumped inside."

The scenes being presented on the screen showed a truly disgusting place, the sky enflamed and the sun a dim bulb through the thick air. Layers of filth coated everything. Only a few trees tolerated the environment wearing wilted leaves on their sickly branches.

Axandra wanted to listen as the man continued to describe Old Earth, but her exhaustion distracted her. Her brain felt mushy, like rotten fruit, and responded slowly even to the most mundane task of blinking her eyes. Seeing a bench nearby, she perched herself on its contoured surface, relieving the weight from her joints. She fought to keep her eyelids open.

Grrrraaaawwl

The Goddess reacted, making the same noise as from the garden, that defensive guttural growl. The presence from the garden followed her here, watching them. Her mind perceived a distorted image of this room and its occupants, as though from a high perch. The Goddess raised her hackles. The internal presence skirted the edges of her consciousness.

Axandra glanced around the interior of the enclosure looking for the source of the vision, even looking to the high, dark ceiling. If the creature was watching, it had to be inside the ship. A brief flicker of movement darkened in the corner of her eye, but by the time she turned her head, she found nothing. The only living things here were humans. She saw no other visible creatures.

Perhaps she overreacted to the sensation. Still unaccustomed to the effects of the Goddess's presence, Axandra could not feel certain about what she sensed. Maybe she now suffered a hypersensitivity to small wild animals. Gworls often nested in unoccupied spaces such as attics and rafters. A gworl might very well be skittering around in the decking, using the space as a comfortable home for a healthy family of rodents.

Weariness began to claim Axandra's senses. She woke so many times through the night with her heart racing imaging someone else standing in the room. Her dreams replayed the intrusion in exact detail over and over. Each waking disoriented her, jumbling time and place and amplifying the fear.

Axandra felt disappointment to miss the direct evidence of the history she often read about, but she was not in the mood to stare at photos on the brightly lit screens. Her interest wandered. Stifling a yawn, she at least tried to appear to be absorbing the lessons the custodian recited. Acknowledging failure, she rose from the bench as the group began to move about the ship.

They visited various compartments of the craft, including family quarters, dining areas and work areas where the crew once maintained the ship or collected data.

The sensors of the ships collected so much data that humans had still not analyzed every bit. Only a handful of scholars were able to dedicate their time to understanding the scientific information about stars, planets and about space itself. Planet-bound now, most people saw little use for astronomy and space science or the minutiae of their neighboring planets.

After a couple of hours, the tour ended, but the councilors wanted to continue to look through the images. The dire state of Old Earth overwhelmed their sensibilities. Their people were instilled with the necessity of recycling and composting everything they used to produce almost no pollution. The custodian helped them compare the deterioration to earlier photos of Earth, when the skies gleamed pristine blue.

With the Councilors on their own to sift through thousands of digital images, the custodian approached the Protectress with a special invitation. The guide offered to allow the Protectress to view a few items that were not on the public tour, gesturing to a door at the far end of the main arena plainly noted as a restricted zone. Barely able to keep her eyes open any longer, Axandra declined, asking to be escorted back to the inn. Miri and the Elite went with her. She was too tired to even sense his disappointment, though it showed clearly on the man's face.

At the inn, in her own room again, she lay down and slept. When she woke, the suns set in the west over the trees. She asked for a light dinner, then returned immediately to bed, foregoing any social events on the schedule. The next day, early in the morning, the entourage climbed back into the cars and started the trip home. At least two Elite remained in the car with the Protectress and always close to her when they stopped along the way for rest breaks and lunch. She took comfort in their diligence.

Chapter 11

Homesick

12th Pentember, 307

Home again, Axandra returned to her submersion in the study of the Covenants and their interpretation. The main duties of the People's Council included the equitable distribution of the world-community's resources and the oversight of social policies. The social rules relied on the citizens to follow them with dedication. From time to time, the interpretation of the laws came into question as a new method or new technology proposed to improve the overall quality of life. Citizens freely questioned anything that concerned them, and the majority of the people decided the final conclusion to any matter.

Axandra focused this time on the Rule of Service. "Everyone is expected to perform service for the welfare and benefit of the community."

She spoke the words aloud as she studied them. To receive benefits, one provided benefits. The prosperity of their people rested on the willingness of each person to share with every other person. Food grown by the community became property of the community. If individuals grew something in their own gardens, they shared their crop with their neighbors, usually in exchange for a haircut or a vase or other desired item. If some-one failed in providing a benefit for the community, the entire community paid their price. While some were incapable of pro-viding substantial benefit in hard labor due to illness, disability or age, those persons were still capable and willing to provide whatever assistance they could through less physical chores.

The Believers in Lazzonir intentionally took for granted that their needs for food and water would be provided for while they stayed in the village. They neglected to bring any resources with them except the clothes they wore. Following the Covenants, the Lazzonirians provided for them anyway, acting true to their creed. No one went hungry as long as resources existed. Unfor-tunately, the depleted resources quickly cost the hosts and their guests health and enjoyment of life. Many people went hungry.

Eryn assured the Protectress and the councilors that the man in Lazzonir who trespassed in the inn was not afflicted by any illness and did not display the same array of symptoms as the man from Cutoff. In Lazzonir, the man shown only the symp-toms of a starving body, but had been hydrated and otherwise in stable health. The man from Cutoff displayed symptoms of malnutrition and dehydration, despite the fact that the people of Cutoff observed him eating complete meals daily up until the day of the murder. He also behaved abnormally, speaking in-coherently and acting violently. The trespasser in Lazzonir be-haved well within the norm for a Believer.

However, Eryn also delivered upsetting news. Reports came from the Believer sect in Northland that many of their members were stricken ill. Their symptoms included weight loss, listless-ness, dehydration, fever and abnormal behavior. Those ailing had all been present at the Landing outside North Compass, Northland, the night the Goddess allegedly appeared.

Whatever manifested itself that night must be connected. Axandra resolved to visit some of the infected personally to see if she could ascertain for herself what they had seen that night. Some members of the sect lived not far from Undun City. Her next tour headed west, but perhaps she could convince the drivers to stop for a short visit at one of the neighboring villages where some of the afflicted lived.

During the two-week break between trips, clothiers fitted Axandra to expand her wardrobe. Her old clothes were those of a simple young woman in a sea-side village who did nothing more than walk the beach and go to town from time-to-time for supplies. The island climate held an almost constant and comfortable temperature suitable for light cottony fabrics, short sleeves, and sandal-like shoes. Occasionally she donned a loosely knitted sweater, if a cool breeze came off the Ocean. Many of the clothes were somewhat worn, at least a few years old. She typically kept few changes of clothes.

Prior to the installation, the clothiers in town offered her a few selections for the spring weather, which felt much cooler than she was used to. The dresses sported short sleeves, but were worn with long-sleeved jackets and longer skirts that made her appear more stylish for the region and, some commented, statelier. Axandra wore these new clothes when she made public appearances and reverted to her comfortable old favorites when she milled about the Palace.

Now that summer came into full swing, the clothiers returned to offer her new fashions. Summer in this part of Eastland bore hot and humid temperatures as the air usually sat trapped on this side of the mountains for days at a time, shielded from any moving winds by the high peaks. Fashion preferred gauzy, translucent fabrics layered in twos or threes. Extremely breathable, the gossamer created wispy dresses and pantsuits.

Axandra picked a few, still prone to keep her wardrobe small. She asked for Miri's opinions once or twice, when she wasn't certain what to think of a low cut neckline or wrap-around smock. The aide complimented that the lady's shoulders and collarbone were very fine features that deserved to be shown.

Then, Miri reminded her that she also needed new sleepwear, as her old nightgowns wore thin.

"And a hat. The sun beats down very hard in the summer," Miri told her, realizing Axandra wouldn't be used to the climate here. The aide already donned the gauzy fabrics of summer in a straight-legged pant of white and a light blue thigh-length tunic. "We should go down to the shops and pick out a hat. Augusta makes very sturdy hats woven of flatgrass."

"That sounds like a very good idea. I haven't had the opportunity to mill about the City," Axandra realized as she slipped on one of her favorite old dresses and tied her long hair loosely at the nape of her neck with a strand of ribbon. She ran her fingers through her hair for the hundredth time since Miri had taken the shears to it the night before, aware of the absence of several inches of brown curls. She told herself again that she liked it shorter. It was easier to manage. "Instead of sitting in the basement all day, I should get out."

"I would be glad to take you, Madam," Miri volunteered with an approving smile. "I can give you a fairly complete tour, and the locals will enjoy a chance to see you in person. The placards just don't do you justice."

Axandra blushed, but agreed with the sentiment. She slipped on her sandals and they headed out immediately.

To Axandra, taking time to mosey on the avenues almost felt like her old life again, wandering to town just to see who was around and what she might like to trade for. Walking with Miri, she chatted a little about the councilors and staff, with the aide offering tidbits of gossip about this person or that person and who was infatuated with whom. Not quite familiar with everyone, Axandra found herself every once in awhile feigning such familiarity, filing away the comments to attach to a face later on.

Miri took her past the Theatre and talked about the concerts and shows that took place often, inviting many visitors from nearby villages to come and enjoy. All manner of entertainment took place there. The building represented the largest indoor venue in the world. At the moment musicians carrying their cased instruments headed into the building for rehearsal.

Most of the architecture in Undun City was constructed from quarried granite and limestone from the foothills of the mountains. The granite came in shades of red and pink, speckled with minerals such as quartz and mica. The chalky white limestone contrasted against the granite foundations as window arches and doorways, all intricately and painstakingly carved with curling forms of birds and leaves and other sweeping abstract designs. No building stood solely for the sake of utility, but each one echoed the artistic nature of their people.

Miri led her at last to the hat shop, actually a part of Augusta's home. A large window in front displayed hats of many-sizes, some with wide sun-blocking brims, while others were tiny, for decorative purposes only. Different colors of flatgrass crisscrossed into geometric patterns. Dried flowers or bird feathers accented some styles.

Inside, Augusta delighted in helping the Protectress choose a topper that was both fashionable and functional. Axandra tried on several with wide brims, but all were just a bit too large for her head. Augusta measured her and promised to have one made for her in just five days. Axandra chose two designs, one a solid color and another with adjoining diamond shapes along the brim.

"It will be a perfect fit, Your Honor," Augusta promised, then busied herself right away on the order, asking the Protectress to choose colors for the dyed portions and the length of wide ribbon that would act as a strap to hold the hat in place when the wind blew. Augusta began weaving even before the two women left the shop.

As they continued on a leisurely stroll, Axandra asked how the woman's service would be repaid, since the Protectress possessed little to give directly to her.

"Don't worry, Madam. Everyone who provides something to the Protectress or the Palace is taken care of. Augusta favors cuts from plants in the garden," Miri explained as they walked along the bricked street. People toiled collecting supplies for their homes or repairing fences or planting some plots with special vegetables and flowers or any number of other chores. Everyone appeared adequately busy. "The Palace always provides for those who serve it. Besides, you will more than repay the community during the length of your service."

"Of that, I am certain," Axandra confirmed. She knew she had barely even begun to perform all of her duties. She did not want to weigh herself down with thoughts of the distant future, filled with both pleasant and unwelcome tasks. Today, she enjoyed being out. She said hellos to many or offered a cheerful smile to those they passed, while the people paid her homage with a bow. Today, everything seemed right with the world.

+++

27th Pentember

On Tinsday, the time came again to pack and climb into the cars. This time they headed to Westland, a longer trip to reach the far side of the continent. They stopped in many small villages along the way for rest and meals. To reach Port Togor would take more than twenty hours of driving, so the time was divided into a two-day trek. On this trip, the Protectress was accompanied by Antonette Lelle and Casper Ross, both natives to this region, as well as Eryn, Miri and a small team of Elite and the Commander, Ty Narone.

Antonette and Casper both sported silver hair, senior members of the council with over fifteen years of service. Their constituents held great respect for them and continued to elect them to their positions. Axandra remembered voting for each of them in her own turn. Once every eight years, the citizens of each region received the opportunity to vote for new representation to the Council, to assure that they were listened to and cared for by those closest to the Protectress. During the ride, both spent a great deal of time talking about their many grandchildren, some as old as Axandra, and their great grandchildren. Each spun the adventures of quite extensive families.

The Westland landscape was primarily formed of flat forest land and lakes surrounded by wetlands. Rivers large and small flowed down from the broad mountain range and pooled in deep basins cut by tens of thousands of years of water erosion. The roads they traveled between townships ran through enclosed tracts of timbers, trees that stood thirty meters high on narrow, straight trunks. The leafy limbs formed a canopy at the tops of the trees, protected from any grazing. Deep in the shade of the trees, the air seemed cooler, despite being deeper into summer.

They visited three villages on the first day of driving for brief rest stops and community chats. Many citizens voiced concern for the ailing Believers, apparently already having heard the news. Healer Eryn assured that anyone ill received appropriate care, as the Covenants provided. No Healer refused aid requested by anyone, despite the patient's beliefs. Axandra tried to steer the conversations back to less depressing news and asked for more opinions on the communications network. Many considered the expansion a beneficial project, giving the community swifter communication to share their resources and to hear from their wide-spread families.

The group stayed overnight in the larger township called Realm, where they toured a recycling facility that reclaimed glass for use as new items. For this regional operation, used glass was collected by toters from nearby villages and towns in the Westland, smashed into bits by large water-cranked augers, and then the materials were returned to glass blowers and molders throughout the area.

The next day, they continued on to the coastal area, surrounded by more watery fens and sandy soil. The types of trees began to change as well, with many of these growing larger leaves and shallower roots. The leather leaf trees and the umbrella trees grew here topped with dates and bowl nuts.

Axandra felt pangs of homesickness, especially when they reached the port. Togor was just a stone's throw from the island where she last lived. She could see the peaks of the archipelago above the blue-green horizon of ocean water. The cool sea breeze kissed her skin, reminding her of many nights on the beach, watching the white waves wash in lit by the moonlight, and the curana leaping and heaving offshore. Jon walked at her side, his thick arms wrapped around her.

She tried to strike him from her thoughts; but after spending the last seven years with him, he had, in many ways, bonded with her.

However, that seemed to make no difference now. Axandra would not have chosen to end the relationship this way. The will of the Goddess pushed her to be the Protectress, pushed her back to Undun. She always believed she did not want to be the Protectress, did not want to live the busy, servant life her mother lived. Now immersed in her duties, she allowed herself to be open to the experience.

The letter Axandra left asked Jon to come to Undun City, to come and find her and let her love him again. He did not come. He sent no words of his own. She forced herself to accept the fact that he was no longer in love with her.

Staring out across the sea from the inn, Axandra still longed to see her old friends. She missed Lilsa most of all, her comrade and counselor. She missed being able to call on Lilsa to commiserate over her troubles.

Below, a flock of helpers prepared tables for lunch on a veranda jutting from the building out over the ocean. Curious onlookers gathered by a short fence that protected the border of flowers planted along the patio. They did not notice her looking down on them from her balcony, carefully hidden in the shadows to avoid attention.

A knock came at the door.

"Come in," Axandra called, sensing her aide outside.

Miri poked her head in. "Madam, I have two visitors wishing to see you," she said warily. "They say they are Jeanette and Dora—"

"They're here?" Axandra burst, striding in from the balcony.

"Yes. Downstairs in the courtyard. You know them?"

"Oh, yes! I'll enjoy seeing them! They're from my old village." She dashed toward the door, her spirits rising. Miri reminded her to put on her shoes before escaping out the door. Down the open staircase, she found the two elderly ladies seated beneath a leatherleaf, out of the sunlight. The two chatted with each other and cracked open roasted nuts to snack on. Gulls swooped down to snatch their snacks, but the ladies deftly fought off the opportunistic scavengers.

Axandra hurried to them, calling their names happily.

Looking up, the two women squinted at her curiously, then jumped up to say hello. They fussed over her for several moments.

"You look so different!" Jeanette exclaimed, framing her hands in midair to better focus on the younger woman's appearance. "Even from the photos. Don't you think, Dora?"

"Feels different too," Dora agreed. "Lovely dress."

"Oh, yes, it just shimmers in this sunlight," Jeanette agreed, reaching out to feel the thin fabric, a deep purple flecked with silver threads.

The friends carried on about how her overall demeanor had changed from the quiet young girl who would help them plant their vegetable gardens to the traveler, the speaker and the Protectress.

"Axandra, it is so good to see you—oh my!—I guess I can't call you that anymore, Protectress—" Jeanette emphasized the title heavily, suddenly remembering the taboo of addressing the Esteemed by her given name.

"It is my name," Axandra insisted proudly. She dropped her voice to a whisper. "Don't worry, I won't tell anyone about your slip. Please, let's sit awhile and visit. I so appreciate that you're here. I was just thinking about Gammerton."

"Oh, as soon as we heard you'd be in Togor, we decided we'd jump the ferry and try our luck at getting an audience. We didn't think they'd let us anywhere near you," Jeanette told her, dismissing the notion that the visit was intentional.

"Not after what happened in Lazzonir," Dora elaborated. Her cocoa and pink hands cracked open a few more nuts and tossed the shells into the flowers. The bell nuts, named for their bell shape, grew thin-shelled and easy to crack with bare fingers.

Axandra preferred to keep the incident in Lazzonir quiet, but obviously the tale spread across the world despite her efforts. "What did you hear about that?" she asked curiously. "How did the story come out?"

"Oh," Dora began, shifting in her seat and thinking it through. Her dark brown eyes gazed up at the lavender sky, glinting in the suns. "It's said that a young man asked to see you, but was denied. He entered the inn anyway and got pounced on by the Elite and hauled out. Some tell he was handled quite roughly. What's your side?" Dora inquired, always looking for another angle to any gossip.

"It didn't happen quite that way," Axandra explained. Then she narrated the tale as she remembered it, with the young man sneaking through her window in the middle of the night and scaring everyone half to death. "I didn't see how the Elite handled him after the initial capture. They acted as they saw fit—believing the man came to do me harm."

"How terribly frightening!" Jeanette exclaimed, overly dramatic. "You poor dear."

"I'm fine," Axandra assured. "It turned out he had no intention of causing any injury. You know, I do feel terrible for running away from the village like that."

"Not even a goodbye from our favorite neighbor," Dora complained.

"I just needed to go as soon as I could," she offered as explanation. "I didn't want anyone to know until I went to the Council."

"It's okay, dear. We forgive you," Jeanette affirmed graciously.

"Goodbye would have been nice though," Dora added, less forgivingly.

Axandra chuckled. They hadn't changed a bit and treated her no differently than before. The casual discourse came as a welcome change to everyone treating her so delicately.

"I don't know if you're at all interested," Jeanette leaned close with a secretive whisper, "in what Jon's been doing since y'left."

Of course he would come up. They saw him daily.

"I suppose I want to get it out of the way," Axandra allowed, giving in to the temptation. She wondered for a moment if she might regret hearing about him. How would she get him out of her mind? She could see and sense that the women were eager for her to know.

"Well," Jeanette began, "for the first few days after you walked out, we were guaranteed to find him with liquor at hand, usually at Kyle's, perched at the bar. He looked extremely upset that you left. Eyes all bloodshot. Bad mood. I don't blame him. You're such a wonderful girl."

Axandra half-grimaced, half-smiled at the comment. Axandra felt she was being mocked, for the elder woman did not say such words as a compliment. Jon was born and bred a Gammerton native. Axandra was not. Most of Gammerton had always treated her as an outsider, and now their actions seemed vindicated. She was not one of their own. Part of her felt satisfied that he felt some grief and regret. Another part felt guilty.

"Then he became more his usual self, cooking and hanging out with the boys in town. Within a couple of weeks, wasn't it Dora? Just a couple of weeks?"

Dora agreed with a nod. "A couple of weeks. Time's gone by fast."

"Well anyway, Jon started to woo that pretty young blonde Anna Milo, but that didn't last long. By the installation, he had moved on to a newcomer to town, a red-head. She's quite enamored with him. They're thinking about getting married."

"Married?" Axandra almost snorted. "We never talked about marriage," she revealed, frowning.

"Oh, sorry, dear, but that's the story. I know it was your decision to go."

"I asked him to come with me," Axandra said hoping to appease the old gossips. She did not need rumors spreading around that she had abandoned her former lover. So far, that gossip seemed contained to the island. "It was as much his choice."

Miri came up behind them. "Madam, it's time for lunch. The Governor and Principal are waiting."

"Just a few more minutes, please," Axandra requested, flashing her eyes toward the aide with a slight curve of her lips.

Stepping back, Miri gave them more time.

"It was so good to see both of you again." Axandra returned her attention to the ladies.

"Oh, we love coming over to Togor once in a while. We're just lucky to get to see you, too. We do miss having you around. Our new planter just doesn't have your personality."

"She's a better gardener though," Dora put in flatly.

"Of course. I must go. Service calls. Please write to me. The next time I come this way, I'll come to see you."

"Oh, you won't have time for us, but thank you for the thought. Just be the good woman that you are. We couldn't ask for a better Protectress," Jeanette praised.

"I always thought you were the Heir," Dora claimed.

"Oh, you did not," Jeanette chided. "Go dear. Your helper is back."

Sure enough, Miri had returned to pull her away.

"Goodbye," she said, then rose to go to her appointed lunch, her satiny dress swishing about her legs as she walked. She glanced back once and gave a wave of her fingers. She thought sadly that this might be the last time she would see them.

Chapter 12

What's in a Name

9th Hexember, 307

Ghastly news arrived at the Palace shortly after the traveling party returned to Eastland once again. This time, the information came over a communicator piped into the Council Chamber over wall-mounted speakers.

The incident occurred near one of the fishing villages along the western coast. The Governor of Westland explained that two hundred curana beached up the rocky shore, literally pounding themselves to death on the jagged rocks.

"Assistors immediately took to boats with nets to try to hold others back from the beach, but the creatures broke through. The animals were frantic, as though trying to escape some kind of predator," the Governor said, the signal crackling through the speaker. Apparently, magnetic interference from looming Soporus interfered with radio transmissions. The quickly approaching planet introduced a host of new atmospheric difficulties. "The Assistors were helpless to stop them from killing themselves."

Axandra closed her eyes, pained to think of the graceful swimmers purposely breaking themselves against those rocks, scenery that she knew well. Curana possessed a high degree of intelligence. In fact, many believed the creatures were sentient beings, capable of the same range of emotions and perceptions as humans. Unlike humans, they lived in perfect harmony with their native world and had no need for cities, cars or other sedentary adaptations.

What frightened the curana so horribly to try to flee to land, that death might be a better alternative?

Two hundred easily constituted an entire pod, a large extended family of both sexes and all ages.

"We are having to take the bodies back out to sea a few at a time and scatter them to the currents so they don't rot in one pool. I've never seen anything so devastating." The crackling voice faded out for a moment as he went on.

"Governor?" called Nancy Morton in to the communicator box in her hand. "Are you still there?"

"—ll here," came the broken replay. *"Sig– — ry weak. We're ha— —ble—."*

At once the signal broke completely, replaced by harsh static and sharp zapping noise that pulsed unevenly within the interference.

"Send Assistors from, uh, from nearby ports with boats to help the, uh, cleanup," Axandra began to order, her words stuttered as sadness swelled up in her chest. She used to go swimming with those creatures. Large and bluish gray with flat wing-like fins, the gentle animals surfaced for breath from the deeper waters. When she swam, members of the pod would circle her, usually the adolescents who were still small enough to enter shallower water, and nudge her mischievously.

She drew in a deep breath through her nostrils to try to settle the flushing of her skin. "And have them patrol the waters near there, to look for anything that might have chased the curana." She knew that few predators would attempt to hunt healthy curana swimming in a pod group, but perhaps such an animal had taken the chance. Curana were quite capable of defending themselves when threatened. Not even a large group of typical predators would make an entire pod flee like this without a fight.

"Very good," Antonette accepted with a bow, her own wrinkled face damp with tears. "We will dispatch Assistors immediately." The councilors on hand instantly set her request into action, quickly clustering in the center of the room with low words to each other. Axandra exited the chamber to allow them to work. They would notify her if they needed her again.

At any given time, at least one councilor from each region resided in Undun in order to take care of the business for their citizens. In between major sessions of the Council, many members returned to their homes to live life as citizens. Most councilors were able to live at home for sixty percent of the each year, depending on their given shifts and duties.

During the first one hundred days that Axandra acted as Protectress, she was introduced to each of the seventeen Councilors in service. Unfortunately, other than her installation, the representatives from the Prophets remained absent, banished since Ileanne had gone missing from their care. In the past, at least one Prophet was available to the Protectress as an advisor on the Council. The majority of the members of the Prophet clan remained under cover of the Storm and unreachable.

Despite her return, the Prophet advisors remained absent from their duties. No one could explain their choice, for few outsiders had intimate contact with any of their people. The Prophets chose to ignore the Protectress' request for a representative to appear again. Not even Tyrane answered the call. She thought that he at least would venture to see her, as concerned as he had seemed about her transition.

The Prophets were the most highly developed telepaths among the human race, and had been so since before leaving Old Earth. Their kind sought each other out and secluded themselves in a community of their own making in a remote area of Old Earth, away from the Normals. In seclusion, the people trained to control their abilities and use their powers with natural grace. Among their own kind, the conversed only mind-to-mind and communed constantly with their contemporaries.

Apart from other telepathic groups, they had built a ship intended to take them to a new star. They joined the other ships of less talented people in the last minutes of preparation. They maintained their separatism on their new world and were hailed as Prophets of the divine by the other voyagers for some of their unique talents, such as rumors of precognition and telekinetic abilities.

For reasons still unknown, the Prophets set their ship down in the center of the desert and under the Great Storm, away from the scattered populations of lessers. Little was known about their way of life, save the occasional visit to Undun. They traveled to no other parts of the world and rarely stayed out of the Storm more than a few hours at a time.

Axandra had questions she wanted to ask the Prophets about what was happening around the world. Could they tell her why the curana had committed suicide so bloodily? Could they explain why the Believers were ill and unable, so far, to be diagnosed, much less cured? And why did the Goddess exist? That was the most preoccupying question in her mind. Perhaps it wasn't one even they could answer. What was her purpose and why was Axandra's family a string of vessels housing the entity? She did not like all of these difficult questions.

+++

During the afternoon, Axandra sat at a large desk in a small room adjacent to the Council Chamber, certifying hand-printed documents that would be placed in the Archives deep in the Palace holds. These notes were intended to be the factual depictions of the events that had occurred over the last several weeks, hand-lettered by the archivists as described in notes made by the councilors' aides and others involved.

Axandra read each, judging their accuracy as she knew it. One detailed her initial arrival to the Palace from the Council's point of view—how she had been tested and confirmed by their approved methods. The account gave no intimation of Councilor Morton's adverse behavior toward the new arrival or any of the doubts Morton had expressed about the Heir's claim. Another transcribed the details of the installation ceremony, from the dress she wore, to the words that accompanied the Gifts, to her speech. She signed her name to each of these as presented. After doing so, she realized she wasn't certain which name she should sign. She automatically signed that name which she had used for the past twenty years, Axandra Korte.

"Oh dear," she sighed, pen hovering uncertainly.

The archivist, who placed the documents before her, raised his eyebrows curiously. "Is there a problem, Madam?"

"Well, I may have just signed the wrong name," Axandra told him, still looking at her sweeping cursive on the paper. Axandra Korte never really existed. *Who am I now?* she thought to herself, troubled that she was forced to ask herself such a question.

No one had called her Ileanne in her presence since she was six. Or was she to sign "Protectress" or something else entirely?

"Let me summon Councilor Morton. She may be the one to help you with that," he offered. He sneaked out of the room and into the Council chamber. He left the door of the office open as he disappeared for a couple of minutes.

Morton was not far away, just outside the chamber in the main hall where she finished a meeting with two other councilors. While waiting, Axandra began to read the next archival record, one describing the intrusion at the inn in Lazzonir. She breathed in deeply, uncertain if she wanted to relive that event at the moment. The physical and mental intrusions still gave her nightmares, even after a few weeks. She scanned the lettering, her eyes picking up the words "Believer" and "trespassing" among the description.

"You needed me, Your Honor?" Nancy inquired when she entered followed by the archivist. She scowled dourly and glared down at Axandra across a hawk nose.

"Yes. This is a bit embarrassing," Axandra admitted with a grimace. She gestured to the papers. "How am I expected to sign my name? What name do I use?"

Morton lifted one of the ledger-sized pages and examined the signature. "Oh my," she said with a sigh similar to Axandra's moments ago. "I'm afraid I hadn't given that any thought."

"If I may, the Protectress has always signed her given name," the archivist offered.

"Then I definitely defaced your work, sir," Axandra said apologetically. "This is not the name I was given at birth."

He took the paper from Morton and examined the signature through a pair of rimless spectacles he produced from the pocket of his shirt. "I see. In this instance, I suggest," he said, tapping the paper gently with the earpiece of the glasses, "that you sign again, beneath your first signature. I will make note that you are also known as 'Axandra Korte.' On the approval document, the transition will make perfect sense, since that is how you were described in the body of that document."

"Very well. But I will have to practice a new signature for a few minutes," Axandra explained. "I've never scripted it in cursive."

He gave her a scrap of blank paper on which she penned the name "Ileanne Saugray." She struggled at first to make the letters flow, spelling it silently on her lips as she slowly drew it out. She had only just learned to spell her matername when she ceased to be the Heir.

Over and over, she scripted the names almost twenty-five times before she felt comfortable enough to sign officially. She decided she needed to practice further to make it feel natural.

Axandra looked to the archivist, signaling that she was ready. He returned with the documents. He had already added the footnote and additional signature line, crafted masterfully in such a short time. She signed her given name on each, still spelling it in her mind as she wrote.

"Thank you, Madam. Please continue with the rest."

Satisfied that she was no longer needed, Morton left without excusing herself. Axandra made mental note to discuss protocol with an expert before bringing up the lapse to Morton. If she was to continue learning and developing in the office, Axandra resolved that she would need to demand respect.

Axandra read through the remainder of the archives, satisfied with the facts as written, though the written details of the intrusion gave her the shivers. Reading the details refreshed the incident in her memory. She felt her relief renewed as well reading Eryn's analysis of the intruder as harmless.

During her weeks of orientation, Axandra learned that these documents would be photographed for additional copies, then loosely bound in the vault. The books would be permanently bound when filled from cover-to-cover. Three archivists served the Palace vault, their sole responsibilities consisting of recording the events in the Palace and the life of the Protectress. The archivists hand-printed each record on linen sheets and made certain the vault remained the optimum environment for preserving the records. The photos were stored at a separate site, a backup in case something happened to the originals. These original records and the copies remained accessible to the public for review at any time and were indexed in the archive books by dates, names, key words and other criteria that would make information easy to find.

And now Axandra became a permanent addition to that record. After the archivist had gone, she sat at the desk for several more minutes, continuing to practice the signing of her given name, though she thought that it would never quite feel like her own. Twenty-one years ago, she had resolved to give it up forever.

+++

Because of the curana beaching, the Council decided to postpone the next tour. Citizens across the continent expressed extreme concern about other strange behaviors emerging in animals. Reports by Watchers of packhounds venturing into the villages during the day came from all over the plains area. No person had yet been harmed—people tended, smartly, to get out of the way—but bustles and crowngoats and other herds were being ravaged more than the natural hunt. Many feared the animals were sick. The Safety Watch cremated the remains of the slaughtered animals and any packhound carcasses to inhibit spread of the sickness.

Astronomers offered that the approach of the sister world might be affecting the animals. The planet grew larger and brighter in the sky as the two worlds approached their nearest pass in over three hundred years. Bona Dea and Soporus revolved in orbits so similar that the planets only neared each other when Bona Dea, the fourth planet, lapped the fifth planet's orbit. This passing took almost a full year itself. The climax of the passing would occur in a few months, just as fall began. The astronomers surmised that the gravitational pull and the intense magnetic field of the planet affected all life on their small world. The humans landed after the last passing and gained no experience with those closest days.

Over the last few months, the scientists scrutinized the sister planet, calculating its expected path and observing its surface through their telescopes. Gray and dead, visible images of the surface revealed that the world once contained water and probably life. At some point, the planet lost its atmosphere and now floated dead in orbit. Slightly larger than Bona Dea, the gray world was otherwise a possible twin in composition, with a similar iron core and carbon rich mantle. Much of what the humans knew of Soporus, they had learned when the ships entered the star system and passed the orb on the way to their new home.

"It is possible," said one of the astronomers, a nasally male voice over the communicator, "that Soporus is also the cause of the Believers maladies. Like our moons, we expect the gravity to have a tidal effect on the Ocean. Every living thing will feel the effects of that pull."

"I understand. Please give the Council a written report on your theories. We'll continue to monitor the overall situation," Axandra ordered. "And hope for the best. Thank you."

"Yes, Your Honor. Right away."

Morton, Osander and Lelle all looked to each other for a moment, gauging each other's reactions and waiting for someone to speak first.

The Protectress took the lead. "If this is the cause, we need to provide this information to the Healers Council so they can disseminate it to all of the Healers. Hopefully it will help them find a treatment."

Osander volunteered to prepare the written report and have the papers delivered by courier to the Healers Council in Bexan by the following afternoon. Everyone agreed that the theory was indeed plausible and a glimmer of hope for those afflicted shown through each of their souls.

Chapter 13

In the Garden

16th Hexember, 307

A cool front dropping over the mountains brought a delicate drizzle to the evening, a welcome break from the hot humid days of summer. The local farmers complained that the fields were dry this year and asked several times already to use more water from the river to irrigate the crops. The Council gave permission to do so, seeing no reason to deny such usage. Right now, the river ran high from the snowmelt on the peaks. The light rain might alleviate a fraction of the river's burden to sustain the crops.

Axandra decided to dress casually and take a quiet meditative stroll in the garden. Lifting her face to the soothing sprinkle of rain, she pushed all thoughts from her mind for the moment. She pulled every remote tendril back into herself and closed them all away, resting her mind in the solitude. The true extent of her fatigue lumped onto her back, and she felt hunched. She'd never imagined talking to be such a taxing occupation. She used to remark that anyone could talk all day as long as they got a meal in the end.

Positioned at several points about the garden, Elite kept their eyes on her. Ty remained wary of any other unannounced visits.

This was one of the few times in her life that Axandra wished to be invisible, so that they could not watch her every move. She strolled deeper into the garden, wondering how far she could go before the Elite lost sight of her and began to worry. A mischievous thought, to play with their minds. She tried to look aimless, but she purposefully went far into the high hedges until she could no longer see a single guard.

Their minds shifted from passive observation to actively seeking her among the growing shadows of the plants. Axandra opened her mind just enough to sense them, touching them faintly so they would not sense her. All four focused on where she was last seen and each waited a few patient minutes for her to reappear. When she did not present herself, they became concerned, but first for themselves. If they reported that they lost sight of her at any time, Commander Narone would knock their service down to the City Night Watcher. At the moment, they did not fear for her safety, assuming the garden a secure niche. Three of the four began to move about the paths in search of her. The other remained at his high perch on a second floor balcony to keep a look out.

She giggled to herself, enjoying this play way too much. Teasing them was one thing. In another minute, she would make herself visible again and give them a sense of relief. She certainly did not want them to be disciplined for her trickery.

Hearing soft footsteps, Axandra pushed herself against the hedge, hoping to remain invisible to them just a bit longer.

But it wasn't an Elite that passed her by.

Invisibility would have been a perfect defense against this unknown figure. The shape of the person in the dim light looked tall and broad, shrouded in a cloak of coarse gray fabric like those the Prophets wore. A hood shrouded the face, but she caught sight of a pale hand clenched around an edge of the cloak. The figure paused a moment and turned toward her, eyes searching. She knew he would see her if he looked this way. The sky was not dark enough to completely shroud her beneath this arbor. Heart racing, brain swirling, she wished only to remain hidden. His presence here disturbed her. No one knew he was here. The secretive actions of the Prophets made her even less trustful of them than ever before.

Axandra saw his face as he turned her way, the last rays of the blue sun lighting his pale skin beneath the shade of the hood. An older man with silvery hair and a hawk-like nose, she did not recognize him. His dark eyes looked all around her, searching for the presence he surely sensed nearby. He almost looked right at her several times, but his eyes never quite focused on her.

Prophets rarely wore their emotions on their faces, making it difficult to know if he felt disappointment, curiosity, or satisfaction to find no one there. She dared not touch his mind for fear the brush would bring his eyes right to her. Without a sound, the Prophet walked away, disappearing around a hedge.

More footsteps came, these heavy and quick. Two of the guards converged on this spot and now their concern focused on her. She had been out of sight too long.

Emerging from beneath the arbor, Axandra stared in the direction the Prophet had gone, but he had vanished from view in the maze. He probably escaped out a nearby gate in the back. But why had he been here at all?

The guards caught sight of her and immediately slowed their frantic pace. Despite their jog and the humidity in the air, they did not pant or even appear to sweat. Each was in perfect physical condition, a requirement of their service.

"Is something wrong, boys?" Axandra questioned, masking her own face with innocent curiosity. The third guard came just a moment later.

"We were about to ask you the same thing," spoke the first. She recalled his name as Ben. He looked a bit cross and relieved simultaneously.

She smiled at them and shook her head. "I'm fine. I was just watching the hover birds. They almost glow in the dark. By the way, did you see anyone else in the garden?"

"No, Madam. Are you expecting someone?" the same guard replied. The other two surveyed the vicinity, acutely aware of their surroundings, always on watch.

"No, but I thought I heard footsteps a few minutes ago." She contemplated if she should tell them the whole truth, and for one of the few times in her life, decided that the full truth would be detrimental. Not noticing the uninvited guest carried a worse penalty than losing track of her for a brief time. "It must've been something on the wind."

"Of course, Your Honor. Are you going to remain out here for much longer?"

The sky deepened to luxurious purple, like velvet sparkling with stars. Wisps of icy white clouds high in the atmosphere caught the last rays of sun and glowed. The rain clouds long since evaporated into oblivion. All around them, the insects began to chirp and buzz and a few nighttime birds swooped down from the trees to snatch a meal.

"No. I'll head in now. Goodnight." She walked back up the path to the Palace doors, aware that only one of her troop followed her in. The others dispersed among the hedges and flowers, probably triple-checking for anything that might make footsteps.

They walked less than half-way back when a shout shot from the back edge of the garden. "Hound!" came the warning. Axandra and her escort stopped abruptly and looked in the general direction of the shout, trying to make out what was happening. They heard a growl and a barking noise not far away.

"Packhound!" Ben told her sharply. "We'd better get you inside." Gripping her elbow forcefully, he steered for the quickest path out.

"How did a packhound get in?" Axandra asked. "They can't jump over the walls."

"A gate must be broken," he answered. His eyes focused on the narrow passage ahead and on getting her through quickly. She could barely keep up with his wide strides. His grip tightened painfully on her arm. For the moment, she made no protest, but tried to move her feet faster.

They heard the growl again and another shout. Something trampled through the vegetation beside them with cracks and snaps. Another sound met their ears, an electric buzz. The noise split the air like a soft crack of thunder.

"Hold your fire!" Ben shouted out. He did not want either of them to be hit by the stunner. He halted the Protectress at that moment and followed the movement in the bushes, waiting to see what came out. From his belt, he produced a small black device which he pointed in that direction.

Axandra sensed the beast, primed with raw instinct and primal intelligence. There was one animal, but it wasn't alone. Something shared its consciousness, controlling it, making it more agile and craftier than it would be of its own accord.

With a snarl, the packhound leapt out from behind the hedge. Facing them head on, the beast stopped in their path. The over-sized ears flicked at nearby noises, but the dark, slanted eyes stared directly at the two humans, daring them to move. At the end of the elongated snout, pink nostrils flared with rapid breathing, matching the rhythm of ballooning ribs. The body of the beast appeared emaciated, with every bone clearly outlined beneath thin skin. It limped to the right. Tongue hanging out of its mouth, drool dripped from its long fangs.

Axandra froze on the spot, uncertain what to expect next. Ben hesitated with his weapon, wanting to avoid harming the animal unless it became absolutely necessary.

The beast rolled back on its haunches, the tufted tail extending for balance. Then it snorted again and charged, powerful hind legs propelling the full body forward.

I have no fear of you! the mind screamed at her.

Ben tried to fire his weapon and nothing happened. He pressed the button frantically over and over, but the device remained dead. His face soured from determination to helplessness. Throwing the device aside, he crouched low, hands out in a defensive posture.

Something had to be done or at least one of them would end up dead. Axandra reacted quickly and instinctively, throwing out her hand with a guttural cry. Power surged through her chest and out through her fingertips in unseen waves.

The next moment, the beast flew backward in the air and sailed in the opposite direction. It yelped sharply, limbs flailing wildly. When the hound hit the ground, it slid along the paved path and stopped when the skull contacted the trunk of a tree with a wretched crunch.

At the same time, the burst knocked Axandra and Ben onto their backs into a patch of flowers. They lay staring at the sky, stunned and breathless. As she stared up at the almost black sky, she felt something else. An escape. The entity in the packhound fled now that its host lay dead. She saw a light flying toward her from above, striking her shoulder before she had a chance to raise her arms in defense. Bouncing away, the light flew up into the sky and vanished among the stars. Heat swelled in her chest a second time.

Gravity pulled hard upon her body as she lay flat on the ground. As the swell of unused energy faded out of her body, pain replaced the electricity. Flame shot through her wrist. Stabbing ripped her shoulder. Each breath caused agony through her torso. She heard her own airway wheezing and heard crying as the anguish overtook her.

Heavy boot heels drummed closer as she lay there, more than the three Elite on duty in the garden. Reinforcements arrived in the form of entire troop of twenty. The Elite gathered around them, some kneeling down to check on Ben, some near her. Others approached the packhound corpse cautiously, weapons drawn.

Eyes squinting, Axandra watched Ben sit up first, shaking his head to clear the daze. He looked around at his fellow guardsman and assured them that he remained unharmed. He looked to the Protectress, his brow furrowed.

Axandra looked up at him, eyes wide with fear. Her brain felt hazy. Bright lanterns made their faces pink, featureless circles floating above her. Help me, she asked of the guards. No one seemed to hear her.

"Protectress, are you all right?" one of the men asked. The voice came at her ears from everywhere. Axandra blinked slowly in response and wheezed again, her chest heavy. Her voice refused to speak. Someone tugged at her arm to help her sit up. She yelped in pain.

"Get her inside. Fetch Healer Gray."

Axandra felt herself lifted from the ground and carried in Ben's arms. Lack of oxygen combined with pain made her ears ring and her vision blur. A new surface gave softly beneath her. She moaned with the change of pressure, feeling no more relieved of the aches.

What just happened? It was like she had hit the creature with a shovel, yet she hadn't touched it at all. The reaction seemed surreal. She had channeled something powerful through her body and that power killed a living creature. The same force hit her with equal pressure when released, and she felt crushed and broken.

The Goddess. There could be no other explanation. The entity was understood only by those who spent a lifetime hosting it.

And she had no one of whom to ask any questions. What have you done? She asked the being. All she sensed was satisfaction.

No one touched her until the Healer arrived, fearful of making her injuries worse. Eryn's face floated above hers, her red hair tied back behind her neck and those green eyes piercing through the haze. The Healer shooed away the Elite with a few words, but gestured someone over. Miri appeared, her young face creased with concern.

"Protectress, you'll be all right," Eryn promised. "The pain will diminish soon."

"What's wrong with her?" asked Miri in a whisper. She held the medicine pack as the Healer instructed.

Eryn did not reply, but immediately set to work on finding out. "I am going to touch you, Protectress. I am going to lay my hands where I believe you might be injured. You do not need to speak."

Axandra blinked hard, trying to keep her eyes open. Her lungs felt so heavy she thought it would be easier to stop breathing all together. She nodded fervently, willing to do anything to stop feeling.

Eryn spoke instructions to Miri, who then opened Axandra's mouth and deposited several drops of strong-tasting liquid that made her tongue feel numb. As she swallowed, the numbness followed the liquid down her throat and into her stomach. The sensation seemed to spread through her body almost instantly. The aching in her muscles eased. The sharp pain in her arm dulled to an ache.

Meanwhile, Eryn touched her arms, first the right, then the left, holding the left longer and squeezing gently. She called out for a splint and bandages. Then she moved her hands to Axandra's torso, pressing gently along her ribs. She listened to Axandra's labored breathing as she did this, her head cocked to one side and her eyes closed.

"Broken ribs," Eryn stated aloud. "Quiet please," she requested, then her chin sank down to her chest and she breathed in deeply.

Axandra felt something happening in her chest. The bones pulled back from her lungs as though Eryn's hand pried them apart. Suddenly, her lungs inflated fully with less pain. The renewed source of oxygen woke her brain and everything seemed clearer.

Still in a trance, Eryn moved her hands to Axandra's temples. "Please relax, Madam. I will go only where you allow me to go. Nowhere else."

Not even realizing that she resisted, Axandra made an effort to open the parts of her mind where Eryn might need to go. The green circle that represented Eryn appeared in the forefront of her vision, tiny at first, but the shape grew more quickly than the last time.

Even understanding that a Healer would never intrude in a person's mind without permission and would never divulge what was found there, Axandra continued to resist. She did not trust herself at this moment to know how to keep compartments of her mind closed. Everything of recent memory smashed and jumbled together. At the front of her mind loomed the packhound and the Prophet creeping through the garden.

Eryn touched her mind only briefly, then was gone.

"She's in physical shock, but she will recover. Her left arm has a hairline fracture in the ulna and her broken ribs bruised the right lung but did not cause a puncture," the Healer announced for someone on the edge of the room. The Healer expertly wrapped the arm with the splint as she spoke.

With her eyes open and her brain refocusing, Axandra found herself in a small windowless room, most likely in the basement of the Palace. Cupboards lined the far wall along with shelves filled with a variety of medicinal herbs and equipment.

An herbal aroma permeated the furnishings. The Healer kept supplies in this room and saw patients if needed.

"She will need to be restricted to rest for three days to let her body heal naturally. Miri, I don't want anyone to bother her during that time." Eryn declared with an authoritative demeanor, a facet Axandra had not formerly witnessed.

"Yes, Healer," the aide responded dutifully.

Eryn moved swiftly away. "Commander, I would like to examine the animal before it is destroyed," she requested, her voice fading as she and, presumably, Ty Narone, left the room.

Miri took over tending to the Protectress, arranging for transport upstairs to the Residence. Axandra sat up with help. With her body almost completely numb from the medicine, she found it incredibly difficult to stand and walk without support, even though she would have preferred to maneuver under her own power. She said nothing, still unable to find her voice.

Once upstairs in the suite, Miri helped her to dress in a nightgown and slip beneath the covers of her bed. The aide asked if there was anything she needed before she went to sleep, to which Axandra shook her head weakly.

"Just think to me, and I will come immediately," Miri instructed, her voice quiet and gentle. The young woman nervously left the room, but Axandra knew Miri sopped in the sitting room where she would probably wait out the night and fall asleep on one of the sofas.

Facing the wide, glass balcony doors, Axandra lay numbly, unable to feel pain, and equally unable to feel sensation along the right half of her torso. The outer doors stayed closed tonight, as they remained since the heat rose and the air cooler activated to keep the interior of the Palace comfortable. Raw to the drama of a mere hour ago, she failed to find a thread to grope and tether herself to the earth. Her brain shutting down from exhaustion, she let her eyes begin to close.

Inside her eyelids, Axandra witnessed the face of a woman, a face quite similar to hers but much older. She realized immediately that this was her mother's face as though looking at herself in a mirror. Elora's words filtered into Axandra's ears as though through a mist.

"My dear daughter, I miss you so much," Elora said. The voice sounded so real, Axandra opened her eyes again for a moment to make sure she was alone. When she closed them again, the woman's image lingered. "You may never realize how deeply I loved you. I wish that I could see you one last time." Those violet eyes expressed deep sadness. In the reflection, Axandra could see this very room. Elora held a picture frame in her hands, to which those sad eyes looked and her long fingers traced over the glass. "I can sense that you are alive, but I won't look for you. I hope that you are living a good life."

The memory continued to play like a recorded message. Was this playback from the memories of the Goddess? The sensation made Axandra believe that this was actually a ghost message, a left over resonance within the room itself. The Goddess chose to playback only those memories that benefited its existence and stifled a great deal more.

"There are so many strange things you will experience," the elder woman told her, those eyes focusing on the mirror again. "I wish I could tell you what will happen. You won't be ready. A mother always worries." The apparition slumped heavily with fatigue. Elora appeared frail with age. She must have staged this mock conversation just shortly before she passed away.

"You will find powers you weren't aware existed, like the power to push with your mind and the power to sway those around you with mere thought. You have not learned how to control them the way my mother taught me, the way I should have taught you. My darling girl." Tears swelled up in those eyes and the face disappeared from the mirror. The memory stopped there.

"Mother?" Axandra called out. "Wait."

But there was nothing she could do to call the image back.

Miri appeared in the doorway, having heard the Protectress' voice. "Can I get you something?"

Axandra pretended to be asleep, and within moments, she was no longer pretending.

+++

17th Hexember

By morning, every nerve in her body hurt. Axandra had no desire to get out of bed or to see anyone. She picked through her small portion of breakfast since her stomach did not want to keep many solids down. Sipping her tea helped relieve the pain.

"The Healer asked me to put the elixir in your tea," Miri admitted as her mistress drank. "She stopped in while you were still asleep."

"That is some splendid stuff." Axandra sighed as her body relaxed. Her left arm felt awkwardly restricted by the splint, lying stiff and immobile at her side.

"It is," Miri agree, smiling briefly. Then her face returned to nervous concern. Her heel tapped on the ground as she sat in the chair nearby.

"Why do you look so worried, Miri?" Axandra asked, for the moment her brain artificially free of any strife. "Or did the Healer tell you something she didn't tell me?"

"It's not that, Madam. It's—" Miri stammered, searching for the right words. "It's that you remind me of your mother."

"You knew her?"

Miri nodded. "I've served at the Palace for five years now. I helped care for her when she became gravely ill."

Axandra felt a twinge of jealously. "You probably knew her better than I ever did." She gave a little laugh at the end to try to smooth over the hurt that influenced the words. The effect of the elixir made the laugh sound too loud in her ears.

Eyes downcast, Miri apologized, "I'm sorry, Madam. I didn't mean to offend you."

"Five years," Axandra tried to wash over it. "You're so young. You've practically grown up here."

"I was seventeen when I moved in. I wanted to serve where I might be the most helpful. You see, I was always very sick as a child, and I'm not very strong. Physical labor tires me too quickly so farming or building isn't suitable. When an opening came to work here, I took it immediately." Miri slowed herself down at that point, as she had grown quite animated with her story. "The Protectress-past used to talk about you all the time. She always said you were alive. She was so convinced of it that I started to believe her too. It turns out she was right. I am—I'm sorry." Miri's eyes flooded with tears, and she hurriedly left the room before letting out a choked sob.

So Miri wasn't just a young girl charged with the new assignment of being the Protectress' aide. Knowing Miri's remoting abilities, Axandra suspected the aide knew more about the Protectress' burden than she let on.

The Goddess rummaged around inside her head again. For a powerful entity, Axandra found that it seemed quiet most of the time and unobtrusive. Only when it decided that she needed to feel the world did it open the floodgates and fill her mind with the voices. Sometimes the thing lay completely silent and almost forgettable. And sometimes, it slithered about the gray matter of her brain like a serpent, creeping here and there as though looking for something. What could it be looking for now?

Closing her eyes, weary of the intrusive sensation, Axandra practiced blocking pathways from the creature. The exercise proved futile, for the entity coiled securely within her brain.

Chapter 14

A Visit from the Prophet

Date Unknown

Riding on Reiko's shoulders, Axandra could see above all of the heads in the crowd. The people were like the sea, undulating as they shifted from side to side, trying to witness the Protectress' arrival.

A silver, electric automobile moved slowly by the crowd and stopped nearby in front of the Principal's house. When Elora, the Protectress, appeared, Axandra felt an urge to cry out to her real mother, to run to her and go home with her. Yet she held back. She looked down at Reiko, her father, and Kari, her mother, the people who had taken her into their home with more love and affection than she could remember from anyone.

When Elora looked her way, waving at the people, Axandra wished to be invisible. She wished Elora would not see her or recognize her and she wouldn't have to go home. Those violet eyes passed over her several times, never focusing on the small girl perched so high. Elora continued waving for several minutes, smiling at the citizens who cheered for her and called to her. She appeared to be looking for someone, someone who wasn't to be seen anywhere.

Axandra remained quiet on her perch and watched her real mother turn away and disappear into the Principal's house.

"What did you think, Little One?" Reiko spoke up to her excitedly. "Isn't she wonderful!"

The child couldn't respond to the question with such enthusiasm. She signaled to be let down to the ground again and took hold of his hand to keep from getting lost in the mass. "Can we go home now?" Axandra asked, tugging at his fingers.

"Already? Don't you want to stay and have lunch?"

She shook her head. "I don't feel very well," Axandra told them. Seeing her real mother made her feel queasy. Reiko lifted her up in his arms and held her close. Even for eight years old, she was tiny and light as a feather.

"All right," he said. "You look tired."

He carried her all the way home.

+++

20th Hexember, 307

After three days of lying in bed, Axandra felt she had taken quite enough advantage of everyone and asked for a warm bath and her casual clothes. She would not spend another minute restricted to her quarters. Her ribs felt normal again, though her arm still ached and itched around the splint. She dismissed Miri's pleas to rest. Now was the time to get back to work. Regardless of her physical state, she was still the Protectress and the people relied on her to perform her expected duties.

Axandra dressed simply in white, wide-legged pants and a sleeveless tunic woven from a rainbow of wide ribbon-like strips. She pinned her hair up in a tousled mass on the back of her head to keep her neck cool. Today promised to be a scorcher, and she intended to remain indoors as much as possible.

Kindly she ordered Miri to take the day off from her duties. The girl had already worked more than her fair share these past few days and was entitled to her own time. Of course, the aide protested, arguing that her duties to the Protectress were of much higher importance than any personal errand. Insistently, Axandra asked her to leave.

"I can take care of my own needs for one day, Miri," Axandra assured the younger woman. "Please, go. You look exhausted. At least go sleep in your own bed for a while. These sofas aren't that comfortable."

"Madam, I—" Miri began to protest. She assumed her charge hadn't been aware of her nesting in the greatroom. "Very well. But I'll return to my duties this afternoon. You need me."

Axandra smiled, endeared by Miri's dedication. "I do need you. But I need you to be at your best when I need it the most. I won't overdo it. I promise. Take the entire day."

"Yes, Madam." Reluctantly, Miri left through the main door of the residential suite, her entire body slumping with signs of fatigue.

Satisfied that Miri was on her way to bed, Axandra also left the Residence. As her Elite fell into step behind her, she noticed a different rotation today. Normally, Ben would be one of her guards at this time of day. He was notably absent.

Not one person inquired about the incident with the pack-hound or how she had been injured. Not even Ty came in search of answers, but that probably had a great deal to do with the Healer's strict orders to leave her in peace while she recovered.

The elixir administered over the past few days made her feel very sedate and almost mindless, so Axandra had concerned herself only with sleeping and eating and not much else. Finding the pain bearable, she refused the medicine this morning.

As she made her way down the wide staircase to the main floor, Axandra gave the matter serious thought. What had she done and how? She remembered clearly how Ben's weapon failed and he was unable to stun the beast. She remembered his thought at that moment, an instant of helplessness. Then one thing came to his mind—he would have to leap at the creature to block the attack. Knowing he'd be killed, she didn't give him the chance.

Slowing her descent, Axandra looked down at her left hand, still wrapped in bandages, and sought to remember the sensation flowing from her fingertips. The effect was not born of conscious intention, but rather the instinct to survive outshined anything of a deeper level.

Without words, the Elite following her waited for her to continue. She struggled with embarrassment for slowing them down, so she continued on her path to the Council Chamber in hopes of finding Nancy Morton. Nancy usually arrived in her office each workday morning by nine o'clock. It was now nine-thirty and Nancy busily read through a thick stack of paper.

"Good Morning, Head of Council," the Protectress said as she stepped into the large office. She set the tone of her visit with a touch of vigor in her voice.

Nancy looked at her and let a brief smile curve her lips upward, softening her usually dour face. "Ah, Protectress. You're looking better than I expected. It's good that you weren't injured more severely." Nancy stood and came from behind her desk, offering a courteous bow and gesturing that Axandra take a seat in one of the chairs that faced in.

"Yes. I feel quite fortunate," Axandra responded, accepting the offer to sit. Morton returned to her high-backed swivel chair. "Pleasantries aside, Councilor, I see that you are perusing a rather large report," Axandra put on a more serious air.

"Yes. More about the Believers and their epidemic. I received it just this morning," Nancy made sure to say, delaying any doubt the report had been kept out of the Protectress' sight for very long.

"Not a good report, I take it," Axandra surmised.

For a brief moment, Nancy avoided looking into those violet, all-seeing eyes. When she did look up, Axandra caught her line of sight immediately. The frown returned, an unpleasant, unwelcoming expression. "It doesn't look favorable. More cases than the Healers first suspected."

"How many" Axandra asked reluctantly, knowing the number would make her heart ache.

"Five hundred three. Currently still within the Believer population, but the Healers fear the disease will spread to others soon. They don't agree with the summation that Soporus is the cause."

"I was afraid of that."

Nancy breathed deeply and noisily through her nose with her lips pinched tightly together. "The high number of sick will strain the Healers and anyone assisting them. And if violence continues to be a symptom, the Safety volunteers will be strained as well."

"Won't the Healers' Council handle most of those details, at least for the medical aspect. I guess we need to recruit more Safety volunteers and improve training."

"Yes, the Healers' Council is already reassigning Healers where they are needed most. I'll invite the Safety Coordinator to a meeting this afternoon to handle the arrangements for additional security."

"Very good."

Though Nancy seemed eager for her to go, Axandra did not rise just yet. The elder woman set her expression in that deep, unimpressed frown, staring at the Protectress across the table.

"Is there something else I can do for you, Your Honor?"

When Axandra started her way here, she believed that Nancy would be the best available source of information about her growing number of questions about the Goddess. But now, she wasn't certain she should confide in the Councilor at all. The emanations Nancy projected sent a discomforting shiver down her spine. She would need to remove herself as gracefully as possible.

"I wanted you to know that Ben, the Elite guard, should be commended for his actions," she told Nancy. "He acted very honorably in my defense against the packhound. I haven't heard about him, and I hope he wasn't seriously injured, or worse, disciplined by Commander Narone."

Nancy leaned back against her tall chair. "I haven't heard a word about Ben, but thank you for telling me. I will see to it that Ty knows your comments." Nancy suspected there was more.

Axandra felt unwilling to divulge further details. She no longer understood the Councilor's intentions.

"Thank you, again, Councilor. If you hear anything about him, please let me know. I want to thank him for his quick thinking."

"Of course."

Rising from the soft chair, Axandra turned to leave the room. She straightened her spine, making herself feel taller and appear poised and confident in her actions.

A shadow moved in the far corner of the room but seemed to disappear as she turned her eyes in that direction. She checked for an open window that might have moved the curtain, but the windows were closed.

Did Nancy know she had a guest? Saying nothing, Axandra left the office, closing the door behind her. The invisible figure would not be able to follow her, if that was his plan. As the door clicked shut, she thought she heard Nancy speaking to someone. Not to be seen spying, she curbed her curiosity and walked away from the office. Instead, she sent out the tendrils of her mind to listen inside Nancy's head, the same technique she was always admonished for as a child, caught snooping in other's brains. She hadn't done so in many years. She found the function easy to perform undetected.

Once voice rang through her ears for just a moment.

"*I detest your methods,*" Nancy said, the voice carrying the resonance of hearing oneself talk. "She can sense you here."

The other voice sounded distorted and incomprehensible. That mind skillfully blocked intrusion

However, Axandra's suspicions were confirmed in part. The Prophets were here secretly. To what end, she was uncertain. Perhaps she was conceited to think it was about her, but other reasons seemed unlikely, especially if Nancy Morton conspired with them. Breaking the connection, Axandra headed back upstairs.

+++

"**Did she see you?**" Nancy questioned the Prophet who stood at the corner of her desk. Tyrane came from the shadow of the drapes as soon as the Protectress closed the door.

"I do not believe she did."

"Did you let the beast in?" Nancy accused, an index finger jabbing the air in front of him. "You could have gotten her killed."

"I did not allow the beast through the gate," he denied stoically, his pale face masked of any emotion. "But I rigged the gate to remain unlocked. The hound could have pushed its way in. We do not wish to harm the Protectress. She is still needed."

Nancy pursed her lips tightly, still dissatisfied with the explanation. She moved on. "So what about Soporus? You were going to tell me what would come with her passing." She fought down her bubbling ire. She began to regret the course of events set in motion by accepting the Prophets into the Palace in stealth. Their ability to conceal themselves from lesser minds made her shudder.

"The approach of the Sister planet brings about a great number of curious behaviors, not all of which can be anticipated," the Prophet told her.

"You refer to the curana and the packhounds or the Believ-ers?"

"All. Their behaviors are most erratic."

"I don't see how it makes them starve when they are eating or rant demented nonsense?"

Though Nancy appeared quite animated on her end of the discussion, pointing this way and that, eyes wide, the Prophet remained undisturbed.

"It is the best explanation for what they are experiencing."

"It's also a heap of compost. Something else is wrong with them and your people know what it is." Nancy stood close to him, poking him in the chest. "You need to help them. You need to fix this before—"

The room dimmed around her eyes. Blinking, Nancy stood staring across the office, uncertain why she had gotten up. Looking about, she thought maybe she was heading to the lavatory. Yes. That must have been it. Funny to forget something like that. Her brain must be tired from reading that dreaded report.

+++

Axandra returned to her rooms for some difficult-to-find privacy. Perhaps if she sorted out her memory she might find the secret to the force she channeled. Perhaps she could use it for a better purpose. She felt deep guilt for having killed the animal, despite its intentions to kill her. Her people spent many centuries removing lethal violence from their lives, and she had taken a horrible step backward.

She stopped in the main room, looking around for something she might use for practice. Her mother's message echoed in her thoughts that she would find unimagined powers. The power to push with her mind being one. She had definitely pushed—and hard—to protect herself from the attacking hound.

Seating herself on one of the solid chairs, Axandra focused on a miniature metal statuette on the tea table. The figurine of bronze represented a tree and was quite heavy for its size.

She breathed deeply, her diaphragm and lungs moving in and out. From her toes, she relaxed each muscle. As this reached her brain, she thought back to the garden, of hiding in the hedges. Then of seeing the Prophet sneak by and the guard finding her. She recalled the intensity of the shout and the sinister growl and the way the noises made her heart race. She remembered staring down the animal, its yellow eyes boring into her with its fixed gaze.

Axandra allowed her soul to summon up the fear of the moment. Her heart raced while, in her mind's eye, she watched the slow motion of Ben attempting to discharge his weapon. His expression changed as he went through his options. To save her, he had one option remaining. Before Ben could intercept the beast, Axandra raised her hand. From inside her heart, the surge grew.

Here, she opened her eyes, ending the memory and transferring the heat filling her chest to her outstretched fingers. The air appeared to ripple like waves on the water.

Startled by the visual manifestation, she jerked back. The ripples disappeared.

Looking down at her fingers, she squeezed the fingertips together. They felt hot like fire and tingled.

Excitedly, Axandra let out a girlish giggle, amazed that anything happened. Calming herself, she centered her mind again and searched for the power in her body's center.

As the ripple flowed from her fingers again, she focused on expanding the energy, reaching out to the statuette. Slowly, the efflux spread farther until at last the border touched the metal. Abruptly, the tree toppled on its side with a clank. Just as abruptly, she withdrew the force.

The mental work drained her strength quickly. At the same time she felt energized and frightened. A gamut of emotions swirled in her. Such power could be useful and tempting. Rumors and myths circled that the Prophets possessed such abilities, though no one alive admitted ever witnessing the use of them.

Her mother's wrinkled face floated in front of her eyes and she thought of those words again. Was this the Goddess? Did it make these things possible?

The Goddess. Another creature to contend with. What other side-effects would she endure while hosting this creature?

More questions reared, and Axandra had no one to answer them. Maybe Tyrane spoke wisely when he urged her to let the Prophets help with the transition. However, she feared being with them again. Just the thought of Tyrane's face made her spine rigid with alarm.

Again, she felt lonely and lost. She breathed out a frustrated sigh. No one to talk to and nothing to do but wait around. She looked about the sitting room, huffing through her nose and pursing her lips as she sought out something to keep her busy.

She resolved to see what else she could do with this new-found power.

Chapter 15

North Compass

The Protectress and her troupe resumed touring the country despite the spreading illness. They headed north, past the tallest of the world's mountains and into rockier country.

Riding in the car with Sara Sunsun, Miri, Eryn and Councilor Homer Spirton, also a native Northlander, Axandra watched as the terrain rose and sharpened, with trees and grass growing sparse. The air became cooler the higher the altitude and latitude. Soon they passed beneath the shadow of the highest peak, Mount Mirage, named after one of the largest ships on the Journey. That very ship rested not far from the base of the mountain, near North Compass, still a couple of hours away.

The women played card games and chatted about things both personal and business.

"Protectress, do you believe the Healers will be able to find a cure to the disease?" Sara asked, her voice soft with concern. She avoided eye contact by studying her hand of cards and rearranging them one by one.

"I have to trust that they will find some kind of treatment," Axandra replied, watching Sara's long pink face, noting the three small brown moles along her jaw line, a jaw rigid with worry. Sara plainly wore her stress on her features.

Homer snorted. After loading, he shuffled himself to one side of the car, reading a thick book and apparently ignoring the other passengers. His deep voice filled the compartment, indicating he was indeed listening. "Your trust is well placed, Protectress. The Healers have a lot of work to do."

Axandra rested her cards discreetly on her lap. "I will always feel I need to do more."

"The Healers Council is already researching many possibilities," Eryn chimed in. "So far, all indicators point toward a parasitic infection. With our combined resources, we should be able to develop a treatment within a few weeks."

"That's good to hear," Axandra agreed, smiling to the Healer gratefully. "Now, about North Compass," she changed the subject. "I understand that I'll be staying at your home, Sara?"

"Yes. Even with the Landing nearby, we don't get enough casual visitors to justify having a dedicated inn. You, Miri and Eryn will stay with Suzanne and I. The others will be in nearby homes. Suzanne is very excited that you're coming." Sara's face glowed when she spoke of her partner, and her green eyes sparkled. She was proud of her hometown. "Then tomorrow, we want to take you to the dig."

"The dig?" Axandra questioned.

"Oh, the archeological dig nearby. They've uncovered something remarkable there, but I won't spoil it. You have to see it."

The card game fizzled out, so the cards were casually tossed back onto the pile. Sara leaned back in her cushioned seat and peeked out the window.

"Those, Madam," Sara pointed toward the pink and gray rocks to their west, "are the Spires. They are unique to this region. Upward forces thrust the rock up millennia ago. Limestone has washed away leaving the granite."

Knife-like protrusions of stone, each one thin and tapered, shot straight into the air in rough rows of ten or so. Some stuck out cock-eyed, but always toward the north.

"Some are over 30 meters tall."

"They are quite astounding," Axandra marveled. Looking ahead, she could see the formations far into the distance. "They cover a lot of ground."

"Yes, right up to the limit of North Compass," Sara said. Then she pointed out a few other unique marvels of the area, including the pygmy crowngoats that pranced among the Spires, and the crested golden eagle nesting on a flattened outcropping.

"And that is a rockwood," Sara pointed to a gnarled, twisted tree that looked half dead. "A conifer. They live for hundreds of years, maybe even thousands. That one hasn't changed much since our ancestors landed. There are only a few this large. We've planted many seedlings recently, but it will be lifetimes before they grow to even a few centims around," Sara explained with a wistful look. "They grow very slowly due to the short growing season."

"Do you harvest them? The Staff is made of rockwood." Axandra thought of the Gift that traveled with them in the storage compartment of this car, just as the other Gifts traveled to their respective regions. The wooden Staff felt heavy like rock.

"No. They would be extinct if we did. Only one tree was ever cut down and legends say that took some doing. Your Staff was made from that particular tree," Sara explained as they passed the solitary tree.

"What else was made from the wood? They are quite thick." Eryn noted, joining the conversation.

"Well, the main beams of my home are from that tree, as is the table I dine on. They were gifts to the first Councilor and it has been the Councilor's home ever since."

The village appeared below them in a shallow valley of the foothills. The shadows of the mountains darkened the town early and lanterns burned along the streets.

"We're almost there," Sara said, just short of cheering. She could hardly wait to reach home. I'm *coming, Suzanne,* Axandra heard Sara's broadcast and blushed at the outpouring of affection Sara threw toward the village.

The cars rolled into North Compass, moving from the gravel-sealed road to carefully placed slabs of slate, each as wide as the car itself. The village sat on a circle rather than a square, with all of the homes front doors facing into the center. At the center stood a bronze statue of a human figure, stylized in sweeping curves. Long arms scooped low as the figure bent its body down in motions of labor. The houses themselves were all built of stone. The oldest, those closest to the center, included metal rafters exposed on the sides of the buildings. Axandra realized that the metal was salvaged from the ships, for it was dark gray in color and some pieces were roughly cut. The special houses were built with exposed timbers bracing the stones—the lumber of the rockwood tree. The rest used metal supports made of new materials mined from the caves and blended into strong but lightweight alloys.

The residents of the village stopped their activities as the cars passed by. Many were smithies, working the metals into versatile objects such as tools and frames for furniture and parts for the electric cars and busses that operated across the continent. There were also spinners and weavers, using the wool from native dardaks and goats collected through the year. Some repaired homes. Others cultivated gardens, eking out the last crops before winter for preserving.

"The community has a very nice greenhouse on the southeast edge of town," Sara described. "We don't get very much sun here in winter, but the greenhouse gives us a few vegetables."

Stopping in the town circle, the cars expelled their passengers, who were relieved to stretch after the prolonged ride. They quickly grabbed light covers to ward off the northern chill. The suns failed to penetrate the overcast sky.

"Come, everyone. Let's get settled in before for dinner," Sara directed, gesturing to other residents nearby. Several locals helped the Protectress' party with their luggage and separated the group into various homes close to the center circle.

From one of the nearby homes, the second largest structure, came a dark-haired woman. Her olive-skinned features appeared steep on her face. She dressed in red with a wool sweater drawn over her shoulders. Seeing her lover home, she smiled with joy.

Sara smiled back to match and gestured for the Protectress to come with her.

Suzanne, Axandra assumed, bowed at the waist respectfully to the Protectress as she approached. "Welcome, Your Honor. I hope you will find yourself at home with us."

"Thank you. It is an honor to stay with you. I've heard a great deal about you, Suzanne."

Suzanne eyed her partner and let her smile spread. "I'm sure she exaggerates my good nature."

"But I say nothing of your jealous side," Sara teased. "Don't keep our Protectress waiting on our doorstep. She isn't used to the cold."

That was true. Axandra had never felt so deeply cold in her entire life, especially in the midst of summer. On the islands, the temperatures rarely dropped low enough to call for heavy layers, let alone cause her breath to mist in the air. She shivered beneath her light wrap.

"We'll get you dressed properly first," Suzanne promised, leading them inside.

After dinner when many had turned in for the night, Sara and Axandra strolled outside in the village, taking a brief tour of the closely packed homes. As promised, Suzanne saw to it that the long-time islander received proper apparel for the northern weather. Though a tad long, Axandra dressed in heavy but soft woven pants of dardak wool, along with socks and a cottony tunic. As a gift, her hostesses presented her with a woolen sweater dyed a deep red, which doubled over the front and tied in place with a silken sash. The wide collar of the sweater was brushed into a soft fluff that felt luxurious around her neck. Even though the temperature dropped, these clothes kept her comfortably warm.

As they walked, Axandra and Sara discussed the members of the People's Council. Sara gave Axandra some insight into the most prominent members, filling in some gaps in personal information that normally took years to acquire. Sara spoke of Nancy Morton's almost permanent scowl. "She has a strange notion that if she shows any happiness her constituents won't take her seriously. She's been like that ever since she was voted to Head of Council. I hear, though, that when she visits her grandchildren, she is nothing but smiles."

"Nancy doesn't seem to care much for me," said the Protectress bluntly. Over the last several weeks, this simply became a fact of life. Axandra no longer committed on trying to change Morton's opinion of her, only to doing the best she could with her given circumstances.

"She makes such comments to the Council," Sara apprised. "Most of us just roll our eyes and ignore her remarks. We've watched you very closely, and we're quite satisfied with the way you handle yourself. Even Osander's grown to accept who you are, and he was the worst of your opponents in the beginning."

"And what do you think of me, if I may be so bold as to ask?" Axandra only posed the question knowing that, of all of her new acquaintances, Sara Sunsun was the most honest and did not shy away from sharing her honesty.

"I am very proud of you," Sara grinned. "You are the most qualified for your service because you haven't been sheltered from living your life as you chose. Most of all, you empathize with everyone. You truly care what happens to every soul." Sara looked over at her and their gazes caught at the corners of their eyes. "I see in your face how worried you are. I know you'll do everything in your power to make everything right again."

"That is all very kind of you to say," Axandra accepted humbly, though she worried she wouldn't live up to such a reputation. "Thank you."

They sauntered along the slate-laid street where the wide flat stone sections lay placed together like a jigsaw puzzle. A light-colored mortar filled the seams. Around the two women, the village rested very still and quiet.

A group of Believers visiting the Mirage Landing promised to stay there, about three kiloms to the East. This group brought their own provisions. After hearing the dire circumstances created in Lazzonir, nearly running out of food, this group did not want to cause detriment to their neighbors. Many citizens begrudged the Believers for their lack of consideration.

"The air here smells so crisp," Axandra observed, taking a long whiff of the frigid air. "And cold."

"Even in summer, the temperature barely stays above freezing at night. We don't have to worry about overheating," Sara informed. She sniffed at the air as well. She donned a fleece jacket to warm herself against the evening dip in temperature. "It smells like mossy juniper. They have very fine needles for an evergreen, and very soft." Sara led her around the corner of a house onto another, narrower street, back toward the Councilor's home. Ahead and behind, Elite monitored their path. "We often use them to scent our closets."

Up ahead, Suzanne opened the side door for them to come back inside.

"Suzanne is everything you described her to be," Axandra complimented. "The two of you seem very happy together."

"Yes, we are," Sara blushed. "Thank you."

There came an awkward pause. A question formed in Sara's mind that she would not speak, for she felt it impolite to ask things of such a personal nature. *Does she have anyone to love?*

"I had someone back in Gammerton," Axandra offered upon deriving the question. She heard a hint of heartbreak in her own voice, a twinge of grief that Jon was gone from her life, even though he had moved on. "He didn't want to leave the island to come with me, so it ended."

"I'm sorry to hear that," Sara sympathized.

"My friends there tell me he's now planning to get married. I guess he isn't terribly heartbroken," Axandra assured. She faced her eyes forward as they walked "I feel better knowing he isn't deeply scarred."

Sara must have caught on to her sarcasm, for she chuckled lightly. "But sometimes you wish he felt worse," she supplemented.

Shrugging, Axandra smiled and gave a slight nod. "Sometimes," she admitted.

"Don't worry. There will be someone better for you," promised Sara, bumping Axandra's shoulder playfully. They went back into the warm house.

Chapter 16

The Orb

19th September, 307

The Northland represented the heart of metal production for the continent. Veins of gold, silver, copper, aluminum and iron ore ran through the stony ground. Miners entered caves from day-to-day and removed the amount required for new manufacturing. Mining was not a full time operation and required special training due to dangerous spelunking in natural caves. The usage of metal was reserved for objects requiring extreme strength, such as building materials and tools. All discarded metal was recycled into new items.

On occasion, the miners uncovered artifacts of a much older civilization underground. Archeologists exposed a great deal of evidence that, in the distant past, another sentient race lived on this world. Traces of their existence remained buried underground, leading humans to believe that a cataclysmic event destroyed those ancient people, leaving the planet inhabited only by the most hardy animals and insects.

Sara and Suzanne eagerly led the Protectress to the archeological excavation near North Compass. Having little working knowledge of the dead race, Axandra asked her hosts to give her some details.

Suzanne offered the lesson, exhibiting a fascination with the old culture that emerged from the ground nearby. "Different tribes of people lived across the continent. This particular group of Ancients were hunters, using the native animals for food, clothing and tools. They made use of every part of the kill. They also made use of stone and metal. They may have been the first of their kind to melt ores and smith them into desired shapes, utilitarian and ornamental."

That morning, they traveled to a remote camp in the foothills of the mountains. Off the established roads, they rode atop dardaks. Unused to any type of four-legged travel, Axandra rode tandem with Sara on a shaggy white female while Suzanne rode alone on a dark brown male. Ty and one of his officers rode separately, hurrying forward like scouts, checking behind rocks and outcroppings for hidden dangers.

The animals trod on four strong legs capable of supporting the weight of several humans, and their long snouts housed a row of sharp teeth in the front and grinders in the back. These creatures were omnivorous, rather than strict herbivores, feeding just as often on rodents as on grass. Two broad ears listened to each and every sound around them. Splayed hooves gave the animals secure footing on rocky surfaces. Prized for weaving warm clothes, the thick fur formed a natural cushion for the riders atop the flat back. At the rear, a bushy tail wagged, swiping away insects. The most unpleasant part of the ride was the smell of digested grass wafting from the rear.

They stopped on a high ridge overlooking the busy site. Down in a spacious rift, the archeologists and their assistants excavated a nine-meter wide, ten-meter long and three-meter deep trench. Ladders descended into the trench and several workers shoveled dirt into buckets to be hoisted up and out of the cavity on a system of pulleys. In the center, still half-buried in the gravelly soil, rested a sizable silvery orb.

Axandra stared in bewilderment at the object. "What is that?"

Near the oblong shape, several people hunched toward the ground with brushes and cameras. Clouds covered part of the sky today, and the surface of the capsule reflected the glare of the sunlight as the rays poked between the clouds.

"You two go on down," Suzanne urged. She pulled out a sketch pad from her pack and dismounted. "I'll be down in a bit." She sketched hurriedly on the paper, outlining the orb, the people and the mountains.

With a click of her tongue, Sara urged the dardak to move forward, down the well-trodden path used by the diggers as they accessed the site.

Noticing the visitors, two gentlemen walked away from the tents to greet them. The men donned dusty button-up shirts and tan twill pants. They each wore heavy boots. The taller man wore a wide-brimmed straw hat, tattered and cracked in some places. The other donned wire-rimmed glasses and a bandana tied about his neck to wipe a bit of dust from his face. The day was not particularly warm, but the suns combined with work prompted the stripping of layered clothing.

The taller one removed his hat as he bowed in greeting. The other stepped up beside the dardak to offer balance for the dismount. Through the touch of his hand, Axandra sensed his delight to have her visit, and not just as a scientist showing off his pride. He wasn't blocking much of his emanations.

She's here, he thought to himself. *She's really here. Don't mess it up this time.*

As she thanked him and said hello, Axandra thought she recognized him from somewhere. She definitely remembered his smile, but she could not remember exactly where she had met him. After crossing paths with so many people in the last couple of months, she often dreamed of faces to which she couldn't attach names.

"Protectress," Sara began the introductions. "This is Quinn Elgar and Tomas Kirk. They are leading the team on this dig, and they are good friends of mine, even though Quinn spends most of his time in Southland." Sara teased her round-faced friend, and her smile proved infectious.

Quinn beamed, his cheeks reddening slightly. Realizing he still held Axandra's hand, he let go with a hurried jerk and dipped in greeting.

"Welcome, Esteemed Protectress. I am so happy you came out here to see us. We—" Quinn gestured broadly toward the orb. "We have made a most remarkable discovery… and probably the most frustrating."

The group walked toward the tents while Quinn and Tomas took random turns explaining what occurred in each area of the camp. Under the tents, shards of pottery and metal tools lay spread on tables, the wooden handles long ago rotted away. These more primitive pieces seemed completely out of synch with the shining metal capsule in the trench.

Gazing from the edge of the pit, Axandra noticed the surface of the orb appeared completely seamless and immaculately smooth, without a scratch or dent. In fact, she watched as circulating dust seemed repelled from the polished surface, leaving no residue. The object reflected almost every bit of light, giving the metal an unnatural and painful glow.

"As you can see, the object appears completely solid," Quinn told her. Axandra felt familiar with the voice and sought to pinpoint the sound in her memory. "There are no cracks or openings, not even a microscopic fissure, and we have used our scanners and our eyes on every available inch of it."

"We've even whacked it with a hammer," Tomas chimed in, acting out a hammer strike. "Accidentally the first time. We found it indestructible. You can't even tell we tried to pulverize the blasted thing." He slipped his hand back onto his bald head and ran his thick fingers over his graying mustache.

Axandra listened to the scientists while watching the workers go about their duties across the expansive site. Everyone present applied her- or himself to a specific task, either hauling buckets of dirt to a discard pile to the south, cleaning pieces in basins of liquid, or packaging the cleaned and cataloged items into wooden crates.

In the back of her brain, Axandra felt a buzzing, a minute, soundless vibration that caused her vision to blur just slightly around the edges like tight ripples in water. The sensation reminded her of having too much wine. The buzz faded away after a moment.

"Some refreshment, Protectress?" Quinn offered, motioning across the camp to another tent storing food and water.

"I remember you," Axandra said as realization suddenly struck. She pictured his face in her mind surrounded by the machines in the Lazzonir.

"You do?"

"Yes, from the Lazzonir. You're a custodian there."

"That's correct," Quinn admitted with barely contained excitement. "I didn't think you recognized me."

They turned slightly toward the dining tent. Sara and Tomas walked several meters in front of them, laughing between themselves.

"You seemed so disinterested in the museum," Quinn stated, reminding her of their past meeting.

Axandra remembered that day, suffering from fatigue and disappointed in her lack of concentration. "I apologize," she told him sincerely, radiating the emotion toward him. "I wasn't feeling well that day."

"So I was told—and saw," Quinn accepted. Nearly everyone had heard about the intruder at the inn. "That bump on your noggin must have hurt. You will have to visit again."

Smiling, she agreed. "I will. I enjoy learning about history."

His proximity emitted waves of adoration and a desire to touch her, though he attempted to keep such carefully hidden from his face.

Quinn was an adorable man. He stood just a few centims taller than she, even in his heavy-soled boots. His round face with its round cheeks dimpled at the corners of his mouth when he smiled. Brown freckles dotted the pale skin on his muscled arms and smooth shaven face. A few dark moles dotted his skin, one above his right eye in a wrinkle of his brow. Thin dusty-blonde hair, which was just a tad long, feathered in the wind. His eyes, his most boyish feature, peered out in grayish-blue, and their expression made him appear many years younger than she suspected him to be. Those eyes sparkled with enthusiasm.

He peered quietly into her eyes for a moment as they walked on, then looked away shyly.

Don't stare, he scolded himself. *Nobody likes to be stared at.*

Axandra decided to add to the conversation. "I don't know much about the Ancients. Only a few tidbits I've read in newssheets," she told him. "How long ago do you think they lived?"

"Oh, many of the artifacts date about seven thousand years. That's not long on a geological time scale," Quinn added. "In the areas where we've found items, they've been buried by volcanic activity or silt from massive floods, covering them rapidly. Here, it was a rock slide that likely buried the pottery and tools, though we've found no humanoid or animal remains. All of these disasters appeared to have occurred about the same time. Now that we have Soporus visiting, we believe She had a lot to do with it. The planet may have veered much closer in the past."

He waved to a bench-style table where metal cups of sunjuice and a covered plate of chewy pastries waited for them.

"However, the large object is distinctly different from anything we've ever found. There are no such materials anywhere else on the planet," Quinn commented, looking back at the shining orb in the trench.

"In other words," interjected Tomas, "we have no idea who made it, what it is or where it came from. It could have been buried here as recently as five to five hundred years ago."

"Why not a month ago?" Sara asked with her teasing lilt.

"Because the soil has settled enough—"

Sara bumped Tomas on the arm and giggled. "Leave it to you to actually answer the question."

"It's what I do, Sara," Tomas reminded in a defensive tone, brushing crumbs from his whiskers with a fingertip. "All day long, I answer questions."

"Though right now we are just creating new ones," Quinn added with frustration.

The buzz came again, this time making her skin tickle up her neck and in her nose. She reached back to sooth the hairs, discreetly leaning toward Quinn. His body offered a momentary shield to the sensation. She noticed immediately how the buzz faded when she neared him. She sneezed suddenly, and the fizzing disappeared from her nose.

"Good health," everyone wished in near unison in response to her sneeze.

"It must be the dust. Thank you." Axandra rubbed her nose with the handkerchief Tomas handed in her direction. Then she continued with the conversation. "So just seven thousand years ago, an entirely different race of people lived right here in this spot." She looked out toward the rocks and soil around her, trying to picture what a camp of these people might look like.

Quinn continued by describing the Ancients, depicting small-statured and heavily built bipeds who wore furs in the cold climate and used fire to cook meat and other foods. The tools found here were forged metal and consisted of long knives and heavy axes. The people were advanced enough to be fully clothed and communicate with a moderately advanced spoken language. No evidence existed of written language other than pictograms. The pottery discovered was often decorated with bas-relief figures of their people and animals. Water pitchers showcased waves of water and fish. Bowls exhibited images of fruit or animals, though the contents had disintegrated millennia ago.

Even though Quinn stayed near her, the buzzing became more incessant. Her entire head seemed to be vibrating, and her stomach began to revolt against the intrusive sensation. Gingerly she sipped her glass of juice. Her tongue felt numb to the acidy-sweetness of the pulpy liquid.

"May I have a closer look at the capsule?" Axandra asked abruptly midcourse.

Eager to comply with her wishes, Quinn gave permission and hopped up from the bench, volunteering a hand to help her up. "As you wish, Your Honor. I'll take you over."

Suzanne finally came down from the ridge and found the group, bouncing excitedly along the way. "There you all are! Did I miss anything?"

"Snack?" Tomas offered her, thumbing over his shoulder.

"Oh, please," Suzanne accepted, grabbing a metal cup and taking a long swig of juice. "It was getting a little warm up there."

Sara lingered with Suzanne and Tomas, waving to Quinn and Axandra. "You two go ahead. We'll be along in a few minutes."

At that moment, Axandra got the distinct feeling that she had been set up on a romantic meeting, rather than an educational one. It may have been Sara's crafty smirk that tuned her in, or the way the trio whispered as they spied on the couple. For the time being, Axandra wasn't opposed to the idea. His affection came as a welcome delight. He genuinely craved to learn about who she was as a person, not as Protectress. Smiling in his direction, she walked with him back to the trench.

Ty, who had stayed in the background since their arrival, jogged to catch up with her. "Your Honor, I do not believe touching the object would be wise."

"I didn't say anything about touching it," she dismissed, avoiding his eyes. "Just a closer look."

Ty eyed Quinn suspiciously, disapproving how closely the two walked together. Then he backed off a respectable distance and followed.

The buzzing in her brain continued to intensify. An image flashed before her eyes, blinding her to the present. She saw a similar orb in her mind, propped inside a cave, glinting with fire-light. A face with pale skin flashed before her eyes, a perplexing vision.

Tripping on the rocky ground, her consciousness returned to reality.

Quinn caught her arm to steady her.

"Sorry," she said, straightening up.

His hands gently gripped her upper arm. She lay her hand over his purposefully, letting the contact linger. His hand felt hot to the touch. The skin felt dry but soft, meant for delicate work. As the contact lasted, his emanations grew stronger. He sought to impress her, to offer her anything to promote further visitations. And he desired to know her in every way. Her mystery intrigued him, this woman who suddenly appeared in his life. She took her turn to blush and avert her gaze.

The vibration plagued her. She wanted the droning to stop. Her neck felt stiff as she resisted the quiver in her muscles.

At the edge of the excavation, Quinn instructed her to climb down one of the metal ladders. For a nervous moment, Axandra feared one of the flashes might cause her to fall. After a deep breath, she swung onto the rungs and climbed down. Her shoes safely touched the bottom a few seconds later. Quinn quickly followed, descending the ladder in the blink of an eye, sliding with his boots scraping down the sides.

As they neared the metal object, another peculiar sensation touched her body, a pulse—subtle and low in frequency. She stopped in her tracks.

"Do you feel that?"

The question prompted the archeologist to regard her with a curious expression. "Um. No, Madam. What do you feel?"

The pulse in the air exacerbated the internal vibration. She blinked and rubbed her eyes to clear them of the blur, but this only made tears flush over their surfaces.

Palm out, Axandra stood motionless and concentrated for a moment on the pulse.

"A thrum," she described, closing her eyes to help sooth them. She felt as though her body turned in a slow circle, even though her feet remained planted in one place. She sensed a knot of heat in the center of her torso. "Every second or so. Very deep."

Copying her movement, the explorer stretched out one arm toward the object. He waited several seconds, then lowered his arm. A disappointed look marred his round face.

"Peculiar," Quinn said softly, a finger tracing his lips as he thought. "Is it rhythmic? Is it centered here?"

Her body swayed again. Her gut flipped and with just a moment's notice, she lunged aside and heaved the contents of her stomach onto the dirt. She crouched low, trying not to fall over. Why couldn't anyone else feel it? The noise flooded her ears.

As he reacted a moment later, she heard Quinn say "Oh dear," then he hollered for help. He hurried to her side, holding her shoulders against her wobble to keep her from tipping sideways into the dust.

"I'm sorry, but I have to leave," Axandra moaned, staying doubled over. Her skin perspired suddenly. Her digestion bubbled restlessly, and again she vomited. Squinting down the undigested pastry she'd just eaten, she felt embarrassment flush through her body. The pulse still throbbed through her and the buzzing filled her ears. She reached up to cover each side of her head, trying to block out the noise.

"By all means. Let's get you out of here." Quinn helped her to her feet and steered her toward the ladder even as she remained half-stooped, her head reeling. With Ty reaching down from above and Quinn pushing from below, they managed to extradite her to the ground level.

From there, Ty supported the Protectress and took her to his dardak. She heaved again before mounting the animal, but there was nothing left in her stomach to expel but bile. Sara gave her a cup of cool water to wash the acid from her mouth and throat.

"I'll be okay," Axandra assured, sensing everyone's concern. "It must be motion sickness." Climbing onto the dardak's back, she wrapped her arms loosely around Ty's torso, and they trotted away. She swallowed down the next wave of nausea, feeling relief the farther they moved away from the site.

+++

After Eryn gave her an extra dose of chickle leaves, Axandra took a few hours to sleep off the raw stomach and headache that came as side effects of–well, whatever she had experienced at the dig site. She wasn't entirely certain the source of the discomfort. Though she was highly susceptible to motion sickness, she always dosed herself with chickle leaves before going on any type of transportation, and had done so that very morning to avoid being sick. The mysterious rhythm and vibration certainly contributed to the upset stomach. The most likely source of those sensations was the orb. And while the object appeared to be a solid globe of shining metal, she felt certain that something lay inside. At the moment, they had no way of distinguishing the contents.

The last time she experienced anything akin to this bout, an earthquake occurred several hundred kiloms offshore of the island. Dizziness struck her with an overall sense of disorientation. The mild sensation lasted a very short time. At the time, she managed to keep down her day's meals. But she hadn't been the only human being to sense the sudden shift of the tectonic plates beneath her feet. Visiting with friends, she learned several experienced analogous discomforts at simultaneously.

After waking, Axandra sat in the main sitting room of Sara's home. Eryn sat with her and they talked quietly about how she was feeling after the brief rest. Axandra assured the Healer that she felt much better and that whatever unsettled her system was gone. She was given an entire sofa to herself, and she took advantage by stretching out her legs along the cushions and keeping warm under a knitted afghan. Ending any further conversation, Axandra took to reading one of the many books she toted with her.

Miri, who had a difficult time sitting still, busied herself by assisting Suzanne washing the dinner dishes and cleaning the table. The chimes hanging high in the foyer rang, signaling visitors at the front door. Miri immediately went to answer the summons.

Hearing voices, Axandra picked out the male voice and recognized the timbre from earlier in the day. Bowing her head back to the book she was reading, she hoped to hide a small smile that curved her lips.

Miri returned to the room, followed by the visitor. "Madam, Mr. Elgar has come to see you."

Flashing coy smiles to each other, Sara and Suzanne encouraged Eryn and Miri to go with them into the kitchen to fetch after-dinner tea.

Washed clean and donning a wool jacket against the evening chill, Quinn bowed stiffly toward her. "Good Evening, Protectress. I came to make sure you were feeling better," he told her, a statement and a question all in one. His thoughts found their way in to her mind again. *She looks better. Good. I've never seen anyone so sick from a cup of juice.*

"I do," Axandra affirmed, moving slightly to sit up.

"My apologies, Protectress, but no one has shown such a reaction at the site. I wasn't aware—"

Axandra stopped him with a wave of her hand. "It wasn't your fault. I'm hypersensitive to motion. Vibrations, too. Travel does a number on my stomach." Waving again, she offered him a place to sit down. She shifted her feet to the floor, clearing a space on the cushions. He accepted her offer and sat on the far end of her sofa.

"You really felt a pulse from the object?" Quinn asked, the scientist in him always seeking out details. She found it an endearing trait.

"Yes. It reminded me of a heartbeat," she described, "a very steady rhythm, but a hundred times heavier than my own heart." Shaking her head, she pushed away a revisiting feeling of nausea. "What made you want to be an archeologist, Quinn?" she asked, shifting the focus from herself.

By the pleased smile on his face, she could see that showing interest in him personally caused him great joy. He relaxed a bit. His shoulders lowered about two inches as he settled against the cushions. "When I was a little boy, I read one of those journals where they made the first discovery of the Ancients—farther north of here. I was fascinated by the similarities with humans. After my service years tending to grain fields and building houses, I trained to go into digging for the Ancients myself. History is so alluring, the patterns of events and fitting together the puzzle. I am happiest when I find a challenge."

"Like this one?"

"Oh-ho-ho," Quinn guffawed. "This is by far the most challenging puzzle yet! A gigantic, featureless orb!" Just the thought of it sent his mind spinning with possibilities. His grayish eyes lifted toward the wood beams in the ceiling, his arms uplifted. "Where did it come from? What is it? What's inside?"

The true Quinn shone through, not the one nervous to impress her, the unreachable Protectress. She witnessed at that moment his passion and his nature. Inquisitive. Compassionate. Intelligent. His first love was his science.

"And you, Protectress? What gave you the inclination to serve the world?"

And funny.

The laugh came out unbidden. Her body relaxed further and her fatigue melted from her shoulders. She listened to her own laugh and realized she missed the sound.

"Of all the choices I had before me," Axandra began, still chuckling through her words. "I guess this was the best fit."

He laughed with her, his eyes twinkling. Then, he sighed, looking down at his hands. He cleaned beneath one fingernail as he said, "I have a confession, Your Honor."

"Oh?"

"I asked Sara if I could see you again. Well, really I asked Sara if I could see you the first time." He tripped over his words. "I arranged to be the custodian the day of your visit. I had to ask for a few favors. Sara helped."

Now Axandra's suspicions about being set up were confirmed. "Really?"

"I just wanted a chance to talk to you, but you didn't talk much. So I asked Sara if she thought I could have another chance."

"I'm glad you did," Axandra told him. Something about his eyes struck her as alluring. The gray-blue circles of his irises swirled like water.

"Oh?" Quinn asked, his blonde, broad eyebrows arched high with surprise.

She held out her hand to him. "Yes. Thank you for today."

He accepted the offer to touch her hand, at first with just his fingertips. Then he clasped his thick hand about her slender one. She likes me! Would it be too much to ask?

"May I see you again?" he asked hopefully.

"I would like that very much."

She thought she heard giggles coming from the kitchen. Then the other women returned, each one smiling secretively.

Suzanne carried a tray of tea and cakes. Quinn blushed and withdrew his hand from hers.

Sara invited him to stay for tea, an offer he couldn't refuse.

Chapter 17

The Believers

20th September, 307

Prior to the Northland tour, a sect of Believers requested an audience with the Protectress on their home soil. They complained of unfair discrimination against them due to the actions of a separate sect and wished that their requests be heard by the Protectress herself.

Though still skittish, the Protectress felt she needed to make a display of fairness toward the group and, with the Council's approval, forwarded a message that they would meet at the Northland Landing at the time specified in the request.

Together with the People's Council, the Protectress carefully worked out how she would address the expected questions. Certainly, they would once again ask the Goddess to show herself, as the group had requested for generations. The answer was always the same—neither the Protectress nor the Council reserved means by which to summon such an entity. The answer did not confirm nor deny the existence of the Goddess but made clear the being would not appear upon demand.

The council members agreed that the most likely questions would pertain to the health and well-being of fellow Believers. Many still ailed from the first alleged appearance of the Goddess.

At this point, five had passed on, hopefully to commune with the Goddess as the Believers sought. A few managed to overcome the barrage of symptoms and clutched at life, plagued with aches and pains and chronic fatigue. The Healers gave no explanation why some improved while the majority continued to decline. There did not appear to be any unique characteristic common to those who beat the symptoms.

The councilors agreed at the same time that an assembly of Healers in the nearby villages and towns would be called to discuss the details of each afflicted individual's health in order to compare symptoms and circumstances. Axandra offered that Eryn coordinate the assembly, as the Healer had already discussed the idea with her. The Protectress spoke at great length with her Healer to try to understand how the affliction affected the people and where it might lead.

At first, the councilors and Ty Narone protested Eryn's involvement, for the Healer's duties were to the Protectress first and the Palace staff second. However, Axandra pointed out that Eryn already spent a great deal of her time away from the Palace treating several of the afflicted citizens living in or near Undun City, aiding the city's Healers in caring for the increasing number. So they agreed that Eryn would lead the assembly. This meeting would be proposed to the Believers to encourage their cooperation.

On the morning of their second full day in North Compass, the entourage proceeded to the Landing a few kiloms outside the village proper. As they approached the monument of the three derelict interstellar ships, they viewed a large encampment of Believers gathered on the open fields to the northwest. The pilgrims housed themselves in colorful oilskin tents grouped in loose clumps. Many people sat in small circles with one or two standing in the center preaching or singing. Creases etched the lethargic faces, and dark circles sank the eyes. They all appeared very thin, save a few with firm faces in sharp contrast to the hollowness of the sick. The healthy ones helped care for those in need.

"They all look so frail," Eryn whispered toward the Protectress' ear.

Axandra nodded in dismal agreement. As the cars pulled up to the main entrance, she let her mind wander out to the people and found little except discomfort and pain filling their souls. There were so many minds in such dire states that she felt it necessary to block them out, lest she begin to echo their symptoms. Eryn warned everyone to be careful with their abilities and aided the councilors and Elite in blocking the onslaught, as she had done back in Lazzonir. Axandra refused this time, believing she needed her mind to be free and open if she were to try to better understand the Believer's plight. As the despair washed over her, she momentarily regretted that decision. With a deep breath, she brought down the curtain in her mind that she could use to shield herself.

Just outside the main door to the museum site stood a frail-looking man dressed in an unadorned brown tunic. He waited there alone, his fingers steepled in front of his chest. His body hunched forward, and he limped when he moved a few steps to greet them, waddling from side-to-side on bowed legs.

"Protectress," he said with much relief and gratitude. "My name is Algin. Thank you for coming. It gives us hope that you agreed to this meeting."

"When the people need me, I will listen," the Protectress pledged, bowing at the waist in greeting.

"Shall we go inside and sit comfortably while we talk? I have arranged for refreshments for you and your group."

"Please," Axandra agreed, almost feeling a need to reach out and steady him as he hobbled in front of her. She resisted, knowing the touch would not do either of them any good and would be quite unwelcome.

They entered the grounded spacecraft and found a small conference room with seats around an oblong table of highly polished wood. The frail man sat in one soft chair while Axandra sat in another and turned to face him. The others continued to stand, allowing the meeting to proceed more intimately.

"The others elected me to speak with you about our situation," he introduced. His voice rasped and shook his ailing body.

"I am here to listen to your needs, sir. I will offer whatever assistance I can give you," she stated in carefully rehearsed words, making no promises. She let the curtain in her mind lift slightly so that she might monitor his feelings while they conversed, even if his face expressed a good deal of his anxiety.

"I know you will," Algin responded, squinting his dark eyes with his thin smile. "I will not mince words. We wish to see the Goddess again. That is our primary desire."

In return, Axandra pronounced, "I am unable to summon such an entity. I regret I cannot help you with this request."

Breathing heavily, Algin smacked his tongue inside his open mouth a few times, wetting his palette and lips. His eyes watched her carefully. Typically, the Believers would not open their minds to anyone outside of their beliefs, but she understood that being the Protectress, she was not restricted by such rules. She sensed his abilities probing her gently. Watchfully, she allowed him only a peek at her thoughts.

He continued his story. "She came here that night. I saw Her myself. She was smaller than I expected—but beautiful nonetheless—a light that hovered over this very ship. We marveled at Her appearance and said our prayers to Her. Then She bathed us in light and we felt as we never had before, as though Heaven had descended on us for a brief moment in time!" Algin smiled in remembrance of the sensation, his arms outstretched toward the ceiling. "She filled us with joy and took away our pains."

Then his arms dropped. Quivering slightly, his lips turned down into a frown. "But now, we are all sick. We have made a sin against Her, and we need to make it right. She needs to come so we can make it right. She will make us better again. Please, you must call Her to us."

Again she said, "I cannot summon the Goddess, sir. What sin do you believe you've committed?"

"We need help!" Algin demanded. His mind pushed at hers more forcefully, tugging at the curtain. The cat opened its eyes and growled at the intrusion, then shrank to the back of Axandra's brain, away from the prying tendrils. As gently as she could, Axandra resisted him.

"The Healers are trying to help you."

"The Healers have not helped. We are still sick. We need the Goddess!" He lunged at her desperately. Ty reacted immediately, grabbing the man across the torso and pulling him back. "Please!" Algin cried out. "Please help us! We are dying!"

Helpless as to what to do next, Axandra searched the eyes of the Eryn and the others, but they were shocked as well. They were not prepared for this situation.

Turning inside her mind, Axandra asked the Goddess in her for guidance. *Can you appear? Can you make them better? What can you do?* she questioned urgently.

A dark sky and a rain of stars overtook her vision, falling at her at astronomical speed. All around her, people fell and lay lifeless on the ground. Then the Great Storm filled her eyes, the swirling mass of colored clouds and lightning striking all around.

What does this mean? she thought in confusion.

Algin wept, kneeling on the floor where Ty restrained him. The old man only wanted one thing, to be well again. In his mind, only the Goddess could cure their ailment. For two months, he suffered through pain and weakness.

"Only the Goddess can help us," Algin whimpered, his face in his hands. "We've always been faithful. Why does She punish us? Why?" he implored, looking up at Axandra with cloudy eyes.

"She can't help you," Axandra said, her own voice filled with his despair. The link to him was too strong now, and he did not want to relinquish his mental grip. Could he sense the Goddess in her? She resisted again, pushing against his offense. "I'm sorry."

A bright flash caused her to shield her eyes with her hand. She turned and hurried from the room, away from Algin. Footsteps echoed in the large open entry way as she headed out the front door. The world dimmed around her, and she feared she might collapse on the floor.

Outside, she stood on the paved walkway and inhaled a deep breath. She looked around at the vicinity trying to remember why she had come out here. She felt tired, her eyes heavy and achy. The sun appeared much higher than she thought it should be for this time of day. On the road, the two cars sat idle, the two drivers waiting off to the side, chatting with each other and sharing a bit of something that was packed in small tan envelop. The wind picked up from the east, blowing in with a hint of moisture that tickled her nose. Perhaps it would rain somewhere today.

Breathing deeply, Axandra attempted to focus on what had just happened, why her emotions swirled in turmoil—she felt sad, terrified and confused. Her heart raced in her chest and every inch of her skin felt hot. She'd never experienced a panic attack like this before.

Eryn came out after her just a second later. "Madam, are you all right? You ran out in quite a hurry."

"I'm fine. Um, I think," Axandra rubbed the center of her chest, felt the fierce thumping of her heart beneath the bone and inhaled deeply, forcing her shoulders up. She gazed out at the airy fields around the ships, expecting something or someone to be there. She found nothing but the short blue-green grasses showing their light sides as the wind blew down the blades like a ripple on the water. "I feel like I've been asleep, like I've missed something. I needed fresh air."

"Well, it hasn't been very entertaining in there. Ty is about fed up with our Believer friends not showing."

Believers. She expected the Believers to be here for the meeting. But no one was here. The fields around them lay empty and appeared undisturbed. Yet, she had just been speaking to someone...

"Madam, you look puzzled," Eryn observed.

"I expected—" Axandra said as she continued to look around for clues as to why her brain felt so disconnected from the present. "I expected they would be here waiting for us—for me. Why wouldn't they come? They requested this meeting. It doesn't make any sense."

"We all expected the whole throng," Eryn reminded. "But I guess they've given up or stayed home. I hear from Healers all over that the sick are bedridden. They have no idea what causes it other than they were all present here the night of your installation. Some suspect contamination of their food or water. I've asked the custodian to check the ships for any sort of leak. It took a slew of toxic substances to keep these ships in space. Radiation or chemical sickness could be possibilities, though we've never experienced such before."

Lips pursed, Axandra nodded in acknowledgment of the Healer's words. A leak of toxic particles offered a less chilling hypothesis. Perhaps radiation explained the glowing light that the Believers claimed to have seen.

Then she realized that a long blank existed for the span of the morning, maybe more. The sun hung noon high, and the last thing she remembered clearly was arriving in the village just before dinnertime.

"Eryn, what did we do last night?"

The Healer took a turn scrunching her face in a curious and concerned expression. "We ate dinner at Sara's shortly after arriving in the village and then all went to bed. You headed in the earliest. The extra day of travel just about did you in."

"Extra day?" Axandra asked curiously crossing her arms over her breasts. The chill of the air got to her skin. "Why did it take an extra day?"

Before she received a response, Ty came stomping out through the main doors of the museum ship, mouth a straight line.

"I suggest we leave, Protectress. Your appointment appears to have been canceled."

Axandra shook her head. "No. We should wait. They asked us to be here. It's very important to them." She wanted to give them a chance.

"We've already waited two hours and my scouts have reported there is no sign of any Believers anywhere."

Two hours. Axandra couldn't remember even coming here today. With her thumb and forefinger, she pinched the bridge of her nose between her eyes, lids shut. She thought the pressure might help clear the haze from her brain. However, the haze remained.

"Exhaustion has a nasty effect on people," Eryn said to her, trying to interpret the visible symptoms. "We should return to our hosts and rest."

"Very well," she acquiesced with a disappointed sigh. She addressed Ty with a pointed finger, "But have one of your guards remain here in case they do come."

Ty agreed. The rest climbed back into the cars to leave. Axandra could not shake the strange sensation that something very odd had happened to all of them, though no one seemed worse for wear, except her.

Back at Sara's house, instead of sitting for lunch, Axandra went straight to her room, requesting that the Healer come with her. She sat tiredly on the edge of the bed and slipped her heavy shoes from her feet. "Eryn, I'm not feeling well."

"I suspected as much," the red-head agreed with an almost annoying tone of mothering. Eryn drew up a chair to the side of the bed and sat eye-level with her patient. "What is the trouble?"

"I keep having flashing lights in my eyes," Axandra complained, squinting as she described it. The bright flashes disrupted her vision frequently since she found herself standing outside the monument. "My stomach is upset. I don't think I could possibly eat lunch. My head aches. I feel somewhat dizzy."

"Remove your sweater, please," Eryn suggested first, helping her untie the sash and pull the thick knit from her arms. Then the Healer asked in her ritualistic manner, "May I touch you?"

Axandra gave a brief nod of permission, but still she winced as the Healer's hands touched her skin. Not because the hands felt cold—in fact, the fingers and palms felt pleasantly warm—but because her mind already felt battered and trampled by someone or something else. The touch only added to her discomfort. Eryn first massaged the palm of each hand briefly before moving the touch up her forearms, over her sharp elbows and onto her upper arms, each brush light and unobtrusive. The green-tinted circle entered her mind's eye and spread throughout her being like a pool of cool water. The warm hands crossed her shoulders, gently pushing away the thin cottony tunic in order to touch her skin directly. Moving further up, Eryn's hands squeezed the back of her neck near the base of her skull, the base of her pain. She moaned in protest, but noticed a moment later that the pain dissipated almost completely. In her mind, the cool green washed away the flashes of light and settled her thoughts to a still, glass-like surface. She felt her body being tipped sideways, a pillow rising to meet her head.

Rest now, Eryn thought softly.

Axandra lapsed into deep sleep, unable to resist.

Chapter 18

New Friends

Even after a three-hour nap, Axandra still felt uneasy and perplexed about everything that had occurred on this tour. She lay in bed for almost half an hour, staring at the ceiling and trying to remember anything from the day before. But nothing was there. It was all blank.

She prodded the Goddess for any clue of why she felt out-of-touch, but the entity ignored her, crouching quietly somewhere in the back of her mind. She wondered if any of her mothers before her had distrusted the creature the way she did or if they had complied to its will happily. If she had stayed with her real parents, would she have learned to welcome it and bend with its whims? Would the transition pass more smoothly?

Finally she felt it was time to get up, before lying in bed felt more permanent. The suns already dipped behind the peaks of the mountains, shadowing the village into early twilight. From the kitchen, the aroma of dinner baking in the wood-fired oven wafted in the air. Voices and laughter met her ears. The others played a game in the main room.

Rising stiffly, Axandra washed her face at the sink in the small bathroom, then brushed through her dark hair, returning the ringlets to a more cared-for look. She employed two silver combs to draw the long strands away from her face. Before she walked out of her room, she found the sweater and slipped the plush knit over her shoulders. The wool felt comfortable against her body, and the sweater offered something tangible she could tie herself to, the very last thing she remembered before today. She received the dardak wool as a most welcome gift from her hosts.

Axandra found her housemates at the short table in the drawing room, a deck of cards strewn about among them while they played a round of gin. Noticing her entrance, they greeted her and urged her to join in the next hand. Miri leaped up immediately, ready to attend to her mistress's needs.

"Sit, Miri," Axandra pleaded, waving the young woman to rest. "I'll get myself a glass of water."

"Don't be ridiculous, Madam," Miri denied, scooting off to the kitchen to take care of the request.

"You're lucky to have someone so attentive," Suzanne observed. She sat on the floor, her long legs stretched out beneath the table, her cards held close to her breast since Sara sat behind her on the chair. Sara casually ran her fingers through Suzanne's raven hair.

"Just like I am," Sara chimed, laying a peck upon Suzanne's head.

"Miri is very in tune with you, Protectress," Suzanne continued, gracing her lover with a genuine smile.

"Yes, she is. Most of the time, she knows what I need before I even think of it." Axandra eased onto the sofa next to Eryn and peeked at the Healer's cards to see if she might be winning. Eryn's meager hand offered little hope for a victory.

"I hope you don't mind, Madam," Sara said, "but I invited a couple of friends of ours for dinner this evening, since it's your last night here."

"Oh?" Axandra responded curiously. "I don't mind, but who are they? Did you clear it with Ty?" She said the last part as a joke, to which they all suppressed a chuckle. Axandra didn't see the Elite guards, but she sensed their alertness. She suspected they stood guard at the two entrances to the house.

"They are archeologists working on a dig nearby," Sara explained. The councilor drew a card from the deck and instantly flipped it onto the discard pile. "One is a long time friend. I've known him since we were children. We were going to take you out to the dig, but our schedule had to change." Sara ticked her head sideways and grimaced with disappointment.

"I do remember you mentioning that," Axandra recalled, straining to remember the exact conversation. "That would have been more interesting."

"Speaking of our guests, I'd better finish setting the table." Suzanne got to her feet and handed her cards to Axandra. "Do try to win for me. I hear you have a knack for this game." Suzanne sprang off to the kitchen, from where Miri returned with a polished metal cup of cool water.

Making an attempt to play, Axandra drew a new card, saw it suited her needs, and ended the game with a winning hand. Disgusted, Eryn tossed her cards at the table. Two of the slick cards continued their path off the far side of the table to the floor. "Again! I don't know if I'll invite you to play anymore."

"Technically, Suzanne won," Axandra defended. "These were her cards. I just got the luck of the draw."

The door chimes rang musically above their heads. Sara hurried to the door, swinging it open. She immediately embraced the first man and greeted the second with a peck on the cheek. "Thank you both for coming. It's so good to see you again."

Axandra rose from her seat and observed the interaction between friends.

"You are looking marvelous, Sara," complimented the second entry, a tall lithe man whose head was hairless but his lip sprouted a thick gray mustache that hid his upper lip. He wore a lightweight off-white sweater over unbleached algodon slacks and freshly-wiped leather boots.

The first man possessed a shorter and bulkier build with blondish hair and a round, whiskerless face. Wire-rimmed glasses graced the bridge of his nose, though he slipped them off and into the breast pocket of his blue shirt. He wore a tan jacket in which threads of green and red blended with the golden wool for an overall rough texture. The jacket exaggerated his shoulders into perfect squares, which disappeared as he removed the coat, softening his physique.

When led to the great room, where everyone now stood on their feet, they bowed in greeting as Sara introduced them. "This is Tomas Kirk," she said of the bald man, "and this is Quinn Elgar. Gentlemen, our Esteemed Protectress."

They bowed again very deeply and respectfully greeted Axandra with her title, to which she responded with a short, gracious bow of her own and wore her most pleasant smile. Both men spewed excitement to be in her presence. They had been looking forward to their dinner here all day. Tomas spoke reverently when he complimented the Protectress' service so far to the people.

The other gentleman, Quinn, clenched his fists nervously at his sides and moved about stiffly and uncertainly, grinning the entire time. Even his thoughts emitted a jumble of nervous excitement. *I'm really here! She's standing in front of me! She's more beautiful than anything I've seen. Is she smiling at me?* Axandra tried not to giggle at him.

Sara continued to introduce Eryn and Miri to the new arrivals. They all returned to their seats while Suzanne came around with appetizers of baked root chips and spreadable cheese. Sara opened a ceramic bottle of wine and poured several glasses to pass around.

Tomas sat in the last available chair, while Eryn shared one sofa with Miri and Sara. This left the last cushion of space on the sofa next to Axandra for Quinn. He sat at a respectable distance and beamed a smile in her direction. His gray-blue eyes met hers, and she witnessed a dreamy pleasure twinkling through them. His youthful eyes made him appear quite boyish, though she suspected he was actually a few years older than she.

Much chatter ensued among the guests and hosts. Axandra, charmed by the blonde man's youthful exuberance, observed Quinn as he answered a question from the Healer as to why he chose archeology as his life service.

Again Quinn's eyes sparkled as he talked about his first love. "When I was young, I first read about the Ancients in a discovery journal and—well, I fell in love with the thought of finding treasure," he said. "It turns out the true treasure is solving the puzzle the Ancients left behind. They are so similar to humans, both physically and culturally." He spoke further of piecing together such a challenging puzzle, and Axandra could see that discovery was his ultimate passion.

"At our latest dig near here, we are finding a great deal of whole pottery and parts of metal tools, all gathered together. It may have been an altar area, where offerings were given to their gods," Tomas explained, taking a turn in the conversation. "We feel certain we're near a large settlement buried somewhere beneath the ground."

"Buried?" Eryn quizzed. "How does a village become buried?"

"Here, it appears a landslide or mudslide covered the entire area. North Compass itself is built on the remains of that slide. The soil here is formed mostly of dry dust and sand and shifts easily when disturbed. Once you dig down about seven meters, you are on bed rock," Tomas described. He took a napkin-full of chips and chomped them down in short order. He leaned over to the tray to get some more. Miri hopped up again, offering to serve more hors d'oeuvres to everyone, relinquishing Suzanne of this duty. No one said anything to thwart her efforts.

Axandra noticed that Quinn took only one, and the chip remained in his napkin, untouched while they sat. He felt extremely nervous. Keeping his body stiff, he shifted away from her a slight bit more, as though afraid he might offend her if he strayed too close. *Don't mess this up,* he thought to himself. His mind opened to her so easily. His emanations practically jumped out at her because she was such the focus of his thoughts. *Act casual. You're not a little boy.*

He looked right at her as he added, "An altar is a good indication of a settlement. People of this developmental stage often lived near the believed homes of their gods."

"Dinner, everyone," Suzanne called from the dining room. In a mass of movement, they all rose from their seats and walked to the large table with their goblets of wine.

While Axandra received the honor of the head of the long table, Sara made certain to seat her guests as she saw fit, with Quinn to Axandra's right and Suzanne at the left. Sara sat at the far end with Tomas to her left and Eryn to her right. Miri did not want to sit with them at first. She was unaccustomed to dining with the Protectress on formal occasions and had so far avoided doing so at every meal. The pleadings from everyone at the table coaxed Miri to the chair between Tomas and Quinn.

As a leafy salad rounded the table, the conversation continued to focus around the archeologists and their findings.

As she listened, Axandra carefully studied Quinn's face, for she felt she recognized him from somewhere. She could not place him definitively, but that was understandable considering the vast number of people she had seen and met over that past few weeks. The sense of him resonated in her with such familiarity, she felt certain she had spent more than just a few minutes with him before. Many of his words sounded familiar as well, as though she had heard some of his stories before. Yet she could not place him.

"I must apologize if I seem rude," she whispered to Quinn as the others became wrapped up in talk about possible tidal floods due to the close approach of Soporus. She wished to be discreet. "But I feel as though I've met you somewhere before."

His round cheeks pinked slightly. "Yes, Madam, you have. I was custodian at the Lazzonir Landing when you toured there many weeks ago."

Thinking back to that day, Axandra found that his face fit into the picture. "Ohhhh. That explains it." She nodded and forked salad into her mouth. The fresh lettuce graced the ceramic plate in a rainbow of colors—deep red, bright orange, and dusty gold—lightly drenched with a creamy dressing.

"I didn't think you would recognize me at all," Quinn told her. "You were very distracted that day."

How embarrassing that he had noticed! She thought she had hidden her distress better than that. "I wish that day had turned out differently," Axandra sighed. "I regret not enjoying the tour. I have an interest in history, especially in the Journey that brought our people here. From what I've read, it's a wonder so many ships made it here, or that any ship survived the continuous dangers of space."

So the table's conversation turned to human history. Quinn brandished his knowledge and his deep curiosity as well as his humor. He described a particularly harrowing tale in which one of the ships that began the Journey, the Orion, was lost when the convoy encountered an ion storm, the first of its kind to be experienced by human beings. The shielding on the ship collapsed under the stress of the ionized particles and the massive vessel disintegrated, flashing out of existence with all souls lost. Fault was laid with the captain of the ship. "Of course, reading history in our books and even in the data records of the ships, we find that the information can be one-sided. The victor of the war often wrote the history of it."

"I think that our ancestors did a fine job of bringing with them a wide variety of points of view," Axandra disagreed, sipping at her blushed wine. "The Palace Library contains literature from all walks of life and from much of Old Earth's troubled past. I've even found two works by authors who believed that telepathic abilities were a symptom of a disease and offered all manner of cures. They are troubling to read, but I do understand why our families chose to leave Old Earth behind, even though it meant they would never walk on a planet's surface again."

"Now, that is an interesting point to bring up, Madam." Quinn steepled his index fingers and tapped them on his chin. He finished the last bite of his salad and last sip of wine and poured himself another, fuller glass. Be careful with her. Don't scare her off. I think she's enjoying this. "The Palace library you speak of is off limits to the public. If you look into the public circulation of books, I doubt you will find those same titles or such variety."

"QE, are you saying that the Protectresship is keeping secrets?" Sara scorned. "That seems a bit impudent, don't you think?"

"Everyone keeps a few secrets, Sara. It's human nature." Quinn stated this fact without accusation or displeasure. To him, it was simply a fact of life.

Eryn prudently stepped in to change the topic. "Are you and your workers going to shut down the dig until Soporus passes?"

"Yes. With so many extraordinary circumstances going on, we decided to shut down tomorrow after we pack up the artifacts we've collected and ship them to Millerton for further study," Tomas advised. "Then all of us'll volunteer where we're needed. Plus, as the temp cools, it's safer south. I'm goin' to move home in Millerton until Soporus shows us her tail."

"To safety," Sara offered as a quick, sobering toast, "and to our friends." They all drank, and a few quiet moments ensued about the table while Suzanne served the main course.

Axandra caught site of Sara and Suzanne winking at one another across the table, and got a sneaking suspicion that she had been set up on this encounter with Quinn for more than cultural reasons.

For the moment, she didn't mind. Quinn made pleasant company, even when he argued with her. He was not afraid to put forth his beliefs and his facts, even if he was trying to make a good impression on the woman he pursued.

The evening went by quickly as the hosts and guests continued to entertain each other with stories and games. They returned to the great room when dinner was finished. For the most part, they kept the topics casual, avoiding depressing talk about Soporus or the Believers or other dreadful subjects.

"So, tell me—us," Quinn stuttered awkwardly in the conversation over yet another bottle of wine. Clearing his throat, he persisted, "Tell us something about where you grew up. I know I'm curious where you've been for so many years."

"Oh, I don't want to bore anyone with my childhood," Axandra attempted to shelve the discussion. She felt her face color with discomfort.

Sara snickered. The woman's skin looked pleasantly pink from the four glasses she'd consumed. "I'm sure it isn't boring, Madam. Do tell. Where did you live? Who did you live with?"

The others prodded her as well, each intrigued to hear some of the secrets she'd been keeping to herself. Miri was the only one who didn't speak up about her curiosity. The aide secluded herself to one side of the room, waiting for someone to need her help.

"Well," Axandra resigned with a sigh. The room became very quiet and everyone ignored their cards. "I lived outside the village of Cherish, in southwest Westland, on a algodon farm with the Kortes. Reiko was my adoptive father, and Kari was my mother." Speaking these words incited a swarm of memories she hadn't paid attention to in years. The faces of those people hovered at the back of her eyes. She missed them. "They had no other children, but they treated me as their own. Nothing much happened. I helped with the algodon field during the growing season and harvest. I went to school in the village. Kari taught me to sew and to cook. Pretty much the same as any other child."

"Where are they now?" asked Suzanne curiously, though the woman suspected she could guess the answer.

"The Kortes were already in their late fifties when I lived with them. Kari passed away when I was fourteen after having pneumonia," Axandra explained sadly. "Reiko missed her very much and never really recovered from the ordeal. He passed away a couple of years later. I had no other family, so I volunteered for service early. I haven't been to Cherish since."

Suzanne's piercing blue eyes glistened. "Oh, you poor thing. I'm sorry."

"Don't be," Axandra excused. "I miss them, but I know they gave their best to me."

Tomas stroked the long whiskers of his mustache and wore a consternated frown. "Pardon me if I seem inconsiderate for asking, but what about your real parents? Did they send you to the Kortes? Why didn't you go home?"

Everyone else in the room, Quinn included, flashed Tomas scathing glares. Each one appeared to have swallowed their tongues in shock.

To evade the question, Axandra poured herself another glassful, praised the flavor of the wine, and then retrieved her cards. "Whose turn was it?"

Other than Tomas, the group uneasily returned to the game already in progress, deciding quickly that the play went to Sara. Within a few minutes, most of them refocused on the fun of the match. Tomas excused himself from the game with a grump.

After a while, the two gentlemen decided—when the ladies began to yawn—that the time had come to head back to their own accommodations.

"Thank you, Sara and Suzi, for the most delicious meal," Tomas said graciously, heading for the door.

"And thank you for the lovely company," added Quinn, though he seemed to be referencing the Protectress more than anyone else. He said the words with such sincerity, his voice melted her heart. "Have a pleasant night and a safe trip back to Undun City."

"Goodnight," Axandra wished them both, then they were out the door into the cold night. The air froze their breath into clouds as they hurried away up the narrow street.

"QE is quite adorable, isn't he," Sara baited, keeping her voice low so that the others wouldn't hear her.

"He is," Axandra agreed simply.

"You know, he passes through Undun quite frequently." Sara and Axandra watched as the men turned the corner up ahead and disappeared from sight. "Perhaps he could stop by some-time."

To this, Axandra made no answer, but smirked and raised her brows in a quick wiggle. Turning into the house, she left Sara to read into that what she wished.

Chapter 19

Force of Will

31st September, 307

The first traces of autumn struck the temperate country-side. Flowers began to fade out and turn to seed, drying in the sun and releasing bits of fluff into the wind. Nuts and fruits ripened, ready for the picking. Some fields of grain already lay bare from harvest, while others were just turning to golden red. Breadbeans, blackcorn and milkseed all awaited the scythes and threshers.

After listening to Ty Narone's arguments, the Council members agreed by vote that further continental travel be suspended until after the Sister Planet made her pass. With the numerous accounts of odd behavior in both people and animals, they unanimously believed the safest and best place for the Protectress to offer her support to the people would be from the Palace in Undun City. Axandra expressed her disappointment to the small contingent of the Council, giving them the same rebuttals she had given Ty. In the end, she agreed to abide by their decision and asked that they act as her physical liaisons by visiting their home regions frequently and report first hand the details of any more disturbing behaviors.

For the next week, the Protectress focused on the reports coming in from the Safety Volunteers who were keeping watch on neighbors and wildlife. Those Volunteers posted in coastal areas reported that rising tidal waters flooded homes near the shore and along some river banks. Due to increased gravitational forces, the tides fluctuated by several meters outside normal.

"Scientific reports indicate the trend of the rising waters will continue until Soporus begins to fall behind in orbit," Morton informed the on- duty Council members. "They recommend we evacuate low-lying coastal areas."

"Then we should begin immediately," the Protectress ordered. "Can we agree today to delegate resources in each region to begin packing residents' belongings and get them moved farther inland?"

"Many could be sheltered with family members. We'll fill the inns and then turn to volunteers to house the rest," Carmen Offut, a representative from Eastland, assured.

"Not everyone will want to be moved, Your Honor." Osander spoke out. "We should grant the Assistors authority to remove citizens by force. It is our duty to ensure their survival."

Antonette agreed with the young man. "I won't sit by idly while the people I know get washed away, not when it could be prevented. We've never had such foreknowledge of a natural disaster. I agree that we should move them, whether they like it or not." As she spoke, her long finger jabbed straight into the top of her desk, emphasizing her last few words.

"Force seems uncalled for, Protectress," refuted Offut. She rose from her desk and directed her words to the others, her golden-brown hands gesticulating as she spoke. "We still have time to persuade them to evacuate. I will volunteer to go myself—"

"All by yourself, dear?" Antonette scoffed. "How long will you try?"

"As long as necessary," Carmen insisted, her dark brown eyes glaring at the elder Councilor. "And I would prefer to have some help, but I will go by myself if necessary. We can't just pick them up and carry them. That would strip them of their dignity."

"Oh, boo!" Antonette jeered.

Casper Ross, with eyelids drooping, rose to his feet, leaning heavily on his wooden cane. He offered somber words. "They should be allowed to do as they wish."

"And why do you say that, sir?" Axandra asked, thankful that Casper's soft voice forced silence to the room.

"The Covenant of Free Will. They have every right to stay to meet their fate, just as you and I have a right to choose our own paths," he lectured. "We have never forced any of our people to do anything they did not wish to do. We cannot make that precedent now. Of course, we are talking about something completely hypothetical. We don't know who or how many, if any, would want to stay put."

"Free Will supersedes everything else," the Protectress agreed. "It is our highest Covenant, the reason our ancestors left Old Earth and brought life here. The people should be left to their own decisions."

"But they should be provided safety," Osander argued forcefully. "Sometimes people are not able to make such decisions for themselves. They become blinded—"

"We will provide the option for them to move. If it is their wish not to take part, we cannot force them to do so," Casper pointed out, a gnarled finger in the air. "I think we should vote."

A quick vote showed four out of six in favor of letting the citizens be. Only Osander and Antonette disagreed.

"Is that enough to follow through," the Protectress asked to the councilors, still uncertain about the protocol of such a vote without the full council present.

"It is, Madam," assured Osander. "It appears that you have won."

"I wouldn't consider it much of a victory," Axandra responded solemnly. "Thank you all for your input. Please inform the Assistance Coordinators what needs to happen and the guidelines we want them to adhere to. Good day." She dismissed the group by turning away from them and hoped she did not let them see her eyes tearing up over yet another impending disaster. There was some clatter as the Councilors rose to leave, but little talking amongst them.

The archivist, who took notes of the meeting, immediately approached, requesting that the Protectress take some time to review his archives so the records could be entered officially. Sucking in her sadness with a deep and noisy breath, she allowed him to take a few moments of her time to do so. Then Carmen approached her.

"Your Honor, if I may speak with you," Carmen posed cautiously. The woman must have sensed her distress.

Another discussion was the last thing Axandra wanted right now, especially if it concerned the matter with which they had just finished. She wasn't sure if she could contain herself for very long. But the needs of the councilors were as important as the needs of the people.

"Come with me." She led Carmen to the small office where the archivist waited with his sheets of parchment. She dismissed him for a moment and gestured for Carmen to have a seat in a comfortable chair facing the desk.

"Madam, I still feel that some of our citizens can be persuaded to change their minds," the Councilor began earnestly.

Axandra halted her with her hand palm out. "Councilor, if you wish to pursue your mission, it is your free will to do so. However, the official view from the Protectresship will be that of choice. Do you understand?"

Carmen sat as the youngest current member of the council at the tender age of twenty-four and had been a member for only a few months, barely longer than Axandra had been Protectress.

Her election came from a very young class of people who dominated the eastern half of Eastland. She still believed that she was going to change the world in tremendous ways with her service. The young woman felt determined to start somewhere.

Slowly, Carmen nodded, her sleek dark hair reflecting the lamplight. "I do, Your Honor. It just so happens that my respite begins next Sunday."

"Perhaps you should plan a trip to the coast," Axandra suggested coolly.

"Thank you for the suggestion," Carmen said as she rose to leave. "Have a good day, Madam."

I wish you Good Luck, Axandra thought to Carmen.

A thought came back to her. *Thank you.*

After Carmen exited, the archivist returned and began to lay sheets before the Protectress on the desk, along with a wooden pen filled with black ink. She asked for a blank sheet to practice on once again. She could not cease thinking of herself in terms of Axandra, the woman into whom she had grown. Ileanne was just an empty name to her, a part of her title, and no longer a person. She scratched out her official signature several times with her left hand before beginning the ritual of reading the depictions and signing off on their accuracy.

Axandra read the details of the trip to the North, following along with the date of their departure and who was in attendance. She agreed with the purpose of the trip, including the expected meeting with the sect of Believers. Then she came to details she did not remember. She read over them quickly at first, as she did most of the documents, trusting that the notes were accurate. But then, as realization sunk in that she recalled no such events, she reread the words slowly.

It was noted that the travel began on Moonsday, the first day of the week. Due to a massive herd of three-horned bison covering the only road, the travelers were forced to turn back and spend the first night in the small village of Barton, just on the border between Eastland and Northland. The herd contained several thousand of the densely-furred grazers. The humans made no attempt to go through the herd or force them to move, lest they cause a stampede or injure one of the animals. The next morning they continued North after Ty sent ahead a scout to see that the herd had moved on, therefore the group arrived in North Compass a half-day later than expected.

Only, Axandra did not remember any such herd of animals—they would have been difficult to miss seeing—and she remembered arriving in North Compass in late evening, not at midday as the narrative described.

With a flare of white light in her eyes, the Goddess flashed an image in her mind, a scene of a two-ton, dark brown beast peering curiously at her as it chewed a mouthful of yellow-striped grass. Behind this animal, the landscape lay thick with them, bison as far as the eye could see. The grazing animals stood squat and wide, pelted in thick fur to warm them in the colder climate. Three horns adorned their flat, bony heads—two between the small ears and one in the middle of the snout. Despite the darkness of the fur, the snouts were pink like new skin.

Shaking her head, she refused to accept the image as a memory and indicated to the Goddess that she would not be tricked. The visual must have come from the memory of some past host. Axandra knew that she had never seen a three-horned bison in her entire life and that had not changed on this trip.

Was the archive written falsely? Should these memories fill the blank hole in her mind? Was it possible to experience this and not remember? There was no indication in the log that she had been injured or taken ill at that time. While human memory was not the most reliable keeper of information, she felt certain these events did not happen to her.

Politely, she asked the archivist whose notes he had used to draw up the report.

"I compiled notes from Healer Eryn, Councilor Sunsun and the Elite note keeper," he responded promptly. "Is there a problem?"

"Did they all mention the bison?" Axandra tried not to give away too much of her bewilderment as she asked, nor accuse him of any wrongdoing. He was a master at scripting these logs, but he had not been at hand on the trip.

With certainty, the archivist answered, "Yes, Your Honor. The only discrepancy occurred with the time of day. Two noted that the car came upon the herd in the morning. The other stated it was afternoon. But when one is on a long drive, it is easy to make such a mistake. Not terribly peculiar."

"No, I guess not." She looked down again at the inked words in graceful print. Small drawings or filigrees always illuminated the top of each document. In this case, the decoration included a few of the bison, barely four centims high, in a line across the header. "Unfortunately, I can't concur with the report."

"Oh, dear," he sighed worriedly.

"I will have to speak with my fellow travelers before I can sign this one," she told him, handing him the sheets.

"I understand. I will hold it until I hear from you. Will you sign the others?"

She glanced quickly at the others. The ones prior to Northland, she agreed to sign. Those that involved the Northland trip, she refused, especially since she was uncertain of the details.

"No trouble, Madam," he told her. Carefully, he rolled the linen-fiber sheets and slipped each into a cane tube stopped on one end with a wooden cap. With the tubes in hand, he excused himself to other duties.

With a mystery at hand, Axandra went in search of the Healer. If she indeed lacked such memories, perhaps she should discover the underlying cause. She thought back to the flashing lights that plagued her at the Landing and wondered if that had anything to do with the blanks.

She found Eryn in the basement of the Palace, working in the small room where the Healer kept her medical supplies and records. The woman busily sorted through vials of herbs, roots and extracts, checking the quantity and quality of each. Some were discarded and replaced with fresh supply. Along the far wall, several plants hung in various stages of the drying process. Today, the Healer dressed in a casual tunic and slacks with her faded terra cotta hair wrapped in a loose knot at the base of her neck. She did not immediately notice the Protectress' arrival.

"Good afternoon, Healer," Axandra said, bringing attention to herself as she waited in the doorway.

"Oh, good afternoon, Protectress. My apologies. I didn't see you there." Eryn stopped what she was doing momentarily to give the customary bow. "Just performing a monthly inventory. We've had a rash of headaches around the Palace these past few days. What can I do for you?"

Instructing the Elite to wait outside, Axandra closed the door and sat on a stool that Eryn motioned to. "I'm not feeling ill, necessarily," she began, dispelling the idea that she had come to cure another headache. "I just came to—well, to clear up a few things for myself."

"Clear up a few things? Have I done something that you dislike, Madam?" Eryn asked openly, though without much concern. "I will treat you in whatever manner you prefer."

"No, nothing like that. It—" Axandra struggled to get the words right, to draw the question into something worth clarifying and not inane babble. "Ever since last Hopesday, I've felt completely out of synch with everyone else."

"When we were at the Landing?" Eryn questioned. "You asked me some curious questions that day. Do you still feel fatigued?"

Fatigue. The spoken word seemed like such a simple answer to the puzzle. Traveling across the continent for many days put great strain on her, both physically and mentally. She did not feel healthy. She did not eat or sleep as well she should. Worry exacted a heavy toll.

Axandra's shoulders slumped a little as she let out a sigh. "Humph. I hope that's all it is."

"You have barely rested since you first arrived in Undun," Eryn offered as an observation. She sat herself down on another stool facing her patient. "Due to the circumstances, I haven't yet made any orders for you to take a vacation. First of all, I know you wouldn't take one. And secondly, the people need you desperately right now. But if fatigue is beginning to affect you so detrimentally, I will make you spend a week with no councilors and no reports. Just food and rest."

"That sounds like quite a wonderful idea," Axandra breathed in agreement, tucking her loose curls behind her ear. "Eryn, I came down here because of the archivist's logs. He wrote in the report that we came upon a herd of bison."

"Oh, weren't they marvelous! You could see them clear to the horizon," Eryn recalled excitedly, green eyes flashing.

In a worried whisper, Axandra leaned close to her and stated, "I don't remember them. I don't remember the cars ever stopping on the way, except for a rest stop, and we arrived at North Compass the same day we left, not the next day. Why don't I remember what everyone else seems to?"

The Healer's gleeful smile disappeared immediately. She did not hide her concern at this unpleasant revelation. Her brows knit together as she peered seriously at her patient. "That is very strange. My first thoughts are fatigue, which does affect short-term memory recall, but you are not to that stage. There is also amnesia, but that usually accompanies severe injury or illness, of which you've had neither in the past several weeks." Those green eyes studied Axandra's face, then moved about her body, looking for any other sign that might give a clue to the disorder.

"What about my headaches? And the lights flashing in my eyes?"

Eryn dismissed those symptoms with a shake of her head. "Typical symptoms of exhaustion and lack of proper nutrition."

"And that isn't all. The archivist said that the notes don't match. Two said the bison were seen in the morning and one said the afternoon."

"It was definitely afternoon," Eryn said, indicating which of these note takers she represented. "We had already stopped for lunch." She continued to visually study her patient without a single touch. Her eyes stopped below her head and to the right. "What is that mark?"

"What mark?" Axandra strained her eyes to try to see, but whatever the Healer saw was in a blind spot.

Eryn asked for permission to touch her skin and proceeded to brush aside her long hair and draw aside the neck of her blouse. "It looks like an abrasion," she said, her cool fingers brushing over a spot just where the shoulder stretched away from the neck, toward the back, "Like your skin took a hard rub."

"I did carry that heavy bag when we got home the other day, just before Miri grabbed it from me."

Eryn narrowed her eyes, unconvinced. "Perhaps. May I offer to see inside your memories? Hopefully I can see what is causing them to hide."

"I beg you to help, if you can. I don't like feeling this way. What if I've lost something important?" Axandra pleaded. Already worried about the lapses, Eryn's lack of answers and serious demeanor only deepened her anxiety. Her primary worry became that she was being stricken with a severe illness, possibly the one that afflicted the Believers. Would she wind up demented and bedridden like them?

The Healer took a cleansing breath, eyes closed. When she opened those eyes again, she looked straight into Axandra, pushing herself into her mind as she laid her fingers upon her face.

The greenness appeared before her, that loose blob of color that slowly clarified into a perfect circle. Gently, Eryn moved about the mind, brushing away the last few days, putting them behind her and searching for just the right moments. She settled upon a point where Sara's house, made of stone and rockwood beams, appeared.

Axandra did not close her eyes, but Quinn's face replaced Eryn's, handsomely adorned with his dimpled smile. He clutched a small hat to his chest as he said "I came to make certain you were feeling better."

"I do," Axandra replied in the memory, though her body did not feel well. She felt heavy, weighed down through to her core.

Then she felt a touch on her hand, his touch. His mind met hers for an instant.

In the depths of her consciousness, the Goddess stirred. It had been resting there, as it had for the past several days. The images of the bison were the first she had sensed of it since returning from the Northland.

Now, it lunged forward with a fury, disturbed by the intrusion. Hissing and snarling, the creature lashed with ghostly claws at the green orb.

Deftly, Eryn dodged the scrape, withdrawing to a safe area in the outer layers of consciousness, where only shallow and short-term thoughts flitted through. The Healer appeared unscathed, to Axandra's relief. Axandra could hear herself breathing heavily as adrenaline coursed through her blood, frightened by the unexpected act. *Stay back,* she hissed at the Goddess.

Treading softly, Eryn approached from another side, coming in from behind the hidden memory instead and disguising herself in the background. This tricked the Goddess briefly, giving Eryn a few precious moments to peer around at the details and stretch the time into the moments surrounding it.

But the Goddess realized that the intruder lingered and attacked once more, roaring angrily and leaping at the circle. Instead of allowing herself to be injured, the Healer quickly exited and released her hold.

Shaking, Axandra whispered fearfully, "I'm sorry!" The thing in her head growled and seethed, its claws scratching at where the Healer had been.

"No apology necessary. The entity and I have had our run-ins before."

The Healer said this so casually, that Axandra almost missed the significance of the statement. She blinked and then stared. "I beg your pardon? You know about it? I-I thought—"

"I have been Healer at the Palace for ten years now and treated your mother on many occasions. The nature of my work allows me knowledge of the Goddess," Eryn explained calmly. "Though I doubt those councilors responsible for the secret realize I know. In this case, it is protecting the buried memories. To what end, I'm not certain, but it's offended that I might see them. I managed just a glimpse."

"Quinn," Axandra breathed out, filling her mind with him in the memory Eryn had examined. "At Sara's house. But we were never alone together."

"At first I thought it was a duplication—an echo of that night." Eryn said, replaying the memory for herself as she looked toward the gray wall behind Axandra. "But the night was surrounded by different events and feelings. You were feeling quite ill when he came to see you." She closed her eyes now, concentrating further. "You reached out for his hand at one point. No one else was nearby, though you heard laughing." When she opened her eyes again, she allowed herself to smile. "You did meet him before that party. But that was hidden from all of us. My memories have been replaced to explain away what is missing, but yours were not."

Axandra started to speak, but found her throat tight and her voice box locked. The right side of her face felt suddenly numb and her eyelid began to twitch uncontrollably. The Goddess scratched, digging into her brain, blocking her from speaking and pulling at her new deductions, dragging them back into that dark places where the other memories lay concealed. Axandra closed her eyes in pain.

Eryn must have noticed her struggle, for the woman grabbed her hands and leapt back into her mind, saturating everything green.

You cannot control her, Eryn told it, blocking another swing of claws that would have slashed the present to pieces. The green oozed, cut to shreds by the razor-like talons.

Eryn? Axandra thought after the Healer, afraid to see the damage. *Stop it! Stop!*

Seething with ire, Axandra slammed a cage over the creature. The bars rattled as it banged against the trap, but the bars held. The Goddess hissed furiously and paced in its cat-like state.

You harm no one, ordered the host.

The greenness of Eryn faded away.

Opening her eyes, Axandra found the Healer drooping backward, slipping from the stool. Eryn appeared catatonic, her eyes open yet unseeing, stupefied by the mental lacerations.

"Eryn!" Axandra tried to call back. The Healer only stared from where she lay sprawled on the floor

"Help!" Axandra called out for her guards to hear. They immediately opened the door and rushed in. "Eryn needs a Healer. Bring one! Quickly!"

Axandra crouched over the limp form, her hands hovering and shaking, afraid that her touch might cause further harm but wanting to offer help. One of the Elite left to get help while the other waited nearby, asking what else could be done.

Axandra could only shake her head. Tears sprang hotly from her eyes as she kept calling Eryn's name, hoping to bring her back. She touched Eryn's face and tried to reach in, finding only green ooze filling the wounded mind, spilling all around her like blood. When Axandra pulled away, her hands dripped with green. Startled, she shrieked and fell backward onto her rear. Looking again, the green disappeared.

Healer Phineas Gage arrived after several minutes. Quickly, he studied the patient and questioned the Protectress.

"Her mind," she said through her sobs. "She's hurt. Please, you have to help her," she begged.

"How did this happen?" Gage insisted.

Choking on her tears, she confessed, "I did it. It's all my fault."

Gage barely touched Eryn's temple. The woman blinked and inhaled a sharp breath, her entire body trembling. Then she lay still once more. Within moments he withdrew his hand. "It is quite severe, but I patched the damage to her mind. It will hold until I summon assistance from the other Healers. We must take Eryn home and have the others meet us there."

One of the Elite hurried off to collect the other city Healers. Another grabbed a stretcher from a nearby wall. At some point, several other Elite arrived to give aid. Soon they lifted Eryn onto the portable stretcher and carried her from the room. Axandra was left where she sat on the floor. She drowned in tears and in guilt and the green she saw everywhere, the essence of Eryn that spilled from her body.

It's not real, Axandra told herself, closing her eyes to the pool of emerald liquid surrounding her. *It isn't really there.* When she opened her eyes again, she sat alone, and the green stain was gone.

Chapter 20

Everything Means Something

3rd October, 307

Axandra waited impatiently for an update of Eryn's condition. She paced her rooms, refusing to eat more than a few bites of any meal, and those only because Miri promised to remain in the bedroom until she put food in her mouth.

This was her fault. She should never have asked for Eryn's help. She should have let things be and taken her failed memory as part of her transition. Her choice to find answers left Eryn badly injured.

Each day for three days, Axandra went over and over the incident and each day her anger with herself grew ten-fold.

Right now, she wanted to take it all back, but she didn't possess the ability to turn back time. No one did.

Her body tense and seething, she turned on the ball of her foot to leave the balcony. A fly buzzed in front of her face. Angrily, she swept an arm through the air to shoo it away.

The table and chairs scraped across the stone and banged loudly against the railing. She stopped in her tracks and stared at the iron furniture in astonishment.

The release the energy felt renewing. Standing in the wind, she felt another surge building, and with a grunt, swept her arms aside again, pushing the table and chairs hard against the Palace wall without a touch. The metal bounced and toppled, clanging against the stones. Grooves marred the white limestone of the outer wall.

Panting, Axandra reviewed the mess. The urge to break something still seethed inside her, the need to transfer all of her frustration to an object that could not defend itself. And as she sought something—anything that would make a satisfying crash—she realized that no matter the circumstances, the necessity of solving the overall puzzle loomed more urgently than before. This wasn't just about her or Quinn. It couldn't be that shallow. Something more sinister loomed, and the effects would touch everyone living on this planet. Being angry at the furniture was pointless.

The surge of energy dissipated from her in that moment. Her hands, which had been clenched tightly at her sides, relaxed and hung open.

Closing her eyes, she let the cool autumn winds blow against her back. Long trails of her hair snaked around her head and face as the wind hit the side of the building and thrust back at her, creating eddies. Birds whistled overhead, flying in and out of their roosts in the decorative finials below the roof. The drying leaves of the trees rattled together below her in distant applause.

Lifting one hand, eyes still closed, Axandra summoned the force again. She practiced this talent in the evenings, when the day wound down and she found herself alone before going to sleep. Practice let her feel comfortable with the vibration which started in the space below her heart and rose up through her sternum. Gently, she lifted the chairs one at a time and righted them, then set the table back upon its base. The table was quite heavy, the heaviest item she had tried to lift so far with this mental muscle. She reminded herself that in her mind, the table could be as light as a feather. The effort eased and soon the arrangement appeared largely undisturbed. She lifted the last, small items, the broken pieces of the flowerpot that so recently decorated the table. She could not repair the damage to the pot, so she caught the pieces in her hands.

At that moment, a knock rattled the bedroom door. Miri entered without waiting for a response, stopped short and narrowed her gaze thinking that her eyes played tricks on her to see the broken pottery floating through the air.

Axandra said nothing. It felt best to leave the matter be, a path Miri agreed silently to take.

"I'm sorry to barge in, Madam, but Healer Gage sent information about Eryn. I knew you'd want to hear it right away." Miri looked tired and frazzled, having spent the past three days constantly checking on the Protectress, worried like a sister that Axandra might do harm to herself out of guilt for Eryn. Axandra could not pretend that such thoughts did not cross her mind every time she closed her eyes and saw the green oozing all around her.

"I do," Axandra replied, coming inside with the broken pieces, the moist soil cold on her hands. She dropped the fragments into a basket near the vanity to be collected for recycling. She stood with her head bowed, waiting for the news. She sensed that it was not pleasant.

"Gage enlisted the help of several Healers in the city to repair the injury, but they weren't able to return Eryn completely to her prior state," Miri reported as unemotionally as possible. "The good news," Miri tried to add a glimmer of hope to her high-pitched voice, "is that she is conscious and able to speak. They say she just doesn't seem to comprehend very well. But Gage assures us that the mind has an amazing ability to heal itself. With time, Eryn may return to her old self."

Lifting her eyes to Miri's, Axandra said, "I'd like to see her."

"That would be wonderful, Madam. Perhaps it will help her recover."

But Axandra desired the visit for selfish reasons. She thought it might heal her own soul if she could see Eryn's green eyes with her essence behind them again, not the hollow eyes that stared up at her from the floor.

"I'll get you fresh clothes," Miri stated, busying herself in the wardrobe to find a suitable outfit for the day's weather. She came back with slacks, a long, scoop-necked tunic with elbow-length sleeves and light wrap to guard against the wind.

In the meantime, Axandra washed and freshened her face, adding powder to her skin to conceal the dark circles under her eyes and the wrinkles that worry creased into her cheeks. The frown would not wash away, adding age to a once youthful face.

Dressed, Axandra stood ready to depart. Miri stepped outside a moment to let the Elite know where they were heading, and the two women exited the Residence and descended the main staircase. In the main entry of the Palace, staff members made themselves scarce as the women passed through. Axandra walked with her head straight, but her eyes cast down. She followed the seams of the marble in the floor, avoiding eye contact with anyone.

Long shadows cast across the floor from the wide doorway. Axandra glanced up momentarily, seeing a silhouette with the southern suns at its back. The double patches of shadow formed the shape of a man.

She looked away once more and thought, Do I know him? When she raised her eyes again, he had come inside where the sunslight from the high windows evened his color. Like being lifted from her feet, she felt pleasure rise up in her heart to find that she did know him.

"Quinn!" Axandra burst happily.

"Mr. Elgar!" said Miri at about the same time, who then glanced at the Protectress with a surprised smile.

"I couldn't have timed that better if I'd tried," Quinn cheered with a boisterous guffaw. Then he bowed in respectful greeting. "Hello again, Protectress."

"I'm so happy to see you," Axandra greeted, hurrying up to him where he stood next to the welcoming fountain. "In fact, I don't think I've ever been so happy to see someone in my whole life." She blushed even as she said the words, embarrassed that she gave it voice. She wanted to embrace him but held back knowing how many sets of eyes watched them at that moment, curious onlookers hiding in doorways and stairwells.

Quinn took great pleasure in hearing the words, grinning as he looked at her face. He felt his trip to be quite worthwhile. "You look as though you are on your way out somewhere," he commented. "Am I interrupting an appointment?"

"Not an appointment," she said. But the smile slid from her face. "I was on my way to see Eryn Gray."

"The Healer? Are you ill?" he asked with concern.

"I'm not. Eryn is very ill, however. She was injured three days ago," Axandra explained, still choking up over the incident. Eyes downcast again, she put her fingers to her lips to staunch the flow of sadness that welled up inside her. She looked to Quinn again, trying to keep her face composed. "I do need to see her. Do you mind waiting for me here?"

"I don't mind," Quinn assured, his tone inflected with a willingness to wait for her any length of time, anywhere.

Turning to her aide, Axandra instructed Miri to take her guest up to the Library and tend to his needs. Miri appeared momentarily disappointed to miss the visit with Eryn, but quickly set her mind to her duties.

"I promise to be back in one hour," Axandra told Quinn.

"Take your time," he allowed, dismissing her self-imposed timeline. "Don't worry about me. I have nowhere to be."

Nodding, she sent him with Miri, then turned and headed out the front doors.

Eryn lived in a house just at the bottom of the hill on which the Palace stood, a convenient location for the Healer of the Palace, accessible on foot and by car. Axandra walked quickly down the slope, eager to see about Eryn's condition and just as eager to get back to the Palace to her guest. On her tail, two Elite kept up easily and quietly. Their duties included being aware of everything around her and they used their eyes, ears and mental senses to do so. With so much peculiar activity going on with people and animals, they applied themselves to this duty more wholeheartedly than ever. Her entourage included Ben, for the first time since the garden attack. At least she could put that worry to rest.

The Healer's home was fashioned of stone blocks, like many of the houses in Undun. The stone had been quarried from the foothills of the mountains and cut into neat building blocks cemented together with pale colored mortar. This house consisted mostly of red-tinted granite, though lighter, grayer stone formed accents around the windows and doors and decorated the corners of the tile roof. Two levels made the house more vertical than houses had been on the islands, where typhoons necessitated low-profile structures.

After Axandra knocked on the wooden door, she was graciously welcomed by Eryn's husband, Marcus.

"Protectress, an honor for you to visit." Marcus bowed deeply. "Come in and I'll take you up to see Eryn." He turned quickly inside, not allowing her to ask any questions. He led her up the curving staircase to a room just to the right of the landing. The interior of the house consisted of long curves and arcs, giving the illusion of the stone as a fluid medium.

Marcus gestured her to the room. Axandra looked at him carefully before entering, sensing his worry and his disappointment with the Healers who had tried to heal his wife. Concern lined his brow and thin mouth. Marcus had darker skin, burnished a deep bronze by the suns. His dark hair looked stiff like wire.

"I am truly sorry for what happened," Axandra apologized to him, hoping he would take some comfort in her words. She certainly didn't. His expression of grief refueled her anger, and her perception that this was her fault.

He tried to force an accepting smile, but it failed into a pained grimace. "Just go inside, please. I hope that your visit will help her. I know some people believe that the Protectress' touch conveys elements of healing."

She wished that such was true. She turned from him and entered the sunlit room.

Eryn was awake, sitting up in a large bed looking at a picture book. She looked up with her green eyes and a simple smile. "Who?" she said. Her voice sounded childlike, high in pitch and soft in volume.

"It's me, Eryn," Axandra said, moving carefully to a chair stationed next to the bed. Marcus must have spent much time in this seat keeping vigil over his wife. "It's the Protectress."

"Who?" she asked again, as though she didn't recognize the woman seated next to her. "Book." She pointed at the hard backed book that lay open on her lap.

"Yes, that is a book," Axandra agreed. "Eryn, how do you feel?"

"Feel?" Eryn echoed, staring back at her. "Feel soft." Her hand rubbed the sheets and mattress.

"No, I mean, how do you feel?" she repeated. "Do you feel well?"

"Feel," Eryn said, then paused, looking around the room. "Sky." She pointed up at the lights hanging from the ceiling.

Glancing out the doorway, Axandra detected that Marcus had left them alone. He must have gone down to keep an eye on the Elite. Slowly, Axandra reached out to touch the hand closest to her. Seeing this, Eryn pulled away. "No," she denied.

"I just want to—to help you." *I can't hurt you any worse,* she thought.

Eryn refused, those green eyes narrowed suspiciously. She kept watching Axandra, not looking away.

Backing away, Axandra gave up this tactic. Instead, she offered to read the book. To this, Eryn agreed. The red head listened intently as Axandra pronounced the words of the children's book and studied the colorful illustrations. Then they read another. After about a half-hour, Axandra rose to leave. She said goodbye and, when Eryn pleaded for her to stay like a girl might do with her mother, promised to come back for a another visit.

On the way out of the house, Axandra thanked Marcus for allowing her visit. He seemed eager to get her out, it seemed. His thoughts circled around the woman he loved and how she would never be the same now. He hated that he thought it would have been better if she had been killed in an accident, rather than turned into this.

Sadly, she began to walk home. She kept her pace slow as she climbed the gentle slope of the hill. While she walked, she stirred the pot of her thoughts, trying to reason out why events developed this way. She could not prevent the disaster that loomed with Soporus' approach, and she believed that she and the Council had done all they could do to ensure the safety of the people who lived on the coastlines of their continent.

On the other hand, everything to do with the Believers appeared to be centered around her, which was a complication she had not expected to have upon her return to Undun City. Her reappearance only fueled their conviction that the Protectress was a part of their theology, and that the divine being they prayed to was intimate with her, making the Protectress more of a priestess than a governmental leader. The Believers continued to make requests that she summon the Goddess to cure them. Short hand-written letters came to the Protectress each day requesting help. She had started to respond to each one, then realized the activity was pointless. The letters, all read, lay on her desk in her study, unanswered.

And what of the covert comings and goings of the Prophets? She began to feel paranoid that someone was always watching her from some secret corner, even if she could not sense anyone nearby. Every little movement she caught in the corner of her eye caused her to start and worry that someone hid in the shadows. She understood, after her own hidden moments in the garden, how one could hide in plain sight. A powerful mind could simply convince the occupants of the room that he wasn't there. The trick reminded her of old stories about invisibility formulas that rendered the consumer completely transparent. The question now in her mind was why they would be sneaking around the Palace in such a manner, known only to Councilor Morton, who had no relation to the Prophets, nor did she care much for their kind. What was their motive to spy on the Proctectress' activities? What was Morton's motive to help them?

The Goddess was the largest mystery of all. It existed as a living creature of energy and had done so for a virtual millennia. That was the extent of the information she could access. The secretkeepers offered little else, for their purpose was only to ensure that an outside party knew of the existence in case of extenuating circumstances. The Prophets, who likely knew the most about the entity, simply refused to appear. Axandra had no way of sending a verbal or written request. Tyrane and his kind were completely sheltered by the Storm.

Arriving at the Palace, Axandra was greeted at the door by Miri, who informed her that Quinn waited in the Library and that she had just taken up a pot of hot tea and light snacks. Putting the lid on her thoughts, Axandra ascended the staircase, each step up matched by an increase in her excitement.

She found him at the large table in the library, his head bowed to an enormous leather bound book. His thick index finger followed along the coastline of a landmass drawn on the pages. He peered through his wire-rimmed glasses at very tiny print in the legends.

Quinn looked up as he heard her footsteps and beamed from ear-to-ear.

"You did wait," she said pleasantly, feeling her own cheeks rounding with a grin.

"Of course," he responded, rising from the tall chair, leaving the atlas behind on the table. She assumed the book contained maps of Old Earth. There were many continents colorfully divided into countries and kingdoms. It was a book that a historian like Quinn could spend hours dissecting and digesting—yet now he ignored it. Was she more interesting to him than a prized piece of history?

His round cheeks pinked slightly as he came forward. He stopped just centims away, one hand touching the corner of the hardwood table, the other hovering in front of him as though reaching out for her. He drew that hand back slightly, uncertain what to do with it in that moment.

"You came down from North Compass?" Axandra inquired, gesturing him to sit next to her where she eased down on a long bench near the wall. He joined her, sitting at a proper distance. He folded his hands on his lap.

"I'm on my way back to Southland to collect some belongings. I need a few things I left at home."

"Oh," she said with some discouragement. He hadn't come just to see her. Her mind reeled, trying to decide how this relationship was going to go. Every look he gave her spoke volumes about his attraction and infatuation for her, yet some of his words seemed to brush that away.

"But I planned on staying in Undun for several days before I go south," Quinn said, sensing her disappointment, "to see you. I-I want to—drat." He stammered, flustered by his own thoughts. The pink in his cheeks deepened to a rosier hue as his eyes dodged about the room. He cleared his throat. "I thought we might spend some time together. I want to know more about you—if that's all right?"

Axandra tried not to giggle, but the moment she opened her mouth to speak, the girlish sounds came out. "It's all right," she said with glee. She reached across the upholstery and placed her hand upon his where his thick fingers rested on the cushion. "I think that's a wonderful idea."

His shoulders dropped with relief. "I can't believe I'm so nervous," he said under his breath. "I have something I should confess to you," he began to say.

"That you asked Sara to set up a way to meet me?" she offered.

Shocked, he looked directly into her eyes. "How did you know?"

"Eryn told me the story while we were on our way back to Undun," Axandra explained. She couldn't contain her laughter completely. His expression amused her. "I'm not making fun of you," she said, hoping he wouldn't take it the wrong way.

"Well, did she tell you why I asked for Sara's help?" he pried. Instead of being mortified, he relaxed. Tension fled his body and his shoulders shook as he joined her laughter.

Breathing deeply to contain herself, she stated, " Apparently—as I was told—you saw me on the pier when I arrived in the port."

"That is true," Quinn confirmed. "I happened to be at the port coming in on a ferry from the coastal islands. I remember it was a very cloudy and windy day. The seas were rough."

"Yes, they were," Axandra recalled with him. "You saw me in that crowd?"

"It certainly was crowded, wasn't it," he agreed. "Somehow, it was as though a sunbeam shown just on you—you seemed to glow. I pushed through the crowd trying to catch up with you, but you disappeared around a corner. I must have looked for you for a half-hour, checking inns and restaurants along the way."

"I went straight in search of transportation to Undun," she inserted into his story. "I happened on the bus depot and a bus that was just about to leave for the City. I wasn't thinking of anything else."

"All so you could come here and be...who you are," he marveled, gesturing at her as a whole. "I never thought I would see you again. When I saw your face on the announcement placard in Lazzonir, I nearly fell backward! I thought there was certainly no way you would ever want to see me. I wasn't going to walk right up to the Palace and say hello. That would be crazy!"

His hands gestured as he talked, animating his story and prompting continued chuckling. It all seemed so comical, how they had come to this point, sitting together. "The Elite would have chased me away. Then I realized that Sara was here all the time, so I asked for her help. I'd never felt so drawn to anything in my entire life—other than digging up the Ancients. I had to know what the outcome would be."

"You certainly were determined," Axandra noted. "Sara seems quite the matchmaker."

"Oh, you have no idea," Quinn hinted, then skipped on. "My little plan seems to be working. Would have worked better if that Believer hadn't ruined things for me in Lazzonir."

She frowned at him. "That isn't nice to say. Many of the Believers are very ill. They can't seem to control themselves."

Clasping her hand apologetically, he sighed. "I'm sorry. I wasn't trying to be nasty."

She drew her hand away for the moment and looked across the library at nothing in particular. She didn't feel very relaxed at the moment. "It's just that I've worried so much about them. The Healers try to help them, but nothing works. And now we have to evacuate people due to the flooding. I'm letting everyone down."

"What? You're not a miracle worker, Protectress," her guest reminded emphatically. "You're a human being, just like the rest of us. You can't fix everything."

"Aren't I supposed to be more?" she asked. She looked into his gray-blue eyes, searching for that answer. Maybe he would know. She didn't know why she thought he would have the answer, but she wished he would say something.

He responded with such certainty she believed every word. "The Protectress is not supposed to be better than everyone else. She is supposed to be just like everyone else. You are the people. And humans have a lot of flaws. You've done everything you have the ability or the right to do."

Quietly, Axandra studied him and thought about what he said. He made such sense. She asked him another question. "Why are you here?"

"Here in Undun or here with you?" Quinn asked for clarification. He smiled as he said it and the tension seemed to fly out of the room. "If you mean here with you—I'm not sure, but I like it."

Smiling, she said, "I like it too."

She offered to let him freshen up for lunch, and after they ate the chef's preparations, they continued to chat and share their ideas with each other. Axandra's calendar was quite clear for the day. Since most of the world's resources were temporarily locked up in evacuating the coasts and redistributing food, most other matters were on hold. She gave him a brief tour of the Palace from the top to the bottom, showing him the Archives in the basement and the art work that graced every hallway and room. In the Library, Quinn pointed out articles about the Ancients in the collection of journals that graced the private shelves. He even found the very one that had sparked his interest in digging up the past. With boyish excitement, he read a few sentences aloud.

After all this, they took a long stroll out in the garden. The sky was draped in twilight with the suns already half hidden by the mountains. They walked in the shadow of the Palace. Around them and above them, five Elite stood watch, their vigilant eyes patrolling this maze of hedges and trees. Axandra was finally learning to ignore the presence of the guards. She wondered if Quinn even noticed them, because he seemed so at ease.

"What is your favorite color?" he asked her. He had been asking questions all day long about what she liked and what she disliked and reveled in their common interests as well as their differences of opinion. In this colorful place, it seemed a natural question to ask.

"Favorite color?" she returned with a question. "Do I have to choose just one?"

"You don't have a favorite?"

"All colors have their place," she stated matter-of-factly. "The green sea, the lavender sky, the blue butterflies, even the brown of the soil. Without each color, there wouldn't be much to see."

"Tell me which color you like the least," he switched the question.

"Black," she answered almost immediately.

"Very interesting," he mused. "And not entirely uncommon. Now, black can be the absence of all light or the presence of all color. Which is it to you?"

"To me," Axandra clarified, "black is a void. It is emptiness."

"Ah. Interesting. Let me ask another one. If you were choosing an article of clothing, what color do you prefer to wear?"

"The context makes a difference, doesn't it," she noted with a crafty smile. They strolled along very slowly, each step a deliberate stall for time. "I look best in pinks and purples."

"Interesting," he hummed, making a metal note. "The sky is purple."

"Must you read so much into everything?" she complained. "Those colors go best with my skin tone."

"Oh, everything means something, Protectress—"

"Please," she halted at the sound of her title, wrinkling her nose at the word. "You may call me Axandra."

"Everything – Axandra?" he questioned curiously, breaking his own thought. "I thought your name was Ileanne?"

She waved dismissively as she started walking again. "It is. But I—maybe I'll explain it sometime. Just not now."

"All right. Well, where was I?"

"You were about to say 'Everything means something.'" She lowered her voice in a sad attempt to impersonate him.

"Right. It does, you know. Every moment has meaning."

"So," she stretched the word coyly. "If I were to hold your hand as we walked, that would mean something?" She reached to her side and caressed his thick hand, interlacing his fingers with her own.

Those round cheeks arched more as his smile spread into that giddy grin. "We both know that would mean a great deal. And, if I were to pluck this bloom, it would mean," Quinn paused to choose a bright pink puff from the nearest bush, "that I am willing to disrupt the life cycle of this innocent plant to give you a beautiful gift."

He gave a twist and the bloom broke from the stem. He presented the sparkler puff to her with a slight bow.

"A gift that will wilt and fade within hours," she said, examining the puff with her nose and eyes. The perfume smelled musky, a subtle scent. The flower was composed of hundreds of tiny, slender tubes. The end of each flared open like the bell of a trumpet and bore a fringe of hair-like wisps.

"Now you read too much," he complained, squeezing her hand.

Stopping on the path, they turned to each other, face-to-face, both pairs of hands entwined.

"What does this mean?" Axandra asked him. The sunslight was almost gone. Each of their faces glowed copper in the light reflected off the high–floating clouds.

"This means that I am being very serious," Quinn told her. "I would like to see you again tomorrow. Will you extend me the invitation?"

"You don't have to leave," she offered in a yearning whisper. Her body tingled and her heart pounded so heavily against her breast she felt certain he could feel the sensation through his skin.

"With so many eyes watching, that may not be the proper thing to do tonight," he whispered back. His voice dripped with anticipation.

Forget about them, she begged in her thoughts.

He heard her. "I can't forget who I'm with right now. I will come back tomorrow." He started to loosen his grip.

She held fast. "At least kiss me?" she begged sweetly.

He responded without delay by pressing his thin lips warmly and firmly on hers, his breath against her cheek. She leaned into him.

Yet he drew away. "I-I have to go." His voice cracked in his throat.

"But we haven't had dinner," she offered, her voice ripe with disappointment.

"Dinner," he chuckled feebly, somewhat out of breath as he increased the distance between them, "will only lead to me staying with you."

"I know," she admitted boldly. "Don't you understand? Come inside. Have dinner. Then we will let what happens happen."

"Axandra—" he sighed. He fought the battle in his brain. Stay out of a desire for pleasure, regardless of what talk would come out the next day, or protect his respect for her and who she was. Strangely, the logical side prevailed in the fight.

She let go of his hands at that moment and stepped back. "Oh, Quinn. I'm sorry. I shouldn't push you."

"I want to—oh, how I want to stay tonight!" He emphasized his words with his hands clasped tightly together, reigned in close to his chest. "But you are the Protectress—the matriarch of the people. I have to respect that. I have to respect you to respect myself with you." *I don't want to wreck the whole thing just yet,* he thought loudly, though she was certain he didn't mean for her to hear his thought.

"I understand. I will see you tomorrow morning?"

"Afternoon," he designated. "I like to hike in the foothills in the mornings. I promised some friends I'd hike with them."

"That sounds quite invigorating." She too held her hands tightly together, resisting the urge to touch him again.

"Yes, it is. 'Til tomorrow." He bowed and strode away quite quickly.

Axandra looked skyward to the emerging stars and breathed in the enjoyment.

Chapter 21

Places

4th Octember, 307

Overnight, a string of storms raged to the southeast. Strong winds damaged villages in their path. Heavy rains brought flooding to small streams and rivers. In some places, hail as large as frost apples plummeted to the ground.

The Protectress was awakened in the wee hours of the morning by one of her Elite, Diane, with news of villages in trouble. Bursts of swirling wind blew wood-framed houses off of their foundations. More than half of a village known as Beeterton lay completely destroyed.

Knowing help was in short supply due to the sudden evacuations, Axandra left with the first group of Assistors. Ignoring Ty's protests, she rode on a bus with fourteen others. While the usual Assistors, those who volunteered regularly for such duties, tried to catch some sleep curled up on the soft seats, Axandra sat awake at the front of the bus. Her eyes followed the headlights cutting a path along a rain-washed road. Once, the bus got stuck in a new wash out. Everyone unloaded while they pushed the vehicle out onto harder ground.

Standing back a safe distance from the rocking machine, Axandra huddled inside her wool sweater and watched Soporus setting in the west, silhouetting the mountain peaks against her gray face. The planet loomed larger now, appearing to be the same size as the red moon, Zanita, two thumbs across at arm's length. In just three weeks, Soporus would dominate the sky.

As the Sister's brightness faded to the west, Axandra witnessed a cascade of meteors streak across the vista. The glowing fragments accompanied the Passing, an event the astronomers listed in their report. Soporus orbited the suns surrounded by a cloud of debris, probably remnants from the impact that robbed the planet of its atmosphere. The fragments rained down each imminent day of the Passing.

By the break of day, the Assistors reached Beeterton and lay their eyes upon the devastation. Splintered wood and broken stone lay strewn across the flat ground. Trees stood stripped bare of their leaves.

The townsfolk clustered in what used to be the town square. Each face looked lost and helpless. Children clung to their parents. Many people held hands with someone nearby, clinging to anything they had left. They stared at the chaos around them.

Surveying the village as she stepped off the bus, Axandra counted the homes still standing. Of some thirty buildings that formed the village, only five stone constructions remained, randomly placed about the village. Even these exhibited damaged, their windows broken and roof tiles missing.

The Assistors immediately began to unload food, water and supplies. The Protectress went straight to the people. The Principal met her just outside the loose circle of townsfolk. The woman's long face contorted between grief and gratefulness as she greeted her leader.

"Protectress! Your Honor, thank you for coming. We can't believe you are here in person." The woman was near tears as she spoke. "You can't believe what happened here." She led Axandra toward a single tent to one side of the square. The tent would soon become the coordinating point for the clean-up effort.

"Bursts came with the storms," the Principal began to explain. "You can see the damage. Four perished—an entire family was killed when their house collapsed. The fourth was swept up by the wind and found beneath that large tree." She pointed to a tremendous trunk that lay diagonally across a portion of the food silo. The body had already been removed, probably to one of the houses for cremation preparations.

"We grieve with you for your losses," the Protectress said tenderly. From her pocket, she offered a handkerchief. Tears streamed down the woman's cheeks. "How many are injured?"

"Four dozen. Scrapes and bruises. No one seriously, thank goodness. Most hurried to stronger houses or basements to take shelter. But we only have a few basements." The principal dabbed at her eyes and then wrung her hands as she looked around her village. "We rarely get storms like this."

"We will have everything right again soon," the Protectress promised, offering her words with sincerity to help calm the woman.

From here, Axandra moved among the other residents, helping pass out water and rations. She visited with nearly everyone, from the oldest to the youngest. The youngest was an infant just hours old. The mother went into labor due to the stress of the disaster and now she had a baby girl. Axandra enjoyed holding the baby for a few minutes. The parents insisted, hoping to bring luck to the child through the Protectress' purported mystic touch. She paid them the honor, though not certain what luck she would bring.

As Axandra visited, she felt the despair around her begin to lift. The faces of the victims changed from sadness to hope.

Soon everyone helped in the clean-up. Donning long pants, a sleeveless shirt and wide-brimmed hat, Axandra put her arm-power to the cause. The first task consisted of setting up rows of tents. A large tent was erected and furnished with tables to give a sheltered place to gather out of the sun and wind. It provided a place to eat, to receive healing treatment and to just congregate.

Smaller tents offered places to sleep. Many of the victims would live in these tents until they could organize more suitable, even if temporary, accommodations. More of these tents would house the Assistors as long as needed.

After this Axandra moved on to sorting piles of debris that used to be buildings, while others went to inspect grain fields and collect any usable food. The debris was sifted into piles of salvage for the rebuilding and piles of recycling, soon to be collected by electric-powered drays. Other Assistors joined her at her pile, lifting and hauling. They worked for hours. The Assistors chatted with each other amiably, tempering the laborious work with songs and jokes. Axandra did not join them in conversation. Finding her offish, the workers moved to different areas of the town. Eventually she worked this block alone.

On two carts, she sorted terracotta roof tiles. Whole tiles she placed on one cart to be moved aside with the reclaimed materials. Broken tiles went into a second cart. Soon the fragments would be dumped into a recycling bin, broken up and reprocessed into new tiles, eventually making their way back here for the new houses.

About mid-afternoon, another busload of Assistors arrived. She glanced over at the bus briefly when she heard the tires crunch dirt and debris. The newcomers began to unload before the vehicle reached a full stop. People shouted greetings across the camp.

Refocusing on her task, Axandra thought of nothing. She emptied her mind of everything except the dwindling pile in front of her and the warm suns bronzing her skin. The work was back-breaking. She began to feel sore in muscles she hadn't known existed. Still she kept working.

Stepping into the midst of a collapsed room, she bent to lift a wooden stick of furniture with her gloved hands, only to find it heavier than she expected. Struggling, she tugged multiple times to work it free.

A dual shadow came from behind her, falling across her back and arms. Her skin suddenly felt cooler with the suns blocked.

"Let me help you with that," said a man. He joined her in lifting and carrying the piece to another cart.

"Thank you," Axandra said, turning to her assistant. She felt stunned to find Quinn standing there. "You? What are you doing here?"

"Helping my fellow humans," Quinn boasted. "I heard more help was needed here, so I hopped on the next bus. Dear, you look exhausted. You need to take a break."

Knowing what he'd say next, Axandra shook her head and turned back to her pile to keep working. "I can't right now," she said firmly. "There's too much to do." She hoisted another whole tile onto her cart, knowing that if she stopped moving, she would feel the need to sit and then she might not get up again.

Quinn's arrival threw a stone into the still surface of her mind and the ripples churned up the worries she suppressed with physical labor. She stood still next to the cart, staring at her gloved hands. Quinn's footsteps crunched over the rubble as he approached behind her.

"Are you all right?" he asked in a whisper.

Her body began to tremble. "No," she rasped, her voice choked by the tightness in her throat. She could not fight the grimace that contorted her mouth and eyes, nor could she stop the hot tears that streamed down her cheeks. Hiding beneath her hat, she didn't want anyone to see. Her purpose was to give them hope and assurance.

"Let's take a little walk," Quinn coaxed, his hands on her shoulders to steer her away from the active part of the ruined village. One of the Elite began to follow them. The two guards were the only ones anywhere near her as she worked. Everyone else left her alone.

"Do you mind, fella?" Quinn confronted the guard.

"Ben, it's all right," Axandra said in a gravelly voice, signally the guard to back off.

"Madam, Ty gave us strict orders—"

"I have had enough of Ty Narone and his orders!" she hissed, glaring up at Ben with burning, tear-filled eyes. "Leave me alone!" Turning on her heel, she hurried away from both of them at a half-run, stopping only when shielded from the villagers by the broad trunk of a naked tree. Above her the stripped branches hung broken and twisted, exposing the bright taupe of wounded wood. She leaned against the rough bark and covered her face.

Quinn's footsteps followed. At the moment, he was the only person she wanted to see.

Axandra took off her woven hat and looked up at him from her seat on the gnarled roots of the tree. He crouched down next to her and quietly put an arm around her shoulders. He sat there patiently, saying nothing but, just by way of his presence, offering to listen.

When she could control her voice again, she began. "I couldn't sleep the entire way here," she said. She spoke softly, even though she sensed no one else around. "I kept going over things in my head, worrying about how to take care of these people on top of everything else. Now we've lost their homes and most of their food. Where are they going to go? When can we re-build this? I don't know these things. I can hear those questions in their minds and they keep looking at me to give them some indication. But I can't." Talking calmed her breathing and the tears stopped flowing. Her eyes stung with fatigue. The muscles in her arms and legs loosened up, becoming more like jelly than muscles. Every part of her ached. "All I can give them is my labor."

"Axandra," Quinn said, speaking her name as though the sound were a treasure to him, a secret only he could speak. He patted her bent knee. "Do you see all of these people? Every one of them will do whatever is in their power to put everything right again. And they will work until it's finished. And each of them knows that they have a limit to what they can give. Each one has a family to care for at home. Some will get tired of lifting and hauling. Others will come to replace them. They do this because they know that alone, one person can't do everything. Only together can things be accomplished. You— the embodiment of everything our people believe in—you have forgotten this. You try to do everything yourself and you never ask for help."

"I don't have anyone to ask," she lamented. "I'm alone."

He chuckled at her expense. "It seems to me that there are about six hundred thousand people on this planet. Surely one of them can be helpful."

"Only you." Hearing her own words, she went rigid with surprise. She hadn't expected to say those two words together and mean it the way it sounded. She had just admitted something that seemed very profound to her own soul.

When she was with Quinn, she didn't feel alone.

"Well, like I said," Quinn responded as though the matter was settled. "I guess I'm right, then. There is one."

An awkward moment of silence passed between them.

"So, can I help you over to the baths to get cleaned up?" he asked, wiggling his eyebrows at her.

"If I weren't so exhausted, I'd think you were being very forward."

"I am being forward," Quinn admitted, getting to his feet with a grunt. "But don't worry about any indiscretions. Frankly, you stink right now."

The reaction he got from her was laughter. The sound began as a small chuckle. Like a leak in the dam, the chuckles broke through into all out guffaws, a deep therapeutic gut-busting that went on for several minutes. He couldn't help but join in and together they released frustrations and worries. At last, when they just couldn't laugh anymore, she leaned into his arms and sighed.

+++

7th Octember

After three days, Quinn decided that it was time for him to finish his intended trip. With the new evacuation orders, he decided he would ready his house for refugees of the tides.

"I really think I should let someone else have the place," he said over their last meal together. "There's a young couple that just got married last month. They are on the waiting list for the next available house. I should give it to them. I'm hardly ever there anyway."

"Where will you call home?" Axandra asked, somewhat distressed about anyone cutting their ties to a place. She had done so twice. First when she ran away, and secondly when she left Gammerton so abruptly. She regretted the cuts now more than she ever expected to.

"My mother lives in North Compass," Quinn told her reassuringly. "That's my true home anyway, where I was born and where I grew up."

A large group gathered together for dinner this evening, all collected under the large tent. The wind blew in from the north, bringing in the arctic chill reminiscent of winter. When the suns went down, the chill bit at the skin.

"That's very generous of you," she praised half-heartedly.

"You don't approve?" he pried.

"No, I don't," Axandra answered honestly. "Everyone should have a place to retreat to, somewhere to 'hang your hat,' as they say."

"I hang my hat wherever I find a hook," Quinn retorted. "I don't feel at home when I'm in Lazzonir unless my friends are visiting. I travel all over. I have friends in many places. To me, it's the people, not the place."

After they ate their meal, Quinn tapped on Axandra's shoulder and they sneaked out of the tent quietly, escaping the eyes of almost everyone except a small girl who watched the Protectress since dinner started. Axandra flashed the girl a playful smile. In turn, the girl smiled, giggled, and shyly hid her face in a blanket.

Outside, Soporus soared in the east. She followed the same path as the suns, rising as Bona Dea turned to her, setting as their world faced away.

The two moons marked the half-way point of the evening sky, close together in their orbits this month. The Milky Way spilled across the southern portion of the sky and dribbled below the southeastern horizon.

She wondered for a moment how the Milky Way looked from Old Earth, then remembered the image of the dirty sky. Icky smog shrouded the atmosphere. Those skies were blind to the stars.

Axandra and Quinn walked hand-in-hand through the village—if it could be called such anymore. Already, much had been cleared away. The main avenue, paved in gray brick, was clear enough to bring in larger carts to haul away more in a single load. Much still needed to be removed. She expected clearing all of the wreckage would take weeks, not to even think about rebuilding. Tomorrow, several of the families would be moved to Undun until their homes were rebuilt.

"Will you be going back tomorrow?" Quinn asked, expecting that she would go with those families.

A chilly blast blew across the open plain around them. She pulled the collar of her sweater up over her neck.

"No. I'm going to stay a few more days. I just want—" She cleared her throat to cease stumbling over her words. "Just a few more days."

"After I'm finished with my house, I'll come back to Undun," he told her. "In a week or so. I want to help as much as I can in Lazzonir. She's almost here, you know." He pointed toward the sky, in the direction of the cratered face of Soporus.

She nodded in understanding. Hidden down the street, away from scrutiny, they stopped.

Quinn's eyes studied Axandra's face. He brushed his fingers across her cheek and leaned close to kiss her lips. The chill left her body. Closing her eyes, she shut out the destruction around them and wished for the moment to last. His touch felt tender but hungry. He wanted to be alone with her somewhere, in a place where they could enjoy each other.

The place wasn't here. They both understood that. When they parted, almost panting, they held onto each other tightly in the dark. She listened to his heart beating in his chest and sighed.

"A week," she bemoaned.

"It will go by quickly," he promised.

"When you come to Undun, will you stay with me?" she invited. She peered at him with bewitching eyes, hoping to make it difficult to say no.

"Yes," he committed. He held her face between his hands, his fingers in her curls.

"The, um, the city players are planning a production on the twenty-first," she told him. "Perhaps we could attend together."

"A play?" Every word between them was spoken to keep them in the present, though each of them imagined what time would be like when they could be completely alone together.

"Yes. The Council agreed that a play could be the perfect entertainment to help people feel normal again. Everyone is growing very weary of the compounding disasters."

Nodding, he agreed that he would see the play with her.

"It's late," he said finally. "We should turn in. I leave early."

She didn't want to let go of him. "I know. Just a few more minutes. I just want to be near you."

He held on tightly, looking up at the stars in the clear sky.

"Shooting stars," he marveled suddenly.

She raised her eyes and saw the streaks of light. Some were short and dim. Others stretched in long slow streams.

"Pieces of Soporus," she explained. "The astronomers tell us by the time she passes us, we'll see hundreds of meteors per hour."

"That will be a brilliant sight," Quinn dreamed. "We'll have to watch."

Reluctantly, she loosened her grip on him. "I should let you go."

"Walk me 'home'?"

It was too tempting. "I'm going to stay up a little longer."

"You shouldn't be out here alone," he lectured. He had spent too many days with the guards around.

"Ben isn't far," Axandra assured him, gesturing with her head toward a nearby pile that was once the public house.

"That sneaky devil."

"He's just doing his job," she defended.

"He does it very well. Goodnight, Axandra."

"Goodnight," she wished. She watched him walk away, etching his stride into her memory.

After Quinn had gone, Ben appeared from hiding and came within a suitable distance of his charge. He spoke first, which was unusual.

"I apologize for the intrusion, Your Honor. But I do take your protection very seriously."

Axandra continued to stare out at the sky, watching the meteors and wondering just for a moment why they were falling so close to the mountains in the west. Out on the plain, she could hear the yipping of the packhounds as they searched for prey. The animals sounded some distance away.

"I know you do," she acknowledged. She tucked her hands into the pockets of her sweater. "I apologize for the other day. I put you in a very difficult position. I know Ty took you off duty because of what happened in the garden."

"The Commander did not remove me from my duties, Madam," Ben explained.

Struck with confusion, she turned to him.

"I asked to be relieved. I failed in my duty that day. It was my mistake that my weapon was not charged. That should never happen, and you were placed in grave danger because of it." As Ben spoke, he stared straight ahead, avoiding direct eye contact. He stood at parade rest, his arms hooked behind his back.

"I wasn't aware of that. I assumed the Commander disciplined you."

"He actually commended me. Since he didn't understand what actually happened, he believed I'd done something to save you."

"Oh." The simple sound gave indication of her surprise at the outcome.

Ben looked at her quite seriously. "If I may ask, Madam, what did happen?"

She dropped her eyes to the dark ground where she scraped the dusty surface with the toe of her shoe. What could she tell him? What did he remember? Should she lie?

She had been raised to practice telling the truth. And despite the over-reaching lie that was her life, Axandra believed in keeping all other truths visible. Besides, among telepaths and empaths, telling lies was usually detectable anyway and therefore pointless. Nevertheless, people still tried to get away with half-truths and deceptions.

"Ben," Axandra began, choosing her words carefully. "Something very rare happened that day, something instinctual and defensive." She watched his face, gauging his reaction. He kept his expression impassive. "You were going to jump in front of that beast to stop it or stall it. I couldn't let you lose your life if I had the power to protect it. The power came to me because I needed it to."

"You saved both of us," Ben said gratefully. "Thank you, Protectress, both for saving my life and for being honest with me. I would not be able to serve you if I did not respect you."

"Those words mean a great deal to me. Thank you."

Ben continued to stand there, guarding against anything else unexpected.

The hour grew later, and the air cooler.

Axandra turned to head back to the tents. "It's time to turn in," she said aloud.

Ben followed diligently.

Chapter 22

Relationships

9th Octember, 307

Thankful to be home again, Axandra walked into the front doors of the Palace with her travel pack hanging from her shoulder and her hat in hand. She intended to go straight upstairs for a much needed bath and a nap to relieve her exhaustion.

Lynn stepped into her path. The young woman, a member of the housekeeping staff, usually worked at Morton's bidding. The two seemed to share the same opinions of the world and of the Protectress. And as she did with Morton, Axandra found the woman's presence unpleasant and distracting.

"Councilor Morton requests to see you in her office," Lynn demanded, standing puffed up like a prairie cock.

Axandra quickly stepped to the side, deciding not to halt her purposeful pace. "Inform the Head of Council that I will be happy to speak with her tomorrow."

The girl slipped in front of her again, blocking the stairs. With a nasty sneer Lynn insisted, "It is a matter of some urgency, Your Honor. She requests that you speak with her immediately."

Matters always seemed urgent when Morton called for her. Though she suspected duplicity, Axandra did not intend to be accused of selfishness if a true emergency existed. "Very well.

Take my bag to my rooms." She dropped the bag heavily on the stone floor and shoved her hat into the woman's chapped hands. Spinning around, Axandra marched back toward the Council wing and into the office hallway that ran along the East side of the Council Chamber.

Morton's door hung wide open when she arrived. The Councilor sat behind her desk studying a sheaf of papers and marking notes with a pen.

"Councilor, I didn't expect you to return from your break so soon," Axandra commented, foregoing any formal greeting. "What do you wish to discuss?"

"Please close the door," Nancy instructed, her eyes remaining on her papers. The tone of her voice signaled displeasure.

After swinging shut the ornate door, Axandra stood in place before the desk, waiting to be properly acknowledged.

Morton did not rise from her seat or look at her guest. Instead, she wet her finger with the tip of her tongue and turned a page of the collection in front of her. "I understand that you have taken up a relationship with a gentleman from Lazzonir. One Quinn Elgar?"

Inhaling deeply, Axandra composed the instant feeling of discomfort that washed through her. She predicted that this conversation would aggravate her, and she vowed to herself at that moment that she would not lose her temper in this room. Such a lapse would only fuel Morton's contempt for her. "With all due respect, Councilor, I do not believe that my personal affairs are any concern of the Council. Now, I was sent in here under the guise that you had an urgent matter—"

"That is the urgent matter!" Morton exclaimed as though the fact was obvious. She rose at last and stood with her hands clasped behind her back, her posture confrontational, chest out, chin up.

"Then I would appreciate it if you would show me the respect to which I am entitled before you begin such a discussion." Axandra hardened her own posture, evading intimidation.

"Respect to which you are entitled, of course." Nancy forced a bow.

Axandra grew more aggravated by the Councilor's actions, but forced down her urge to shout about it. "You seem to harbor some negative feelings toward Mr. Elgar."

"I have met Mr. Elgar before, and I am informing you that he cannot be trusted."

Brow wrinkled, Axandra peered back at the Councilor's dour expression. The elder woman clearly intended to dissolve the romantic relationship. Would Morton go so far as to embellish a few tales to slander Quinn's reputation? Touching the Councilor's mind, Axandra found that the details about to be revealed were true, at least from Morton's perspective.

"Please elaborate," Axandra prompted.

Morton took a few steps forward, forcing a condescending smile on her wrinkled lips. "Your Honor, you are in a position that people—well, people want to get close to you. You can't give yourself away too quickly."

Facing the Councilor, Axandra set her jaw. "What do you want me to know?"

Nancy motioned for her to sit on the nearby sofa, but Axandra refused. The moment this conversation ended, she planned on racing out the door.

"Very well, I will tell you what I know. About twelve years ago, Quinn Elgar was a Believer, and a quite outspoken one." Morton began.

The words intrigued Axandra, especially if they were to be believed. Morton continued the tale, explaining that the younger Quinn was determined to prove that the Goddess actually resided in the Protectress, not just that a link existed between the two, which was the typical teaching of the cult. For months, he harassed the Palace staff and the Council members. He also attempted to contact the Protectress directly. He was caught trespassing in restricted areas of the Palace several times and in the Residence once.

"He is only wooing you to finally prove his theory—he wants access to the Goddess, like the other Believers," Morton warned.

"Twelve years is a very long time, Councilor," Axandra sighed disappointedly. "The Quinn Elgar I've come to know is sincere, honest and has only one passion—history. He's given no reason for me to believe otherwise. Good day." Without waiting for any further accusations or explanations, she exited the room, walking with her shoulders back, chest out and chin high, her best imitation of a woman with no doubts.

Unfortunately, Morton succeeded in sowing a seed of doubt in Axandra's thoughts. After spending four days very close to Quinn, sharing their stories and their dreams, not once had he mentioned having belonged to the Believers. And the topics of religion and spirituality came up many times over the course of their conversations, so he certainly had the opportunity. He offered insight into the creeds of the faith, explaining for her why they refused healing aid from non-believers. He also revealed that they refused to share their minds with anyone outside their own sects. Believing themselves to be a chosen group of people, they did not wish to taint their thoughts with those of other religions or secularists. Accepting sin into their minds would cast them out of the Goddess's good graces.

Why would he not mention a period that greatly impacted his life?

Morton was not the only current inhabitant regularly availing the Palace twelve years ago. Marta, the groundskeeper, had been employed here for the last fifteen years, she'd been told. Marta was the most senior member in service at the establishment.

Axandra summoned Miri in the manner to which she had become accustomed, sending out a brief emanation of her need for the aide. Miri always appeared promptly, usually bringing with her whatever her mistress desired. This time, Miri came with Marta in tow, bringing the elder woman into the study. She also brought tea service and a snack of fresh fruit cut served in very small cups, barely large enough to hold one quarter of a frost apple.

The Protectress noticed daily that her portions seemed slightly larger than anyone else's. And sometimes she received a double ration. She had an inkling of where the extra came from. Miri seemed to have lost some weight in recent weeks. The loss showed most noticeably in her face. The young woman's cheek-bones sharpened beneath her pink skin

Unfortunately, Axandra lost weight as well, most noticeably in the way her clothes hung loosely on her frame and her cheeks appeared sunken. She started slimming when she left the islands. She didn't eat as much as she used to. Stress stole her appetite and her sleep.

"You asked to see me, Your Honor?" Marta inquired, standing near the doorway after she entered.

"Yes, Marta. Thank you for coming," Axandra greeted with a friendly smile. She motioned for the gray-haired woman to have a seat in one of the comfortable chairs grouped around an elaborately carved tea table, while she moved to sit in another. "How are the garden plants holding up without the usual rain? Everything still looks very green."

"Oh, I'm allowed a ration of water to provide 'em, those thatin need the moisture," Marta said gratefully, her speech thick with an accent Axandra recognized from the south central forest lands. "Most of th'plants don't need much. They just aren't flow'rin like they usually do. They're hardy. They'll survive."

"I'm glad to hear that. Marta, how long have you been at the Palace?"

The woman's faded blue eyes circled around to the ceiling as she mentally counted the cycles. "Oh, I'd say 'bout sixteen an' a half years, Mad'm. Long enough. Not that I'm ready t'take my leave. Serving this place's been my calling." Axandra accepted the tea Miri handed her and reached out to the tray to add sugar. Marta made herself comfortable, sinking into the cushion of the chair.

Axandra thanked her aide and dismissed Miri from the study, asking that the aide run her a warm bath so that she could clean up after her long trip. The aide excused herself and exited through a second doorway directly into the great room.

"I was wondering about something that I think took place about twelve years ago. With everything that's going on with the Believers, someone mentioned that one tried to come into the Palace—"

"Oh, you're talkin' 'bout the one that sneaked up here to the Res'dence. Oh-ho, that young man was a rascal. It'n started one day when he showed up in the kitchen—came in through the side door down by the recyclin' an' compost bins," Marta recounted, one hand shaking loosely in the air as she spoke. That hand pointed in different directions as the story continued, pointing out where each instance took place. "He kept rantin' about the Goddess an' the Protectress and ev'ry few days, the Elite'd catch him somewhere else in the Palace. Once upstairs in the Staff quarters, another down in the basement near the bunker. Finally they caught him in this study, prowling around. He was given no uncertain terms that he was not to show up here again. And he ne'er did."

"Do you know his name?"

She shook her head, her lips pursed in a thoughtful frown. "No. Can't say I ever heard his name. Cute fella though. Little young for me. He couldn't been more 'n nineteen or twen'y then. Don't know if he ever found what he was lookin' for, but he ne'er came back. Who told you 'bout that? With all the heck you've been through, who'd want to worry you with old stories."

Axandra said nothing in reply to the question. "Thank you, Marta. I was just curious about the story. It seemed like a stretch of someone's imagination, but I think you've filled in the gaps."

"Glad I could help. Thank you for the tea. Ya'know," Marta began to comment, "Ya're a lot like your mother. She always did like to hear the scuttlebutt from the lips of the staff, rather'n those stodgy Councilors. Knew she'd get the story straight from us. Knew we're the real eyes and ears of this place. Well, I'll let you get to that bath. And you can have my fruit. You look like you've lost three kilos just this week."

"I worked very hard in Beeterton," Axandra justified, standing with Marta out of respect. "Have a good afternoon."

"Same t'you, Your Honor." Marta escaped through the main door, slipping on her work gloves as she walked away. She would go straight back to her chores.

Steam billowed from the bathtub, filling the bathroom with the aroma of herbs and oils in which to soak. As she undressed to slip into the long tub, she asked Miri how quickly she could send a letter to North Compass.

"I would like to write to Councilor Sunsun," Axandra explained.

"I believe we could get it there by tomorrow," Miri offered. "But isn't Mr. Elgar in Lazzonir?"

"The letter isn't for him. I know I'll see him on the twenty-first."

"I'll check on you in twenty minutes," the aide advised, "just in case you fall asleep."

Axandra agreed that was a distinct possibility. The heat mixed with her fatigue sedated her mind and body. A bath had never felt so luxurious.

+++

"You did what!?" Miri shouted at Lynn, her face instantly red with anger. "Why you wretched, little… toad! The Protectress' personal life is no business of the Council, and you had no right to inform anyone of their relationship."

Lynn pushed her light brown hair behind her ear. She actually smiled at Miri's agitation. "I see it as my duty to inform the Head of Council about anything suspicious that's going on in the Palace, personal to the Protectress or not. Our Esteemed leader should put more priority in improving her precarious reputation."

"Precarious—" Miri stuttered. "Our Protectress is loved by everyone—"

"Not everyone. You blind fool." Lynn derided. "She's got you so wrapped up in her masquerade of the helpless, uneducated stranger that you don't see what she really is, a conniving harpy." Turning, Lynn started for the door of the laundry room, taking her basket of linens in her hands.

"I don't know what lies Morton's been feeding you, but you are the one who's blind," Miri cried after her. She found herself crying, disgusted that Lynn would take such an attitude about the Esteemed.

Ever since Ms. Korte's arrival, Morton mongered in rumors and half-truths, trying anything to discredit the woman who claimed to be the Heir. The councilor had been sorely disappointed when all of the evidence proved the Heir's claim. Forced to declare Axandra Korte the Protectress, Morton became insufferable in her disdain. Miri could hardly bear to face the Head of Council without visibly cringing. The negative emanations buffeted her mind like a storm-fed wind.

Having spent so much time close to the Protectress, guiding her in day-to-day activities, traveling with her on those long roads, listening to her lilting voice touched with an accent spoken by those of the sea-side, Miri felt nothing for the woman but admiration and love. Even the brief touches of mind-to-mind, when the Protectress summoned her assistance, gave insight into the woman who was queen. Those thoughts projected worry for the people and concern that she acted appropriately. Whenever the Matriarch spoke, she did so honestly. She asked questions when she needed information. She requested those things she needed to keep her life simple.

And there was always that struggle with the thing that lived inside her, as Elora had struggled before her. No one suspected that the lowly aide knew the secret of the Protectresship. No one had any inkling of how many times she brushed the presence and how Elora, ill in her dementia, spoke to her plainly about the creature. The Protectress-Past prayed for the thing to die with her. Even then, Elora knew that the creature's death was impossible, and so Miri knew it, too. The creature would seek out the Heir if she were alive and bring her back here. Elora always believed that her daughter lived, and even regretted the fact at times, knowing the life her daughter was destined to suffer.

Fleeing the laundry room, Miri escaped outside the Palace through a doorway at the end of the narrow service hall. Outside, she crouched behind a tree by the garden wall and hid with her tears. She came to this place when she needed a moment alone. Here, away from everyone, she could think. And right now she needed to think. She thought of Elora, her frail, feeble body bedridden those last months. She thought of the woman's face, cracking with dryness as she spoke of her daughter, wishing she could see that little girl as a woman.

Thinking of Elora reminded Miri of something she had seen in that old woman's mind. She wanted to remember those thoughts now, though she had not given it much consideration before. In her dying days, the woman's mind was a tumult of stray memories and feelings, bits and pieces of which stuck now in Miri's mind. She kept them like a shrine to the woman who, other than Miri, had died alone.

A man's face caused Elora to feel hopeful, not the face of her late husband nor of anyone that Miri had ever met. The man was a Prophet. She could tell by his pasty skin tone and those all-seeing eyes. He had a round face and a hawk-like nose. His brown hair lay in short waves over his scalp. She committed this face to her memory, for he suddenly seemed important. Frustrated, Miri found that she could not remember the words that accompanied the image, only the feeling, that sense that he alone could help her.

Miri, a fairly adept telepath herself, let her mind float to that of her mistress, intending to take a small peek. She found the Protectress fast asleep, her mind blank. She wasn't even dreaming.

Hearing footsteps nearby, she quickly straightened up and pressed her tunic with her hands. She wiped the tears away from her eyes. Peeking around the tree, she found Mikel walking toward the tree. He served as an Elite, a rather young recruit. He joined the force just a month before the Heir arrived. In his dark gray uniform, he looked quite handsome and appeared older than he actually was. He searched for Miri.

"Miri, are you all right?" Mikel asked softly when he came near the tree. She stayed hidden behind the thick trunk.

"Yes," she replied, cringing when her voice cracked.

He removed his cap. His chestnut hair lay flat and limp underneath as a result of a arduous day of service and training. The breeze caught a few strands and lifted them. They stuck there, pointing diagonally into the air.

"I heard you yelling at Lynn. You ran out so fast—I just wanted to check on you," he told her awkwardly.

Wiping her face again, Miri made certain her cheeks felt dry, though she couldn't do anything to tame the redness that stung her eyes. She revealed herself, carefully folding her arms behind her back. "You heard that? I wonder who else did," Miri probed.

She felt embarrassed for losing her temper, an unbecoming lapse for the Protectress' personal aide.

"Just about the entire Kitchen," Mikel said, then realized he should have kept his mouth shut. Miri's eyes shot to the ground, disheartened. He whispered to her, "Lots of people agree with you. Morton's been acting crazy these last few months. Lynn is about the only one that can stand her."

Looking up at her companion, she raised her eyebrows hopefully. "Is that true?"

"I would never mislead you," he promised.

Smiling, she nodded, accepting his words.

Chapter 23

Desperation

19th October, 307

More questions surfaced than answers when the subject came to the Prophets and their connection to the Goddess. What was their connection? Why did they protect the secret of the creature? Was there some hidden purpose to allowing it to, or even helping it to survive all these centuries?

In her studies of the Official Archives, Axandra only found references to the Goddess in connection to ceremonies or encounters with the Believers.

Having lived among the Prophets, she knew a few facts about their kind. They were the descendants of the Journeyers on the ship called Prophet. The independent generation ship joined the fleet of twelve on the trek to claim this world. On Earth, these people consisted of a collection of the most gifted telepaths known. Hiding from the Normals, they formed a secret community to keep them safe and allow them to develop their talents unhindered. Arriving in this system, they secluded themselves away from those less advanced.

After the first few years of strife, the Four Regions nearly ignited in civil war. To prevent destruction, the Prophets emerged from the storm and gave Amelia Saugray the first title of Protectress, bestowing upon her the ability and authority to speak for the entirety of the people. A common emblem united the people as one.

Since then, the Prophets only showed themselves when the time came to train the Heir or at the installation of the new Protectress. The vast majority of citizens did not even give them much thought. Some viewed the Prophets as only a legend, a story to explain how the Protectresship came to be. Most of the less-gifted never saw a living Prophet.

The best source of answers to the questions would be the Goddess, but Axandra kept the creature caged in her mind, protecting herself and others from its dangerous actions. The Goddess hissed and sulked in her cage. Since the creature no longer acted as an ally, Axandra planned on keeping it locked away and powerless.

The second best source would be the Prophets, but they remained secluded in their stormy fortress. For a normal person, passage through the ravages of the Storm was impossible. The deadly barrier afforded the separatists impenetrable protection.

There was a secret to getting to the Haven safely. When she had been taken through, young Ileanne witnessed an incredible display—the winds of the storm parted with the wave of a hand, giving them a safe passage straight into the Haven. The passage closed behind them as soon as they traveled through.

The trick would be discovering how to summon the passage to appear. She had actually seen the portal twice, once in and once out. She didn't have any idea how the passage appeared the second time. She wished for the passage to help her escape, and the opening appeared moments later. Not wasting time to wonder how, she took off through the safe tunnel.

Would it be that easy to get back in?

First she would have to elude the watchful eyes of her Elite and her aide, for they would never allow her to place herself in such danger. If she wished to make a surprise visit to the Prophets, a great deal of planning was required just to make it outside of the city.

Axandra gave this idea serious consideration and formed some rough plans in her mind while she made notes of her questions on paper. After Soporus passed and the flooding crisis dealt with, she would make an attempt to reach the Prophets.

On her calendar, Axandra requested time to visit those in the city ailing from the still incurable illness. Many Believers remained afflicted but alive, saved from perishing by the adept skills of the Healers. By now, most of those Believers first sickened had passed from this existence. Only a handful clung to life. She intended to find out why these few managed to carry on.

Today, she visited Sue Randas, a citizen bedridden due to her still unknown ailment. She suffered hunger, dehydration and fatigue.

The ailing woman lay in her bed in a room of muted light—the suns deflected through lace curtains. In the outer room, devout Believers gathered together and sang.

Oh Goddess and our Protector
Bring us peace within
To ourselves and those around us.
We are here gathering
To ask for your embraces.
Shine light upon our faces.
Heal our sick and wounded
So they may with us be.

The voices swelled in mistuned harmony and gave an eerie atmosphere to the small home. When the hymn finished, the group began to utter soft prayers. To Axandra, the prayers sounded like incoherent mutterings.

Healer Gage explained that Sue was forty-four years old. Beneath the coverlet, the woman's body lay wasted to bone. Her face appeared ashen and hollow, eyes sunken into dark circles. Every vein showed through her translucent skin. Axandra would have thought her to be in her nineties.

Quietly Gage stated his suspicions that the epidemic was of a parasitic nature. "Intestinal parasites often cause such symptoms," he explained, "because they steal the nutrients that would normally be absorbed in the intestines. I have treated Sue with the extracts that aid in digestion, helping her retain more of the nutrition from her meals. However, I have not found the parasites themselves." He also confirmed that he was not able to touch the patient's mind due to her beliefs. "When she was still able to speak, she often prayed for the Goddess to forgive her sins."

Nodding to acknowledge the Healer's words, Axandra spoke softly, announcing her visit to the patient. Sue did not stir, and her eyes remained closed.

"Perhaps," the Healer spoke softly, "if you held her hand, Your Honor, she will sense you are here."

She squinted at him, shaking her head. "I'm not a Believer. I don't want to—"

"You are their link to the Goddess. She will welcome your touch," he assured. "It was the last thing she asked, for you to come and see her. She wants to make her peace."

A service Axandra always avoided was sitting with the dying. Anytime she received a request to volunteer for such service, she traded it to teach the children their lessons or take food to the homebound. Though death was part of life, sensing the ending moments always caused her severe depression. Others were much more capable of offering comfort in those last moments.

She would not be able to trade this time. Timidly, though trying not to show it, she clasped the dying woman's hand between her own. The bony limb felt cold and lifeless.

Yet Axandra sensed a trace of warmth in the body. Sue welcomed the Protectress inside her mind, into a small place, a warm place. All the dark space tugged at the edges of the light, trying to obliterate this last thought.

Axandra felt the strong pull of the darkness, the nothingness, like a vacuum. Resisting, she held herself in place. *I am here, Sue.*

It's all I have left, the woman thought to her. *My sin has taken everything else from me.*

In this small room of memory, a young child sat on the floor playing with blocks. Sue, a healthy and vibrant young woman, joined the girl in her play.

Axandra understood this was Sue's daughter, though she did not know how old the memory was. There was no evidence of a young child in the present house.

You have not sinned, Axandra tried to convince the woman. *What has done this to you?*

Axandra heard a growling somewhere deep in the darkness that surrounded the memory room, the same familiar growling from the garden and from the *Lazzonir.*

Thank you for coming. Now I may rest.

Soon the room dimmed to match the darkness. In a slipstream of rushing light, Axandra watched Sue fly away from her. Thrown back, Axandra felt the weight of her own body falling and stretching. Out of the dark, sharp teeth rush at her. Her chest burned as a fang caught her skin. Abruptly, she slumped back into the real bedroom, back in the present.

The Healer also touched Sue, finding no pulse in the still form. Others stood in the room now where they had not been before, a man in his middle years and a younger woman. They each touched the dying woman. The Healer must have summoned them when he knew the end neared, so that Sue would be surrounded by her family.

Rising from beside the bed, Axandra felt as though her body spun against the room. The square walls bowed outward. Forcing herself to focus on the family, she reached out to each of them.

"I grieve with you for your loss," she sympathized with them, sensing their sorrow through their touch. The emanations added to the disorientation she felt.

"She is with the Goddess now," said the daughter, smiling through her tears. "Thank you."

Axandra stumbled out of the house on uneasy feet. In the outer room, the gathered Believers began to sing again.

> *Oh Goddess and our Protector*
> *Bring us peace within*
> *Our Sister lives on with you...*

Gage followed her outside, stopping her on the walkway. Turning back to him, she found she could barely focus on his pockmarked face. The scars of a childhood disease appeared grossly oversized to her swimming eyes.

"Madam, are you all right?" Gage inquired with seriousness, his eyes looking her over from head to toe. "Are you getting enough to eat? Eryn's notes mentioned that you have sudden drops in blood sugar—"

"I'm fine," Axandra snapped, refusing to admit her weakness. His face wobbled back and forth in her blurry vision. She wanted him to stop moving.

Taken aback by her tone of voice, Gage took a step backward. "Very well. Thank you for coming. You have given great comfort to this family."

She only nodded. Focusing became more difficult with each passing second. She wasn't certain she would be able to walk all the way back to the Palace.

Gage almost turned away, but at the last moment, his eyes focused below her chin. "What is that mark?" he questioned, reaching to touch her skin. "Was that there when you arrived?"

"I have to go," she said, hurrying away from him before his fingers could make contact. The two Elite quickened their steps to keep up. Saying nothing, Axandra concentrated on making her way home. Head bowed, she watched carefully each step she took, thinking of nothing else but climbing the hill without fainting.

In the Palace, Axandra felt drained of hope. She felt her soul darken, as though a piece of her flew away with the dying woman. No matter what happy thoughts she tried to muster, they turned to thoughts of despair and desolation. A bird's song morphed into that creature's growl. Trapped in these feelings, she fled immediately to her Residence, blocking any attempts to offer her comfort or aid, and shut herself behind the layers of doors.

In her bedroom, she closed the drapes, shutting out as much light as she could.

Then she hid under her covers, shrouded in solitude. She sobbed into her pillow, dumping the dregs of her wounded soul into the darkness of the space.

+++

20th Octember

Morning came in brilliant sunslight, casting the bedroom in shades of purple as the rays penetrated the thick drapes. Buried beneath her quilts, Axandra ignored the sunshine. She couldn't tolerate such brightness.

The death drained so much from her. She wondered how the Healers could deal with the sensation over and over, each transition ripping them apart a little piece at a time. She felt a new respect for those performing their life service caring for the dying. She wanted to avoid that sensation forever.

The door to the room creaked slightly when it opened. Axandra knew that her aide had arrived, and she felt guilty for having treated everyone so rudely the night before, Miri especially. To avoid facing up to her actions, she pretended to be asleep, which was a silly attempt. Miri would know that she was awake with a simple passing thought.

The aide did not speak. The only sounds came from the soft friction of her padded shoes on the rug and the clatter of dishes as a tray came to rest on a small table near the balcony doors. Then the drapes were drawn back with a scrape of the wooden rings against the metal rod, flooding the room with light. The doors to the balcony opened with a click and the noise of birds and the wind in the trees broke into the silence.

The revelry of nature overpowered her senses. Axandra buried herself deeper still.

Miri stood beside the bed when she spoke at last. "Madam, I am not here to force you from bed. You may remain there as long as you require."

Axandra sighed in relief. She wanted to be left alone.

"But I thought I would remind you that today is the twentieth. You said that Quinn should be arriving on the twenty-first for the play."

The one thing in the world that could make her shed her cocoon was Quinn. Just the mention of his name brought a bit of peace to her soul, for the word instantly brought his sweet face to her mind. Pushing the covers down below her head, she found Miri looking at her and smiling.

"I thought that might work," the aide gloated.

Axandra blushed at the truth.

As Miri pulled the quilts away, folding each of them at the end of the bed, she remarked, "He has a very interesting effect on you."

"He does?" Axandra acted innocent. She sat up, leaning against the lacquered headboard. She still wore yesterday's clothes, having come straight into bed from her visit. The pants and tunic lay wrinkled and twisted around her body. Her braided hair came loose everywhere. Bits of curl clung to her cheeks.

Miri looked dreamily toward the sky as she said, "Your entire face lights up just thinking about him. Your smile is so contagious."

Again, Axandra blushed. This time, she rolled herself out of bed on the opposite side of where Miri worked and made a quick escape to the bathroom. She looked at herself in the mirror, trying to catch a glimpse of this look that Miri talked about. There, on her lips, arose an intoxicating smile. For the first time in months, her face shone with a natural glow. She'd gotten so used to seeing a glower when she looked at her reflection, the face of a worn out old woman. She'd forgotten when she used to be beautiful—and it wasn't that long ago.

A knock came at the door and Miri's muted voice asked, "May I draw you a bath?"

"Yes, please," Axandra responded, opening the door for the aide. Studying her reflection, she thought about how thin she looked. Her wrists, naturally thin, bristled with boney spurs. Her elbows poked sharply out when bent. She realized she had not kept up with her meals, but she didn't realize she was wasting away.

"When did I start to look like this?" she asked herself aloud.

"Excuse me?" Miri inquired over the splashing of water in the tub. Coming over to Axandra, the aide offered to undo her braid and brush her hair. "Madam, I don't know if this is my place, but you look as though you haven't eaten for a week."

Axandra balked that the deterioration was so obvious. Her thoughts of Quinn fleeing her mind, her face returned to an unhealthy sag. "I don't know what's wrong with me. I haven't felt hungry." She circled her fingers around her arm, measuring just how thin she had become. She looked at her collarbone in the mirror. The shape protruded sharply beneath her skin.

"These last few days," Miri told her, "you've looked worse. I'm sorry to say so. Wait, what is that?"

The younger woman noticed the spot where Axandra fingers came to rest, an irregular patch of angry red skin on the left shoulder, blotched with broken capillaries. The area was the size of a red tealeaf, about seven centim long. Leaning closer, Miri studied the rash directly, her soft fingers brushing the skin to feel its texture.

"Did this happen yesterday?"

"I-I don't remem-member," Axandra said, worry straining her voice. She imagined that such an injury would have been received with pain, but she did not recall—

Pain. That burning in her chest when the creature in Sue's mind chased her, those teeth catching her for just a moment before she escaped.

"Madam?"

She stared at her own lavender eyes in the mirror. Her hands dropped into her lap. The puzzle pieces snapped into place. The sighting of the Goddess at the Landing, the sickness, the packhound, the hissing she heard when things were quiet... The creatures were the light and the infection! When the Believers looked upon the light, dozens of the parasites attached to them, making them sick. The man who had committed murder must have been the first infected. He showed the same symptoms of malnourishment and fatigue and madness. The parasites not only stole their host's nourishment but the very essence of the host. Somehow, the curana became infected, too, insanely bashing themselves upon the rocks. She witnessed one of these entities flee the packhound, but had not linked its presence to the emaciation of the animal until now.

Her own parasite did the same thing. The Goddess shared their nature. They were all the same race of creatures. Was she going to die this way?

More than ever, Axandra wanted to know why the Prophets kept this thing alive. The women of her family had been nothing more than vessels to sustain it, idolized by the people because of the side-effects of an infection. The only thing that separated the Goddess and the rest of her kind was that she didn't destroy the body as quickly, at least not in her prior hosts. Most of the Believers perished within a few months of their infection, while the Protectress survived for a few decades.

Yet such an infection explained why all the Protectresses-Past lived considerably short lives. Elora had lived to be fifty-seven. Before her, Cassandra had barely reached her sixtieth birthday. The longest-lived had been Amelia, the first Protectress, but she had not been named so until she reached her forties. At this rate, Axandra could not expect to live to be forty.

Miri's face moved in front of her own. The pleasantness erased, replaced with a seriousness Axandra had not seen in the young woman before.

"Ileanne," Miri spoke the name, a breach in protocol when addressing the Esteemed Protectress, but the sound captured her attention. "Don't let it destroy you the way it did Elora. You can fight it."

"How do you know?"

"Because she fought it to the end. She wanted it to go with her to the grave. She didn't want it to find you."

Amazed, Axandra could only stare at Miri.

"I can't explain why," Miri continued. "I could never decipher the reason why."

"Did she believe I was alive?"

Nodding, Miri said, "She knew you were alive. And I'm telling you, you can fight it. I'll find a way to help you."

Axandra grabbed hold of Miri's hands, holding them like a lifeline. "We have to find a way to help the others. There has to be a way. I have to see Eryn."

Confused, Miri pursed her brow. "Eryn? But Eryn is—"

"I know, but she may have the answer I need." Axandra attempted to explain what had taken place at the time the Goddess tore Eryn's mind apart. "All because I couldn't remember a day's worth of events."

"But, Madam, I was there too. The bison were real." The woman said this with a taint of doubt, suddenly questioning the memory. Miri wanted desperately to believe the bison were a true memory, but at the same time, wanted to believe her mistress told the truth.

"For me, it never happened. Eryn tried to help me find out the truth. The Goddess struck her down to protect the truth, and then the thing scratched it out of my brain. I think Eryn still has my memories."

They both jumped as a loud splash of water struck the stone floor. The tub overflowed, a wide stream of water pouring over the side. Leaping up, Miri hurried to turn off the spouts, her clothes soaked as she leaned over the brimming tub.

"Ummm. The bath is ready," she deadpanned, panting from the rush. The simple words lightened the atmosphere. Both women laughed helplessly. Miri grabbed several towels to mop the floor. "Hop in. I'll let Marcus Gray know that you're coming." Miri headed for the exit.

"Miri, wait."

The aide stopped at the summons and looked back attentively.

"Thank you," Axandra expressed graciously.

"All part of the service," came the humble reply.

+++

Eryn's home was a quiet and peaceful place. Marcus was beginning to come to terms with his wife's disability. When he greeted the Protectress today, he seemed in much higher spirits, smiling as he bowed and motioned her inside.

"She's greatly improved since you last saw her," he stated proudly. "Her mind is recovering more rapidly than Healer Gage anticipated. He thinks there may be a chance she'll be herself again within a year, though with some amnesia."

While Axandra ascended the stairs, Marcus offered the Elite refreshment. She was grateful he would keep himself occupied while she visited. She did not suspect he would approve of her probing the woman's frail mind.

Instead of lying in bed, Eryn was up, seated at a writing desk to one side of the large drawing room. Full bookshelves lined the outside wall of the room, while immediately to her left, the wall displayed a collection of different harps. She wondered curiously for a moment if Eryn was the harper or Marcus. Either way, the instruments did not appear to have been touched recently.

"Good Morning, Eryn," Axandra announced herself, masking her voice with cheerfulness.

The straight red hair rippled slightly as the Healer turned her head toward her guest. "You," she responded, smiling, her now customary greeting. Eryn recognized familiar people only on the basis that she knew them, but not that she could remember a name. Then she returned to work on a drawing in front of her. She used a variety of pigmented pencils. "Sit there."

Already, Axandra sensed a difference in Eryn's capacity. She was more cognizant of her surroundings this time. Her words actually made sense in the circumstances.

"Eryn," Axandra addressed as she took a seat on a soft chair nearby, facing the desk. "I came to ask you a few questions. Is that all right?"

"Yes," Eryn said with confirming tone. "Quinn."

Distracted by the mention of his name, Axandra frowned. Perhaps she assumed too much improvement. She wasn't thinking about him, at least not consciously.

"I'm sorry, I don't—"

"You like Quinn," Eryn said with a girlish twinkle to her voice.

"Yes, I do," Axandra agreed, wondering how he became a topic of conversation. "But—"

"He likes you, too. Very much."

"I believe he does," Axandra agreed. Her frustration already grew. She was not in the mood to sort through layers of cryptic nonsense. "Eryn, I wanted to ask you about memories. May I—may I touch you?"

To this, Eryn cringed, a frightful expression on her rosy face. "No. No touch. No more pain." She pulled away slightly, even casting her eyes away from the Protectress, a defensive posture.

"It can't hurt you again," Axandra tried to convince. "I won't let it."

"No," Eryn insisted. She returned to her drawing, her eyes darting at her visitor suspiciously.

So much for that plan. She did not want to force herself on the woman. The trauma could cause more damage.

"All right. I won't. Can I ask you to try to remember something for me?" She tried to catch Eryn's line of sight, to get the woman to stop drawing and look her in the eyes. Eryn avoided her, focused only on the paper.

"I remember … Quinn," Eryn said smiling. "Digs in the ground."

Sighing, the Protectress settled her impatience. She should have known this would not be as easy as she hoped.

"Yes. Quinn is an archeologist. He digs for artifacts left by the Ancients."

And so the conversation continued in a similar manner for the next hour, always about Quinn, but nothing that Axandra didn't already know about him. Eryn spoke of his eyes and hair, then of the dinner party where they had met. She even spoke of his desire to see Axandra again as though it hadn't happened yet. But Eryn didn't know that Quinn had already visited or that he was coming back tomorrow. When Axandra tried to tell her these things, the ill woman could not grasp the ideas. She continued to speak as though trapped in the past.

Finally, exasperated with the process and noting that Marcus prowled anxiously in the corridor, Axandra rose to leave.

Eryn rose, too. "Wait. This is yours." She held out the drawing.

"No, Eryn. That is your drawing," Axandra refused. She was not in the mood to accept gifts.

"Take it," Eryn insisted, pushing the paper at her. "It is yours."

Not even glancing at the pencil drawing, Axandra rolled the large paper into a tube. "Thank you, Eryn. Good Day."

Disheartened by the lack of progress, Axandra hurried home to formulate a new plan.

By the time she returned to the Palace, the lunch hour had passed. The dining room was being cleaned and swept. Rather than intrude, she headed upstairs to her rooms, sending a thought to Miri to have lunch brought up to her balcony.

She carried the rolled up drawing with her. When she reached the landing of the third floor, she unfurled the long paper and glanced at the image. Eryn seemed to have quite an imagination to draw this picture. From a high point of view, possibly a ridge, the artist looked down at a collection of tents and people. Distant mountains formed the backdrop. In the center, the focal point of the image, a large round object rested in a trench, surrounded by men with shovels and buckets. Though the human figures stood in the distance and their facial features drawn as indistinguishable marks, one of them reminded her of Quinn.

Glancing up to see where she walked, Axandra spied a pink puff on the window ledge across from the staircase. Pausing, she blinked, making certain she wasn't just seeing things. In a few steps, she collected the bloom and lifted it to her nose.

The musky perfume immediately brought Quinn's face to her thoughts.

Turning toward the main door to her Residence, she saw other flowers, like a trail, running right to her door. Collecting the blooms, she made her way to her home.

She nodded a greeting to the two guards, each of which kept his face impassive. Whatever they knew, they kept secret.

Inside, she looked for Quinn, finding him seated on the sofa, his eyes momentarily absorbed in a book.

"You're here!" she burst joyously, skipping to him and wrapping her arms around his thick torso just as he was able to get to his feet. "How did you get in here?"

"Miri was kind enough to let me in," he explained, squeezing her tightly in his arms.

"And the flowers?" she asked, holding up the small bouquet. "The garden's stopped blooming because it's so dry. Where did these come from?"

"A friend keeps them in her garden. She's kept them well watered."

"I didn't expect you until tomorrow."

"Is that a complaint?" he teased.

"Oh no!" she reassured quickly, her eyes brimming with tears. She rested her chin against his shoulder. "I'm so glad you're here."

"Good," he sighed. "I think I'll stay awhile." Gently, he lifted her chin so that he could kiss her. It was a soft, pleasant kiss, one shared between lovers who had been apart, now reunited.

Backing away a step, he just stared into her eyes. "Their color is so remarkable," he declared of the violet irises. His hand cupped her cheek. She welcomed the touch, nuzzling against his palm. His fingers felt rough from working.

"Do you know what you are doing to me?" Quinn asked. Beneath her hands, his heart beat rapidly in his chest. His skin felt hot and his cheeks flushed bright pink like the flowers.

"I know what I want to do to you," Axandra said with a saucy grin. She made certain to send her thoughts to him through her fingertips.

He blushed, his round cheeks rosy. He wasn't wearing his glasses, so the lines around his eyes weren't hidden. They crinkled to fill his face with his smile.

"Tell me what you want, Quinn," she said, her fingers plucking at the buttons of his shirt, "and I will do it. Even if you want me to do nothing. I just want to be near you." She slipped one hand between his collar and his neck, her long fingers combing his clipped hair, pulling him closer.

He looked at her face with longing. "I wanted so badly for the time to fly to get back here with you," he admitted to her. He reached up for the hand that rested on his chest, caressing her fingers that so earnestly wanted to open his shirt. "I want time and the world to stand still now so that I never have to go."

Hungrily, he pressed his lips to hers, feeding her desires with his own. She felt herself lifted into his arms and carried to her soft bed. She fumbled with his buttons while he pushed the fabric of her dress from her shoulders. His lips traced her collarbone from her shoulder to her throat. In his mind, he showed her everything he wanted to do for her and sought permission.

Willingly, she gave it.

Chapter 24

Clues

20th Octember, 307

Axandra woke somewhat groggy and found the suns hanging at about three o'clock in the sky. She couldn't believe after all that excitement that she dozed off. Beneath the airy algodon sheets, she lay nude, her long hair tousled across the pillows. Stretching, she twisted around to take in a view of her room.

Quinn was gone. Where had he disappeared to? She feared for a moment that he had run off, back to North Compass or Lazzonir, suddenly needed somewhere.

Then she chuckled at herself for being impractical. She could find him easily, especially now. Their minds intertwined in such a way during their lovemaking that she felt as though he left a part of himself attached to her. She closed her eyes for a moment, thinking of his storm cloud-blue eyes. A part of her floated outward, unhindered by physical being. Along the way, she touched several minds—the guards outside, Miri, Marta, that distasteful Lynn. Then she found him. He existed above her in space. She heard musical tones through his ears, hammers on metal strings. The staff common room held a piano.

Slipping back into her dress, she collected her mass of wavy locks into a simple ribbon at the base of her neck. She skipped from her bedroom, humming a lively sea-shanty she'd known since childhood. The uplifting ditty told of clear skies and good fishing.

Barefoot, Axandra padded out of the Residence and headed upstairs, noting the curiosity of the guard that followed her. He would never ask. None of them would ever ask. They watched and protected her from trouble.

On the fifth floor, Axandra heard piano music coming from the common room. The corridor was empty of any people, not that she cared. She followed the music to find him, already knowing that he was alone.

She hid just outside the doorway. Inside, Quinn perched on the bench in front of the large wood-encased instrument, his fingers pressing the keys tenderly as he played the piece. He played from memory, his eyes watching his own fingers. The piece covered the keyboard in smooth arpeggios and expansive chords, struck out at a gentle walking pace.

"Come in," Quinn called without missing a beat. She slowly walked forward, wary of ruining the tune. She waited behind him until the piece ended.

"That was quite beautiful," she praised softly, trying to retain the mood. She placed a hand on his shoulder, unable to resist the need to touch him.

"Thank you," Quinn accepted. "It's unusual to find an original instrument in such superb condition," he commented. His right hand stroked the clear lacquer directly above the word Wurlitzer, admiring the grain of the wood shining through. "It's difficult to find a piano at all, they take so much time to construct. This one—this is almost five hundred years old."

Quinn spun on the bench to face her, meaning to leave the instrument behind. He had slipped on his same clothes, but left the top few buttons open and rolled up his sleeves.

"You look rested," he observed, caressing her hands. She peered down at his smiling face, her own cheeks glowing.

"I didn't realize I was so tired," she apologized. "Will you play some more?"

"You enjoyed it? I missed a lot of notes on that one." He attempted to be modest.

"I didn't notice."

He received her words with a nod. Patting the bench beside him, he turned back around and paused a moment to consider what to play.

He kicked off a quick tune of eighths and sixteenths, his fingers blithely bouncing over the keys. Fingers crossed over one another to reach each key in time. A few ivories slipped untouched beneath his fingertips. The music lasted less than a minute, barely time to for her to blink.

"Oh," she expressed when it ended, mildly surprised how quickly it was over.

"Not to your liking?" he asked attentively.

"After the first one, it wasn't what I expected." She felt sheepish about what she said. She felt she didn't have time to enjoy something so short.

"All right," he accepted. As he thought about what to play next, his fingers tapped out chord progressions on the keyboard, major to minor and back again. "Let me try another one."

After a moment of silence, he played. All the while his eyes roamed over her face and body. He appreciated her as he would the sunrise, for she brought light to him like the suns brought a new day. She blushed at his romantic thoughts, but did not hide herself. She watched him in the same way.

The piece sounded very peaceful and serene. Axandra let her eyes close and listened to each note. The hammer operated by each key struck a metal string. The high strings sounded crisp and clean, while the lower notes echoed over their own harmonics as the coils vibrated against each other. The musician played the music at an unhurried pace, as though holding back each passing second and stretching the very fabric of time. With each phrase, she breathed deeply.

Quinn touched her shoulder when the music ended, bringing her back to the present stream of time. She found her head resting upon his shoulder.

Now that he was finished with music, she sensed his concern for her. He thought she looked faint, and he worried that she looked thin.

"Are you hungry?" she asked, thinking of her own stomach. A growl came from her midsection. "I didn't eat my lunch. There was too much distraction."

"That sounds like a fine idea," he agreed. "Hop on my back." He stood, turned his back to her and crouched low enough that she could climb on.

"What? That's ridiculous!"

"No, it's not," he urged playfully. "You're light as a feather. I'll carry you down to the kitchen."

Since she did feel weak and wobbly, she agreed to climb on his back, her arms draped over his shoulders and her legs about his waist. He locked his elbows around her knees and started off singing a song.

There was a lad, A stout young lad
With arms as strong as a bear.
He had fair skin and a freckled face
And ginger was the color of his hair.

Quinn's tenor tones rang against the stone walls all the way down the main staircase. Her weight cost him no effort as he descended the dozens of steps. She giggled as she held on, laughing at him and at the poor guard who seemed utterly confused by the situation.

As they arrived just outside the dining room, Quinn let her slip gently to the floor. "Front door service, Madam. Let me get the chef." He marched ahead of her as they entered the room. The tables were all set for dinnertime, with fresh tablecloths, utensils and napkins. Pulling out a chair for her at a table near the kitchen entrance, he left her momentarily to enter the kitchen and obtain nourishment.

Axandra heard some commotion as she waited, voices in the kitchen. Someone yelped, startled by the stranger, but seemed quickly calmed. The voices quieted to normal tones. Colors popped in front of her eyes the hungrier she got. She despised the sensation and wished she had eaten an earlier snack to avoid it. She did not want an outturned stomach to ruin the rest of the day. Again. Quinn's early arrival boosted her failing spirits, and everything felt so right at this moment.

When Quinn returned, the chef followed him carrying a small silver tray with goblets of cold water and a saucer holding a cone fruit. The fruit had been sliced to open like a flower.

"Good afternoon, Your Honor," the chef greeted with a brief but respectful bow. "I saved your lunch from earlier, since Miri brought it back to me. It will be warmed shortly. This should appease your immediate hunger." The chef placed the delicately prepared appetizer on the table between their two seats. He waited while she took a petal of the "flower" and crunched it between her teeth. Then he disappeared back into the kitchen.

The overly sweet fruit instantly inverted her off-balance blood sugar and the flashing lights dissipated. Quinn sat to her left at the large round table, one of four set in the room, each able to seat twelve diners at a time. Each table sat adorned with centerpieces of live plants, some of which bloomed with delicate white flowers and their vines trailed across the surfaces. The dining room was typically used by the Councilors and staff for meals. Axandra usually took her meals on the veranda or in her rooms, away from the others.

"Feeling better," Quinn asked, breaking off a fruit petal from the core for himself.

Sucking the juice from another chunk, Axandra nodded. "Yes. I sometimes get light-headed if I don't eat. I guess I haven't had anything since breakfast." The crisp flesh tasted fresh, as though the fruit had just been picked from the tree.

The chef sent out two shallow bowls of thin soup and chunks of warm crusty bread. Flecks of herbs seasoned the vegetable broth, but there were also tiny black pieces of something she didn't immediately recognize. The specks felt like fish bones on the way down her throat.

"Chef," she summoned, as he lingered nearby. "What is in this soup?"

There came a lengthy pause, during which the chef avoided eye contact. "Oh, well—we were looking for another source of protein to supplement everyone's diet. Fish are somewhat difficult to come by right now."

Bumping her shoulder with his own, Quinn whispered, "It's probably better that you don't ask."

But her brain already wrapped around an idea of what types of living things provided protein. She realized the black specks looked like beetle parts. Covering her lips with her hand, she repressed the urged to vomit.

"Actually," the chef continued, "it did help with another problem that we were having down in the store rooms—"

"It's delicious!" Quinn praised the chef boisterously, interrupting any further details. "Thank you. We will enjoy it. Perhaps you have a dessert we can share?"

"Dessert? Yes, of course." Chastened, the chef scuttled back into the kitchen.

Replacing her spoon upon the placemat, Axandra moved the bowl toward the center of the table. Her appetite fled.

In a somewhat bold move, Quinn placed his hand in the path of the bowl and pushed it back toward her. "Eat the soup," he insisted quietly. He was nearly finished with his own already, black specks and all. "You need to eat."

While she agreed that she did need to eat—since this morning's revelation as to what was happening to her body, she thought to herself that she should eat everything within sight in hopes of fighting the deterioration—she simply could not bring herself to take even a spoonful. She could only think of beetles as large as her foot ambulating over the ground, thin legs and shining black shells. She reached for her bread and spread the airy surface with butter, saying nothing to him.

"We're not leaving the table until you eat the soup," Quinn promised, like a father would to a child who refused to eat. "It's actually very delicious."

"I don't think I can."

"Take your spoon and put the soup in your mouth. I know you can do that."

She glared at him fiercely. "I don't appreciate your patronizing tone," she hissed.

"I'm not patronizing you. I'm telling you to eat the soup. You are wasting away and I–I can't stand it." His voice sounded apologetic and sad. He looked away from her, folding his hands together in the air. "I just found you. I don't want you to vanish."

For some reason, the words he spoke went deep into her soul. No one else could make her feel so important. She knew she was important. The entire population looked to her with reverence. But she was important to him for a different reason. He needed her in a different, more intimate way.

Grasping the spoon in her fist, she shook it at him. "Fine. But don't blame me if it comes back up on your shoes."

He only chuckled at the threat and waited patiently for her to finish her meal. She managed to swallow most of it by avoiding the hard beetle parts. The black bits rested at the bottom of the bowl.

"That will do," he dismissed at last. "Thank you."

"What would you like to do for the rest of the afternoon?" Axandra asked, shifting Quinn's focus from her health to more amusing endeavors. "I only want to check on the reports of the tides. I'm very hopeful that the flooding won't be as terrible as the scientists predicted."

"I'll follow you in whatever you do," he offered submissively. "I have no other plans."

"You seem lost without your work," she observed in a soft voice. She felt such as she looked into his gray-blue eyes.

"Today, I am not lost," he corrected. His hand connected with hers in a tender embrace.

"Well, I wanted to ask you to help me with a little research," she explained, smiling at him demurely.

"Oh?" he perked up.

She beckoned him to come with her. As she rose from the table, she found that her body felt energized after eating a full meal. They proceeded hand-in-hand across the main hall to the Council wing, stopping in a small office only briefly to retrieve a sheaf of papers from the desk where the reports were left for her. Then they headed up to the second floor and to the Library.

"I have a lot of questions about the Prophets," she explained, opening up to him about her private thoughts. "And since you are an expert in history and very inquisitive, I thought you might enjoy helping me find the answers I'm looking for."

"A challenge!" Quinn reveled, rubbing his hands together eagerly. "There isn't much known about them, but perhaps your Library holds a few secrets to discover. What questions do you have?"

She waited until they entered the book room before she told him. She closed the wide double doors, shutting out the Elite and signaling not to be disturbed. "Councilor Morton doesn't like me questioning such things," she complained when she sensed his curiosity about why she shut them in. "Well, Morton doesn't like me being with you, either."

She moved across the room to open two of the large windows and let in the crisp autumn air. Icy, thin clouds gathered in the southwest, shading the suns' descent to the horizon. In the shadows, the air cooled quickly, though the rest of the day passed in pleasant warmth.

"Ms. Morton seems to have a poor attitude about many things," he criticized. "I have never met her personally, but I've heard many remarks about her—such as if she ever smiled, her face might crack."

Axandra chuckled, remembering how pained Nancy Morton looked when she forced her thin lips to curl upward.

"It's a shame she makes your life so...well, unpleasant, to put it nicely," he said.

"You make up for it all," she told him. A little flattery didn't hurt.

Quinn slipped on his spectacles and began to peruse the shelves, pulling a few titles here and there and peeking at the prologues or printing details. "Is there an index to the books?" he questioned, thinking such would speed the search.

"Here," she directed him to the small cabinet near the corner window. Index books lay in small sliding trays. One listed the collection alphabetically by title, another by author and a third by topic. Looking inside the third index, the thickest, they found these entries to be page by page, giving space for a detailed synopsis of each piece of literature and leaving room for additional entries as the Archivists added new works. "Will this help?"

"It is an antique method, but it will help," he assured, turning directly to the P section of the index. "It will give us some idea what we have to work with. What are you looking for specifically?" he asked again.

She considered the man next to her for a moment, taking a step back from her growing love for him and her desire for him. Searching him, she looked for anything that might cause her to distrust or misjudge him. She thought of a way to test him.

"Quinn, I must ask something of you. I just want to hear it from your lips."

Slowing in his progression of turning pages in the book, he tensed slightly, anticipating what she might ask him.

"Go ahead," he granted.

"Did you attempt to find the Goddess? Were you a Believer?"

Turning to her fully, he straightened his posture. Removing his glasses again, he took her hands in his and looked directly into her eyes. "Yes, I was a Believer; and yes, I made such an attempt. You heard this from someone?"

"From Morton," Axandra said. "And from Marta and Sara after I asked them. It was quite a story, but I'm certain there is more to it than they know."

Nodding, Quinn agreed to her assessment. "I was nineteen at the time," he narrated. "I was young and impressionable and joined the Believers because I was looking for a place to belong. My father passed away when I was very young and my mother— well, she's never found me to be acceptable. I was talked into attempting to find the truth about the Goddess, that she was really a part of the Protectress, not just an invisible entity that watched over us. I succeeded in making an ass of myself. The last time I was apprehended by the Elite, I decided that I was done with the nonsense."

He held back something. While he was not lying, he was not offering everything. "I see the story didn't scare you away."

"No. Sara assured me that you had long since left the incident behind you."

"She's a good friend," he said with relief.

Axandra drew close to him, slipping her arms beneath his and circling his warm body in a welcome embrace. She tilted her lips toward his ear and whispered, "Did you find what you were looking for?"

His breath caught in his lungs, and the muscles of his back tightened in a nervous moment. He wouldn't lie to her, and she strategically asked a very specific question.

"Yes," he replied very quietly. "But what I found was not what I expected."

"It isn't what I expected either." With her words, she sent her thoughts to him, how the Goddess came into her and the changes that took place since that day. Intrigued and appalled by the events, Quinn's face displayed his reactions. She tried to show him everything, holding nothing back. She didn't want to leave any unintended secrets. She didn't know how long the sharing went on. At last, he seemed to push her away. His lungs pushed hard in his chest. To let him catch his breath, she released him.

"I understand why you ran away," he said after a moment of absorption. "I understand a lot of things now."

"So, my quest is to find a way to get to them," she said, returning to the index, "so that I can get rid of her."

For many moments, he could only stare at her, as though he saw a different woman in front of him now, one more burdened than he could have imagined, and one stronger than he had ever suspected.

Axandra found that the sharing had gone both ways, because she could see in her mind a memory of his past. He had known since their first meeting that she was not alone in her body, for he had seen it in Elora. That distant day in the Palace, he managed to confront the Protectress, when he was still a boy sent on missions by adults who used him for their own purposes. Elora spoke to him as though she expected a casual visitor. When he looked in that woman's lavender eyes, he witnessed the creature that diseased her and robbed her of her youth. At that moment, everything in the Believers doctrine fell away as lies. He never went back to the sect. He never told anyone what he had seen—until now.

"Do you think the Prophets can do that?"

"I believe they are the ones who help keep her alive," Axandra offered her conjecture. "They transfer her from one woman to the next, like pouring wine from one cup to another. What if they don't pour the cup?"

So they set to work, pulling references, reading passages, but found nothing that, between the two of them, they didn't already know. When darkness fell, they felt tired. Asking for a light dinner, Axandra took Quinn back to the Residence and, after eating, retired to bed. Quinn stayed, as he promised he would. He lay spooned behind her as she stared out the open window at the bright stars.

"Quinn, did I tell you about the first time we talked?" she asked him, trying to remember through all their time together if she had shared the reclaimed memory with him. Even recent days seemed like distant past, her recollections fuzzy.

"No, not really. You mentioned we had met that day that everyone seems to remember differently." His words sounded hurried, indicating that he harbored a deep curiosity toward these memories and a lingering uncertainty about the reality of them. He accepted his own memories of that week as true and factual, for nothing seemed out of place to him. He worked at the dig and he talked with her at the dinner party, invited by his friend Sara Sunsun. When Axandra attempted to disorder his memories of that time by implying that something completely different had taken place, he resisted. He struggled with the implication ever since. He wanted to believe her.

Axandra tucked a stray curl of hair behind her ear and watched the flicker of candle flame by the window as she concentrated on what she remembered. She rolled onto her back in order to explain face-to-face. "I can only remember that evening," she began to explain. "I know I wasn't feeling well. I was on the sofa in Sara's house, after dinner." As she noted the time in her story, she noticed Quinn's eyebrows wiggle with puzzlement. "I remember you coming in. The others ducked away somewhere. We were alone."

"Alone?" he asked. He still tried to compare these new details to his memory of the dinner party.

"Yes, alone. You sat next to me. You said you wanted to make sure I was all right." Her fingers absently brushed the collar of his shirt as she watched him. "As though something had happened earlier that day, at another time we had been together."

"Maybe something that caused you to feel under the weather?" he proposed.

"Perhaps," she said with a light nod, her thoughts turning inward again as she attempted to pull something new into her mind.

Quinn captured her wandering fingers and pressed them to his lips. "What happened next?"

"I think we just talked for a little while," she said, this part of the memory blurred. She could picture his face and his hands, but could not remember any words spoken. "I remember that I laughed at something you said to me. And you told me about your love of archeology. I know that when you rose to leave, you asked if you could see me again and I said I would like that. I was struck with such a strange sense of déjà vu at the dinner party that next night. I think our conversations must have been very similar. I just wish I could remember earlier that day." She sighed, laying her own cool hand on her cheek. She thought her cheeks must have looked very red, as warm as her face felt. "I'm certain we'd seen each other somewhere, for you to ask about me the way you did. Sara said she was going to take me to your dig, but we arrived so late—"

Suddenly, something new appeared in the center of her mind, something very clear. She saw the dig in her memory, the tents, the people, all below her as though she stood on a high ridge.

Quinn leaned forward into her line of sight. "What is it, Axandra? Is something wrong?"

Without a word, she leaped from the bed and dashed into the great room.

Where is it? Where is Eryn's drawing?

Now she concentrated on remembering where she put the roll of paper. She hadn't looked at the sketch for a couple of days, not since Quinn's surprise arrival. All she could remember was how happy she was to see him. Everything else slipped away from her. Striding toward the sitting furniture, she looked at the table, on the floor, then on the shelves along the walls.

"Where is it?" she hissed, frustration peaking.

Quinn followed her across the large room. "Where is what? What are you looking for?"

"A roll of paper," she explained, making a vague gesture with her hands. "A drawing. Eryn gave it to me. She said it was mine. I didn't understand what she meant at the time—"

Spinning to her right, she kept looking, frantic to try to find it. She needed to see the picture. The drawing would help solidify the rest of the scene.

Quinn searched the far side of the room. "Here!" he called out. "Is this it?" He turned from a table in the corner and held out a loose tube of paper.

"Yes! Yes! Look at it!" she urged excitedly, hurrying over. "I remember this now."

He unfurled the heavy paper and oriented the drawing to be right side up as they both examined it. "This looks like my dig!" he exclaimed. "What in blazes is that thing?"

The large graphite-gray orb dominated the image, tucked into a trench in the center of the dig site. Workers dug all around the object, holding buckets and tools. Tents shielded their finds from exposure to the sun. As Axandra looked at the image, she felt as though she walked straight into the scene. She stood on that ridge, the wind tugging at her braided hair. Sara stood beside her, pointing out what the diggers had discovered. Suzanne sat down to sketch a drawing much like this one.

"Sara did take me to the dig," Axandra told him. "They brought me to see this... thing. But something made me ill—there was... a vibration in the air or in the ground and I—"

With a flash of light, her brain split open. That pain only lasted a moment before being overtaken by the burning in her head. The Goddess, the cat, broke free of her cage and scratched at her, shredding the pieces of her mind into ribbons that slipped away into a swelling fog.

"Ouch!" she cursed, rubbing the boney protrusion above her left eye. "Stop it, you wretched thing!" She slammed a mental box down around the Goddess again, this time in a sealed trap without seams, one the Goddess would not be able to remove on her own.

"Are you all right, Axandra?" Quinn's bifurcated brow expressed frightful concern about her sudden suffering. His hands reached out to steady her.

Patting his wrist, Axandra exhaled slowly and nodded. "Yes, I'll be fine. The Goddess does not like me knowing anything about this object. And it's apparent the Prophets didn't either."

Confused, Quinn struggled with arguing about the orb's existence and just letting the subject be. He decided, with great difficulty, to set the matter aside and, instead, delve more deeply into enjoying the pleasant night in the company of the woman he was in love with.

"You're sure you're all right?"

"Yes," she assured. Straightening her posture, she pasted on a smile.

"Tomorrow, I promised my services to the public food pantry," he told Axandra. He combed his fingers through her dark hair. "And I left my trunk with my friends on the far side of the city, which I need to retrieve for my clothes. Shall I meet you at the Theatre before the show?"

Axandra felt mildly disappointed that they would be apart again. As the passing of Soporus grew nearer, she became more nervous about what unexpected trials might befall the people. Squeezing the arm that circled about her waist, she acknowledged his plans. "You are a model citizen," she praised, though her voice sounded less than congratulatory. "Yes, I'll meet you at the Theatre."

"I'll wait by the Dancing Fountain," he instructed. He kissed her earlobe.

"All right," she agreed.

Quiet moments passed as they returned to lay on the mattress, though neither was yet asleep.

Quinn spoke again, breaking the silence. "Why is the Protectress falling in love with me?"

She made a small laugh in her throat. "Some mysteries may never be revealed. Thank you for being here," Axandra said to him, running a finger along his chin. The stubble of a beard grew in, rough against her skin like sandpaper. "You make me feel... safe and happy."

"You're welcome." He kissed her softly on the lips. Then they said goodnight to each other.

Chapter 25

The Play

21st Octember, 307

At the appointed time of the evening, Axandra descended the hill walkway to the Theatre. She donned a formal silk gown of violet and lavender hues, and she wore her hair pinned up at the sides but left cascading down the back of her neck. Over her bare shoulders, a silk wrap protected against the chill that blew in with the northern wind. Taking her time, she appreciated her surroundings. The leaves of the trees transformed from summer's green to reds and golds. Fallen leaves scattered in the breeze. The sunset cast the sky in pink and orange. Soporus did not rise until late in the evening, so the stars had an opportunity to show themselves early.

Below her, Axandra glimpsed the crowd gathered on the avenue in front of the performance hall, waiting for seating to begin. She hoped the people would use the opportunity to take their minds off strife and enjoy entertainment. The sight of the crowd imbued her with satisfaction, as well as doubt that she would be able to locate her companion with any ease.

The patrons stood grouped together as friends in various small circles on the brick walkway. A great deal of chatter and laughter filled the air all around. Smiling faces paused in their conversations to wish the Protectress a good evening as she passed among them. She made certain to return the consideration.

Vendors near the front of the building announced their offerings, from wine and ale to small sandwiches. Ushers in blue jackets with brass buttons guarded the main doors, waiting for the signal that the house was ready.

For several minutes, Axandra searched the crowd, unable to see the way to the fountain Quinn described to her that morning. She sought a statue of three dancers made of bronze, their arms and legs extended in vigorous action. Finally, she spotted Quinn from the back. He was engrossed in a conversation with a group of attendees, his voice carrying over the crowd as he told a story that produced laughter from his friends.

As the Protectress approached, the others in the group noticed her first. The conversation ceased and each began to bow to greet her. Quinn, realizing what was happening, turned in her direction. Smiling pleasantly, he bowed slightly, then raised his smoky eyes to hers.

"Protectress," he greeted formally, remembering his manners in company.

"Mr. Elgar," Axandra replied in kind. "I'm so pleased you accepted my invitation." She knew her broad smile betrayed their relationship as something far more than acquaintances. She couldn't help herself. She reached immediately for his hand.

He drew that hand up to his heart, clearly throwing caution to the wind. The gesture grabbed the attentions of those gathered nearby, causing raised eyebrows.

"Protectress, allow me to introduce you to some friends of mine." Quinn went around the circle of four women and three men. They served as historians, archivists, teachers and one as a tavern keeper. Quinn spent a great deal of time in Undun City, the hub of his travels, thus he had acquired many acquaintances in relation to his work—and some that weren't.

"You know," said Ella Bercaw, swirling her glass of wine as she spoke, "the Protectress-Past used to sneak in the side door when she came to a show—if she came at all. She hated crowds."

"Ella!" exclaimed Derrick, her apparent companion. "Show respect, please!"

"Respect?" Ella scoffed. "It's difficult to respect someone who's been hiding for twenty-one years. But now you're here, acting as though you were never gone."

"Ella!" Derrick admonished a second time.

"I've made no excuses for my absence," Axandra reminded, trying not to take personal offense at the woman's accusatory tone. "I have returned to fulfill my duties, and the people have welcomed me. That's their choice."

"Not everyone welcomes you back," Ella spat.

Derrick tugged at her arm, pulling her back. "Ella, stop this!" He struggled to draw her away, while Ella hissed at him. The others stood by awkwardly, unaccustomed to such uncouth displays.

"We—Uh, we apologize for our friend, Your Honor," the tavern keeper said. "She gets unruly when she's had too much wine."

"You don't need to apologize," Axandra assured them. "Everyone is entitled to her opinion."

"Well, since my companion has arrived," said Quinn to excuse them from the uncomfortable scene, "I am obligated to fetch her some refreshment. Enjoy the remainder of your evening." He bowed to his friends and walked away, towing Axandra with him. A short distance away, he apologized as well. "I'm sorry about Ella. She holds a grudge against the entire Protectresship."

Quinn led her toward one of the vendors and procured a glass of wine, a small burlap bag of roasted nuts and a piece of fruit. She devoured them readily, her stomach rumbling. Lunch suddenly seemed a day ago, and she hadn't snacked during the afternoon while joining Healer Gage on rounds to see several of his regular patients. As she ate, Quinn pointed out the architecture of the building, which was similar to the design of the Palace, with many decorative finials and castings around the windows and doorways. As they wandered around the promenade, the Elite struggled to keep her surrounded. The pair changed direction often and had no exact destination at the moment. This made the guards nervous. One surged ahead to clear a path to the main doors. The other two marched behind her. The three felt relieved when one of the blue-suited ushers finally approached the Protectress.

"Good evening, Esteemed Protectress." The graying man bowed in greeting. "Please allow me to show you to your seats. We have prepared your private box on the second level."

Axandra thanked the usher as he led them in. Seemingly out of nowhere, two more Elite appeared. Narone sent them ahead to secure the interior of the Theatre, clear of any apparent threats. She wondered if the scrutiny of the guards produced the wait for seating. Directed up a flight of stairs, she and Quinn passed through a wide curving corridor around the outside of the performance hall to a narrow door. Here a compact enclosure contained two comfortable chairs upholstered in gold fabric, complimenting the deep reds of the carpet and curtains that draped the viewing portal. Along one wall stood a small rectangular table set with a green plant and a chilled bottle of wine. Two fresh glasses and finger napkins rested next to the bottle.

"Compliments of the starring actress, Your Honor," the usher explained of the wine. "She hopes you will enjoy the show."

"This will be appreciated," Quinn assured, reading the hand-printed label on the blue glass bottle.

The usher quickly tied back the curtains, opening the small alcove to the main hall. They peered down at the darkened and shrouded stage and at the main gallery of seats below, which began to fill as the ushers allowed the audience to enter from the avenue. Chandeliers hung from the high ceiling, shedding dim light below. To enhance the focus of the stage, the walls of the hall were lacquered black. The pit conductor prompted the attention of a small ensemble of brass and woodwinds and directed them in a lively prelude.

Axandra stood near the edge of the box, looking down upon the other spectators. Whispering to their companions, several looked in her direction or pointed her out. Many rumors circled the City about her attending or not attending the play. The Protectress' seats had remained empty for a few years now. Some didn't believe the new Protectress would actually show, considering the multitude of crises occurring at the time and the wavering of public opinion. As Quinn peeked over with the Matriarch, some gazers became more inquisitive, wondering who accompanied her and the tone of the relationship.

Axandra felt confident that she sent the right message to the people. She was a citizen, just like them, and she enjoyed a good distraction now and then.

"Have you ever been to this Theatre?" Quinn asked, handing her a fresh glass of the wine and relieving her of the empty challis.

"Once," she replied, noting how the hall, which moments ago echoed with each noise made by the ushers and musicians, was now muted by the bodies filling the seats below. "When I was a little girl, my parents brought me to a concert." She moved a short distance to the chairs and sat down. Her full skirt filled much of the space around her. The air inside the theatre felt just as cool as the air outside, so she drew her wrap more tightly around her shoulders.

Quinn settled himself into the seat beside her and reached for her hand, holding it firmly in his grasp. "Axandra," he whispered, relishing the sound of her chosen name, even though, in public, the spoken word breached etiquette. No one was around to hear him. "Thank you for inviting me tonight. I really appreciate coming to the show."

"You're welcome," she said kindly. She watched his gray-blue eyes highlighted with candlelight. "And thank you for coming. I appreciate the company. I may always be surrounded by people, but I don't really have anyone I can share things with."

"Well, some of those Elite are rather stoic," Quinn pointed out. "I know they take their jobs seriously, but they could loosen up once in a while." He crossed one leg over the other, aiming his body toward hers in the chair. He looked extremely handsome in his silk suit of dark blue, especially as it collected the dim candlelight and glowed back at her. The jacket boasted a high square collar cut out at his throat that dipped to reveal a pristine white button shirt with silverwork buttons. The tan of his skin seemed to be fading since he hadn't spent his working day outdoors for the last few weeks.

She reached up with her right hand and cupped his cheek, feeling the skin shaved smooth and soft. He smiled as she touched him and the muscles played beneath her hand.

"People sure do like to stare at you," Quinn commented. Even he could sense the attention from the audience below.

"I'm sorry," Axandra apologized, though she didn't remove her hand right away. She wanted to kiss him to show her appreciation, but thought he might be embarrassed to give everyone a show. "I'm not really used to it either. These last few months have been very ... trying. I hope the play is more entertaining than we are." She chuckled with him and let her hand drop away.

Very shortly, the overture ended, and the heavy curtains swayed as they swept aside. The room darkened all around until the couple could barely see each other except for the bleed from a tiny circle of light centered on the stage. As the female lead of the play came forward into the light and began a soliloquy that set the story, Axandra leaned over quickly and stole a kiss from her companion. He smiled at her and mouthed, "You're welcome," then settled in to watch the play.

"Earth is behind us. We can never go back," the character's voice projected with a sorrowful tone. "What lies in front of us is hope for the future. I feel…" She paced to one side, her lips to her clasped hands. Looking up again, she said, "I feel frightened! And happy. And sad!" The emotions played upon her face. "And excited. I look forward to the adventure, though I know I will never see what comes at the end of this Journey. Neither will my children. The New World is just too far away." She looked into the imaginary distance, as though she looked out a window. The lights gradually illuminated the set behind her, the interior of a spaceship. "I know we will reach it. I see it in my dreams—the most beautiful world!" She closed her eyes and lifted her shoulders with a deep breath. "People will breathe clean air and swim in clean water. The little ones will run through the grass, like I did when I was young, before all the grass died."

"Mama, do you see it yet?" A little boy in pajamas called as he scurried onto the stage from behind a set wall. He wrapped his arms tightly around the actress's leg and peered up at her hopefully.

She chuckled at his enthusiasm. "No, Darling. Not yet. But look! There's Saturn! We're the first ones to see the rings so close—and we'll probably be the last," she whispered aside as the boy turned away and shouted, "Marta! Marta, come look!"

Now an older girl, maybe ten, appeared. She joined her mother and brother at the imaginary portal. Her mouth gaped in astonishment. "Oh, wow! It's more beautiful than I imagined!"

The family marveled at the imaginary planet through the pretend window in front of them, then the mother shooed her children away to get ready for school.

"I do wish I could see it," she said earnestly, her hands clasped together in front of her. She rose on her tiptoes, pushing herself higher toward the audience. The stage darkened for the next scene.

As the lights brightened during the final curtain call, Axandra rose to her feet for the actors, joining the house in their ovations for the entertaining story and well-played characters. The applause lasted for several minutes, and the cast and crew bowed and waved graciously in thanks.

The door to the box opened to allow the usher to return. "Madam, I have been asked to extend to you an invitation to meet the company, if you would like."

"That would be wonderful! Thank you!" She clapped excitedly. Turning to Quinn, she asked, "Will you come with me?"

"Of course," he accepted loudly over the continuing applause. "Willa Caple is another friend of mine," he said of the leading lady.

"You certainly do have a lot of friends," Axandra commented, adding a false note of jealously to tease him.

"It comes with the travel," he explained, hardly phased by her tone of voice.

The usher led them down through the corridors to the backstage doors. Backstage, the lavish interior appeared markedly absent, replaced by the utility of ropes and weights, cables and lights and pieces of the set that rolled on and off stage. They followed the usher to a large greenroom, where he asked them to wait. A short table sat with beverages and a small selection of fresh fruit. A meager offering for a reception, but with recent mandates to store more food for winter due to flooding and drought, this was all that could be spared. Beverages flowed plentifully, as most of the alcohols had been fermented from previous years' harvests. Lately, many people found solace in spirits. The drinks helped people laugh.

Which is how Axandra felt right now, blissfully cheerful. Her head buzzed from the three glasses of wine she'd already consumed, thanks to Quinn's attention to her glass. Her muscles felt loose, and her mind felt free from any worry. While they waited, she kept hold of his hand and kept him close. Wrapping one strong arm around her waist, he drew her closer still, signaling that he didn't mind.

"Wasn't that a wonderful performance!" Axandra praised, thinking her voice a bit too loud in the cozy room. Picking at the display of fruit, she popped a red berry into her mouth.

"Superb!" Quinn agreed, taking another glass of wine for each of them. "I usually find works about the Journey quite fascinating, even if they are about fictional characters. We can only imagine what it must be like to leave one's home and never have the opportunity to go back."

The actors began to arrive, stripped down to dressing robes and makeup still on. First to arrive was Willa, the star, who was clearly much older than the character she portrayed. Excitedly, she cheered Quinn's presence and embraced him in a quick hug. Then, reminding herself of the Protectress, she bowed and spit out titles and gracious thanks.

"You are so lucky to have Quinn," Willa blurted, winking at her old friend. "Ever the gentlemen and the most honest person I've ever met, despite his previous reputation in this city."

"It's a good thing she already knows the stories," Quinn sighed, his cheeks blushing for Willa to hint at his secrets. "You might have scared her away."

"Nonsense!" Willa scoffed playfully. "She knows she's got a good thing. My dear, your cheeks sure are rosy!" Willa's boisterous voice overpowered every other person in the room, since the place now steadily filled with actors and other invited guests, all milling around to give respects. "You are much prettier than your posters."

Axandra smiled in thanks and watched Quinn interact with the gathering crowd. She remembered how shy and how awkward he had been when they first met and how much he tried to please her and gain her attention. Now that they spent some time together, he loosened up. He still wanted to please her and he still worried there might be something about him she wouldn't like. He guarded his embraces with the others, not wanting to seem overly intimate with any of them.

Axandra wished she could be so free with strangers. She had always experienced difficulty opening up to anyone unfamiliar. She chalked it up to her secret identity—her no-longer-secret identity—which she kept safely hidden away for so many years. Like any old habit, her closed personality proved difficult to shed.

Her observations were cut short by the ground jerking beneath her feet and the resultant outbreak of screams and shouts from the green room occupants. The movement came suddenly and with enough force to upset Axandra's balance. She grabbed hold of Quinn's upper arm for support.

"An earthquake?" Willa exclaimed and questioned at the same time. "Not in three hundred years—"

The ground continued to oscillate beneath their feet, rattling glass inside wooden frames, toppling glasses and loosening artwork from the wall mounts. People fled from the building into the avenue, scrambling in all directions, completely panicked.

The Elite moved in, taking immediate custody of their charge. "We must move you to a safer location."

"Safer?" Quinn barked. "It's a bloody earthquake! Where do we go?"

Encircled by the gray clad bodies of her guard, Axandra had little choice but to follow their lead through the nearest exit onto the paved courtyard south of the Theatre. The tremors subsided momentarily as the group proceeded to the car. Though she had walked down, Ty insisted the vehicle be at the ready, and now she approved of what formerly seemed a pointless waste of resources. This geographic area was not prone to noticeable quakes.

The interior of the car muted the cacophony of the crowd running away from the theatre. Unfamiliar with such sensations, the townspeople earned every right to be frightened. Hopefully, the relatively mild shaking failed to impart any serious damage. If the people would slow down to assess the situation, they would realize their panic was unwarranted.

Quinn slid into the seat next to her. "People need to slow down. If that was the bulk of it, they've nothing to worry about. I've been through worse."

"So have I," Axandra agreed. Nevertheless, she linked her fingers with his and grasped his hand tightly for comfort. "Mr. Narone, any sign of the Safety Watch? We need to control this crowd. These people are extremely panicked."

"Yes, Madam. The uniformed volunteers have just arrived," Ty reported from just outside the open car door. The Commander pulled the door closed as he joined them in the compartment. Through the slot, Ty instructed the driver to head for the open fields east of the city as a temporary safety zone. They would be away from buildings and people. A moment later, the vehicle inched forward, parting the mob centim by centim. Several minutes passed before the car increased speed and reached an open street.

"What would cause an earthquake here?" Axandra questioned.

"Soporus, most likely," Quinn replied. "I imagine the gravitational pull of the passing planet is increasing pressure on the seismic plates."

"Even here? We're not on a fault line, are we?"

"Not directly. But the mountain range sits upon a seismic zone. Those mountains are young and still rising. They move so smoothly and steadily, we just don't experience notable tremors," Quinn answered studiously.

"It's dark out here," Ty commented, clearly unhappy. "Pull over here. Stay in the car. We'll idle here until we can ascertain if the quakes are over."

"I think that was it," Quinn said, attempting to display relief so that the emotion would spread. Even through his meager empathic tendrils, the concern from the guards felt stifling. At least the distance from the city's population freed him of any additional discomfort.

For a time, they sat in the car and waited with barely a word.

The driver spoke on the radio to the station within the city proper. Ty eyed the driver and listened in on the conversation. Two other guards scanned the darkness around them diligently. Hands still clasped, Axandra and Quinn said nothing aloud. He thought of the pleasant solitude of the Residence and how shortly they would go there and end this episode. She echoed his unspoken sentiment.

"Do you hear that sound?" she questioned aloud to everyone. "What is that? It sounds like thunder."

Narone's face brightened with recognition. "Hooves. Move! Move!"

From the darkness came the fastest of the animal herd, crossing the road in front of the forebeams. Antelope, bustles, and bison stampeded the open land, no doubt fleeing the upsetting quake. However, it was too late to avoid the impact of bison horns into the right side of the metal casing, tearing easily through and sending the car sliding a meter left. Dents appeared as hooved antelope leapt onto the roof and over. Another strike lifted the tires and the following impact flipped the car twice over. Resting on its side, the car became an undesirable obstacle and more of the animals steered clear on either side.

Axandra found herself at the bottom of a pile of bodies in an even darker night. Shoving, she struggled to free herself from the crushing weight. Bodies moved, some on their own, others with assistance. Finally, the last weight lifted aside. Quinn knelt in the debris next to her, guiding her into a sitting position. Without the compartment lights, she could barely make out his shape.

With blinding brightness, a torch came on, casting distended shadows wherever directed. Enough light spilled over to aid Axandra in finding Quinn in fair condition.

"Dammit," Narone cursed. He surveyed an immobile body. Axandra knew already what he would announce.

"Diane is dead."

The confirmation sparked tears in her eyes, though she barely knew the woman. For one of the guards to lose their life in duty brought her great sadness and a strong sense of Honor. Diane was the first. This woman would be remembered for her sacrifice.

"Injuries?" Ty requested of his charge, shining the beam directly at her.

"Nothing readily apparent," Axandra replied. "But my entire body hurts at this point."

The Commander assessed Quinn next. The Protectress' companion sustained a shallow gouge in his upper arm where one of the horns impaled the car into his flesh. He felt lucky he did not sustain a deeper wound.

The driver, appearing to cradle a fractured arm, operated the radio to call for assistance. A quick response assured that mere moments would pass before aid arrived.

"I need to get out of here," Axandra insisted, tugging at Quinn's arm as she rose to her wobbly feet. "Is it safe?"

"Safer to stay inside, Madam," Ty reported.

With her chest tightened and breathing constricted, her heart raced faster than those fleeing animals. Axandra did not accept that option. Attempting to maintain some composure, she hissed barely above a whisper, "I very much need to get out of here."

"I think she's right," Quinn advocated. Her pulse thrummed against his fingertips. "For her health."

A moment of quiet contemplation passed before Ty acquiesced to the request. "Very well. I will hoist you out. Stay near the car."

"Of course. Please."

Ty leapt up and with muscular hands and arms, raised the entire weight of his body high enough to secure a foothold and climb completely onto the topside of the overturned vehicle. He lay on the mangled door hanging his arms down, and with ease, he hoisted the petite Protectress up and out. A soft thud could be heard as she slid down the roof to the ground.

"Mr. Elgar," Ty prompted. Quinn brushed his hands on his pants to rid them of moisture and dirt. Knowing he weighed a bit more—well, a good amount more than the Matriarch, Quinn felt uncertain of the outcome of allowing Ty to hoist him through an opening just wider than his shoulders.

"Coming up." Raising his arms to meet Ty's, Quinn locked hand to wrist. He tried not to kick his feet as he was lifted from the ground.

The night was extremely dark. Neither moon rose at night this time of the month and Soporus dominated the sky only after midnight. Starlight cast the faintest glow over the landscape, silhouetting geographic obstacles in black relief.

Darkness certainly did not mean loneliness out here. The human abilities to read each other's emotions also allowed them awareness of the living world. At this moment Quinn recognized the instinctive nature of a few grazers trailing after the stampede. The different animal species separated back into homogenous herds. Predators lurked nearby as well, having followed the stampede in order to catch an injured animal. The predators were eating their fill for now and lacked interest in the human morsels.

One mind he expected to find was missing.

Spinning a complete circle immediately, he burst "Where is Axandra? She's gone!"

Quinn noticed that Ty and the driver both appeared dazed and wobbly. Neither comprehended his declaration immediately.

A knuckle to his eye corner to fight off the wooziness, Narone examined his surroundings.

"Curses! What the hell happened?"

"Someone was here," Quinn realized. It wasn't a definite statement, more of a deduction. The Protectress had just been abducted into the darkness. The only people Quinn knew to have such stealthy skills were Prophets. Between this knowledge and Axandra's aforementioned fear that the Prophets worked secret plans allowed him to derive the answer.

"They've taken her to the Haven. They were here, they took her right out of our hands. Those bastards."

"Sir, I don't understand. She has to be here, nearby. They can't have gone far."

"You don't understand. It's been at least an hour. They blanked us."

"Then where is the rescue party? They should have arrived already," Ty argued, completely denying such a possibility.

"They were blanked too. You have no idea what these people are capable of. We've got to hurry." Quinn oriented himself toward the pale lights of Undun City. They were a few miles out, a least an hour's walk back. "If they've already made it to the gateway, we'll lose them. They're the only ones capable of getting into the storm."

"Sir, we don't have any way back."

"We've got legs."

"We have no hope of reaching the mountains on foot."

"We've got to do something!" Quinn shouted, feeling his face blaze with anger at the absolute resistance. "We can't wait here! Do you want the Protectress lost?"

For what Quinn suspected would be a rarely witnessed event, Ty Narone lost his temper. Flying at Quinn with rage to match a cornered packhound, Narone jabbed him in the chest with the blunt end of his stunner. "What do you expect me to do? You are telling me that I have to contend with people who possess mystical powers of persuasion and invisibility who live in a highly protected fortress beneath an impenetrable storm. I have a broken car, a dead guard and no way to track the invisible culprits. Tell me, sir, how in bloody hell you expect me to mount a rescue!"

Quinn Elgar had faced the tempers of other men and women before. Despite the cultured philosophy to avoid conflict, humans were still animals by nature and were unable to completely suppress the need to take a swing at each other to blow off steam. One particularly frightening contender was his own mother, whose temper flared on a regular basis like a pulsating star. Usually, Quinn backed away to diffuse the situation, gave a little space to avoid getting a lot of knuckles in his mouth.

Tonight, Quinn leaned into the assaulting weapon. "I expect, sir, that you will get on that radio, reinitiate the rescue party and send someone after the bloody culprits to track them down until we can catch up with them. What you do not want is for those Prophets to cross into the Storm and close the gateway without us. I will start walking now and meet the rescue on the way. Move!"

Taken aback, Narone stumbled back a step, his stunner dropping away in a trained motion to avoid accidental discharge. "Yes, Mr. Elgar. Take this with you," he acknowledged, handing Quinn the stunner before he moved in the direction of the car to use the radio.

During a past stint with the local Safety Watch in Lazzonir, Quinn was familiar with the stunner and its functions. He held the weapon in hand and started off on a direct route across the plain back to Undun City.

Chapter 26

Rescue Party

21st Octember, 307

About halfway back to the city, Quinn and the guards met the rescue bus. Ty ordered them immediately to the mountain gateway known to lead into the Prophet Haven, ignoring their questions about salvaging the car and belongings. Expressing the urgency of the situation, he ordered the driver to exceed the recommended speeds to make up time.

As the vehicle sped along the paved roads, Ty stood in the narrow aisle of the bus facing the gentleman with whom he had so recently clashed. "Mr. Elgar, unfortunately, I believe we are far too late to catch up with the Prophets before they enter the Storm. If they are the only ones capable of opening the gateway, how do you propose we are going to get her back?"

"As far as I know, the Prophets are the only ones with the ability to open their own gate," Quinn reasserted. "However, I happen to know a man outside the Storm who can do it."

"Outside the Storm? Who is this man?"

"He used to be a Prophet. He left."

Narone actually chortled. "Prophets don't leave their own kind. Sometimes I think you are full of bustle crap."

"My travels have taught me a lot of facts most people just aren't aware of," Quinn said, trying not to sound haughty about it. He'd traveled to every Region, scores of towns and villages across the continent, a dozen islands, and along the way he'd met hundreds of people. The one he thought of happened to live in Undun, an older man who spent his time keeping the garden of a simple house on the farthest west edge of the city. In his twenties, Quinn had met the man on a late evening hike. At that time, Quinn had just decided to leave the Believer sect in favor of a less warped methodology. Patrum sat on a boulder as though waiting for the young man to happen by. Recognizing him immediately as a Prophet, Quinn was fascinated to learn that Patrum also left his sect to pursue different beliefs. With the bond struck, Quinn kept up with Patrum mostly through letters. Though unfortunate the circumstances, the time had come to rekindle the face-to-face relationship.

"Number 26 on Boulder Road," Quinn announced the address.

When they pulled up outside the small house, Quinn hopped out of the bus and hurried through the high-grown hedges that concealed the structure from the roadway, then up to the door. He knocked with a shaking hand, now that the enormity of the situation bullied through his brain and punched up the adrenaline production.

"It must be time."

Narrowing his focus, Quinn squinted into the dimness in front of him. Vaguely, he could make out a human shape. "You're here," Quinn said with relief, almost in tears.

"Of course," said Patrum, holding out a welcoming hand. "I've been expecting you. Come inside. I have a few things we will need to take with us."

Patrum led Quinn and Ty from the street into his darkened house. Not a single candle lit the inside. Dark curtains draped each window, hiding any movements from those that might be in the street.

"I'm so glad you're still here," Quinn praised. He paced the floor in the great room, barely able to see the furniture to keep from smacking a shin. "We have to hurry. The Prophets have taken Axandra–uh, the Protectress—probably to the Haven. We need to get there before something horrible happens!"

"Patience, my friend. We have some time. You are very lucky. Had I been with the thieves, I would not have left anyone behind." Patrum first went to the far side of the room. With a soft scrape, a match burst into a brilliant flame, which the man used to light a lantern. The room brightened with a soft yellow glow.

"You may have left the fold, but you still think like them," Quinn sneered.

To his credit, Ty's outward emotions remained in check, despite the sudden intensity of distrust that sparked within. "I understand you were once a Prophet. As the commander of the Protectress' personal guard, I implore you for assistance."

Smiling kindly, Patrum nodded. "I was a Prophet, some time ago. May I ask who you are?" Even as he asked the question, he moved about the house. His next stop was the kitchen, which lay separated from the great room by a single narrow wall, leaving much of the two rooms open to each other. Rattling dishes, he fetched cups and a pot of hot water. From the pantry he pulled three different jars. With all of this he returned to the great room.

"My name is Ty Narone," replied the Commander.

"You also served Elora," Patrum assumed.

"Yes, I did, but only for a short time."

Gesturing to the cups, Patrum urged them to drink. "This tea will help strengthen you and protect you once we're inside." He poured three cups of steaming water, then blended the herbs from each of the three jars into each cup. Then he served them where they stood.

Quinn blew on the tea to cool it, hoping to avoid scalding his tongue. Ty eyed the drink suspiciously.

"Tell me how you knew to expect us, sir. I am afraid I do not understand your relationship to this matter. Your assistance will be useful getting us inside the Haven, but after that, my men and I will take over the operation."

"It was many years ago that I knew Elora personally. As a Prophet, I understand the events that are taking place now, and what the Prophets intend for the Protectress. Elora once asked me for help to save her daughter. And I intend to. But the ritual will not take place until Soporus rises tomorrow, when she's at last closest to us."

"What ritual?" Quinn demanded loudly. "This has something to do with the Goddess, doesn't it."

Patrum sipped his own cup. The Prophet's demeanor seemed inappropriately subdued, as though they had all the time in the universe to stall before mounting a rescue. "Quinn, they intend to strip the Goddess from her."

"What! Won't that—" He couldn't bring himself to say the words. The breath left his lungs in a wheeze.

Ty scowled. "What will happen to the Protectress? What about the Goddess?"

Patrum answered the men's questions openly and at length. "This planet was not uninhabited when humans arrived here. The Great Storm is a nest of creatures that feed on the physical and emotional energy of host animals, especially sentient ones. The Prophets fought with the creatures—we call them Stormflies—and somehow managed to make a compromise with them. One human would be sacrificed per generation, a being that could withstand the implantation of one of these creatures and then funnel the necessary energy from the people to the nest, allowing both species to occupy the same space and survive. The Goddess is a creature that has lived within the Protectress as long as the office has existed. The arrangement has suited us well for centuries. Elora was the first woman to resist the siege, to try to end the curse. She wanted life to be better for her child. Because Elora fought and because Ileanne fights now, the truce is broken. The Prophets have every intention of taking the Goddess out of Ileanne and implanting it in a new vessel, one willing to accept the responsibility, and resume the truce with the Stormflies. Once the Goddess resides in the host, she cannot be removed without damaging the host. Nor can the Goddess live outside of host for long," Patrum explained, his lips turned down in a dour scowl. "Elora's request was that I save her child completely from this fate, but I arrived too late to prevent the Sliver from being delivered. I failed her."

"Sliver?" Quinn was too upset to drink the bitter-smelling drink. He set the cup down on the small table next to him and wrung his hands together. "You mean the thing the Prophets put in her before she ran away from the Haven. She shared that memory with me when she told me about the Goddess."

"Yes. When she was six years old, the Prophets implanted the Sliver. It acts like a homing beacon for the Goddess, so that she can find her new host quickly no matter where on the planet the intended host may be. I was supposed to keep Ileanne from receiving it, therefore preventing the Goddess from ever finding her." The older man sounded ashamed of himself. "The elders decided to perform that ritual earlier than planned."

"Then you helped the Heir escape from the Haven," Quinn stated, piecing together the old stories he had heard about the once-missing Heir. He was only a youth when Elora's daughter disappeared without a trace.

Patrum nodded shortly. "Yes, I did. Only she never knew I was there. I made certain she survived the passage out, and I made certain that someone took her in without question. Then I watched her and waited for the time when she would have to remember who she was. I knew the Goddess would find her and bring her back here."

"But you've lived in Undun for that last fifteen years," Quinn reminded. "You weren't watching her that whole time."

"I didn't have to be near her to see her," said Patrum, tapping a finger to his temple. "She lived a very content life."

With his elbows leaning heavily against his knees, Quinn rested his head in his hands and tried to think. What were the facts? He knew that a strange creature inhabited Axandra. He knew that it was killing her anyway, robbing her body of the nutrients that kept her alive and wrecking her internal organs. He now knew that the woman's mother understood future events decades ago and gave up her only child in a thwarted effort to save the girl. He knew removal of the parasite was Axandra's ultimate wish, to be free of the thing that was killing her and killed all her mothers before her.

"Where did the Goddess come from?" Quinn asked Patrum, daring to think that the old man would know the answer to this question, too. He looked across the room to that pale, wrinkled face and the head topped with thick grayish-brown hair and stared deeply into the dark brown eyes. "Why have they kept it alive? Why not just finish off the Stormflies and be done with it."

"A very good question," Patrum said flatly. "No one quite understands why the one creature is used in this fashion, or how it works. The Prophets believe the Stormflies are strong enough to wipe out the entire human race on this world. What I do know is this: the Great Storm is a tenuous prison for those parasites. Ever since our planet began its pass of Soporus, the Storm has weakened, allowing the entities trapped inside to escape and infect your people. I don't know if this was expected. The elders always kept those secrets to themselves—probably for the best. Your dear Axandra, as you call her, will not be the last host, but she will be the last of her family line."

Hope quickly drained out of Quinn. A dozen men versus hundreds of Prophets all bent on one thing. He looked in his own mind, attempting to see the future, and saw only failure.

One last thing seemed strange to him. "Why did Elora ask you for help?"

For a man always prepared with knowledgeable answers, Patrum sat temporarily speechless. His mouth hung open slightly as he sought a safe answer to the question. "She and I were friends. I helped her make her transition when she received the Goddess."

"When was that?" Quinn probed.

"That was twenty-eight years ago," Patrum replied, seeing no way around the answer.

"Axandra is twenty-seven," Quinn said flatly, his reason clear.

"Is she?" Patrum responded with mock innocence. He cleared his throat and moved forward in his chair. "The two of you must drink so that we can leave. Without that tea, the Prophets will quickly be onto us and our journey will be for naught."

Resigning any further questions or protests, Quinn retrieved his cup and drank, his head nodding as everything fell into place. He never believed in predestination before today, but his mind began to embrace the concept that his entire life seemed wrapped into this moment.

Quinn had one goal, to save the woman he loved. He was not alone. Patrum pursued the same goal. Hope returned. The tea made him feel stronger, as though he were invincible.

Rising, Patrum stepped into the next room and returned with an armful of coarse cloaks. "Put these on. They will help with our disguise. I will be able to convince the Prophets that we belong, at least long enough to get close to Ileanne. You must remain quiet and allow me to answer any questions we may be asked. This will not be easy."

"We understand," Quinn said after a brief glance to his companion. "Thank you for your help."

"You're welcome. And thank you," said Patrum. "It's time to go."

Chapter 27

The Ritual

22nd Octember, 307

Cold. Hard. These were the sole sensations that returned to her body as her mind rose to consciousness. Axandra kept her eyes closed at first, not daring to know her whereabouts. She remembered the Prophets appearing on the prairie and remembered the noise they used to drown her senses and cause unconsciousness.

The realization arrived that she was in danger.

She began to sense people all around her, hundreds of them. The Prophets. They brought her to the Haven. Their thoughts began to filter in.

> *She hurts the people…*
> *A new One will take her place…*
> *The Stormflies will be appeased…*
> *When will she awaken?*

Among the thoughts swirled a melting pot of emotion—triumph, sadness, regret, concern, curiosity. Overall, there hovered a sense of relief, as though a long struggle neared its end.

At last Axandra opened her eyes, looking up at the open sky, directly into the crackling, swirling mass of the Great Storm. Inside the Storm, tiny firefly lights flickered and danced.

She lay flat on her back on a stone altar. She had been here before, during the ritual of receiving the Sliver, the beacon that allowed the Goddess to find her. Where would the creature be without her? In the Storm? Lost? Or seeking a new host?

These questions didn't matter. She carried the creature. Soon, the Prophets would reveal the purpose of the Goddess. Axandra feared the outcome did not bode well for her.

Trying to move, to relieve the numbing pain in her limbs, she found herself restrained to the altar without physical bindings. Her captors held her there with the strength of their minds. She could only turn her head to the side to see the gathering. They stood clustered together close by, all eyes upon her.

Why have you brought me here? she thought-asked them. Her captors' minds grew quiet as they realized she could hear them clearly. Soon all she heard was the sizzling of the stormy mass above the arena. Will someone answer me?

The eyes of the group shifted as someone moved in the periphery of her vision. Straining against the invisible bonds, she tried to follow the figure. Turning her head, she found herself looking at an enormous silver orb, which she recognized from the dig in North Compass.

This explained why the memories of that day had been erased. The Prophets brought the orb here for the Goddess. Like thieves, they pilfered the artifact, and everyone that witnessed its existence paid a dear price.

"Community," Tyrane, the elder, raised his voice and his arms to gain their attention.

Axandra sensed their focus transfer almost wholly to him. As Tyrane spoke, she felt a vibration begin to permeate her body. She remembered the sensation from the dig, whenever she neared the orb. In her eyes, the colors melted together and poured into her brain. With her vision blurring, her stomach began to churn. The internal buzzing drowned out the old man's voice.

She felt an urge to touch the orb, but she could not extend her arm.

Not yet, Ileanne, said Tyrane's voice in her mind.

The cat-goddess purred. Axandra found the creature uncaged and pacing the full breadth of her mind. Offering artificial affection, the Goddess rubbed against the walls of her thoughts, opening memories and touching off sensations of sexual excitement and desire, causing her body to respond earnestly. She battled down the reaction, unwilling to be seduced into readiness to accept whatever was coming to her.

The time is coming, came Tyrane's voice again.

"Our time of true peace comes again," he announced aloud, smiling triumphantly. "Tonight, we recreate the truce and renew our freedom from their onslaught."

Time for what? Axandra asked him. She tried to open her mouth and speak aloud, to draw the attention of the others. They restrained her from any movement. Her jaw locked, and her voice stilled. Legs numb against the cold stone, her joints ached from the chill.

The Goddess needs to perform her duty or every one of us will perish, Tyrane said firmly. *You broke our truce and threatened humans with extinction. Your services are no longer required.*

The buzzing intensified, eliciting a moan of distress. In response, the mental grip tightened.

"When Soporus rises, the Goddess will be free to move to a new host, the one who waits quietly in slumber," Tyrane continued, his face to the East, where the first light of the sister planet appeared on the horizon.

A new host? Why will you kill me for this creature? Axandra's mind screamed out. No one reacted. She thought Tyrane must be blocking her thoughts from reaching his followers. She felt in her very center that she could not be freed of this thing without giving up her life, no matter how badly she wanted to be free.

Had you stayed with us, you would have understood your purpose, but you have fought the Goddess and now you must be sacrificed for the greater good of our people.

No! She struggled, trying to force them to lose their hold on her. *No! You can't release her!* Axandra cried out in her mind with every ounce of her strength, broadcasting her thoughts wide to warm them. *She won't keep her promise!*

Many began to lose their focus on her restraint. Their minds scattered from their purpose. As she felt a loosening of her limbs, she knew they heard her. Tyrane could not hold her by himself.

Soporus quickly climbed the sky. The dead world appeared twice as large as the two moons side-by-side and lit the ground in gray light bright enough to read by.

Either you die and the Goddess finds a new host, or we lose this war, Tyrane revealed to her with resolve. *Your mother was not strong enough to end it, nor are you. I hoped that bringing you home would convince you to continue your purpose. You cannot forsake what needs to endure.*

Axandra continued to fight to free herself. Sweat broke on her skin. She grunted as she pulled her arms up from the stone.

What did you do? Axandra suddenly understood that Tyrane would commit any act to ensure his truce continued. Elora died prematurely at his hand.

He smiled down at her, a sickly sweet curve of his thin lips. *Only what needed done.* "Now."

By no will of her own, her right arm extended straight from her side, sweeping toward the object next to her. The silvery surface burned her skin even before contact, the temperature too hot to measure. Axandra could not scream or recoil. Every atom in her body quaked until she felt certain she would be pulverized into dust.

Across the arena came a shout. Axandra couldn't believe her ears. Quinn was here, trying to rescue her. But she couldn't answer him.

The metal of the orb began to melt away around Axandra's hand. Where no seams existed, an opening materialized. An interior light glowed, illuminating the body of a young woman. Unmoving, she appeared to be asleep or in a coma. Her breasts rose slowly with controlled respiration.

Axandra's skin boiled where the molten metal poured. Every nerve in her body inflamed, her muscles went rigid. Weakened, she could no longer fight her captors. Struggling for breath and sobbing, she could no longer hear any noise except the rush of blood in her ears or see anything except lightning or feel anything but agony.

The Goddess rose to the surface of her brain, now a violet sphere of light. The color grew bright in her left eye, blinding her vision.

With a jerk, Axandra felt her body lifted into the air. She floated momentarily, no longer weighed down. She felt nothing, not pain, not cold, not even the air around her.

A frail shell lay beneath her as she drifted upward. The skeleton protruded from the skin. The once rosy cheeks looked hollow. The eyes sank in dark circles and stared lifelessly upward. Those eyes looked green again. She had forgotten that her eyes were naturally green.

How very fragile the human form could be. How easy to rob it of its life.

No, you can't take me with you. I won't become a part of you, Axandra denied the Goddess, pulling herself back down. She endeavored to make her essence heavier and sink back to her body. All she had to do was imagine she was made of lead.

+++

Quinn's shout gave away their disguises. Realizing there were interlopers in their midst, a group of Prophets turned to them, hands open in their direction. He felt himself grabbed by the arms and trapped, even though they did not touch him. Patrum and Ty froze too, unable to move.

"You fools! He's killing her! She doesn't deserve to die!"

As his voice carried across the arena, Quinn watched helplessly as Axandra's hand touched the silver orb. The surface of the metal glowed hot blue around her fingers, blistering the skin instantly. Smoke and the sick smell of burning flesh assaulted his nostrils.

Roaring, Quinn fought against the trap, pushing with his feet until he could feel himself making headway against them. He strained as though he forced a boulder uphill.

Part of the capsule melted away, opening to reveal hidden treasure. Light contained within the shell illuminated the body of a girl with pale flesh and cropped chestnut brown hair. By the smoothness of her unblemished face, Quinn judged her age as no more than seventeen, but he had no idea how long she'd been confined within the capsule. Her features suggested she belonged to the Protecting family.

Ever the scientist, Quinn hypothesized that the Prophets, through their warped wisdom, created an alternate host body decades ago, in order to prepare for any disaster that might befall the only living Heir to their truce. With only one daughter born each generation, the Prophets understood the need for emergency preparations.

The girl slept a few moments more as the capsule's interior controls altered the environment from stasis to revival. The child's eyes fluttered open, gauged her surroundings and squinted with immediate confusion.

Quinn could not care one iota less about the mystery of the orb now. Axandra was still alive, but he could sense her life force fading. Since his weak abilities no match for the power of those occupying this arena, he briefly wondered how he sensed her so clearly, but this was another mystery for which he did not have time. He needed to get to Axandra, to stop the Prophets from killing her. He pursued this need relentlessly. While the Prophets stood astounded to behold the new arrival, Quinn forced his way through the throng. He could see Axandra just ahead.

A light appeared from Axandra's eye, a small violet radiance that shimmered and swirled as it ascended into the air. The very air seemed to change, to become sweeter and more peaceful. He felt almost euphoric, despite the very real fact that Axandra lay lifeless on the altar.

As he neared her body, the euphoria drained from him. Boney limbs drooped from the edge of the stone platform. No breath moved in her lungs. Her eyes stared, open and empty.

The Prophet elder reached up to cup the entity in his hands, but it pulled away from him, moving back down toward Axandra's body. The entity's shape distorted, shooting violent arcs in every direction. The bulb began to split.

Quinn lost sight of the body and the purple light as the Prophets shifted around him, moving in closer to the altar to witness the result of their ritual murder.

Shoving through again, he next saw the old man with the Goddess enclosed in his hands. The gray haired elder stepped toward the girl in the capsule. By the time the child realized her circumstances, Tyrane would deliver the gift.

"Tyrane, Stop!"

Quinn nearly fell flat hearing Axandra's voice.

Patrum and Ty somehow reached her side—he'd lost track of them in the melee—their hands upon her body to help her sit up. Very much alive, Axandra confronted the elder, but not without anguish on her features. She tucked the severely wounded hand close to her body, blackened and withered. Blood and fluid smeared across the loose gray shift she wore. She gasped with pain, her lips twisted grotesquely and her brow creased deeply between her eyes.

Tyrane turned back to her, eyes narrowed angrily. "You cannot live," he growled. "The Goddess must live. She will end this struggle you and your mother brought on us. It is your fault the people are sick and dying."

"She will end it by destroying us!" Axandra screamed. Her body quivered with exhaustion and shock from her injury, yet she stayed upright, facing her captor. "She has no intention of resuming peace!"

"You lie!" Tyrane hurried to finish his act of delivery. "Take this new body, Goddess, to use as your own, to feed your sisters and sustain their existence—"

"No!" Quinn leapt at the old man, tackling him at the knees and knocking him to the hard floor. Limbs flailing, Tyrane released the entity, which flew up into the air as though pitched.

Of its own will, the violet orb sped to the body in the capsule, was absorbed through the left eye, and immediately integrated its physical form with the soft tissue of the brain. The face, a moment ago young and confused, displayed age and experience centuries beyond what any human could hope to achieve. The entity completely usurped the mind of the surrogate.

Placing her bare feet on the stony floor, the new hybrid being appraised the crowd of Prophets staring up at her.

"This body is so young," the Goddess exclaimed rapturously.

"It isn't going to work, Tyrane," Axandra called out. "The people won't accept her. You have to stop this. The Stormflies aren't going to wait anymore."

"It has to work," the elder insisted. "Our two peoples have lived this way for centuries, benefiting each other, keeping peace."

"They don't want our peace." Trying to stand, Axandra slipped her feet to the floor, only to find her emaciated body too weak to support her own weight. Ty held fast onto her arms to keep her up while Patrum circled the altar to assist. Quinn was almost there, his drive to reach her only strengthened by seeing her reanimated.

The host flashed a sardonic smile at the injured human female before her. The violet eyes of possession surveyed Axandra from top to bottom. Her opponent appeared to be in no condition to possess consciousness, let alone stand up.

"You know more than I can safely allow. Please die." The host/Goddess raised her splayed hands toward Axandra. The space between them rippled.

Defensively, Axandra raised her good arm to shield herself. A nearly invisible bubble blocked the rippling air, causing the force to ricochet out in all directions.

"Stop them! Do something!" Quinn shouted at the Prophets. Stifled by the din, no one seemed to hear him. From behind, he received a kick in his kidney. Doubled over in pain, he turned back to find Tyrane on his feet and swinging around for another swipe with his leg. Catching the man by his ankle, Quinn set him off balance and sent them both tumbling to the ground.

"They are going to kill everyone!" Quinn shouted at Tyrane, trying to make him understand.

"You are ruining everything!" the old man screamed, drawing back his fist to strike a blow. Quinn easily evaded the move, propelling himself onto his feet—

Only to be knocked flat again by a flying body. Prophets were being tossed aside like rag dolls by the new host. Invisible yet crushing blows sent the Prophets careening in all directions.

Axandra shielded herself with the bubble of her own making, holding off the crushing mental force aimed at her. Ty pressed behind her, trying to keep the woman on her feet. Patrum could not be seen on the far side of the action. Quinn marveled for a moment at his love's ability to protect herself. He realized that many of the Prophets tried to use similar powers, but the Goddess thwarted their efforts with simple flicks of her wrist.

"Goddess, be patient!" Tyrane begged of the new vessel. "We will deal with the traitor. Allow me to help you learn about our ways. This body has been asleep for a hundred and fifty years. A great deal has changed."

Laughing derisively, the host/Goddess mocked the elder. "As if I don't already know? I've seen it all, human. I was there through all of it. There is nothing you can teach me now."

Quinn moved into the crowd, avoiding more men and women thrown in his direction. He hoped to get near the being unnoticed and use his physical strength against her. It was a slim hope, but one he felt he could not abandon.

Under the pressure of the assault, Axandra's defense weakened and broke. She toppled backward onto Narone. The energetic force wrapped around her and lifted her into the air. Suspended above the stony ground, she writhed and screamed as the ripples enveloped her. Slowly, her body spun and tilted, worked over by the onslaught of energy.

From the far shadows, Patrum leaped into the path of the torturing force. As the rescuer became enveloped in pain, Axandra slumped to the ground, right into the arms of her commander, who lifted her easily and moved to the far side of the stone platform for protection. Patrum's shrieks took over where hers ended.

Furiously, the host narrowed her eyes and raised her second hand directly at the meddling man. The ripples lengthened into waves as she increased her destructive power. The force expanded outward in a sphere, touching the Prophets in the front lines and causing them to drop and thrash in agony.

Patrum's cries immediately ceased.

"You believe yourselves superior, that you captured us and kept us alive. We are tired of this game, and we are ready now to take you all," the host/Goddess proclaimed. Raising one arm to the open sky, she released a spray of lightning that slashed a hole in the clouds like sharp scissors through cloth.

Quinn looked up at the sky full of shooting stars and felt terror. They fell far and wide across the sky, reaching distances beyond the Great Storm. A bolt of lightning struck the lip of the arena, sending down a shower of rubble. People threw up their arms to protect their faces.

Quinn reached the capsule. He leaned against the massive structure to catch his breath, hiding a moment. The screaming cut into his heart.

The metal orb rocked slightly as his weight pushed against the side. Giving a shove, he found its balance unstable.

Looking across the stage, Quinn's eyes met Ty's. Eyes narrowed, Quinn attempted to find some way to convey what he was about to attempt. Somehow, the effort seemed to work, for Ty gave one brief nod of his head in approval.

Quinn shoved against the metal orb with all his might, trying to get the pod to roll. Simultaneously, Ty lunged, shoulder forward. The commander struck the girl with a crushing force, driving her body against the metal capsule. He moved back immediately as the orb rolled in his direction. There came a sickening crunch and a gargled shriek that soon stopped as the heavy capsule came to rest again. The ripples and waves that distorted the space in the room abruptly ceased.

The Stormflies swooped down. Many of the Prophets turned their attention to the raining fire, lifting their hands in unison and building a shield over the gathering. Fingers of lightning showered down among the Prophets. Some lost footing and collapsed to the stony ground with shrieks of pain. Others guarded themselves with bubbles of their own energy which absorbed and nullified the electricity from above. The combined strength of the individuals caused the atmosphere around them to quake and rumble. The sensation struck Quinn with a wave of nausea. Guts flipping wildly, he lost his footing.

The Stormflies swirled around the arena, their miniscule forms striking any human object in their paths. Axandra raised an arm weakly to block the next attack. Her left arm twisted oddly, her hand dangling from a broken wrist. Ty shouted in protest and clambered to place himself between his charge and the showering assailants, a possibility he had long trained for. The commander didn't even give it a second thought.

Quinn examined what little of the body he could view from beneath the massive orb. He assured himself he killed this girl because he had to save many others, but the self-assurance felt weak.

He witnessed the purple spirit rise out of the crushed body, wobbling in the air. With a quiver, the entire thing broke free of the corpse and reshaped itself into the ball of light. Righting itself, the entity made a beeline for the next available body, a young Prophet woman attempting to pull herself to her feet after being knocked down.

Too late to call out a warning, Quinn realized the Goddess could easily leap from host to host in this environment. The woman of pale skin lurched as the light overtook her, then her face adopted the same ancient expression of rage.

Growling like a prairie cat, Quinn plowed forward head down, directly into the host's sternum, knocking her flat against the ground.

The woman only laughed and teased, "You'll never win." Then the life behind the host's eye blinked out, the body dead. The violet essence that was the Goddess rose out of the body and upward.

Quinn fumbled to capture the creature in his hands, just as Tyrane had held it, but the entity slipped between his fingers and escaped into the dissipating mass of clouds that so recently housed the Stormflies.

A thousand results swirled through his head realizing that the Stormflies had just loosed themselves upon an unsuspecting world of humans.

But right now, he had more important matters.

Bodies of the dead and the dying lay everywhere in the arena. Several of the Prophets moved forward, tending to Tyrane, the young sleeper and the Prophet woman who most recently hosted the foul Goddess. Quinn paused to evaluate Patrum's condition. Finding the ex-Prophet lifeless, he joined Ty next to the Protectress.

"She's alive," Ty whispered to Quinn. He feared an open announcement could bring unwanted attention. The overall emotion of resentment hovered in the arena, directed toward the woman Tyrane labeled "traitor" only minutes ago.

Axandra clung to life despite being horribly battered. Bruised, her skin changed into shades of blue and purple. Blisters and burns blackened her right hand. Crushed bones disfigured the other. She coughed and blood trickled from her mouth.

Ty pulled off his cloak to cover the injured woman. Lifting Axandra's body gently, Quinn cradled her against him. Instinctively, he sent his mind into hers. He sought out her consciousness, her very soul, and embraced it with his own.

"Axandra?" Quinn whispered and was rewarded by two slits of eyes. Throat tight, he lost his physical voice.

Don't leave, he begged, his thought-voice filled with grief. *You're not supposed to die now.*

I am not ready to go yet, Axandra responded, clinging to him and entwining her essence with his like twisting ribbons in the wind. His presence could sustain her until she could be healed. He vowed he would not let her go.

Chapter 28

Healing

25th Octember, 307

The Prophets, expert healers using their strong mental arts, set immediately to work to heal the woman they had so recently intended to murder. For thirty hours, they sat with their hands on her skin almost around the clock, many taking shifts to focus on healing her damaged organs and broken bones and controlling her pain.

The broken bones mended rapidly. Cuts and bruises disappeared quickly with the aid of salves and ointments.

The worst physical injury, the burnt flesh of her right hand, did not heal with such speed. The Healers willed the tissues to restore, as they would with a typical burn caused by fire or heat. This flesh did not respond in a typical manner and refused to regenerate. While they did not abandon all hope of completing the task of healing their patient, the Healers reverted back to non-telepathic methods in order to do so. With surgical instruments, the Healers sloughed away dead skin and removed dead muscle. These methods left the hand disfigured. To prevent infection, the open wounds were wrapped in bandages soaked in a solution of potent herbs and extracts that were often used by Healers outside the Prophets realm to anesthetize the pain and promote healing. The Prophet Healers felt these methods less efficient and apologized for their necessity. With regret, the Healers reported their fear that she might lose one or two digits due to the severity of the injury. They monitored the healing and hoped they would be proven wrong.

With Axandra's vital functions stabilized the Healers vacated the room to allow the patient to rest. Quinn never left. He held Axandra's hand or touched her face, all the time in contact with her, connecting himself to her and maintaining her life and her sanity.

Inside, she faced strange demons. Old faces became new to her again, memories that had been suppressed by the Goddess returned to her, even from her childhood. She wrestled with new truths that had been hidden from her so that she would fulfill the needs of her symbiont. She had been used, like her mother before her, in a complex web of lies and deceptions, all to bring them to the time when the Goddess and her kind planned to take the planet from the humans, with no remorse for complete destruction of humankind.

The origin of the creatures remained unclear, especially now that the memories of the Goddess had been stripped away. Quinn believed the creatures traveled the galaxy, preying on the bodies of physical creatures, consuming nutrients directly from the blood. Their queen, a most powerful being, had apparently been hosted by a select human woman for centuries as part of the truce that kept the Stormflies from completely invading the human interlopers to this world. Possibly these Stormflies arrived millennia ago. Perhaps these creatures caused the disappearance of the Ancients. Quinn doubted he would ever get to test his hypothesis, and would probably never find any evidence to prove his presumptions.

On the third day, early in the morning—well before the dawn—Axandra stirred. Quinn felt her move beside him. He lay next to her on the wide spread of pillows and cushions, enveloping her with his arms as she slept. She shifted, suddenly restless. In the candlelight, Quinn saw her face and watched her grimace with lingering pain.

Axandra opened her eyes, disoriented to find herself in near darkness. Her expression changed to relief when her eyes settled on him.

"You're here," she breathed out a sigh and tried to smile.

"I haven't gone anywhere," he said, kissing her unbandaged hand. The other, the one burned, lay at her side wrapped in thick bandages, likely the source of her pain.

"The creatures...?" she questioned, unsure what specific question to ask.

"Will have to be dealt with. The Stormflies are out with our people," he explained. "The Goddess is out there with them."

"Did we warn anyone?"

He nodded. "Days ago. Ty sent a messenger back to the Council with the details," he told her. "Word back is the people are all aware of the signs, what to look for and report. Hopefully most will be able to avoid possession, but if people are affected, the guards will do their best not to harm them until medical help arrives."

Then, lastly, as she grew tired already, she asked, "And the toll?"

"I ... don't know right now. I haven't been given anything. Ty might know."

Nodding slightly, she accepted his response. For now she gave no opinion.

"I'm very hungry," she said to him.

For the moment, Quinn allowed himself to return to his self-appointed task of nursing her back to health. "Eat this," he offered, reaching behind him to the tray that held the staples of food and water. And for a while, as she nibbled tiny bits of dried fruit, they lay side-by-side quietly. He felt relieved beyond measure that she was recovering. She felt grateful to be alive. Together, they cherished each other's touch and welcomed the exchange of emotion between them. She nestled against him, her skin touching his, enveloped in his radiating warmth.

+++

25nd Octember

"**Head of Council,** we have received a message from Commander Narone." Ben began and completed his announcement before he traversed the space of her office.

From behind a desk littered with tea cups, half-eaten sandwiches and sheaves of paper, Nancy Morton rose to meet him.

"Spit it out," she ordered impatiently. After receiving word that the Protectress had been abducted, and that Ty Narone was leading forces to retrieve her, Morton had spent the night here, in her office, waiting for any sign that the incident was over. What she expected to happen, what Tyrane told her would happen, was for the woman known as Axandra Korte Saugray to cease existing. Needing Morton's aide in his plan, Tyrane had explained that within the Great Storm lived an entire population of creatures who needed human kind in order to survive. The Goddess residing inside the Protectress acted as a funnel, drawing in the emotional energy of the human population through the host and channeling the fuel to the Storm to be consumed by the mass. Since the Heir refused to cooperate, a new vessel would be installed, someone trained and willing to accept the responsibility. Without the host, the Stormflies would take it upon themselves to gather their needed sustenance. The effect of such had been unexpectedly witnessed in the recent murders and unusual animal behaviors.

Holding the good of the people higher than the well-being of one woman, Morton agreed to allow the Prophets access, in stealth, to the Palace and the Protectress' home.

Trying to avoid feelings of guilt, Nancy kept the young woman at a distance, spurning any attempts by the Protectress to strike an emotional attachment. Nancy assumed her efforts would prevent this ache in her heart, this sorrow and apprehension. Buried within, a miniscule light of hope blinked. Perhaps the Protectress survived.

Ben read from a sheet of parchment long with hand-written notes. "The Esteemed Matriarch has sustained serious injury, but she has survived her ordeal. Of greater importance, the following information needs disseminated to all villages and persons for their safety. Creatures known as the Stormflies are moving about the continent. The creatures are responsible for the violent behavior and fatal illness people have recently experienced. They are known to enter through the eye."

Ben paused. "The remainder of the report contains instructions for the Healers, Elite and Safety Watch volunteers."

"She's alive?"

"Yes, Ma'am," Ben confirmed.

Tyrane failed. Now the Stormflies would decimate the human population. Internally, Morton cursed the Heir for her selfish short-sightedness.

"Good. Tell Narone to get her back to the Palace as quickly as possible. With a flick of her fingers, she dismissed the guard and turned away to her window. Her chest stung.

Nancy never expected such a cataclysm in her lifetime. She wasn't certain she was prepared to make the decisions required to enter into a war, especially with life forms so vastly different from human kind.

As she felt her heart explode inside her chest, Nancy realized she was a great fool to think she would be allowed to live with the knowledge the Prophets had shown her. She collapsed upon the floor, her eyes open only to darkness.

+++

Each day, Axandra grew stronger. Her body ached in places she hadn't been aware could feel pain, but the discomfort only reminded her that she survived an event when she had been expected—and almost willed—to die.

While she endured the pain of her body by reminding herself that it would all pass in time, she struggled to comfort herself when her mind became filled with disturbing revelations. Past memories surfaced that had been taken from her long ago, shielded from her by the entity for its own purposes. Warnings in her mother's voice told her to run away, to escape the Prophet before he could take her under the Great Storm. Elora did not want Ileanne's fate to be sealed by a race of people warped by decades of seclusion.

Images of her father surfaced, showing her the way he looked at her when she was a child. He would often send her away from him, not to be bothered by her questions or her needs. His blue eyes burned holes in her every time she tried to approach. When her mental abilities first began to manifest at the age of four, she sensed the reason why he treated her so horribly. Not so much in direct words, but in images of another man's face and a flash of passion that Elora felt for that stranger. As a child, she did not understand why her father would picture his wife embraced in someone else's arms and the intense anger the image stirred in him. As a woman, however, Axandra recognized jealousy and understood betrayal. A man knows when something has been stolen from him. Her father refused to care for the child who was not his true daughter.

Axandra did not know who the other man was, nor did she believe she would ever discover his identity. The truth gave her no benefit anyway. It was much too late to reunite with her lost family. Her mother was gone. The man she thought was her father was gone. She suspected that her real father was gone as well.

On the fifth day of her recovery, Axandra dictated that she was to be taken home to Undun. Both Ty and Quinn advised against traveling. Commander Narone relayed reports that incidents of violence spread slowly across the continent. For now the crimes appeared isolated, a single infection in a hundred kiloms.

"You may be safer here, Madam, since your location for now is undisclosed to the general public. The Stormflies may use the information against you," Ty recommended.

"Then I suggest you make it safe to return home, Commander," the Protectress delivered her ultimatum. "You have two days to direct your squads to prepare for my arrival. If we are in the middle of a dark time, the people need to see that the Protectress is willing to get herself dirty, even if I am in harm's way. They need to see something to help them endure."

Once again quashing his own protests, Ty bowed respectfully and agreed to the terms. "We will be ready. I will arrange for transportation."

Quinn watched the exchange and marveled at how the petite, mindful, observant countenance that Axandra normally displayed could so easily be replaced by the commanding, unyielding figure he watched now. Certainly, a person in her position needed to be both. He wondered how often he might feel the stinging end if he chose to continue down this path. He decided within only a few seconds that his love for her would endure, no matter which face graced his presence each day.

Stabbing pain shot through her arm, traceable from the burned wrist through the bent elbow and all the way into her upper back, causing Axandra to hunch toward her right and seize the offending limb hard against her body. Curses trapped behind pinched lips swirled about in the forefront of her brain, battering anyone nearby with any remote talent.

Quinn felt all of it, and now that he had spent unceasing days and nights with Axandra during the course of her healing, he understood why. Each time they touched, she left a piece of herself with him, a thin strand that linked her vast mind with his. Each consecutive contact left another strand, braiding together with the last. The strands might fade slightly if the couple was separated by time and distance, yet each reunion strengthened the existing bonds. Quinn had never experienced this kind of bond with anyone he'd ever known. He did not know if the ability was unique to Axandra, or perhaps unique to the Prophets, of which she was unwittingly a part. He recognized that the bond drew them closer together than he ever hoped to be with another human being, even if the connection meant each and every pain she endured belonged to him as well.

The bond offered him the opportunity to uniquely aid his wife by allowing him to absorb some of the pain and substitute comfort. As tiring as it was to offer this benefit, he continued to do so. Sitting next to her, Quinn clasped her good left hand tightly between his.

"When we get back to Undun," Axandra began, "I want you to know that you are free to go. You don't have to stay with me. You're not obligated."

"That is something we can talk about another time," Quinn refused. "When we get back to Undun, I will have the rest of my belongings from Lazzonir sent up. There is no point in leaving them in Southland."

"I have a lot of work to do with the Council when I return. Things are a mess."

"Yes, they are. There is a lot of cleanup to do. I have two capable hands …" He stopped himself hearing the words and thinking about her disfigured limb. How insensitive!

"Yes," Axandra agreed, forgiving him his words, "You do. I know you will use them wisely."

Chapter 29

Returning Home

29th Octember, 307

From the northwest, a single car drove into the city. From watch on the third floor of the hilltop Palace, Elite Guard Mikel Waters spotted the incoming vehicle. Mikel whistled from the window down to Ben in the courtyard, where he stood speaking with Councilor Sara Sunsun, whom had just arrived from North Compass.

"Small car coming in from the mountain road," Mikel called out, pointing in the distance. "My bet it's the Protectress."

Ben peered in the same direction, but seeing outside the city was more difficult at ground level.

"Thank you," Ben called back.

"I'll wait here, if you don't mind," Councilor Sunsun requested.

"Very well. Healer Gage should arrive momentarily. He asked to be informed when the Protectress returned." Ben gestured for one of the guards posted at the front entrance. Per Ty's remote commands, additional Elite were posted throughout the structure, always in pairs to be alert of any Stormfly activity.

"Will Gage be assigned to the Palace as Gray's replacement?" Sara asked.

"I would not know that, Ma'am," Ben replied.

The Councilor pursed her lips to keep her comment to herself. Most people did not like Healer Gage due to his gruff bedside manner. Gage typically emitted a cold aura and masked his face from any outward signs of emotion. Sara doubted the Protectress would care to have the sour man as her permanent physician.

+++

Axandra's companions woke her when they reached the outer edge of the city, where the rutted dirt tracks melded with the brick paved avenue, the street that would take them straight to the hill.

Groggy from her nap, she yawned and stretched her limbs before pushing herself upright in the seat. She used Quinn's lap for a pillow and lay across the wide bench. Across from her sat Ty and Odon, a Prophet Healer. He accompanied her to continue the treatment of her burns and of her overall health. After just the last week, Axandra had already regained some of her weight and her skin tone returned to a healthy alabaster glow. She began to look like herself again, except for her green eyes.

They all noticed, she could sense, but no one said anything to her about them, not even Quinn, who stared into her eyes every chance he got.

She saw herself in the mirror just that morning, before they left the Haven. Axandra marveled at her own recovery, unable to believe the stick figure from before looked human again. The eyes, so like a stranger's, looked back at her. Green and bright. No longer the unique color of violet. Thinking of the old color made her queasy, like everything else artificial about her recent life.

She felt satisfied with green. These were her eyes and the things they saw were hers alone.

Faster than wildfire, the news of her impending arrival reached the ears of the Palace staff. By the time they reached the Palace circle, members of the staff gathered in the courtyard and front hall to greet her.

"Look at all of them," Quinn marveled, counting the number of people standing outside. "Word travels fast around here."

"More are coming up the hill," Ty alerted, pointing back down the slope. Droves of people moved in their direction. They all wanted to see the Protectress for themselves.

The moment the car stopped, Quinn hopped out, not waiting for the drivers to open the doors. He offered his assistance to Axandra, for which she smiled gratefully. Sitting so long in the car had brought the aches back to her bones and muscles.

When she first appeared, every single person within sight held their breath. Even the wind died down for a moment. Then cheers arose, along with clapping and whistling. The attention was quite embarrassing, actually. She didn't know if she deserved such a welcome. The Stormflies, floods, and drought threatened their established way of life.

Unbidden, their thoughts struck her. Their numbers focused solely on her. She listened for a moment, her eyes roaming over the crowd.

She's alive! (What happened to her? She looks so beaten) Who kidnapped her? (Did you hear she almost died?)

"Wave to the people," Quinn prompted, touching her shoulder. She managed to lift her good arm and motion vaguely to the still growing crowd. Their faces blurred together. Feeling lightheaded, she covered her eyes with one hand. As she swayed, she felt strong hands steady her. They were Quinn's hands.

"Are you okay?" Quinn asked in a whisper close to her ear.

"I'll be all right," she assured, though her head pounded with the ruckus of those around her. She attempted to shake off the disorientation and turned to the members of the staff waiting to welcome her home. They all smiled at her. She felt their relief wash over her. Some were surprised to see her again.

Sara Sunsun, who waited patiently to the side, made her way forward and gave each Quinn and Axandra a tight embrace. "It's good to see you both here again.

"Thank you, Sara," Quinn accepted her hug eagerly, glad to have the comfort of an old friend.

A contingent of guards lined the circle, keeping the increasing crowd in check at a decent distance. Ty barked curt orders in a few directions, his eyes evaluating the situation, counting heads, and weighing sides. "We should move inside."

"Thank you, Commander," Axandra accepted, feeling beleaguered after the trip.

Marta heard and snapped at everyone, ordering them to get back to work. "We'll have time to celebrate later," she told them. "We've your rooms back in order, Your Honor. You go on upstairs and get in bed. You look be—Hmm-mm. You look exhausted."

Axandra was glad Marta recalled her original choice of words. "Beat" seemed completely inappropriate considering her bruised complexion.

Three Elite fell into step behind her as she proceeded inside the main hall supported by Quinn's bent arm.

"I hate to jump into the deep end of business right away, Your Honor," Sara said, donning her Councilor cap as they processed upstairs. "With Nancy Morton's passing, the Council has scheduled an emergency session to elect a new Head of Council, and then to immediately discuss and pass orders for dealing with recent and future crimes."

Reminded of Morton's sudden and unexpected death, Axandra paused her steps to reflect for only a moment. In her desire to do what was good for the people, Morton had committed crimes against the Protectress and others. While the Healers diagnosed the cause of death as a cardiac arrest, a shadow of suspicion led to rumors that the condition was forced by unnatural means. "Who is expected to be elected?"

"Antonette Lelle. She immediately stepped up handle matters when Nancy passed. It's only been a week, and we've seen marvelous things from her," Sara explained. "She has always been willing and ready to step up when needed."

Continuing up the stairs, Axandra nodded approval. Councilor Lelle would quite possibly improve upon the job that Nancy Morton left behind. "When will the other Councilors arrive? When is the meeting scheduled?"

"I was the last one to arrive, Madam," Sara admitted. "We are set to gather at two this afternoon."

That did not allow much time for rest, Axandra lamented to herself. Aloud, she announced, "I will be ready to attend."

"Axandra, I don't think—" Quinn protested, followed closely by Healer Odon's echo.

She halted them both with her bandaged hand sweeping between them. "I will be there." She gave no room for further argument.

Sara, choosing to stay out of the debate, bowed her head and dropped away from the group to return to the main floor.

Reserving further remarks until they reached the residential suite, Odon protested more insistently, "Protectress, you have recently undergone physical and psychological trauma beyond which most people can survive, let alone recover from in such a short time. Returning to your duties is out of the question. You are placing yourself at risk of infection, as well as psychic and mental breakdown."

"And who is at fault for all of those things, Odon?" Axandra spat at the Prophet. She had managed to contain her frustration for the duration of the trip thanks to fatigue. Within her private walls, she allowed herself to vent. "Because of your people, I have no choice but to return to my duties immediately in order to ensure that my people have a fighting chance against an enemy that has the ability to infiltrate any of us on an atomic level. You have performed your duties as required, and I thank you for your assistance. Now that I am home, your services are no longer required."

With a locked jaw, Odon silently spun on his heel and left.

"Was that really necessary?" Quinn questioned.

"Don't start," Axandra snapped, then she took a momentary pause to inhale a settling breath. "Please. If I could just climb into my bed and stay there for a week, I would. I need you to help me, Quinn. I need support."

Against his better judgment, he promised, "I'll do my best."

"Thank you. Let Healer Gage in. I am going to change."

"Let—" Confused, Quinn started to ask how she would know that anyone was coming to the door when no one had knocked. The knock itself interrupted him, and upon opening the inner door, Quinn came face-to-face with Phineas Gage. "Uh, good morning, Healer."

"Good morning, sir. You are?"

"Quinn Elgar. A friend of the Protectress. She is expecting you. She'll be ready in a moment." Quinn gestured that the Healer come in.

"That is acceptable. Since you are here, perhaps you can begin the explanation of what injuries the Protectress sustained so that I may continue her treatment."

"Certainly, and while we're on that subject, I'd better warn you about her plans." Quinn offered the Healer a seat and dove directly into a very long story.

Chapter 30

What About Tomorrow

3rd Decamber, 307

"**Good afternoon,** Councilor Lelle," Axandra said to Antonette as she stepped into the large office. The woman appeared in the midst of moving in her things, though her election took place several weeks ago. "And, though it is a bit late, I'd like to extend a personal congratulations on your election as Head of Council. I expect you will perform excellently in the position."

"That's what everyone must think," the old woman said humbly, turning away from the crate on the desk. "Since they voted me to the top. Thank you, Your Honor. I will strive to do my absolute best."

Axandra did not doubt Lelle would do just that. Antonette assumed responsibility for defraying the crises that arose in the aftermath of the Passing, from the housing shortage across the continent, as well as coordinating massive food shipments to be disbursed evenly among the affected population. The other Councilors followed her example and accepted her delegation of jobs that needed doing. In the near future, the Protectress expected similar leadership in dealing with the continuing threat of the Stormflies.

"And so I come to avail you to perform in your official capacity on a matter of a personal nature," the Protectress declared as the purpose of her visit.

"Certainly. What is it?" Lelle asked eagerly, a toothy smile filling her wrinkled pink face.

Stepping forward, Axandra held out a single sheet of paper and paused a moment while Antonette glanced at the ink. The gray brows knit in confusion.

"This is a petition to formally change my given name from Ileanne to Axandra," she explained. "I thought the approval might need to come from a higher power than the principal of Undun."

"Well, that might be. Hmm, a very curious proposal. I thought—well, I'm not sure I understand." After stumbling through her statement, the councilor looked up at her perplexed. "Why would you do this?"

Having anticipated the question, Axandra pointed at the middle paragraph of her petition. "As I described, I have used this name for over twenty years. It is my foremost identity. It's who I am."

"I don't pretend to understand what you went through while you were incognito," the woman began, pacing a few steps to the left, tapping the corner of the paper on her crooked teeth. "But coming home, you are Ileanne. You have reclaimed her identity. Your parents named you this."

Pursing her lips in disappointment, Axandra realized she hadn't expected much resistance. She was Protectress and granted certain liberties. The change in name affected few, namely herself and Quinn, but mostly how she signed official documents. How did she explain the desire to distance herself from a name associated with a lost child and a man she'd never met until five minutes before he died.

"Councilor, I left Ileanne behind a long time ago. I am not that little girl. I grew up as Axandra and that's who I am today," she stated, her voice soft yet dramatic. She felt strongly that she deserved this one favor. "Each time I sign that name, I feel like I'm stealing someone else's identity. It's uncomfortable, and frankly stirs up some very unpleasant memories. I want that name laid to rest out of respect."

"That's a heart-felt argument," Antonette remarked. She looked over the hand-written paper again, her nostrils flaring slightly as she considered the implications. "Your reasoning is sound, and I have no good reason to deny you this wish. You have performed a greater service to the world than even I can comprehend." She accompanied these words with a glance at the heavily bandaged hand. Parking herself in the tall backed chair behind the desk, Councilor Lelle took up her pen. In a quick scribble, she signed her approval, then called for an aide to witness her signature. Finally, she stamped the parchment with the Head of Council's seal, a circle dotted with stylized heads to represent the people. The seal took up nearly six centims of the page. "It is official, Your Honor," she declared, smiling again as she lifted the paper back to its owner. "Take it to the archives to record, then the name is yours to use as you wish—not that you haven't for a while."

"Well I did compromise a little," Axandra pointed out. "Thank you very much. I appreciate your understanding."

"As I said, you deserve it."

"Good day," Axandra wished, turning out the door again. In her hand, she held the document with a delicate touch and headed directly for the Archives in the basement holds. From this day forward, she would always be known as Axandra Saugray.

+++

Evening settled over the east. The last brilliant rays reflected orange and pink on the underside of the heavy snow-filled clouds moving in on the cold front. Snow would cover everything by morning.

After changing the dressing on her hand, with Quinn's assistance, Axandra ventured out onto the balcony. She and Quinn donned their jackets and sweaters against the cold wind. The air smelled of the crisp, dry scent of ice. Clouds of breath formed from each of their noses as they stared out toward the prairie. Axandra stayed close to her companion, shielding herself from the gusts and gleaning comfort from his warmth. Wrapping his arm around her shoulders, he drew her closer still.

"I haven't seen snow since I was a child," she mentioned, trying to remember what a white world looked and felt like. She'd been five the year of her last snowfall. Since then she had lived further south, where it hadn't snowed in the last fifty years.

"Well, if it isn't too cold, perhaps we should join the kids for sledding tomorrow," Quinn suggested with all seriousness. "The hill makes a perfect run, though you have to watch out for what's at the bottom."

Sledding sounded like fun, she thought at first, but then considered her hand and the lingering soreness of her bruises and thought the better of it. She didn't need to add other injuries to her abused body, as least not intentionally. "Maybe," she said in a doubtful tone. "Maybe we can just stay in and keep each other warm."

She heard the soft puffs of escaping air that came with a restrained chuckle. Turning her eyes to him, she witnessed his smile. "Is that such a bad idea?"

"No," he said, unable to fight the grin. "Not at all, my dear. You just can't seem to get enough of me, is all."

"When Spring comes, I'll be traveling again and so will you," she reminded. "I want to take advantage of our time together. Admit that you feel the same way."

"You already know how I feel," he claimed, dodging the request.

"That doesn't matter," she scolded lightly, kissing the fingers of the hand that draped around from behind her shoulders. "I still like to hear about it. Don't let me think you don't care about me."

"You know that isn't true," he pouted. "I do care about you, very deeply. So deeply, in fact, that I don't even know what to say."

"Just say you'll stay with me," she requested, as she had many times. "You don't have to promise to stay forever, just for the night."

He pursed his brows curiously. "What about the next night?"

"I'll ask you about that tomorrow," she promised.

Shifting, Quinn turned his body toward her and leaned on the stone railing. She felt his eyes look over her, study her, and try to decide if she played a game with him. "What if I want to stay for a long time? Can I just tell you that now, so you don't have to ask me tomorrow?"

"What if you change your mind?" she tempted. She worried for a moment that he grew tired of her teasing, until he flashed a coy smile her way.

"Change my mind?" he said, pretending to mull over the proposition. "I never even thought of that. I guess I could change my mind and go home. That might save me a lot of work." He stroked his stubbly chin and stared up at the clouds in thought. "Oh, but I've put so much effort forth already."

Axandra bumped him with her shoulder playfully. "And every bit is appreciated," she told him gratefully.

"Well, I'll think it over tonight and let you know in the morning," he said at last.

She moved into his arms again and looked into his eyes as they reflected that last bit of light in the air. "I love you, Quinn. I want you to know that. I've loved you since …" Her voice fell silent, trying to decide when the notion first occurred to her. It wasn't really the day they met—she'd barely even remembered his face from that day in Lazzonir, and the day at the dig were events only she remembered. But that was the day, walking among the antique pieces, listening to him described the Ancients, sensing his protective aura and seeing the way he smiled at her. She chose something simpler. "I've loved you all this time."

"And I love you," he responded sincerely. "I will stay with you as long as you will let me stay."

"And what if I want you to stay forever?" she asked, wiggling her eyebrows.

Instead of allowing himself to be pulled into the circular logic, he bent his lips to hers for a tender kiss. She giggled at him at first, then just enjoyed the moment. She felt safe and warm and loved and everything in the world seemed right. In the morning, she would worry about her people again, about their homes, about their health and their rations, and about their opinion of her. Tonight, Quinn was the only person to exist.

THE END

About the Author

Elizabeth N. Love is a small town Kansas native. She first became interested in story writing at the age of nine when a class project required the students to complete a children's book to be read by first grade students. Since that time she has rarely been seen without a notebook or computer at the ready. Elizabeth holds a B.A. in English with an Emphasis in Creative Writing from the University of Kansas.

In 2001, she received 5th Place Honorable Mention in the Science Fiction Writers of Earth annual competition, in which her short story Look Through went up against over 230 stories from across the globe. Her main reading and writing interests are fantasy and science fiction.

Connect With the Author

Twitter: @bee_writerbee
Facebook:
https://www.facebook.com/pages/Elizabeth-N-Love-Author/586497788065264
Tumblr: http://writerbeelove.tumblr.com/
Blog: http://writerbeeblog.wordpress.com/
If you like what you read, be sure to leave a review at the bookseller's site.
Thanks for reading!

Lightning Source UK Ltd.
Milton Keynes UK
UKHW020318270221
379474UK00010B/554/J